FAMILY FORTUNES

A crisis in the Adams family...

The 1950s are in full swing, and the Adams family is blessed with many new additions, including Anneliese, whose German ancestry makes her less than popular with the neighbours, and Joe and Hortense, newly arrived from the West Indies and working hard for Matt and Rosie on their farm in Kent. Sammy, meanwhile, has trouble with the newly formed trade union at his factory, and the shadows of the war continue to haunt the family when Felicity's hopes for an operation to restore her sight are threatened by an extraordinary revelation.

FAMILY FORTUNES

Family Fortunes

by

Mary Jane Staples

Magna Large Print Books
Long Preston, North Yorkshire,
BD23 4ND, England.

British Library Cataloguing in Publication Data.

Staples, Mary Jane
  Family fortunes.

  A catalogue record of this book is
  available from the British Library

  ISBN 0-7505-2254-2

First published in Great Britain in 2004 by Corgi

Copyright © Mary Jane Staples 2004

Cover illustration © Nigel Chamberlain by arrangement with
Alison Eldred

Published in Large Print 2004 by arrangement with
Transworld Publishers

Magna Large Print is an imprint of Library Magna Books Ltd.

Printed and bound in Great Britain by
T.J. (International) Ltd., Cornwall, PL28 8RW

THE ADAMS FAMILY

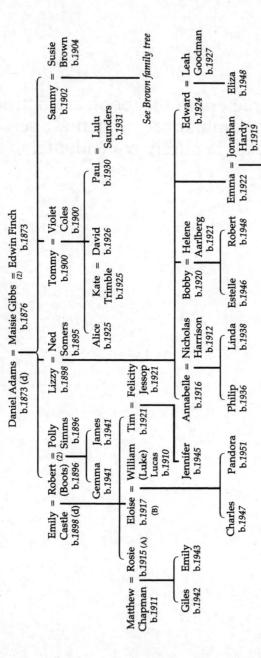

Daniel Adams = Maisie Gibbs = Edwin Finch
b.1873 (d)   b.1876 (2)   b.1873

Emily = Robert = Polly   Lizzy = Ned   Tommy = Violet   Sammy = Susie
Castle (Boots) (2) Simms b.1898 Somers b.1900 Coles   b.1902 Brown
b.1898 (d) b.1896 b.1896   b.1895   b.1900   b.1904

                   Gemma James   Alice = David   Kate = David   Paul = Lulu
                   b.1941 b.1941   b.1925   Trimble b.1926 b.1930 Saunders
                                                    b.1925   b.1931

                                                                    See Brown family tree

Matthew = Rosie   Eloise = William   Tim = Felicity   Annabelle = Nicholas   Edward = Leah
Chapman b.1915 (A) b.1917 (Luke) b.1921 Jessop b.1916 Harrison b.1924 Goodman
b.1911   (B)   Lucas b.1921 b.1921   b.1912   b.1927
                         b.1910

Giles Emily   Jennifer   Charles Pandora   Philip Linda   Estelle Robert   Bobby = Helene   Emma = Jonathan   Eliza
b.1942 b.1943   b.1945   b.1947   b.1951   b.1936 b.1938   b.1946   b.1948   b.1920 Aarlberg b.1922 Hardy   b.1948
                                                                                          b.1921   b.1919

                                                                                                          Jessie
                                                                                                          b.1946

(A) – adopted   (B) – by Cecile Lacoste   b. – born   (d) – deceased

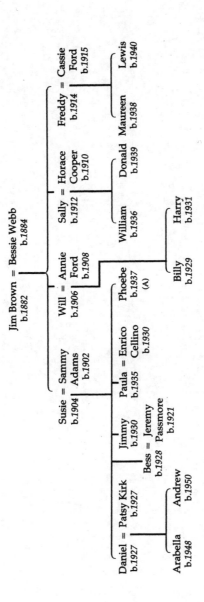

THE BROWN FAMILY

Chapter One

It was close to midnight on New Year's Eve, 1953. The vast crowd in London's Trafalgar Square, waiting for Big Ben to strike the hour, was agog with anticipation. Down in Kent, in a Maidstone hospital, a woman was close to giving birth to her first child.

Big Ben struck, and the chimes boomed. In Trafalgar Square, high on his lofty pinnacle, Nelson looked down on thousands of people bursting into revelry, beginning with a rousing rendering of 'Auld Lang Syne' as 1953 gave way to 1954.

Ten minutes later, hardy cockneys and other intoxicated people were splashing around in the fountains. At half-past twelve, down in Kent, Bess, the eldest daughter of Sammy and Susie Adams, was happily delivered of a baby boy, much to the delight of her husband, Jeremy Passmore.

At a later than usual breakfast on New Year's Day, the phone rang in a handsome house on Denmark Hill, South-East London. Sammy, a little bleary from a New Year party, answered it.

'Hello, someone can't sleep?'

'You're still in bed, Sammy?'

'No, I'm up, but I've still got my eyes shut.'

'Great party, was it?'

'Hold on,' said Sammy. 'I think I know you.'

'You should,' said Jeremy Passmore, a resident American who farmed in Kent, 'I'm married to your daughter Bess.'

'Now I get it,' said Sammy, 'you've got news for me.'

'Yep, I promised to let you know,' said Jeremy, 'you're a grandpa again. Bess has had a baby boy. Gary. How'd you like that?'

'Love it, don't I?' said Sammy. 'Never mind my hangover, I'm chuffed for you and Bess. How is she?'

'I'm reporting that mother and child are doing fine.'

Sammy turned from the phone. 'Hey, family,' he called, 'New Year's a yell. Bess has had a baby boy!'

There were shouts from the kitchen, followed by a surge into the hall of Susie, daughter Phoebe and son Jimmy.

'Who's on the phone?' asked Susie, blue eyes sparkling. 'Who's giving you the news?'

'A new dad, name of Jeremy,' said Sammy.

'Let me talk to him,' said Susie, and she did, for several minutes, while Phoebe, nearly seventeen, reminded her brother Jimmy that everyone had been a baby once.

12

Jimmy said that kind of daft information could only come from a girl, and that he preferred not to think about the time when he wore nappies.

The arrival of the infant became a New Year's Day cause for further celebration among the many members of the Adams family. The matriarch, Chinese Lady, said there was going to come a day when she just wouldn't be able to count them all. No-one believed her. Everyone knew that so far she'd never lost count of any of them.

Only a day later, her son-in-law, Ned Somers, was discharged from King's College Hospital. He'd spent many weeks there slowly recovering from a stroke. His wife, Lizzy, was happy to have him back home, although his speech was slightly affected and the right side of his face a little slack. However, there was no real impairment of his brain, and Lizzy gladly took on the task of being a watchful and encouraging wife again. He'd had other setbacks in the past.

On the second Saturday in January, an ex-German army nurse, Anneliese Bruck, who had known all the horrors of war on the Russian front, was married to Harry Stevens, a widower and a writer. The ceremony took place in a Camberwell church. The bridesmaids were Harry's daughter Cindy, twelve, and Irena, the three-year-old daughter of Brigid, Anneliese's sister. It was a well-dressed wedding, the bride in immaculate white, the bridesmaids in apricot and the groom in a fine-fitting tailored suit of dark grey.

Harry had suggested a quiet wedding.

'No, no,' said Anneliese, a striking and elegant blonde, 'this is to be my one and only wedding. So you see, Harry, I must have a white gown, a veil, a bouquet and bridesmaids. Oh, and you most of all.'

'Well,' said Harry. 'I suppose–'

'Harry, you love me, don't you?'

'Hopelessly,' said Harry.

'Hopelessly? How wonderful. So we shall have a wonderful wedding, yes?'

So they had a white wedding. In addition to Brigid and her English husband, Major Gibbs, those present included friends Colonel Lucas and his wife Eloise, French-born daughter of Robert Adams, still known as Boots, and Boots himself, together with his wife Polly, his son Tim, and Tim's wife Felicity, blinded by a bomb blast during a wartime air raid on London. Anneliese had first encountered Tim when he was a wounded prisoner of war of the desert campaign, and she a German army nurse. On the day of the wedding, Anneliese and Harry became related in friendship to the Adams family.

It was midwinter, so they spent their

week's honeymoon at the Majestic Hotel, Brighton, while Harry's lively young daughter, Cindy, stayed with Tim and Felicity. Tim saw to it that she didn't miss school, and Cindy came to wonder at how capable Felicity was as a blind woman.

Brighton had something to offer newly-weds in the way of entertainment, summer and winter. There was also a long promenade for walks in the tingling, invigorating seaside air, Anneliese wrapped in a new fur coat she had bought for herself. It made her look strikingly rich. Well, as an heiress, she was materially rich, and there had been arguments with Harry over her wish to settle on him half her fortune of a hundred and twenty thousand pounds. Harry said no to begin with and a positive no to end with.

At night, they made love. Anneliese, such a cool and composed woman on the surface, surprised Harry with her ardour.

'Again, Harry, do it again.'

Harry, perforce, had to request an interval for restoration of his capability. He was just another bloke, he said, not a Hercules. Anneliese said he wasn't just that at all, he was the kindest man in the world, which was why she loved him and wanted him to love her.

'I still need another ten minutes before I can operate again,' said Harry.

'Operate? Operate?'

'Yes, and can you face up to it without an anaesthetic?' asked Harry.

Anneliese found that very funny.

It was wonderful to have discovered a man with not a single trace of spite or aggression in him, a man who could make her laugh. Her history took in years of searing shame at all the savagery inflicted on innocent people by Himmler and his unforgivable SS. Those years had made her think she would never laugh again.

Now she had a gentle English husband and Cindy, a sweet stepdaughter. Life, after all, had relented. It had blessed her and brought laughter back.

She pressed close to Harry, and Harry stirred.

Another child arrived the following month. Kate, a daughter-in-law of Tommy and Vi Adams, presented her husband, David, with a son in February. It was Tommy and Vi's first grandchild, and it was also the first time in Tommy's life that he got a bit legless. He overdid the celebrations. Vi, the soul of equability, said she'd excuse him as long as he didn't do it again. Tommy, slightly blurry-eyed, said he might need a bit of help come the new day. The day's already come and it's over now, said Vi. Yes, this one, said Tommy, but Lulu's day is on the way. Lulu, their other daughter-in-law, was married to their younger son Paul, and over three months pregnant with her first child.

Kate and David named their infant son Douglas. David said he'd be a great help on their farm. Not just yet, said Kate. Well, no, not just yet, agreed David, say in a year or two.

Their invaluable farmhands, Enrico Cellino and his wife Paula, a daughter of Sammy and Susie, were delighted for Kate and David. The event gave Enrico cause to regard Paula with the soulful eyes of a romantically speculative Italian. Oh, no, you don't, said Paula, I'm too young at the moment. She was a month short of nineteen. It's not going to happen till I'm twenty-one, she said. OK, not half, you bet, said Enrico. He spoke what he considered the right kind of English.

Another wedding occurred on Easter Saturday. Sammy and Susie's younger son, Jimmy, married Clare Roper, a cockney girl from Bow and a stunner of face and form. She was the granddaughter of Gertie and Bert Roper, stalwarts of the Adams garments factory for many years until their recent retirement.

Chinese Lady thought Clare just the kind of wife Jimmy should have. She was no mouse, she had a lively spirit, lively enough to make sure Jimmy didn't lord it over her.

17

In helpful advisory fashion, Chinese Lady spoke to the eighteen-year-old bride at the wedding reception. You have to remember, she said, that husbands like to be lords and masters, which is something that shouldn't be encouraged, so make sure you don't bow down to Jimmy, then you'll both enjoy the right kind of marriage.

'But, Grandma,' said the happily flushed bride, 'I'm not thinking of bowing down to him, anyway.'

'Well, I'm pleased to hear it,' said Chinese Lady, 'but you have to watch them. Fond as I am of my own, that Boots, well, all his married life he's acted like an airy-fairy lord. Didn't Polly tell me once that she never knows what to do with him? As for Sammy, he's been a good boy on the whole, but Susie still has to watch him and keep him in order.'

'Oh, I'll keep my eye on Jimmy, Grandma,' said Clare, and whispered an aside to Jimmy's American sister-in-law, Patsy, a little later. 'Patsy, isn't Jimmy's grandma funny?'

'Funny? Grandma Finch?' said Patsy. 'A star turn, Clare, to whom we should all bow down.'

'Bow down?' said Clare. 'Bow down?'

'You bet, ducky,' said Patsy. 'Your Jimmy and my Daniel have both got plenty of say-so, and so have my dad-in-law Sammy and his brothers, but Grandma Finch is boss. So bow down to her.'

'Oh, help,' said Clare, wondering if any other families talked about bowing down. What a comical lot the Adams were.

She and Jimmy honeymooned at St Ives in Cornwall, where the Atlantic rollers surged into the beautiful bay and foamed over the golden sand of the beach. Their hotel fronted the bay, and since Easter was the beginning of the holiday season, other visitors helped to create the typical English seaside atmosphere of jollity.

Clare and Jimmy were happy, being very much in love. But although Clare was a modern young lady who read modern novels that touched on subjects hitherto left in the dark, and knew more about what a wedding night entailed than pre-war brides, she was actually nervous and even a bit shy when Jimmy slipped into bed with her. She hadn't thought she would be, since she'd hardly been able to wait for her wedding day.

'Jimmy, the light, you haven't turned it out.'

'Well, I thought I'd first see how you look in your nightie.'

'No, you can't, it ain't fair.'

'D'you mean there's not much of it, that it's a shortie? Well, you darling, let's have a peep at it.'

'No, you can't.'

'Yes, I can, unless you mean I mustn't.'

'Yes, you mustn't, you've got to have some respect for me modesty. Oh, Lor'.'

Her pink silk nightie was off-shoulder and low-cut, her rounded pippins in danger of tumbling out.

'Well, aren't you a lovely girl, Clare? Clare? You're blushing.'

'I should think I am. I didn't know you were going to keep the light on, did I?'

'There we are,' said Jimmy, and switched off the bedside lamp.

Intimate togetherness began.

Then, after some exciting minutes, 'Oh, me nightie, what's happened to it?'

'It's somewhere in the bed, but need we bother with it?'

'Oh, Lor', I don't know what me mum would think.'

'Well, she's not here and we're not going to invite her. Wow, you darling, aren't you gorgeous?'

Rows of flashing dots followed. Well, what bride, modern or old-fashioned, could find words at such a moment? Or needed to? Flashing dots said it all.

It was that kind of a beginning for Clare and Jimmy, just as it had been for Anneliese and Harry, although in the latters' case the act of love wasn't unknown to them. It was simply a typical example of ardently wanting each other.

In May, Lizzy and Ned's younger daughter Emma presented husband Jonathan with a second child. A boy named Mark. Chinese Lady felt herself on the verge of bewilderment.

'Edwin, oh, Lor', how many's that?' she entreated her husband.

'Great-grandchildren?' said Sir Edwin. 'Offhand, Maisie, I couldn't say. I suggest that sometime today we make a list.'

'I don't know I'll be able to keep up otherwise, Edwin.'

'I'll leave a space for the next,' said Sir Edwin.

'What next?'

'Um – there's your granddaughter-in-law Lulu,' said Sir Edwin, 'I believe she's expecting in July, isn't she?'

'Oh, my goodness, so she is,' breathed Chinese Lady, 'I forgot. I just don't know where I am, that's what it is.'

'Shall we have a cup of tea, Maisie, and make up the list while we're enjoying it?' suggested Sir Edwin.

'I'll put the kettle on,' said Chinese Lady, 'that'll make me feel more like myself.'

Life was running richly for the family, for Tommy and Vi's other daughter-in-law, Lulu, was indeed delivered of a child in July. A girl. Husband Paul was allowed to see Lulu a little later. He expected to find her pale and exhausted, but she was flushed and even triumphant.

'What a great girl you are,' said Paul, kissing her forehead.

'What a happening,' said Lulu, 'and to me of all people.'

'Natural,' said Paul, 'and I'm proud of you. You'll make a lovely mum. Where's the infant marvel?'

A nurse came in, carrying the swaddled babe.

'It's all yours, Mrs Adams,' she said.

'And mine, I'm proud to say,' said Paul, peering at the pink face that was slightly crinkled. 'Hello, little lady.' Little Lady let out a newborn baby's cry. Paul, delighted at being a dad, said, 'What's up, can I help?'

'Not just now,' said the nurse, 'it needs its mother.'

Lulu sat up and the swaddled infant was placed in her arms.

'Buzz off, Paul,' she said.

'Buzz off?' said Paul. 'What for?'

'I'm shy about what's going to happen next, said Lulu, loosening her nightdress.

'Oh,' said Paul. 'Oh, right,' he said, and made himself scarce.

Lulu's voice followed him.

'This is going to sabotage my political career.' Lulu was still a Labour Party activist of serious intent.

Too true, thought Paul, since Little Lady

won't let politics interfere with her needs.

When he visited the following day, mother and child were on very good terms with each other, and Lulu had decided to name the infant after one of her political idols, Sylvia Pankhurst, the fiery Communist daughter of Mrs Pankhurst, the leader of the suffragette movement before the First World War. Sylvia was also the name of Lulu's likeable stepmother.

Paul didn't argue, he was too entranced by Lulu's achievement.

He brought mother and child home four days later. Their Brixton house received them as a family. Lulu placed the sleeping baby in a pram that stood in the hall. Upstairs, in the marital bedroom, was a new cot. On the kitchen table was a shining white baby's bath, in which were two new sponges. And beside the bath was a parcel of new white towels, soft and fluffy, and a box of pure white nappies.

'I've a feeling,' said Lulu to Paul, 'that you're already conniving to turn me into a middle-class frump with a sponge in one hand and a nappy in the other.'

'Nothing of the kind,' said Paul, 'it's just that my good-natured mother has been helping me to get everything ready for you and our little girl dumpling. And I'd like to say, Lulu love, that a sponge and a nappy aren't frumpish, they're the tools of a devoted mum.'

'And a devoted dad,' said Lulu.

'Do I like the sound of that?' asked Paul.

'You'd better like it,' said Lulu. 'We've got equal responsibilities as parents. So see to it that you take your turns, boyo.'

'At what?' said Paul.

'Sponging baby, bathing her and putting on a clean nappy,' said Lulu.

'What, at the offices?' said Paul.

'Here, when you're home,' said Lulu.

'I'm not sure–'

'I am,' said Lulu.

'I think my immediate future is going to be complicated,' said Paul.

'You'll adapt,' said Lulu. 'My dad said he did.'

'He changed your nappies?' said Paul. 'Well, I like your dad, but as a babe, didn't you find him a bit heavy-handed?'

'Would it surprise you to know I don't remember?' said Lulu, curling up on the living-room settee.

'I bet it would be an eye-opener if you could,' said Paul. 'Feeling a little tired, Lulu love? Well, you stay here and I'll make you a cup of tea.'

'Thanks, I'd like that,' said Lulu. 'And see to the infant if she wakes up.'

'See to her?' said Paul. 'What if she's hungry?'

'Nature had an unfair moment when she arranged that kind of responsibility to the disadvantage of women,' said Lulu. 'Some subhuman male ape must have got at her.'

'I don't think I'll complain about not having a bosom,' said Paul, and went to put the kettle on.

The little lady, on her first day at home, slept on in her pram.

Chapter Two

'Uncle Sammy,' said Paul on his arrival at the family firm's offices after a long weekend of paternal responsibilities, 'I don't think Lulu will be coming back to work for quite a while.'

'Quite a while?' said Sammy. 'That won't do, me lad. I'm expecting her not to come back at all. She's got a new job, a full-time one. So don't talk in some opposite direction, or your grandma will get to hear and give you a talking-to.'

'Have to point out, Uncle Sammy, that Lulu doesn't believe in living with the kitchen sink,' said Paul.

'Well, we all know that, don't we?' said Sammy. 'But it ain't natural, a mother going back to her commercial job. Might I ask who's going to look after the infant if Lulu's not there?'

'She's already talking about placing her in a local crèche as soon as possible,' said Paul. 'Say when the infant's three.'

'Well, I ain't in favour,' said Sammy, 'and if your grandma finds out, nor will she be. Our Emily was the only family wife and mother she allowed to have a job, and that

26

all started because your Uncle Boots was blind for four years. Talk to Lulu.'

'Uncle Sammy–'

'It's an order,' said Sammy. 'I've got problems enough trying to get manufacturers of manmade fabrics to supply the factory with all it needs for its customers. Once deliveries start to be unreliable, customers go elsewhere. Which I'm against. It's the start of business ruination. You got that, Sonny Jim?'

'What I've got, Uncle Sammy, is an order to talk to Lulu,' said Paul.

'That's the stuff,' said Sammy.

Paul talked to Lulu that evening. It didn't do any good. Lulu simply reiterated her intention to have a career that might help her political ambitions.

Down on their farm in Kent, Bess and Jimmy were delighted with the progress of their infant son. The child, thriving, was a chubby bundle of joy. They had one problem. Jeremy's widowed mother, having indefinitely postponed her return to Chicago, was still with them and becoming very possessive towards baby Gary. Her attitude seemed to suggest he was as much hers as theirs.

Bess had a helpless feeling that her mother-in-law could become a permanent presence and a dominating figure in the life of the boy.

'Jeremy, can't you point her back to Chicago?'

'Honey, I point her in that direction every day.'

'It's not working.'

'Unfortunately, my sister and brother-in-law failed to find the right kind of guy for her.'

Jeremy's sister and husband had promised to do what they could to find an irresistible suitor for the restless widow, who had inherited a fortune from her late husband. There had been possibles, but none proved as irresistible to her as she, with her riches, was to them. What Jeremy and his sister Louise had in mind was the certainty that if she did marry again, she'd spend her time moulding her new husband into shape instead of taking up permanent residence with her son and daughter-in-law.

'Tell her,' said Bess, 'that your brother-in-law has made a transatlantic phone call to say your sister's having a crisis and can she fly home at once.'

'If my sister were having a crisis, Bess, my mother would expect me to fly home with her.'

'Tell her you can't possibly leave the farm at the moment, and that you'll follow in a day or two.'

'And what happens when she discovers my sister is all right?'

'Cable your sister and tell her to lock her up.'

'Holy cowboys, are you that desperate, Bess?'

'I'm desperate to ensure Gary doesn't begin to feel she's his mother, not me.'

'We'll work on it, Bess,' said Jeremy.

'Get going, then,' said Bess, an equable woman of twenty-six, but strongly against letting little Gary be smothered by her mother-in-law.

Jeremy encountered Guy Burke-Browning the next day. They met in the village of Bromley Green, Jeremy there to collect a large amount of cattle feed, Guy passing through on horseback. He was a man of sixty, with aristocratic connections, the owner of an ancestral pile, and a rakish lifestyle. He had never married, preferring gambling, the excitements of Monte Carlo and the occasional love affair to the frightful cost of keeping a wife in the same style as himself. As it was, his own expenses meant he came close to being stony broke all too often.

Pulling up when he saw Jeremy alighting from his farm truck, he hailed the American.

'Hello, hello, Jeremy old boy, still treading fields of cow-pats, what?'

'Hello yourself,' said Jeremy, 'long time no

see. Thought you were still in Monte Carlo.'

'Would have been, but the ready ran out,' said Guy. 'Had to leave in a hurry, damn it. Matter of honour to go back sometime and settle my hotel bill, but a crashing bore to have Pinky Stebbings send me a bank statement this morning.' Mr Stebbings was the local bank manager whose round, rosy face had earned him his nickname. 'Dashed if there weren't red marks all over the account. None of my business, of course, but d'you get bank statements like that, Jeremy old boy?'

'Thankfully, no,' said Jeremy.

'Ah, well,' said Guy, 'point a jolly old finger at yours truly. A fool and his money, what? You Americans handle it more wisely.'

'Oh, the wise skinflints pile it up, count it, hoard it, and wait for more to roll in,' said Jeremy. 'But I doubt if hoarding is more enjoyable than spending.' Jeremy liked the man, and if Guy's long acquaintance with the fleshpots was reflected in his raffish looks, he still had the charm of his kind. Ladies regarded him as slightly devilish, even at sixty, and accordingly the odd widow or two had ideas about him. However, he couldn't afford any of them as a wife, and they certainly couldn't afford him as a husband.

'I've a few regrets,' he said, 'but no complaints, what? How's your sweet Bess, Jeremy?'

'Flourishing,' said Jeremy. 'A week after you left for Monte Carlo, she had a baby boy. First thing in the morning of New Year's Day. He's flourishing too.'

'Well, glad tidings and all that,' said Guy. 'Congratters, and many of 'em. Lovely lady, your Bess. Charming gel. Made you a proud father, has she? Never had any children myself, never had a wife. Too busy with my bally irresponsibilities, don't you know. Look here, I'll be passing your farm on my way to an appointment. I'd consider it a favour if I could drop in on Bess, eh?'

'She'll be pleased to see you,' said Jeremy. 'You can meet the infant – yup, and my mother too. She's been staying with us for a while.'

'Right, good show,' said Guy, and rode off, whistling to his nag. He might be stony broke, thought Jeremy, but never sour. He always talked in a cheerful if outdated way.

When Jeremy slogged his weary way into the farmhouse scullery that evening, Bess slipped quietly from the kitchen to halt his further progress. She closed the door, shutting them off from the house proper.

'Tired?' she said.

'Whacked,' said Jeremy, 'and if you'll open that door I'll point myself at a highball before my feet give up.'

'Dear man, you can have two highballs in

31

just a few minutes,' said Bess. 'D'you know what you've done?'

'I sure do,' said Jeremy, 'about twelve hours of hard labour.'

'You'll recover,' said Bess, 'especially when I tell you that in encouraging Guy Burke-Blooming to drop in—'

'Burke-Browning,' said Jeremy, loosening and kicking his boots off. They landed with thumps on the stone floor.

'Oh, but he is blooming,' said Bess. 'At least, your mother thinks so.'

'Enlighten me,' said Jeremy.

'Well, he dropped in, he met our infant and then your mother,' said Bess. 'My dear, it was instant chemistry.'

'Instant?' said Jeremy.

'Perhaps not immediately instant,' said Bess. 'Perhaps as soon as I put in a few words of my own, which made Guy realize your mother was a rich widow who comes of an old American family, and she realized he was an English aristocrat and a bachelor. That, I thought, was what you wanted me to do when you invited him to pop in.'

Jeremy's smile was broad.

'No, you take all the bows, Bess,' he said, 'I never thought of that angle. I guess I still had a fixation on someone from my mother's own back yard, Chicago. But an English charmer? Clever girl. How did it go with the two of them?'

Bess said she made coffee, left them together while she took time seeing to Gary, and an hour later they were still chatting flirtatiously. Jeremy pointed out that Guy had had an appointment to keep. Well, you know Guy, said Bess, he can walk round an appointment and then offer an apology that will make him completely forgivable. However, on this occasion he broke off his close engagement with Jeremy's mother to phone the man in question and tell him that frightfully sorry and all that, but he simply couldn't make it today.

'He's an old charmer all right,' she said.

'Is my mother charmed?' asked Jeremy.

'Is she? Not half,' said Bess. 'He's coming here to pick her up tomorrow and entertain her at Browning Hall for the day. She's frantic about whether or not she has a regal enough day dress.'

'Frantic? Regal?'

'Jeremy, she's fascinated.'

'Fascinated and frantic? My mother?'

'After he'd gone, I told her he was the Honourable Guy Burke-Browning, due to his aristocratic lineage.'

'And what did she say to that?'

'I think she was a little breathless at that stage,' said Bess, an impish smile making her look girlish. She knew her mother-in-law considered herself one of America's elite in that she claimed descent from the country's

33

Founding Fathers, and that accordingly she would see aristocratic Guy as a very suitable second husband. And Guy, of course, would see her bank balance as the one thing that would induce him into marriage at last. 'Jeremy, it's my guess that by the end of her time with Guy tomorrow, she'll have offered to pay for the roof repairs to Browning Hall. Guy won't hide the fact that he's broke. He's an honest old bounder.'

'Suffering angels,' said Jeremy, 'what have we got now, Bess?'

'Happy possibilities,' said Bess. 'Now you can have your highball.'

'I'll double the Scotch content,' said Jeremy. 'By the way, is Guy an Honourable?'

'I'm sure I've never heard him say so,' murmured Bess, 'but it's not the kind of thing he'd throw into a conversation, so he could be. Oh, when your mother talks to you about him, as I'm sure she will, don't forget to tell her what a fine English gentleman he is.'

'A fine English gentleman?' Jeremy laughed. 'Coming from an American, that'll sound as if I've gone native.'

'It'll be for a good cause,' said Bess.

A month later, down in the garden of Kent, Bess and Jeremy threw a party, at which the engagement of Guy Burke-Browning to Mrs Rose Passmore of Chicago was announced.

Among those who found the announcement unexpected, some whispered comments were exchanged.

'Chicago? That place? Well, my word.'

'Yes, what happened to her husband?'

'Put in a sack with lumps of concrete and drowned by one of those gangsters, perhaps?'

'Lord, that could happen to Guy.'

'That's if they go to live in Chicago.'

'You wouldn't get me there, not even if the mayor offered me a sackful of gold.'

Outside of such whispers, Mrs Passmore senior sailed about in a new creation, dispensing gracious words to all and showing not the slightest hint that she had anything to do with Chicago gangsters. At fifty-six, she had made herself look forty-five, a feat of miraculous endeavour. Guy looked what he was, a raffish sixty still able to exude charm. That was easy enough. He was marrying a fortune and looking forward to putting stony-broke days well behind him. In fact, much to Mrs Passmore's delight, the honeymoon was to take place in Monte Carlo, never mind the expense to her purse, or the fact that she was going to settle his outstanding hotel bill.

She was no longer obsessive about her role as little Gary's paternal grandmother.

Jeremy, incidentally, had bought Bess two new outfits for being such a clever girl.

The marriage took place in the Burke-Browning family chapel three weeks later, Jeremy's sister and brother-in-law, over from Chicago, in attendance.

The following day, bride and groom disappeared from sight, going off to Monte Carlo for a prolonged honeymoon that would undoubtedly cost the bride more than a few dollars, which she would fork out with never a quibble, so taken was she with her charming and sophisticated husband.

Bess and Jeremy felt as free as God's air, and celebrated with champagne and a reckless bedtime. Some weeks later she told him the result of their heady celebration.

She was pregnant again. Her mum and dad, Susie and Sammy, were delighted to receive the news. Chinese Lady, however, wondered if one day the uncountable number of her great-grandchildren might get into the newspapers and make people talk about her.

'When that day does come, Ma old girl,' said Sammy, 'we'll let Queen Liz know and I daresay she'll send you a congratulatory postcard of Buckingham Palace.'

'Sammy, don't be disrespectful about our Queen,' said Chinese Lady, 'and don't call me old girl or Ma. It's common.'

'OK, Ma,' said Sammy, 'hearing you loud and clear.'

Chapter Three

The independent school for girls a little west of Clifton in Bristol was surrounded by a high brick wall, and could not be seen except through its iron gates. A man, alighting from his parked car, walked to the gates and made his observation of the school's frontage. It was covered by Virginia creeper, now beginning to turn a September red. It framed the many windows and the double front doors. The noticeboard, fixed to the wall on one side of the gate, informed the public that the school was for girls from eleven to seventeen, and the headmistress was Miss Hilda Lee, BA.

Hilda. The man smiled. How many headmistresses were called Hilda? More than a few.

From where he was, the building sounded as quiet as if it were void of staff and pupils. Deceptive, for summer holidays were over. He looked at his watch. Nearly four o'clock. Two cars arrived to park behind others already there. At a minute after four the double front doors opened, noise erupted, and a teacher stood by as a flood of girls swarmed out. In their striped blazers, white blouses, blue skirts and light boaters, they were a picture of life and animation, most of them dancing teenagers of the musical Fifties.

The man returned to his car to stand beside it. A bus rumbled by and pulled up at the school stop. On came the girls, the gates opened and they poured out, some running to the bus, some heading for the parked cars, and some beginning a walk home.

The flood of vivacious girlhood seemed endless, the sound of voices a sing-song chorus in the light, sunny air. Two senior girls, satchels swinging, cast their eyes at the waiting man as they approached. He was a dark, saturnine figure, sinewy of body, his medium grey suit well tailored, his head bare. To some girls he might have seemed dashingly devilish. At any rate, one girl actually winked at him as she passed by with her friend. He heard a muffled giggle.

Modern misses, even schoolgirls, he thought, could frighten a modest man with their boldness.

The flood subsided. The bus, full up, moved off, and parental cars drove away. Silence returned, except for the lingering echoes of the young and vital.

The man waited in patience. Two teachers, spruce in dark blue costumes, came out, said goodbye to each other, and went their separate ways. One glanced at him, a slight note of suspicion visible. She stopped.

'May I ask if you're waiting for someone from the school?' she asked.

'Aye, you may,' he said. 'I'm waiting for a lady.'

'I see.' But she was still suspicious.

'For Miss Adams.'

'Oh. I see. Yes.' She went on her way.

Not until four-thirty did the lady he was waiting for emerge into his vision. Seeing him she came to a full stop. She stared.

'Aye, it's me, Alice,' said Fergus Mac-Allister.

'So I see,' said Alice Adams, daughter of Tommy and Vi. Now twenty-nine, she hadn't seen this vigorous Scot for several years. He had wanted to marry her. She had chosen to put her career before marriage, and that sent Fergus back to his home in Aberdeen. He had written once or twice, not to pester her, but to ask after her and to let her know he had taken up with a bonny Scotswoman whose head wasn't filled with learning. He was now well into his thirties, but had changed little in appearance. He still looked like a pirate. She smiled. 'You're very recognizable,' she said.

If he hadn't changed much in her eyes, she came to his own as an adult and extremely attractive woman in a dark blue costume, blue-eyed and serene. Hatless, her fair hair shone in the September light. She was now twenty-nine, he knew that.

'You look, Alice, as if you've calmed down,' he said.

'Calmed down?' said Alice. 'What do you mean? I was never a spitfire.'

'No, but always making a challenge of whatever I said to you.'

'Whatever was provoking, you mean,' said Alice. 'What brought you here, and how did you know about this school?'

'Will you no' let me drive you home to your lodgings and talk on the way?' suggested Fergus.

'Well, thank you,' said Alice, 'it'll save me waiting for a bus.'

Fergus opened the door to the passenger seat and she slipped in. He put himself into the driving seat, started the car and drove off, heading for the busy centre of Bristol.

Alice asked him again what had brought him to the school, and he said he was in Bristol to take charge of a new factory at Filton. The family firm in Aberdeen, built up by his father, specialized in the manufacture of precision instruments, and was presently expanding, hence one new factory in Reading and another in Filton. He was now residing in Bristol and had been for three days. He decided to find out if Alice was still living in Bristol, so he called on the only address he had of her. There, he was told by the landlady he could find her at

Clifton Lodge School.

'So here I am, y'ken,' he said, 'and it's fine to see you again, Alice. But I'm no' intending to bother you, so dinna be worried on that score.'

'Well, you're married, aren't you?' said Alice, as the car began to catch up with the traffic.

'That I'm not,' said Fergus, 'for the lady changed her mind.'

'Why?' asked Alice.

'We called it off by mutual consent,' said Fergus, 'we didna suit each other. What about you, Alice, you're still no' married?'

Alice said she was still happy with a career, although she'd suffered a disappointment. At a time when her qualifications enabled her to apply for a post at the university as a tutor, she did so. But there were three applicants, she said, and she was one of the unlucky two. However, she was recommended for a position as English teacher at Clifton Lodge School for Girls, a private establishment run by its governors.

'I won't say it's as fulfilling as a tutorial post would have been, but I'm happy enough,' she said.

'Well, I know fine how much a bookish career means to you,' said Fergus.

'Bookish?'

'Aye, as I remember, you were never happy except with your nose in a book of learning,'

41

said Fergus.

'That's fighting talk,' said Alice, remembering all too well the verbal affrays she had had with him over preferring classic literature to dance halls.

Fergus, threading the car into a stream of traffic, said, 'It's no' my wish to fight with you, Alice. That's all in the past, although I will say that when you had sparks in your eyes, you were at your best.'

'That's absurd,' said Alice. 'No woman is at her best when she's in a temper.'

'As I recall,' said Fergus, going with the slow traffic flow like a man without hurry on his mind, 'it made you throw your books at me.'

'So?' said Alice, guilty of the charge.

'I thought you always came alive when you parted from your books in that fashion,' said Fergus.

Alice laughed. She was not nearly so touchy about her scholastic self these days. She had survived years of listening to quips and sallies about 'bluestockings'.

'Fergus, you're talking utter nonsense,' she said, 'and you're already forgetting your intention not to fight with me. You should know, incidentally, that teaching is nothing to do with being bookish – look out, there's a van trying to lean on you.'

'So I notice,' said Fergus. 'Well, I'll give way, for it's a fine afternoon and I'm no' in the mood to tangle with anyone.' He slowed to a crawl, and the van, a small white one, filtered aggressively in to show him its dusty rear.

'I don't remember you as a man willing to give way,' said Alice.

'One lives and learns, Alice.' Fergus smiled. 'So here we are, then, neither of us married and both on our way, I fancy, to becoming a couple of old bachelors in time.'

'Is the prospect for you a worry?' asked Alice.

'I canna say it's making me fret,' said Fergus, 'and I'm too busy with the responsibility of getting the factory into production to bother with social commitments just now.'

The traffic ahead was crawling. The white van stopped and Fergus pulled up behind it. Out of the van leapt two men in caps, jerseys and jeans. One rushed to the passenger door of Fergus's Austin car. He wrenched it open, laid a heavy hand on Alice's left arm and yanked.

'Out, out!' he hissed, and he literally pulled her from the car. The violence of the action caused her to stumble and fall to the pavement. At the same time, the second man, a leather Gladstone bag in one hand, had the driver's door open and was glaring at Fergus.

'Out, and quick!'

'Be damned to you,' said Fergus, blood up at what had happened to Alice. But out of the car he came, and without hesitation. His purpose, however, was not to surrender his car, but to knock the man off his feet. He found himself staring at the wicked snout of a revolver. He checked in shock, the Gladstone bag swung viciously and knocked him aside. Then both hijackers were in the car. The driver of the vehicle immediately behind Fergus's Austin was staring in disbelief. Further back, other drivers were sounding impatient horns, and Alice was picking herself up off the pavement.

The man at the wheel of the Austin reversed it. Its tail hit the front of the car behind, much to the fury of its driver. The Austin shot forward on a forceful turn of the steering wheel and drove out wide of the stationary van. Away it went at speed. Ahead, the traffic had dispersed, giving the hijackers a clear run for a while.

'Fergus!' Alice was beside the stunned Scot.

'Damn them,' said Fergus, 'I want my car back. The van, Alice, if they've left the ignition keys in, let's use that. No, you stay here.' He darted to the van, while a cacophony of impatient horns caused pedestrians to stop and stare. In the vehicle, the keys were still in the ignition. Fergus switched on, started the engine and then found Alice up in the passenger seat.

'I owe them something,' she said, 'so get after them, Fergus.'

She had not seen the revolver, and Fergus did not at this moment mention it. Time was of the essence. Away he went, and after a few minutes he saw his dark blue Austin in the distance. It had caught up with the slow traffic. He then communicated a dire fact to Alice.

'I have to tell you, Alice, that one heathen is armed,' he said.

'Armed?' said Alice.

'Aye, so he is, the ugly beastie, with a revolver, so whatever happens, keep your head down.'

Ahead, the Austin swerved, came out of its line and sped up the outside of the crawling traffic, risking life and limb on the wrong side of the road. Alice held her breath, waiting for the moment when surely reverse traffic would appear and either block the Austin or smash into it. The driver and his partner in crime were lucky, however, and the car made a good two hundred yards before it had to force its way back into line. Alice and Fergus heard the angry horn of a driver pressurized into giving way.

Fergus, catching up with the slow traffic, reduced speed.

'We'll lose them,' said Alice, vibrating at the violent way she had been yanked from the car to the pavement.

'As long as we keep them in sight, we'll no' lose them, Alice,' said Fergus. 'Are you hurt?'

'Bruised,' said Alice. 'Fergus, as soon as we spot a policeman, we must stop and inform him.'

'Aye, we'll stop,' said Fergus, keeping his eye on the line of traffic heading east, 'and you'll get out and talk to the law. I'll go on, although I'd say that by now at least one police car will be haring around.'

'Why are you sure you won't lose them?' asked Alice, adrenalin high.

'The luck of the game,' said Fergus. 'My petrol tank needs filling. I was intending to get that done on my way back to my lodgings in Filton. What's in the tank now, Alice, willna take the heathens more than fifteen miles.'

Alice sensed his determination. He was that kind of a man, of course. He had served with a Highland Division of Scots during the retreat to Dunkirk, and then during the advance into the Low Countries following the Normandy invasion. If she felt keyed up, she also felt tingles of excitement at being with him in this pursuit of an abominable quarry. She kept her eyes open for any sign of a bobby on the beat. She asked Fergus if he understood why the men had abandoned their van to hijack his Austin. Fergus said it was almost certainly because they'd committed an armed robbery, and that a description of their van would have been made known to the police.

'Fergus, then the police will now be on the lookout for us,' she said.

'For this van, yes, so they will, Alice,' said Fergus, 'and I'll lead them all the way to the spot where the Austin will run dry.'

Some of the traffic was diverting north and south. In the distance, the blue Austin kept going, taking advantage of moments when overtaking was possible. Each time this happened, Alice and Fergus had a clear view of the car.

In a while, the traffic ahead was thinner and clear of the city limits. It was moving faster on the road to Kingswood. Fergus overtook some tail-enders. The small van was capable of turns of speed.

'Fergus, how many miles have we come now?' asked Alice.

Fergus glanced at the mileage figures.

'Nearly ten,' he said, 'so sit tight, Alice.'

'I haven't seen one policeman,' she said.

'That's the way of it,' said Fergus, who did not seem in the least worried about what might happen if or when they caught up with a stationary and dehydrated Austin. 'When you need a bobby, there's never one in sight. And when the last thing you want is to be fashed by one on account of sinking a wee dram or two, a whole platoon turns up to surround you.'

'Fergus, are you saying you've been charged for being drunk and disorderly?' said Alice.

'Well, lassie, I'm saying that in my time in the army I've been picked up by the redcaps, but I dinna know any Highland laddies who haven't. Now, have those heathens spotted that we're trailing them?'

Alice, pulses quickening as the Austin clearly showed itself in another overtaking manoeuvre, thought it about three hundred yards ahead. Its overtaking burst was done at reckless speed.

'I think they have,' she said.

'It's no' a bother,' said Fergus, 'we dinna need to ride on their tail.' At that point, they heard the faint wail of a police siren far back behind them, while noting the Austin had taken a right turn onto the Bath road.

'Fergus, do we stop for the police?' asked Alice.

'We'll stop when they catch us up,' said Fergus, and kept going. He turned onto the Bath road, a winding course. The Austin was out of sight. The police siren was still distant.

'Fergus, where's the Austin?' asked Alice, heart beating fast now.

'Well in front, I fancy, Alice, and we'll no' see it till we hit a straight stretch,' said Fergus.

What a cool one he is, thought Alice.

They overtook a cyclist and then the road was clear up to a distant bend. Behind them the police siren was suddenly louder. Fergus, glancing in the wing mirror, saw the patrol car career into view. He drove fast for the bend, and the clanging police car flashed its lights. Coming out of the bend, he saw his Austin a hundred yards ahead. It was at a standstill. Doors opened and the two men leapt out, ran across the verge, jumped a gate and sprinted fast across a field to a wooded stretch. One man was carrying the Gladstone bag.

The loot's in that, thought Fergus, and pulled up. The police car shot by and tucked itself in at an angle between the van and the Austin. That blocked the van. Two uniformed officers emerged, but did not advance to the van. They quickly tucked themselves behind their patrol car, using it as a shield against any possible gunfire. One shouted.

'Get out and stand with your hands up!'

Fergus and Alice alighted. At the sight of Alice, a picture of respectability in her costume, the policemen gaped.

'The men you want are running,' said Fergus. 'There. Look.' He pointed. The police officers, now not sure of themselves, turned their heads. The running figures were halfway on their sprint for the wooded stretch.

'What the hell–?' One policeman made known his confusion.

Fergus explained rapidly, and since he was wholly credible, and Alice, in her obvious respectability, even more so, the policemen wasted no more time, apart from telling them the men had committed an armed bank robbery. They called up their station, gave details of the situation and what they were about to do, try to track and locate the offenders. Help was needed in view of the fact that one was still armed. They asked Alice and Fergus to stay where they were and wait for another patrol car. Then, without further ado, they climbed the gate and set off in pursuit of the wanted men, by now out of sight.

Alice and Fergus were left to keep an eye on all three vehicles, and to wait.

Chapter Four

Alice and Fergus, waiting, had their eyes on the woodland. Both were unsure of what might happen if the policemen caught up with the two men. The revolver might or might not play a deadly part.

'Exactly how do policemen act when confronting an armed robber?' asked Alice.

'Sensibly, I hope,' said Fergus.

The occasional car passed, going wide of the obtruding rear of the police car, drivers casting inquisitive glances.

'I'm supposed to be going to the theatre this evening,' said Alice. 'I've arranged to meet a friend there at seven-thirty.'

The time was well past six.

'I'll do my best to get you there,' said Fergus, 'but it'll depend on putting some petrol into the Austin's tank.' He had checked and found it as empty as he'd expected. 'I'll no' be able to move it as it is.'

'You're not to worry about my theatre seat,' said Alice, 'the situation here is too fraught. I'm fraught myself. I still feel as if I've been roughed up by some smash-and-grab gang.'

'You were,' said Fergus, 'which was one

reason why I was against letting the heathens get away. Your parents won't like hearing about it. I willna be surprised if they tell you Bristol's no' the place for a young lady.'

'It'll depend on exactly what I tell them,' said Alice.

'Whisht, lassie, Bristol and its bank robbers will be featured in tonight's news, and in every paper tomorrow,' said Fergus. 'You'll no' be able to play it down.'

'Oh, Lord,' said Alice wryly.

'And if the police manage to make an arrest,' said Fergus, 'there'll be a trial, at which we'll be among the witnesses.'

'That's it, make my day,' said Alice.

'Oh, you're a fine lassie, Alice,' said Fergus, 'turning never a hair when others would have thrown a wee fit or two. Your parents will be proud of you.'

'I couldn't resist joining you in the chase,' said Alice. 'Fergus, you're a brave man.'

'There's a difference, Alice, between being brave and being in a temper,' said Fergus. 'I dinna go for a woman being handled like a sack of potatoes.'

'It made me furious,' said Alice.

'So there we were, both of us in a temper,' smiled Fergus, 'and here we are now, waiting for more police and the chance to find some petrol.'

'I think our waiting's over,' said Alice.

It had lasted twenty minutes, the waiting, but now the distant wail of sirens reached their ears. Within a further minute, two patrol cars came rushing up to park behind the van and disgorge seven police officers, two of them in plain clothes. They closed in on Alice and Fergus.

One of the plain-clothes men spoke.

'I'm Chief Inspector Bradley of Bristol CID, and this is Detective Sergeant Moss,' he said, indicting the man beside him. 'Are you the lady and gentleman who used the suspects' van to follow them and gave my officers some very helpful information?'

'We are,' said Fergus, 'and if you've got time, I'll put you fully in the picture.'

'Go ahead,' said Chief Inspector Bradley, a man of burly authority. His men were crowding and quivering like ferrets after a brace of rabbits.

Fergus gave a second explanation, with a little more detail this time. It caused Chief Inspector Bradley to issue orders that sent the five uniformed men over the gate and at a pell-mell rush for the woodland. Two of them were armed. Another was running in the wake of an Alsatian dog that was straining on its leash.

'Now, sir, could we have your name and the lady's?' asked the chief inspector.

'I'm Fergus MacAllister, and the lady is Miss Alice Adams.'

Sergeant Moss made notes.

'Well, we have to thank you both for your help and initiative,' said the chief inspector. 'I'm relieved, however, that while you knew your car would run out of petrol, you kept your distance. Armed robbers don't operate every day in this country, thank God, but when they do, they're dangerous. If we make an arrest, you won't necessarily be required to identify the men. The bank cashier will do that. You and Miss Adams will only be called on if the cashier has any doubts, and I don't think he will. You will, however, definitely be called as witnesses at the trial, and if you'll give my sergeant your addresses, you'll be free to go.' He glanced towards the woodland. The five policemen and the dog had disappeared. 'This may be a long wait for me.'

Fergus and Alice gave their addresses to the sergeant.

'We may be free to go, Chief Inspector,' said Alice, 'but unfortunately, Mr Mac-Allister's car has run out of petrol.'

'Oh, yes.' The chief inspector nodded. 'Sergeant Moss, I believe we can oblige Mr MacAllister.'

'Right, sir,' said the sergeant, and opened up the boot of one of the patrol cars. He hefted out a petrol can and handed it to Fergus. 'Here's a gallon, sir, with our compliments. Someone at the station pointed out

54

that according to the message we received, you were probably stuck with an empty tank.'

'A gallon is a great help, so thanks for the gesture,' said Fergus.

'No more than you deserve, Mr Mac-Allister,' said the chief inspector, eyes scanning the green fields and the dark mass of trees.

'You don't need to keep my car?' said Fergus.

'If we make an arrest, sir, we can offer the prosecution all the evidence they'll need,' said Sergeant Moss.

At the moment that Fergus and Alice were able to begin their drive back to Bristol, the quarry had been run to earth without a fight, and from her seat Alice saw the police and their prisoners emerging from the woodland. The dog was frisking around on the heels of the handcuffed men. She wound down her window.

'Congratulations, Chief Inspector!' she called.

'Much thanks to you two,' he called back.

'We did it, Fergus,' she said, 'we ran them down for the police. I'm thrilled.'

'Touch and go here and there, lassie, touch and go,' said Fergus, heading for the city. 'Now, about the theatre–'

'Oh, it's too late for that unless we dash

and scurry,' said Alice, 'and I'm not going to do that. Besides, I'm starving and if I went to the theatre with my stomach as empty as it is now, I'm sure I'd rumble at all the wrong moments. It's *Macbeth* at the Bristol Old Vic, but I can give it a miss this time. I'll phone my friend.'

'Well, I'll drop you at your lodgings–'

'But aren't you starving too?' asked Alice, feeling revitalized and not at all unhappy about missing *Macbeth*.

'I'll rustle up a wee plateful at my lodgings somehow,' said Fergus, 'or find a restaurant.'

'Fergus, I can cook for both of us,' said Alice, 'and feel I should.'

Fergus thought about the invitation as he drove through the balmy September evening. All his old feelings for the daughter of Tommy and Vi Adams, two people he liked and admired, were resurfacing. While he hadn't been able to resist looking her up, he was quite sure it would do him no good to attempt any renewal of their former relationship. It had taken him some time in those days finally to realize Alice preferred a career to marriage. Eventually he had stopped pressing her and made a firm break by returning to his home in Aberdeen. There he had opted for a career of his own, in his father's engineering firm. True, he had taken up with a bonny Scotswoman, but they weren't really suited, and there were occasions when his thoughts compulsively returned to Alice. But no, it would be a mistake to suppose he could change her mind now. She had made it clear she was happy with her life as it was. She had her friends, one of whom she'd arranged to meet at the theatre. A man of her own bookish kind, no doubt.

'It's a kind thought of yours, Alice,' he said, 'but no, I won't intrude. It's been a pleasure to see you again, and I daresay the chase has left us with something to remember–'

'Fergus, stop being absurd,' said Alice. 'You know very well it won't be an intrusion, and I'd be as mean as an old goat if I didn't offer to cook for both of us.'

'No, I'll no' take advantage,' said Fergus, 'and the fact is, I need a bath more than food.'

'Well, be cantankerous, if you must,' said Alice, feeling not only offended, but dismayed by his attitude. She lapsed into silence, and nothing was said by either of them until they arrived at her lodgings in the heart of Bristol. Fergus got out, went round and opened the passenger door. Alice slid out with a swish of her skirt, an indication of ruffled feathers.

'Here we are, lassie,' said Fergus.

'Don't call me lassie,' said Alice edgily. 'I suppose you'll at least tell me when we can see each other again?'

'For old times' sake?' said Fergus.

'Why for old times' sake?' said Alice. 'We're still friends, aren't we, and friends meet, don't they?'

'Are you on the phone?' asked Fergus.

'Yes,' said Alice, and quoted her number.

'I'll call you now and again,' said Fergus.

'That's it, overwhelm me,' said Alice, wondering why she was feeling sore at his resistance to her offer of hospitality.

'There's still time for you to get to the theatre,' said Fergus.

'With a sandwich in my hand and my clothes feeling wrecked?' said Alice. 'I think not. Goodnight, Mr MacAllister.'

She climbed the steps to the door of the lodging house, inserted her key, and opened the door.

Fergus, suddenly uncomfortably aware that his reservations had made him commit the sin of ungraciousness, called out to her.

'Alice, so sorry. Look, may I change my mind, may I join you for a wee bite of supper, then, if it won't put you to too much trouble?'

Alice turned at once, a smile of relief displacing hurt. Well, it was a relief to know their eventful and adventurous afternoon wasn't going to end in a disagreeable way.

'Fergus, yes, do come up, it'll be no trouble at all,' she said.

Twenty minutes later, after he had used her bathroom to give himself a welcome wash and brush-up, and Alice had made her phone call to her friend, they were in the kitchen. Fergus was helping her prepare a quick supper of cold ham with a tomato salad and hot sauté potatoes to give the meal a little body. He was attending to the latter, having sliced some leftover potatoes to fry them lightly in the pan. Alice had mixed the salad and was making a dressing of oil, vinegar and just a tiny amount of garlic. Fergus had said yes to that, although she could have told him her parents regarded garlic in the same way that Grandma Finch did: it was one of those Frenchified foreign condiments that ought never to be seen in an English larder, and certainly nowhere near an honest ham salad.

'Potatoes ready, Alice,' said Fergus.

'Salad ready,' said Alice, and they sat down at the kitchen table. She helped herself to ham and salad, and he helped her to hot sauté potatoes. Then he served himself. 'Can you make do without wine or beer?' she asked. 'I'm fairly abstemious at home, and enjoy a giddier way of life only when I'm dining out.'

'Giddier?' said Fergus, who couldn't imagine her dancing on tables, and, in fact, had never known her to be other than modest in her behaviour. 'What does that mean?'

'Oh, as much as two glasses of wine,' said Alice. Smiling, she added, 'And perhaps a wee dram of Tia Maria with my coffee.'

'That's reckless living, I'll no' deny,' said Fergus. 'As for now, Alice, I'm happy with what's in front of me.'

'We'll share a pot of coffee afterwards,' said Alice, applying the dressing to her salad.

'I willna say no to that,' said Fergus, fully relaxed now.

'I'm just pleased that you changed your mind about coming up,' said Alice. 'I wonder what's happening to the thugs?'

'Pound to a bawbee they're locked up in a police cell by now,' said Fergus, already making inroads into his meal, 'and I wouldna be surprised to know the Alsatian is on guard with its tongue out. Alsatian police dogs with the rank of sergeant, y'ken, have a taste for heathens.'

Alice laughed.

'With the rank of sergeant?' she said.

'Promotion comes quickly to those that can chew up a bank robber or two,' said Fergus. The atmosphere in this small kitchen was cosy and light-hearted by now, Alice a pleasure to be with. If she had never been an outgoing or vivacious woman, she was still very natural in that she never made any attempt to be other than what she was, a quiet and studious person. As a soldier for many years, he had known far too many of the other kind, the kind that targeted men in uniform.

'I don't think I'll ever be chewed up,' said Alice, 'for I'm certain I'll never rob a bank.'

The conversation continued in this way all through the meal, then while Alice was making coffee, and during the time they spent drinking it. One could have said they were consciously dawdling at the table. Certainly, they did not bother to move until Fergus looked at his watch.

Then he said, 'The nine o'clock news, Alice, might we listen to it before I go? It might feature the robbery.'

'Oh, yes,' said Alice, 'let's listen to the radio in the living room.'

Her living room was as cosy as the kitchen, and very feminine with its curtains and chintzes. Alice switched the radio on, and they made themselves comfortable in armchairs.

The news arrived. It began with international affairs, including one more confrontation between the East and West, all to do with the suspicions with which Communist Russia and China regarded the Western democracies. Then came a dramatic account of a daring bank robbery in Bristol, the quick getaway of the two men in a white van, and their subsequent vacating of the van to take violent possession of a car in which a young couple were travelling.

'Young couple?' said Alice. 'What will people think of that?'

'Your guess is as good as mine,' said Fergus.

With astonishing courage, continued the announcer, the couple used the van to set off in pursuit of their stolen car, keeping it in sight until it ran out of petrol, when a police patrol car arrived in time to spot the men running over a field in a bid to escape capture. After quick words with the fearless couple–

'Fearless?' Fergus showed a broad grin.

–the two police officers communicated a message to their station and then gave chase. The young couple, continued the announcer, waited until other patrol cars arrived, when a body of police officers joined the pursuit. The suspected robbers were caught, placed under arrest and were presently in custody to await trial. The young couple, their car refuelled, returned home after being commended by Detective Chief Inspector Bradley of the Bristol CID.

'Returned home?' said Alice.

'Oh, aye,' said Fergus, his grin broader. 'Between a reporter's phone in Bristol and the BBC in London, I think you and I have been married off, Alice. Watch out for that reporter getting hold of your name and address, and calling on you.'

'Or you,' said Alice. 'Publicity I don't

want, do you?'

'I'm no' inclined to be turned into meat for hungry newspapers,' said Fergus. He came to his feet. 'Lie low, Alice, and I'll do the same. Now I'll be on my way, while thanking you for a fine meal and for showing what a bonny comrade you are in a crisis.'

'Fergus, I'm delighted to have seen you again,' said Alice, 'and you have my phone number.'

It was an invitation to stay in touch.

They said goodnight to each other, and Fergus drove off in his Austin, which was undamaged except for a dent in the bumper, the result of the collision with the car behind.

Chapter Five

It was a few minutes after nine-thirty when Tommy took a phone call.

'Hello, Tommy Adams here.'

'It's Alice at this end, Dad.'

'Well, what a coincidence,' said Tommy, 'your mum and me have been talking about you for the last ten minutes, and your mum's having fits about what sounds like American gangsters running wild in Bristol. It's been on the television news. D'you know about it?'

'Yes, Dad,' said Alice, 'and I thought I'd better phone you. First off, you'll be pleased to know I'm still alive.'

'Eh? Jesus Christ,' said Tommy, 'you weren't in the bank at the time, were you?'

'No, Dad,' said Alice, 'it was when the ugly brutes were making their getaway through the city that Fergus and I became involved.'

'Fergus? Fergus? Alice, what went on, what happened?'

'Did you hear the BBC announcer mention a young couple?' asked Alice, who knew she had to give the full story to her parents before the trial brought everything into the open.

'Yes, your mum and me both heard that,'

said Tommy. 'So help us, don't tell me the couple were you and Fergus.'

'Listen, Dad.' Alice described what had happened, and if Tommy nearly dropped the phone once or twice, that was to be expected of any appalled father. Only his stalwart self made him retain his hold.

'Bloody hell–'

'Now, Dad.'

'Never mind my language,' said Tommy, 'the bugger could've broken your neck when he pulled you out of Fergus's car. If your mother had known what was going on at the time, she'd have had a real fit. And so would your Aunt Victoria.'

Everyone spoke of Vi's mother as Aunt Victoria, even her grandchildren. To her face, of course, Alice, David and Paul called her Grandma.

'Oh, it's all over now, Dad,' said Alice, 'and Fergus and I are still in one piece. What did you think about the BBC calling us a young couple?'

'I suppose their local bloke thought you were married,' said Tommy. 'And so you should be,' he muttered under his breath.

'But young,' said Alice, laughing. 'I'm thirty next birthday, and Fergus is well into his thirties.'

'I ain't amused,' said Tommy. 'I'm thinking that when Fergus's car ran out of petrol, Bill Sikes and Charlie Peace might have waited for you and Fergus and shot you both, instead of doing a quick scarper.' Bill Sikes was the brutal burglar featured in *Oliver Twist* by Charles Dickens, and Charlie Peace a notorious real-life crook of years ago.

'Oh, I think that if they'd come for us at that point, Fergus would have run them down with their own van,' said Alice. 'He wasn't in the mood to play games.'

'Glad to hear it,' said Tommy. 'Where is he now?'

'He's probably just arriving at his lodgings in Filton,' said Alice.

'Well, next time you see him, tell him he's a bloke after my own heart,' said Tommy, 'but not to take any more liberties with my daughter by pursuing dangerous geezers with her. Listen, are you by yourself, Alice?'

'Of course,' said Alice.

'Well, you shouldn't be,' said Tommy. And you wouldn't be, he thought, if you and Fergus had been churched. But he and Vi had long given up nagging Alice about her unmarried state. They had agreed she had the right to live her own kind of life. 'You could have a nervous breakdown tonight.'

'I don't think so, Dad,' said Alice, 'I'm fine, really.'

'You sure?'

'Quite sure. Give my love to Mum and Aunt Victoria.'

'Well, all right,' said Tommy, 'just take care now.'

'I will. Goodnight, Dad.' Alice rang off.

Tommy put the phone down and returned to the living room to acquaint Vi with events. On the way, Vi's mother called down from the landing. She was living with Tommy and Vi, and had her own two rooms upstairs.

'Tommy?'

'Yes, Mum?'

'There's been some shocking news about Bristol, which is making me worry about Alice.'

'It's OK,' said Tommy, 'she's just been on the phone to let us know she's all right. She sent you her love.'

'Well, I hope you told her there's safer places than Bristol,' said Aunt Victoria.

'Mum, you could live down a mine, right out of the way of crooks,' said Tommy, 'but large lumps of coal could still fall on you.'

'Well, I never,' said Aunt Victoria, aged but still capable of delivering a rebuke, 'it's not like you to give me sauce, Tommy.'

'No offence,' said Tommy, and joined Vi in the living room. He gave her details of his phone conversation with Alice.

Vi, as a loving mother, might have gone a bit over the top at what had befallen Alice in company with Fergus, but didn't. She wasn't the kind of woman to let her imagination run away with her. She could be shocked, of

67

course, but never in any hysterical way. Tommy, in referring to her having fits, had opted for exaggeration, but had not fooled Alice, who knew her mother was the soul of placidity.

'My goodness, Tommy,' said Vi, quivering a little, 'it really was Alice and Fergus that were mentioned on the news? They were the young couple?'

'Alice laughed about that,' said Tommy. 'Beats me that she doesn't mind being old and unmarried.'

'Tommy, she's not old,' said Vi, 'and I'm sure that being with Fergus helped her to cope with things.'

'I don't like what "things" might have meant,' muttered Tommy.

'Still, as long as Alice is all right,' said Vi. 'My, fancy Fergus turning up again. D'you think he's still keen on her?'

'Could be,' said Tommy, 'but according to Alice, he's in Bristol to get a new factory running.'

'Still, that could mean there's hope yet,' said Vi.

'All I know,' said Tommy, 'is that the pair of them only escaped by the skin of their teeth. I'm waiting now to read what me newspaper says in the morning.'

His newspaper made a front-page splash of it, with a photograph of the relevant bank, and a well-drawn diagram of the route taken by the robbers. There were no names, except those of the bank cashier and the chief inspector in charge of the case. But there was quite a bit about the couple who'd given chase in the suspects' own van. It didn't, however, refer to the couple as young. But it did give out the news that the gun used by one of the suspects had not yet been found.

Of course, in Bristol, eager news hounds were trying to trace the couple, but without any help from the police.

Alice turned up for her day's stint at the girls' school, and said not a word to anyone about her involvement with yesterday's excitement. She preferred to carry on quietly until the trial caught the attention of her friends and colleagues.

The days went by, the Adams family feeling quite proud of Alice, although Chinese Lady, inevitably, said she hoped the newspapers wouldn't make Alice look unrespectable when they reported the trial, which she was dreading herself. It could mean the family being talked about again.

A young, up-and-coming band, specializing in the new music trends, gave a concert in late September at a London arena. Teenagers and young men and women packed the venue for an evening of fired-up rock 'n' roll.

The arena boomed with the sound of the revolutionary music of the Fifties, the music that was driving all conventional dance-hall melody to near oblivion, except to the ears of people as old as thirty or forty, the kind who had probably danced a waltz at their wedding receptions. The youngsters of the Fifties, however, jived, twisted, rocked and rolled, their enthusiasm reaching a peak during the final numbers.

BBC television covered the concert. At home, Boots and Polly watched the screen in company with their twins, Gemma and James, soon to be thirteen, an age that would allow them to become part of the fashionable new world, the world of teenagers.

'Oh, just great,' breathed Gemma, eyes glued to the black and white images. 'I don't know why our music teacher is still gone on Ivor Novello's music. Look at all that super rock 'n' roll. Mummy, why didn't you and Daddy take me and James there?'

'Because you're both too young,' smiled Polly, 'and because your father and I still prefer the Charleston.'

'The Charleston?' James looked as if an elephant had walked in with a trunkful of bananas. 'The Charleston? Dad, that went out with the dodo, didn't it?'

'I don't think the dodo went for good,'

70

said Boots, trying like a tolerant old dad to come to terms with the spectacle of near-to-hysterical young people, and the vibrating sound of modern music. 'You can still spot the occasional specimen tottering out of a West End Club.'

'You and your funnies, Dad,' said James.

'Could someone stop talking, please?' said Gemma, eyes mesmerized, ears quivering.

'Dear child,' said Polly, 'never during my lifetime will I allow a rowdy television rodeo to do away with conversation.'

'Rodeo? Rodeo?' Gemma couldn't believe her vivacious mother had suddenly gone potty. 'Mummy, that's American cowboy stuff.'

'Isn't it what we're watching?' asked Polly.

'Mummy, no,' said Gemma 'it's– Oh, blow, it's going.'

The BBC coverage of the concert had come to an end in order to make way for what Gemma considered a boring pro-gramme.

'Bedtime, children,' said Polly. It was ten-thirty, half an hour later than usual for the twins.

'No, just a few more minutes while I get something,' said James. He darted to the sideboard, opened its cupboard and delved. He pulled out photograph albums, and selected one. It was old, but its leather cover was still in good condition. He placed it on

71

the coffee table and opened it up, revealing the title page, which was headed MY TWENTIES.

Boots, Polly and Gemma crowded round to look. James turned pages containing old photographs of Polly and friends in sepia, and snapshots in black and white. James was after finding a special item. There it was, a large studio photograph of Polly as a Twenties flapper in a silk dress with a fringed hem that flirted just above her knees, her stockings a shining white. Around her head she wore a bandeau with a feather. Her bobbed hair came to curling points that touched her cheeks.

'What's the fuss?' said Gemma. 'We've seen that lots of times. It's Mummy as a flapper.'

'Yes, but it's a reminder now,' said James.

'Is it?' asked Boots, who could always find something amusing about life and people, even idiots and politicians. 'Of what?'

'Of how Mum looked when she was doing the Charleston,' said James.

'Spare me,' said Polly, but regarded the photograph as if nostalgic memories were stirring, as they were. The Twenties had been the giddy years of the flappers, of the Bright Young Things. They had been the years when she had first come to know Boots and to fall recklessly in love with him, and he, much to her bitter disappointment, a married man with old-fashioned ideas about faithfulness. How restless and frustrating the following years had been, for not at any time would he accept her as his lover, his mistress.

She glanced at him now. He smiled, affectionately, and she knew he was remembering her wild years too.

'Mummy?' Gemma was curious.

'Yes, young lady?' said Polly.

'You look ever so far away.'

'I'm thinking, darling, of the Charleston and my kind of music,' said Polly. 'The whole so much more delightful than what we've just seen and heard.'

'Mummy dear, I'm sorry to say you're just not with it,' said Gemma.

'Never mind, darling girl,' said Polly, 'I think I'll be quite happy to manage without it.'

'Oh, dear,' said Gemma, 'I think Mummy's getting a bit old-fashioned, James.'

'Oh, that's all right,' said James, 'I expect Dad will see that she doesn't join a knitting circle along with old Mrs Butterworth.'

'Oh, man, I hope not,' said Gemma.

'Oh, what?' said Polly.

'Oh, man,' said Gemma, up with modern parlance. 'Well, I mean, old Mrs Butterworth knits and sucks peppermints.'

'Bed, both of you,' said Polly.

James, a good lad and as easy-going as his father, put the album back in the sideboard, and he and Gemma said goodnight to their parents, Polly receiving a kiss from both, and Boots accepting a smacker from Gemma. Up the twins went to bed.

Polly smiled wryly at Boots.

'There's something on your mind,' said Boots.

'Yes, my flapper days, old fruit,' said Polly, svelte in green silk crepe. She never put on weight or lost any, and so she was still slender and firm of figure. She and Boots had both turned fifty-eight, which Polly thought a sickening indictment of old Father Time's callous indifference to what his accelerating hand could do to women. As she had recently said to Boots, by now the old goat ought to know that most women dislike growing old at the speed of light. Boots, of course, in his airy-fairy fashion, suggested she should call on the old goat and get him to take his foot off his accelerator. That's easy for you to say, said Polly, you're carrying your years without having to watch out for wrinkles. Mine, she said, are simply waiting to catch me off guard. A keen observer could have said that at the moment only some tiny crow's feet had caught her napping. Polly, like Sammy's wife Susie, was a well-preserved woman who naturally objected not only to growing old, but looking old.

'Your flapper days, Polly,' said Boots, 'were hysterical.'

'Don't you mean historical?' said Polly.

'That too,' said Boots. The phone rang. 'Who the devil can that be?' The time was not far short of eleven o'clock, and he and Polly were ready for bed themselves.

'Keep calm, old sport,' said Polly. Boots went to answer the call. It took him a few minutes to return, his expression very sober.

'Polly, dear girl,' he said, 'it's your father. He collapsed a little while ago, just as he and your mother were about to retire. Your mother thinks we should go over. I think we must.'

Polly looked anguished. Her father, General Sir Henry Simms, had celebrated his eightieth birthday only a week ago. He had seemed a little frail, but was nevertheless bright in his manner, and had made the wittiest of speeches. Polly had always been devoted to him. Outside of Boots and her children, there was no-one she loved more.

She came to her feet.

'Yes, we must go, darling,' she said.

'You put your hat and coat on,' said Boots, 'and I'll dash up and let James know we'll be out for a while.'

He did so, having first to shake the boy awake gently. James understood.

'I'll be all right, Dad,' he said, 'so will Gemma. You go with Mum. Dad, I hope Grandpa – well, you know.'

'I know, old chap,' said Boots, and hurried

downstairs to Polly.

They drove into Dulwich Village under a dark sky, a dark brooding sky in their imagination. When they arrived at the handsome mansion, the front door was open, the hall lights on. Charles, the butler, appeared, treading softly.

'How is he, Charles?' Polly's question was quick and anxious.

'Weak, I'm afraid, Miss Polly.' Since his inception, Charles had called her that, just as his predecessor had. Her marriage had made no difference. 'He's up in the bedroom. Lady Simms and the doctor are with him.' He closed the front door quietly, and Polly and Boots hastened up the staircase to the main bedroom. Lady Simms was standing by the bed, the doctor seated on a bedside chair. Silver-haired Sir Henry was lying on the eiderdown, a blanket over him. His eyes were closed, his face pale, his breathing faint.

Lady Dorothy Simms, Polly's stepmother, turned.

'Polly – Boots – so glad you're here – so worried about Henry,' she whispered.

'Is he so ill?' asked Polly, looking down at the man who had always been the most affectionate and indulgent of fathers.

'Dr Wilson–' Lady Simms was halted by a catch in her voice. 'Dr Wilson is as worried as I am.'

Sir Henry lay motionless as the doctor

looked up at Polly.

'It grieves me to say so, Mrs Adams, but I doubt if he'll last the night. His heart is giving out, his pulse fainter by the minute. I doubt if he would survive the strain and effort of being transferred to an ambulance and the journey to hospital.'

'Yes, if nothing can be done, let him remain here, at home,' said Lady Simms. Seventy-two herself, her distress was visible.

So was Polly's. People who did not really know her thought her flippant. That had always covered deeper emotions. As an ambulance driver during the First World War, she had known heartbreak over the slaughter of the men she always called her Tommies. During the years following the armistice of 1918, she had known the giddy way of life taken up by young men and women who felt victory had given the country nothing, and given it that at the expense of nearly a million men. She belonged to the generation of women who lived during the restless Twenties with the ghosts and the shadows of the men who had gone, and so they plunged with baby-faced young males into hectic rounds of false gaiety. All was epitomized in Noel Coward's satirical but moving musical saga, *Cavalcade*.

Only Polly's encounter with Boots had saved her from caring for nothing except her ghosts, her shadows and her wild existence.

Boots induced in her a need for a new beginning, and the Second World War gave her a compulsive wish to do her bit again. It also, in the most tragic way, gave her Boots, for his wife Emily was killed in an air raid. Although she was sincerely sorry for Emily, the day of Polly's marriage to Boots was the day when every emotion was charged with genuine happiness.

But now, to lose her father? He was eighty, yes, and his long life had been complete and fulfilling, but could she call that a con-solation?

A warm hand took hers and lightly squeezed it. Boots whispered.

'Let him know you're here, Polly.'

She leaned, she bent her head and kissed her father on his pale forehead.

'Daddy old darling, wake up and say hello to Polly,' she whispered. 'Boots is here too.'

The dying man's lips moved weakly. His eyelids fluttered and opened. His eyes looked blurred. His lips moved again, and the faintest of smiles touched his face.

'Polly ... dear girl...' The words were hardly audible, but Polly heard them.

'Hello, old soldier, we're all present for inspection,' she whispered. Ever since the opening months of the Great War, Polly had had an affinity with men who wore khaki in the service of their country, and her father had worn his with distinction. 'Papa?' That was an endearment, something from her youth.

The blurred eyes closed again, the lips shrank, and perhaps General Sir Henry Simms heard the call of the trumpets then, for the lightest of sighs emerged and his failing body relaxed.

'Oh, my God,' breathed Lady Simms.

Dr Wilson drew the blanket aside, and conducted a prolonged examination of the old and venerable warrior.

'Doctor?' It was a throaty whisper from Lady Simms.

'I'm so sorry, Lady Simms, so terribly sorry,' said Dr Wilson.

'He's gone?' said Boots.

'I can only say he at least went peacefully,' said Dr Wilson. Although that was a phrase used so often that it had become trite, he hoped it was of some comfort to the suddenly bereaved wife and daughter.

'Such a fine man,' said Lady Simms huskily, and broke down. Polly, emotional herself, did her best to console her stepmother.

Boots looked down at the man he had known as an acutely far-seeing commander and a stalwart friend. He did look peaceful, yes. He looked, in fact, more peaceful than waxily dead. It was his Old Contemptibles of the German Kaiser's war who always said old soldiers never die, they simply fade away.

To what?

Boots touched Sir Henry's lifeless hand.

'Ride your chariot of fire, General,' he said.

Chapter Six

The death of General Sir Henry Simms rated a front-page paragraph in some newspapers. The obituaries were more detailed, touching on his career from his years as a cadet to his time as a corps commander during the Second World War. It was noted that he had had the courage to stand up to Haig midway through the First World War to criticize the tactics that led only to battlefield slaughter.

Members of the Adams family who had know Sir Henry well began to send messages of sympathy to Lady Simms, and to condole with Polly.

'You sign it too, Puss,' said Tim, Boots's son and an ex-commando of World War Two. He had bought a suitable card for Lady Simms.

'Where is it?' asked Felicity, his ex-ATS wife.

'Here,' said Tim, and guided her hand to the card lying on a table.

'All I need now is a flash of light,' said Felicity, whose blind eyes had been experiencing moments of blurred vision for many months. She called them her flashes of light, and was forever hoping they were a signal of eventual recovery. With her left hand she touched the card, and ran her fingers over it.

'You're there,' said Tim. Felicity knew where the pen was. She picked it up and poised it above the card. 'Go ahead,' said Tim.

'I'm waiting for vision,' said Felicity.

'You might have to wait all evening,' said Tim.

'I don't think my will-power could last that long,' said Felicity, and signed her name with a blind flourish, which made it look as if it had been written aboard a heaving ship. 'How's that?'

'Just the job,' said Tim, proud of her. Not even in her worst moments during more than twelve years of blindness had she ever given in to complete despair. 'Damned shame about Polly's dad slipping away like that. She was very cut up when I phoned her.'

'Feel glad she's got Boots,' said Felicity.

'He's a steadfast old lad,' said Tim.

'I think of him as a delightfully reassuring man,' said Felicity. She always felt close to her father-in-law, even if he was only a voice to her. She had never seen him. She only knew from what she had heard about him that he was very distinguished in his looks, entirely whimsical by nature and, according to Susie, a darling man. Felicity had discussed blindness with him at length, since he himself had been blinded during the first hideous battle of the Somme. She knew about the operation that had restored his sight four years later, although his left eye remained permanently impaired. Naturally she longed to see husband Tim again, and daughter Jennifer for the first time, but she also had a strong wish to see exactly what her father-in-law looked like. But then, people's personalities did make their claim on the senses. 'I'll go to the funeral with you, Tim,' she said. 'You and I should both say our goodbyes to an old soldier like Sir Henry.'

'So we should and we will, Puss,' said Tim, who knew that as a one-time ATS officer she considered she was an old soldier herself. And so she was, having been attached to 4 Commando and its complement of bruising, primitive, fearsome men in Troon. And no old soldier could have fought her war-inflicted blindness more courageously than she had.

'Edwin, it's sore and grievous for Lady Simms, and for Polly and Boots,' said Chinese Lady.

'Yes, I know, my dear,' said Sir Edwin Finch, 'Polly was extremely close to her father, and Boots had a great deal of affection and admiration for him. They were at

Dunkirk together, Sir Henry being the last general to escape the Germans on that dramatic retreat to the sea. The War Office heads weren't too pleased with the closeness of his escape. The capture of a general by the enemy isn't welcomed by any High Command.'

'Edwin, I don't want to listen to any war stories,' said Chinese Lady. 'They remind me too much of that madman Hitler. You can come out for a nice walk with me and I'll post the card and letter we're sending to Lady Simms.'

She had written the card and Sir Edwin had written the letter.

'Very well, Maisie, a little walk, then,' said Sir Edwin.

She looked at him, her eyes showing a touch of concern. He was one year older than Polly's father had been. She couldn't say he looked frail or stooping. No, his back was still straight, his features leaner, perhaps, but still firm. His hair, however, was silvery. Chinese Lady felt a tug at the heart at the thought of him slipping away as suddenly as Sir Henry.

Determinedly, she put it out of her mind.

All the same, she said, 'We don't have to walk in any hurry, Edwin.'

'Well, a hurry isn't necessary, Maisie,' smiled Sir Edwin. 'On the other hand, I'm not yet an old man.'

'No, just getting on a bit,' said Chinese Lady.

'That is, I'm not yet infirm,' said Sir Edwin, 'and we'll enjoy a very pleasant walk at our usual pace.'

'Just to the pillar box and back,' she said.

The fact that she herself was seventy-eight bothered her not at all, even if her dark brown hair did show liberal streaks of grey. Other people might be old. She didn't consider she was, especially as she was still active. It was a fact that women lived longer than men, and widows always outnumbered widowers.

Chinese Lady, however, had no desire to outnumber her husband.

'What about a decent wreath for the funeral, Susie?' asked Sammy of his illustrious wife. Well, when she was dressed in her best, he reckoned she was as illustrious as any royal duchess, especially as she still owned a good figure, even if she was fifty. He himself was fifty-two.

'I'm not a great lover of wreaths, Sammy,' said Susie, 'they look waxy and mournful.'

'Aren't they supposed to?'

'Mournful doesn't suit Polly's dad,' said Susie, 'he was always such an alive gentleman.'

'Much to me sorrow, Susie,' said Sammy, 'he's stopped being alive, and that's genuine mournful for him and everyone who knew him.'

'All the same,' said Susie, 'I'm going to suggest we order a lovely floral spray from the florists, something bright and colourful that would be a kind of celebration of his life. That's what we'd like, wouldn't we, Sammy, a celebration of his life?'

'Well, I don't think Polly would want any of us to celebrate his death,' observed Sammy. 'It would look like we were glad to see him go.'

'We'll have a card put with the spray,' said Susie, who liked to do things in what she felt was the right way. 'We'll write "To Sir Henry, in happy memory of his long life".'

'Long and esteemed life?' suggested Sammy.

'Honourable?' suggested Susie.

'Esteemed and honourable?' countered Sammy.

'From Sammy, Susie and family?' said Susie.

'Tell you what,' said Sammy, 'I'll ask Boots about the wordage.'

'I adore Boots, as you know,' said Susie, 'but–'

'Susie, might I point out, as I have before, that I ain't in favour of you adoring me educated brother?' said Sammy.

'Sammy, we'll decide on the wording ourselves,' said Susie. 'I'll let Boots and

Polly see the card at the funeral.'

'Well, all right,' said Sammy, 'but don't do any adoring in the churchyard, or it'll look sacrilegious, and the vicar won't like that, whoever he is.'

'I'll be very respectful, Sammy.'

'Well, both of us should be, Susie. Polly's dad was a high-class military gent.'

'Yes, Sammy, I know,' said Susie.

Bless my Susie, thought Sammy, she's illustrious all right. I think I'll buy her a tiara for Christmas, if old Eli Greenberg or Rachel can point me to a shopful of sparklers run by an obliging son of Moses who likes to bargain. A bloke can't bargain with Bond Street jewellers. They all wear Sunday suits with pearl-button waistcoats.

'Bobby, *chéri*,' said Helene, the handsome French wife of Lizzy and Ned's eldest son, 'I am so sad for Polly.'

'We all are,' said Bobby, much like his Uncle Tommy in his stalwart physique. 'Polly had a very special affection for her dad.'

'Such a distinguished man,' said Helene, who had met Sir Henry and Lady Simms at the home of Grandma and Grandpa Finch on special occasions. 'The kind of Englishman French people see as very civilized.'

'How do they see the rest of us?' asked Bobby, watching the children, Estelle and

Robert, playing in the garden.

'But you know,' said Helene.

'True, I did meet a few during our times with the Resistance, and I know how they saw me,' said Bobby. 'As a bit of a peasant.'

'Ah, yes,' murmured Helene. 'You remember the one called Paul?'

'What about him?' asked Bobby.

'He asked me once if it was true I was going to marry you. And when I said yes, he said "Good God, why?" And I said, "Because I'm an idiot."'

'That makes two of us,' said Bobby.

'Yes, we are two idiots together,' said Helene. 'Are we to go to the funeral?'

'Well, I shall go, out of respect for Sir Henry's achievements in both World Wars,' said Bobby.

'Then I shall go too,' said Helene.

Bobby smiled. His robust and spirited French wife was one with the family in her sentiments, even if she still thought some English people were stuffy and some quite mad.

'Matt,' said Rosie to husband Matthew, who was filling in a monthly return for the Ministry, 'we must go to the funeral.'

'I knew you would want to,' said Matt, 'you were among the ATS personnel attached to Sir Henry's headquarters. And I'd like to go because I think he and Boots were both responsible for persuading the army to overlook my gammy ankle.'

'It'll take up the best part of our day,' said Rosie, now thirty-nine but, unlike Polly had been, not in the least worried about reaching the dread age of forty. Rosie had the same kind of philosophical approach to life as Boots. Since one couldn't hold back advancing years, then enjoy what were left. And she did enjoy her open-air life on the poultry farm, where a small flock of sheep shared the large field with a multitude of chickens, and trained ferrets put paid to infiltrating rabbits.

'I think we can leave Hortense and Joe to take care of things,' said Matt. Hortense and Joe Robinson were their West Indian helpers, who had taken to the work as happily as plumbers to the prospect of several cups of tea. It was Joe who had trained the ferrets. 'One thing I couldn't ask them to do is fill in any of these forms. Burn my damn old braces, Rosie, I can't for the life of me think what the Ministry clerks do with all this information.'

'They file it,' said Rosie.

'What for, a rainy day?' said Matt.

'No, to keep things tidy,' said Rosie.

'How'd you know?' asked Matt, a sinewy son of Dorset.

'Guesswork, old love,' said Rosie. 'For the funeral, wear your dark grey suit, a white shirt and a black tie.'

'Have I got a black tie?' asked Matt.

'You will have by the time we're on our way,' said Rosie. 'I'll see you do.'

'Mista Chapman, Mista Chapman, sir?'

Hortense was calling from the open kitchen door. Matt came out of the little room he used as an office, walked through the kitchen, followed by Rosie, and found his buxom helper waiting for him.

'What's up, Hortense?'

'That damn ole cockerel Obadiah, Mista Chapman, he ain't nothing but a pain,' said Hortense. 'He's pecking at the hens and drawing blood, and he ain't treating the young cock Elijah right, neither. He's turned into a killer, Mista Chapman, like some do, so best if you let Joe wring his neck.'

'Tell Joe to go ahead,' said Matt.

Hortense turned and bawled.

'Joe!' No answer. 'Joe, where is you, you done gone sleeping, you lazy ole black bones?'

'That I ain't, old woman.' Joe appeared by the shed used for grading eggs. As usual, he wore a grin as wide as a barn door. 'I'm here, ain't I?'

'Mista Chapman says go ahead!'

'Chop Obadiah?'

'Right now,' called Hortense.

'That'll make things a mite more peaceful

round here,' said Joe.

Rosie, going back to the office with Matt, said, 'Yes, we can leave things to them on the funeral day. Matt, they're jewels.'

'They like the work,' said Matt, 'and it's better for Joe than a job as a dustman. Dustmen keep close company with house-holders' discarded kipper bones.'

'Do people still eat kippers?' smiled Rosie.

'Well,' said Matt, 'down in the land of Dorset, at Weymouth by the sea, there be one thing for always, kippers for Friday tea.'

'One day you'll run out of Dorset doggerel,' said Rosie.

'One day,' said Matt, 'and then I'll borrow some from Somerset.'

'Oh, joy,' said Rosie, and out she went to pack ten dozen new-laid eggs for delivery to a country hotel.

The funeral at Dulwich church was a tribute to Sir Henry, attended as it was by a representative of the top brass, by two serving generals, several retired generals, deputations from the British Legion and Old Comrades Association, some surviving Old Contemptibles, several veterans of the Second World War, three ex-ATS officers who had been on his staff, and close relatives and friends.

Boots thought it a military tribute to a man who had earned not only the respect, but also the affection, of all who had known him in his active days. He had represented the era dominated by the Kaiser's war and gone on to make his mark in the war against Hitler.

Boots remembered the nightmare retreat to Dunkirk, seated beside Sir Henry in a battered and limping car that finally gave out. Then he and Sir Henry had joined the straggling column of beaten and weary men on the final stage of the slogging march to Dunkirk. Sir Henry had been over sixty then, but had never once wavered on that retreat.

'Boots?' whispered Polly, as they came out of the church in the wake of the coffin. Preceding them were Lady Simms and her elderly brother. 'Boots?'

'I know, Polly. Memories.'

'I'm full of them.'

'France and Flanders, Polly?' said Boots. Their wreath was one of Flanders poppies. 'And ambulances?'

'And everything since then.'

'All touching your father?'

'And you, darling. I love you dearly.'

Boots glanced at her. The clouds of early autumn were reflected in her dark sienna eyes. A little mist gathered.

Whatever some people might say about her, thought Boots, Sir Henry's daughter was a woman of emotions and feelings under her vivacious and sometimes flippant exterior.

Her tears spilled during the final moments of the burial when a bugler of the Scots Guards sounded the haunting notes of the Last Post. Lady Simms crumpled a little. Chinese Lady, never known by her family to give way, did so on this occasion as the bugler's tribute died away. Boots himself, arm around Polly, set his mouth in a firm line.

Chinese Lady and Sir Edwin, Bobby and Helene, Sammy and Susie, Ned and Lizzy, Tommy and Vi, Rosie and Matthew, Eloise and Colonel Lucas, and Tim and Felicity, were among the many mourners who watched in silence as handfuls of earth began to shower the coffin.

Eventually, Tim said, 'It's over, Puss.'

'With some men, and some women, it's never over,' said Felicity.

Rosie moved to join Boots and Polly. Boots thought that if mourning black could suit any woman, that woman was his adopted daughter, with her corn-gold hair and her marvellous blue eyes. He kissed her, and she kissed Polly.

'Rosie, dear old thing, so glad you came,' said Polly.

'Well, you and I, Polly, did have our years in khaki,' said Rosie. 'So I had to come along with Matthew. I'm sad, Polly, yes, but very proud to have known your father. The service was lovely, but far too moving for my heartstrings. What did you think, Boots?' Rosie had long addressed her adoptive father by his nickname.

'I thought it a fine farewell to a fine man,' said Boots.

That evening the rain poured down and turned the topsoil over the grave to mud, which might have been a reminder to the old warrior of the mud of Flanders.

Chapter Seven

Lulu's spectacles regarded Paul darkly as he made ready to depart for work the following morning.

'You don't call this fair, do you?' she said.

'Don't call what fair?' asked Paul.

'You going off to continue your career,' said Lulu. 'And leaving me here to be a mother to our child.'

'Lulu love, you are its mother,' said Paul.

'And you're its father,' said Lulu.

'Yes, I'm proud of that,' said Paul, 'but, unfortunately, I'm not equipped to be its mother as well. Well, you know, bosoms and so on.'

'Ha-ha, I don't think,' said Lulu. 'What an out-and-out rotter. Giving me a baby and sabotaging my own career.'

'I'm proud of that too—'

'Of sabotaging my career?'

'No, not that,' said Paul. 'Of proving my manhood.'

'My eye,' said Lulu. 'Look at what's happening, and what I'm missing out there. New attitudes, new music, a new kind of women—'

'What's a new kind of women?' asked

Paul. 'New framework, like muscles in place of – er – well, bosoms?'

'Have you got a fetish about bosoms?'

'What's a fetish?' asked Paul.

'Something weird,' said Lulu.

'You've got me there,' said Paul. 'I only know about yours, Lulu love. It's nicely shaped, and it's turned out useful too. Our little Sylvia dotes on it.'

'Oh, very witty,' said Lulu. 'Don't you realize my present circumstances are tying me down?'

'Only for a few years,' said Paul. 'As soon as Sylvia's old enough to go to school–'

'That won't be for five years, you beast,' said Lulu.

'You'll still be young,' said Paul.

'Oh, rats,' said Lulu.

'Want to know something?' said Paul.

'Tell me,' said Lulu.

'I like you as a wife and mother,' said Paul.

'Buzz off, or I'll chuck something heavy at you,' said Lulu, and Paul made a wise exit. 'And don't come back,' she called.

'No, all right, not until I've finished work,' called Paul.

Lulu, hearing the front door close behind him, began her first necessary activity, that of attending to her infant. At ten o'clock she put Sylvia, fed, washed and freshly nappied, into her pram, which was standing outside the front door. After the night's rain, the morning was bright and clear, and Lulu believed that time in the fresh air was good for the health of the babe. At eleven o'clock she would wheel her to the shops.

At ten-thirty she was in the front room, tidying up while wondering exactly how she had come to be what she had always planned not to be, the equivalent of a commonplace, middle-class housewife. Well, of course, it was the result of being daft enough to fall in love. Falling in love had a shocking effect on the most intelligent women, it turned their minds mushy, and well before they could recover they found themselves married and enslaved. Look at me, she told herself, I'm chained to the kitchen sink and to housework, while Paul's out in the world meeting challenges.

The curse of it was that she liked being married to him, which meant she was in a hopeless position.

She heard a slight sound then, like the murmur of a woman's voice. She moved to the bay window. Through the right-hand pane she saw a young woman leaning over the pram, talking to the infant, cooing to her. She had the waterproof cover unfixed, and her hands were in the pram. A shock sparked through Lulu. The woman was undoing the holding strap.

She rushed to the front door, pulled it open and darted out.

'What're you doing, what're you up to?' She almost shouted the words. The young woman straightened up, the baby in her arms. Beneath the brim of her hat, her eyes looked hot, her face pale.

'He's mine,' she blurted, 'you stole him from me!'

Lulu had heard about women who, having lost a child through illness, went peculiar and searched around for a replacement. She steeled herself for a confrontation that would avoid a tug-of-war. Little Sylvia was awake, her eyes blinking.

'Are you accusing me of stealing your baby boy?'

'Yes, and you did,' said the young woman.

'That child is a baby girl,' said Lulu. 'Be good enough to put her back in her pram.'

'It's not a girl, it's my baby boy,' said the young woman, cradling the child tightly. Little Sylvia began to cry. The young woman turned and attempted to make a run with her.

Lulu sprang like a tigress, planting herself in front of the crazed woman, whose eyes looked this way and that in search of escape. Lulu reached. For a moment, the woman clutched the infant tighter. Sylvia yelled. Lulu took hold of her. The restricting arms loosened and the woman relinquished the child. She stared in despair at Lulu.

Lulu felt an understanding.

'I'm so sorry,' she said. 'What happened to your own child?'

The woman dropped her eyes and whispered, 'Someone took it.'

Lulu, doubting this, said, 'Was it ill?'

'Someone took it.'

'Your doctor?'

'Yes, that's right, he took it to give to his wife.'

Lulu decided that if there was some truth in that, it was to do with having a dead child removed by a doctor into the care of undertakers.

'What did your husband say?' she asked. She was being very gentle, and Paul would have been surprised at her deep note of compassion.

'He was very upset.'

'Talk to him,' said Lulu.

'Yes.'

'You can have another child.'

'Yes, I'll talk to him. We're both very upset still.'

Lulu's cradling arms had quietened Sylvia, and she said, lightly, 'Say goodbye to my infant.'

'Goodbye, baby,' said the young woman, and walked away. She turned. 'I'm sorry,' she said, and walked on.

Lulu watched her go, then placed Sylvia back in her pram. But she wheeled the pram over the front step and into the hall.

The babe slept.

Lulu was certain of one thing now. Nothing, after all, was as important to her as her child and her husband. That meant she could more easily put up with her status as a lower middle-class wife and mother.

And even with enslavement. For a while.

She had a story to tell Paul when he arrived home in the evening. Paul listened, first with disbelief, then intensity.

'Jesus,' he breathed, 'are there really women so out of their minds that they're driven to run off with someone else's baby?'

'You must have heard of that happening,' said Lulu.

'Perhaps I have,' said Paul, 'and perhaps I haven't thought it believable. I mean, could any woman live her life like that, knowing the child she was bringing up had been stolen from its real mother? Lulu, thank God you saw her in time, otherwise she and Sylvia would have disappeared from sight and sound.'

'I felt terribly sorry for her,' said Lulu.

'Then you're a sweetheart,' said Paul, 'and for that and for saving us from losing Sylvia, we'll all go out on Saturday, and I'll dip into our savings and buy you a new dress, one with a flared skirt over frilly net.'

'Well, thanks for the thought,' said Lulu, 'but that kind of dress?' Her spectacles glinted. 'Haven't you done enough turning me into a house slave. I'm not going to be turned into a teeny-bopper as well by wearing a dress like that.'

'Lulu, you'd look an eyeful,' said Paul.

'Nothing doing,' said Lulu. 'Try me with something smart and dignified.'

'Dignified?' said Paul 'You're only twenty-three. You don't need to look dignified at that age. Wait till you're sixty.'

'At twenty-three, I don't want to look like a giggly teeny-bopper, either,' said Lulu.

'Fair enough,' said Paul, 'you're the heroine, Lulu, so you choose.'

'Black's smart,' said Lulu.

'Black?' said Paul. 'Don't do that to me. My parents, aunt and uncles are all in mourning for the loss of an old family friend, Sir Henry Simms.'

'So help me, what have I done, marrying into a family on close terms with titled aristocrats?' said Lulu. 'Don't you know titled aristocrats rose to wealth and power on the backs of their serfs? For a working-class woman like me, my marriage could alienate me from my roots.'

'Oh, well, together we can both grin and bear it,' said Paul.

'I've had a thought,' said Lulu.

'About my turn to get supper?' said Paul.

'Yes, it's time you got on with it,' said Lulu, 'I have to give Sylvia her bath and her bedtime feed.'

'Hold on, what about this thought you had?' asked Paul.

'Oh, yes. I think,' said Lulu pensively, 'I think I like being a wife and mother.'

'Lulu?'

Lulu smiled, and her spectacles shone in friendly fashion. She came to her feet, gave Paul a light kiss, then went to fetch the child she had rescued from an unhappy, deranged young woman.

On Friday morning, Boots and Sammy were at the firm's garments factory in Bethnal Green, talking by pre-arrangement to the directors of two companies from Manchester whose excuses for late delivery of fabrics were legion. Finally one admitted the trouble lay with the trade union bloody-mindedness of their workforces. Mr Donague said he was well aware that late or unreliable deliveries could cause customers like Adams Fashions to cancel and go elsewhere. But it was difficult to offer guarantees when production was periodically disrupted by union walkouts. Shop stewards as good as ran some firms, a new and aggravating development, by heck.

'That kind are Commies,' said Tommy, who was also present, the meeting taking place in his office. 'Ought to be put on a fast train to Moscow.'

'Look here,' said Boots, who had a talent for taking effortless charge of a situation, 'let's have all the facts, Mr Donague.'

Mr Donague glanced at his rival, Mr Ball, who was in the same rocky boat as himself.

'The facts are, Mr Adams,' said Mr Ball, 'that our timetable for output and deliveries are at the mercy of our shop stewards.'

'You're actually serious?' said Sammy. 'That kind of kiss-my-elbow stuff could lead to a shutdown of your factories.'

'We know it, the shop stewards know it, but they lead the workforces to believe the walkouts will get them a large increase in their wages,' said Mr Donague.

'Well, haven't you told your workers what it really means?' asked Tommy. 'That they'll lose their jobs if shutdowns happen?'

'Managerial staff aren't allowed to address the workers,' said Mr Ball.

'Eh?' said Sammy.

'What?' said Tommy.

Their Bethnal Green factory never suffered trade union troubles. All their workers were non-union. Sammy had always believed in a direct and friendly boss–workers relationship. He'd known arguments with trade union organizers who'd had the gall to threaten to close his previous factories down unless he allowed his workforce to join. With the support and backing of his machinists and seamstresses, particularly that of dear old Gertie Roper he'd won every argument and repaid his workers for their loyalty.

'I'm listening to old Mother O'Reilly's cousins, am I?' he said.

'You're listening to rising power, Sammy,' said Boots.

'Don't think I don't know who's got the power and who's doing the real talking,' said Sammy. 'Trade union bosses.'

Mr Ball said there was another fact, that he and Bill Donague had come down from Manchester specially to advise the Adams brothers that unless they unionized their workforce, he and Donague wouldn't be able to supply them at all.

Mr Donague put in his piece, saying that all other suppliers would have to cut the Adams factory out. Not that it would happen overnight, no, but their factory would come under gradual pressure.

'Gradual pressure, of course, means the trade unions will baulk at putting our workers on the dole at a minute's notice,' said Boots.

'That's my guess,' said Mr Donague, and suggested the Adams brothers should think about the long-term dangers of sticking with non-union labour. 'It's up to you gents, by gum.'

'At the moment,' said Sammy, 'I don't feel like a gent, more like a common geezer

104

loaded with an aggravating headache that's turning me a bit spiteful.'

'What's to be done?' asked Tommy, looking at Boots, the family's lifeboat.

'We think about it,' said Boots, 'as Mr Donague suggested.'

'I ain't in favour of being ordered about by fat trade union bosses who wear bowler hats and smoke cigars,' said Sammy, at which Mr Ball closed his eyes and prayed that that impolitic comment hadn't drifted into the wrong kind of lurking ears. He and Mr Donague knew by now that trade union officials were sensing the extent of their power. A union-backed workers' front could collapse their own companies. It would mean the workers bringing about their own unemployment, but the gormless lot couldn't or wouldn't see their jobs were on the line.

'Mind you, Sammy,' said Tommy, 'there's not many non-union workshops in the country. I suppose we're lucky to have lasted this long.'

'Hold on, Tommy, watch what you're saying,' said Sammy, 'that kind of remark is no help to my present condition.'

'Well, we'll leave the problem with you,' said Mr Donague.

Mr Ball promised he and Donague would keep in touch and do their best to persuade their workforces to let them make some deliveries, which they might do if they knew the Adams factory was considering unionizing their own workforce.

'How kind,' said Sammy, with heavy sarcasm.

'Give 'em our regards,' said Tommy.

The three brothers said goodbye to the two directors, then began a conference, Tommy first letting his secretary know they weren't to be disturbed, and that any callers with urgent problems were to be referred to Mister Jimmy, Sammy's son.

Chapter Eight

Boots opened the informal proceedings by pointing out there was an immediate solution available, that of the whole of the factory workforce accepting trade union cards.

Sammy said he didn't see that as a solution, only as a bucketful of trouble, especially if the elected shop stewards turned cussed. It wouldn't be long, he said, before they claimed their responsibilities were a full-time job, and you can bet, he said, that the local union boss would come along and tell Tommy to accept the claim. The local union boss, said Sammy, was a big bother.

'Big Brother,' murmured Boots.

'Big who?' said Tommy.

'Oh, an unseen power figure in a futuristic novel by George Orwell,' said Boots. 'It's called *1984.*'

'What's futuristic?' asked Tommy.

'In this case,' said Boots, 'it's a warning of what total state power could do to people. Turn them into robots.'

'All fitted up with knobs and wires?' said Sammy. 'I don't fancy that, you could go up in sparks if someone touched the wrong knob. Anyway, what's Big Brother or Big

Sister got to do with our problem?'

'If you think deeply about what our friends from Manchester said,' observed Boots, 'you'll realize workforces are being increasingly controlled by the unions, not by their employers.'

'They've been conniving at that for years,' said Tommy.

Sammy said that once Tommy, as factory manager, lost control of all the workers here, he'd lose his self-respect as well. They all would. And costs of running the place would go up. They always did when trade union rules took over.

Boots pointed out the obvious, that if they remained non-union, they'd almost certainly find their friends from Manchester were right. Unionized manufacturers would stop supplies. The post-war Labour government strengthened the power of the unions, and the unions were beginning to use that power.

'That's it, fill me with joy,' said Sammy.

'I'm rapturous meself, I don't think,' said Tommy.

'Whatever we do,' said Boots, 'there's something extra we should consider, and that's making the factory independent of suppliers.'

'Come again?' said Sammy.

'Adams Fashions has an import licence,' said Boots, 'one that you and Rachel applied for, negotiated for and won. Compliments to you and Rachel, Sammy old lad. Let's use the licence to import the raw materials we'll need to manufacture our own fabrics.'

'It grieves me, Boots, to hear you talking so ignorant,' said Sammy, shaking his head in sorrow for a brother who hitherto had always proved highly intelligent. 'We ain't equipped for that kind of manufacturing, nor don't we have the right kind of workers.'

'Skilled labour is still available,' said Boots, 'and we've room to build an extension to the factory, and to equip it with all the necessary machinery. That could take six months, but we're solvent to the point where we could subsidize all costs for even longer than six months. Don't you fancy that, Sammy, manufacturing our own yarn and fabrics, and being independent of suppliers?'

'Blind Harry,' said Sammy, 'why didn't I think of that? It's one more natural step in our expansion.'

'Which I personally like,' said Tommy.

'Like?' said Sammy. 'I'm seeing rainbows. We'll get the property company working on the project, we'll get Tim and Daniel to apply for planning permission, and work out the size of the extension with the architects. You're right, Boots, we're so solvent we've got thousands of quids ready to be tapped, and rents coming in from the new block of flats.'

Their property company had developed an acquired site in Camberwell by erecting a three-storeyed block of very desirable flats at reasonable but profitable rents, a repeat of a development in Southwark. Boots had invested fifty thousand pounds in the project, the money coming from the sale of a German estate. That estate had belonged to the German husband of one Elsie Chivers, an old friend of the Adams family who had had a particular affection for Boots. On her death during the Second World War, she had left all she owned to Boots, and that came to include her late husband's estate. Boots had sold it to the administrator for fifty thousand pounds, and that was the sum he invested with the property company.

'Yes, we've got the rents coming in nice and steady,' said Tommy, 'but we haven't recovered the costs yet, have we?'

'Those costs, Tommy, are being recovered by the rents,' said Sammy. 'and there'll come the day when every rent is profit.'

'Meself, I'm not a financial expert,' said Tommy, honest, sensible and conscientious, but not up with his brothers' mental prowess. 'Still, I thought I'd raise the point.'

'Your privilege, Tommy,' said Boots, always the one who held the family and the business together. 'Well, then, we've agreed this new proposal, but not the matter of unionizing the workforce here.'

Someone knocked on the office door. Someone, a lady, called.

'Mister Tommy?'

'All right, come in, Maud,' called Tommy.

The door opened, and Tommy's secretary, Maud Galloway, showed herself, a homely woman in her late twenties.

'Mister Tommy, I know you mentioned you weren't to be disturbed,' she said, 'but Mr Burridge is here and says he's got to see you.'

'Barney Burridge?' said Sammy.

'That's him,' said Tommy. 'Well, I suppose it is. Is it, Maud?'

'Yes, that's him, Mister Tommy,' said Maud.

Barney Burridge was the local trade union convenor, who made regular forays into the Adams factory to insist on the right to find out if the workforce was being denied the privilege of joining the relevant union. Invited to accept the privilege, Tommy's workers always gave Burridge the thumbs down. They knew who put the jam in their doughnuts. It wasn't any union.

'Let's see him,' said Sammy.

Maud ushered the man in. Barney Burridge was big and burly, and, like most politicized trade union officials, capable of delivering a speech if asked a question he couldn't answer. Members of Parliament had the same kind of talent.

Dressed in a bowler hat and a blue suit, Burridge came to a stop when he saw

Tommy and Sammy were both present, in company with a third man. He had never met Boots, and Boots only knew of him through Sammy.

'Hello, hello,' said Burridge, 'what's this then, Tommy, a deputation? Well, I'm used to deputations, I've been part of one meself on occasions. I stood side by side with Ernie Bevin once, y'know, when we had something to say to a saucy industrialist who was trying to downgrade his skilled workers. Well, glad to see three of you ready to open up a discussion with me about your non-union workforce. Let's get down to it, shall we?'

'We're busy,' said Tommy, 'and seeing I don't remember inviting you, forget any discussion.'

'Now, now, Tommy,' said Burridge, taking his hat off, buffing it with his elbow and putting it back on, 'you know I've got an open invitation to drop in whenever I'm passing to see that you're not depriving your workers of the chance to join the union. Regarding which, let's have a sensible discussion and no arguments, eh? It's what I'm here for.'

And what you've caught us on the hop for, thought Sammy.

'Be our guest,' he said, while Boots thought that as the subject was obviously going to relate to that which they'd aired themselves, unionism, then Burridge might

112

as well get on with it.

Burridge began to talk, fluently, making the point that in the area covered by Bethnal Green, Stepney and Whitechapel, the Adams factory was the only non-union shop, which was aggravating all honest trade unionists in the East End.

'What about the dishonest ones?' asked Boots, putting the question mildly.

'Dishonest?' said Burridge.

'I think you implied there were some,' said Boots. 'Not many, of course, but some.'

'No such thing as a dishonest trade unionist,' said Burridge. 'Dishonest in respect of not being true to union principles, that is. What they get up to in their private lives doesn't concern us. The point under discussion, he said, was that the Adams workforce was being deprived of the advantages and protection of the union, which situation had come about because the union wasn't being allowed to put its case.

'You're slightly out of order,' said Boots.

Burridge gave him a look, but couldn't see anything contentious about this interloper's friendly smile. Sammy grinned. He knew Boots. Burridge didn't know him at all.

'As a trade union official,' said Burridge, 'I'm never out of order, I make my points in keeping with all the rules and regulations, and accordingly I avoid slip-ups.'

'Nevertheless,' said Boots, still mildly, 'I

think you've just put your foot on a banana skin.'

'Objection,' said Burridge.

'Overruled, me lord?' said Sammy to the ceiling.

'I think Mr Burridge knows that the factory management has always allowed him or any of his brother officials, at times of their own choosing, the freedom to address the workers,' said Boots.

'Who is this bloke?' asked Burridge of Tommy.

'Colonel Adams, my elder brother,' said Tommy.

'Colonel?' said Burridge, and gave Boots another look. This time he thought the smile was a bit aggravating. So he said he wasn't going to be put off by even a bleedin' general, never mind any colonel. It was his opinion that addressing the Adams workforce hadn't paid off because the fact was they were primed to say no. Bribed, possibly.

'I think you've just turned opinion into fact,' said Boots.

'I'll be frank,' said Burridge, 'I don't like the way you talk. It leads to arguments, and I'm not here to argue, just to put my case.'

'Carry on,' said Sammy.

Burridge carried on. First, he said, there's the well-known fact that a non-union workforce is exploited by the management in not being paid approved union rates.

114

Second, low wages–

'Never mind second,' said Sammy, 'our workers are paid above union rates.'

'Well, you would say that, Sammy,' said Burridge.

'I'm saying it too,' said Tommy.

Burridge said he wasn't convinced and that he'd like to make his second point, which was that low wages enabled the Adams factory to undercut their competitors. Which fact, he said, is also getting up the noses of every union shop in the area. Accordingly, he said, you've got to come into line, you've got to get your workers into the union or else.

'Or else what?' asked Boots.

'You'll be picketed until you do,' said Burridge. 'Now, we don't want to quarrel about these problems. The union believes in friendly and sensible negotiations, but in certain cases there comes a time when the only option is effective action.'

'Well,' said Boots, still in mild vein, 'suppose you talk to our workers while you're here?' He consulted his watch. 'They'll be having their lunch break in half an hour. You can address them in the canteen.'

'Nothing doing,' said Burridge. 'I've talked to 'em before, but of course, they're all primed to turn a deaf ear. I wasn't born yesterday, y'know.'

'If you had been, you wouldn't be wearing a suit and a bowler hat,' said Tommy.

Burridge laughed, good-humouredly.

'Too right, Tommy,' he said. 'No, I'm making it your responsibility to do the talking, to let your workers know they need the protection of a union, and persuade them to take up membership, when we'll be pleased to come and hand out union cards.'

'I feel like someone's hitting me over my head,' said Tommy.

'It's not a good morning for mine, either,' said Sammy.

Burridge went on to say that unless agreement was reached, the first pickets would be in place early Monday morning, when no goods would be allowed in or out. This would continue until–

'All right, we know,' said Sammy.

'Think it over,' said Burridge. 'I'll give you reasonable time, up to first thing Monday morning. Well, it's been a pleasure, having a friendly discussion with you gents and avoiding arguments and aggravation.' He glanced at Boots. 'Just about, eh, Colonel? Very sensible. Good day.'

Off he went, as jauntily as a large rolling sailor.

'What dropped on me?' asked Tommy. 'I feel flattened.'

'I feel a draught,' said Sammy. 'The bugger's left the door open.'

'Do the talking at lunchtime,' said Boots.

'To the workers?' said Tommy.

'We'll have to,' said Boots, 'it's unavoidable. We'd almost reached that conclusion before the bowler hat walked in. Let's settle for playing ball with the union and for the consolation prize.'

'The consolation prize being this new development?' said Sammy.

'That's the way I see it,' said Boots.

'Right,' said Sammy. 'I'll talk to the workers at lunchtime.'

'Let Tommy do that,' said Boots. 'He looks after their welfare, listens to their problems, and serves as their kind uncle. Yes, your privilege, Tommy.'

'I'll give it a go,' said Tommy.

He did so later, in the canteen. Women and girls, machinists and seamstresses, maintenance men, van drivers, heavy-duty men, all listened in complete silence to their factory manager advising them why it was necessary to join a union.

The silence was broken by a woman chargehand.

'Mister Tommy, we'll get mucked about, we'll get told to join strikes, and we'll get paid union rates.'

'What you'll be paid, Flo, will be the same as we're paying you now,' said Tommy.

'With bonuses, Mister Tommy?'

'With bonuses,' said Tommy, 'and the usual canteen Christmas party.'

117

'Well, all right, Mister Tommy,' said Flo, 'but there'll be a riot if what orders we get from the union don't suit you and yer brothers. There's nobody here that's going to be party to upsetting you and Mister Sammy and Mr Adams.'

Boots was always respectfully referred to as Mr Adams, which sometimes riled Sammy, even if Boots was the eldest and senior.

'We can always talk about anything that's going to upset any of us,' said Tommy, as stalwart and reassuring a figure as ever, and accordingly much sighed over by machinists married to men who didn't even know how to put the family cat out at night.

Voices were raised.

'Good on yer, Mister Tommy, we'll join the union if we got to, then.'

'Don't you worry, Mister Tommy, we won't let 'em muck us about.'

And so on.

Jimmy, Sammy's younger son, and personnel manager, spoke to his dad and his Uncle Boots before they left.

'What went on this morning?' he asked. 'Must've been something drastic for you to do a turnabout on our principles.'

Sammy put him in the picture, and Jimmy made the observation that trouble wouldn't be long in coming, that it would come in the form of the workers having to walk out to support every factory that went on strike.

'If that happens,' said Sammy, 'I'll talk to the managements of other factories facing the same problem, and persuade them we've all got no option except to threaten a shutdown that'll put thousands out of work.'

'Good on you, Dad,' said Jimmy, 'let's meet any charge of the union brigade with the best form of defence. Something like a three-pronged attack from the family's trio.'

'That's favourite,' said Boots.

'Well, if you say so, me lord, it's got to be,' said Sammy. 'Meantime, Tommy had better let the bowler hat know we're playing ball, even if it hurts me considerable.'

Chapter Nine

Sunday morning at the house of Harry and Anneliese Stevens in Camberwell Road. Harry was having a word with his thirteen-year-old daughter Cindy, before she went out to meet one of her school chums.

'Don't forget we're having some friends to tea this afternoon,' he said.

'What friends?' asked Cindy, looking nicely dolled up in a snug winter coat and a blue and white woollen hat. Her light brown hair was in ribboned pigtails. She was her easy-going dad's best pal, as well as an affectionate stepdaughter to Anneliese, whom she liked very much. Originally, she hadn't been sure it was wise of Harry to take in a German woman as a lodger. However, she soon came to admire the striking blonde lady, and then to see her as a romantic prospect for her widowed dad. 'Yes, what friends, Daddy?'

'Mr and Mrs Robert Adams,' said Harry. 'You know them, you met them at the wedding. Mr Adams is the father of Tim, whom your stepmother nursed when he was a wounded prisoner of war.'

'Oh, yes, that Tim,' said Cindy. 'I stayed with him and his wife Felicity, while you went on honeymoon. They were ever so nice, but isn't it a shame that Felicity's blind? Still, she manages jolly well.'

'Yes, she does,' smiled Anneliese, whose nightmares of the war were receding now that she felt happy and secure in her marriage to Harry. 'When Tim's parents arrive for tea this afternoon, Cindy, we'd like you to be here. We did mention it to you two days ago.' Anneliese's English, after a year in England, had become more fluent than ever, although she still retained the slightest of accents, which charmed some people.

'Oh, yes, I remember now,' said Cindy. 'Very well, Mother,' she added in a precise grown-up way, 'I'll be pleased to attend.'

'Very decent of you, young lady,' said Harry, a writer of short stories who now had a novel under consideration by publishers. His agent had passed it to them. Since his marriage to Anneliese, he needed an income well in excess of fees for the short stories occasionally accepted by magazines. The fact that Anneliese had inherited a fortune made no difference to his fixed belief that a man should support his wife, and that the other way round was the wrong way. The Fifties might be a time of radical changes in society, but that didn't alter his belief.

Anneliese had wished to settle half her fortune on him. He had said a very definite no. She had tried again later on, saying it was right for a wife to share what she had with her husband. Harry said he'd never heard of that right, was she sure it was laid down somewhere? Yes, in the laws of marriage, in the exchange of worldly goods, said Anneliese. No, I don't get any of your worldly goods, you get all mine, said Harry, and it's unfortunate that I don't have any right now. Yes, you do, said Anneliese, you have this house. Oh, and your typewriter. Harry said he didn't think bricks and mortar meant anything other than giving them a roof over their heads. And I can't endow thee with my typewriter, he said, I need it to help me earn a crust or two. Well, never mind, Harry darling, said Anneliese, what you have endowed me with is yourself and Cindy, and peaceful happiness. All that is far more than I ever expected. She considered Harry the kindest and most civilized of men, as far removed in character from an SS thug as a friendly dolphin from a vicious shark.

As to his insistence that a husband had to be the breadwinner, the dear man's income as a writer of short stories hardly allowed him to fill that role comfortably. So she made contributions to the household budget in subtle ways, such as paying the laundry bills and doing the day-to-day shopping at her own expense. Harry never asked pertinent questions, and when she bought a family car, a new Austin, he only said well, it was hers, of course, and that she was entitled to spend her money in any way she liked.

Cindy was thrilled by this exciting acquisition, and hugged her lovely stepmother. She had no inhibitions about showing her affection, since her natural mother had died when she herself was too young to remember her. Harry was entreated by Anneliese to be the family's driver. She could drive herself, but she felt that one way of giving Harry a proprietary interest in the car was to have him in the driving seat. Harry, whose admiration for women generally had been enhanced by the qualities of his first wife, nevertheless owned almost every man's conviction that women drivers were a danger to themselves, their passengers and other traffic. Accordingly, Anneliese's entreaty fell on fertile ground, much to her pleasure. His first encounter with the car was to manoeuvre it through the alleyway that led from Camberwell Road, and to park it in the spacious front yard dividing the rear of a shop from the house.

'Oh, my word, that was super,' said Cindy, her grammar-school education and her years with her well-spoken father having endowed her with speech somewhat superior to that of the Camberwell cockneys. 'Daddy, you only had inches to spare coming through the alleyway.'

'There, you see,' smiled Anneliese, blue eyes a fascination to Harry. 'I simply could not have done that myself. I know I would have scraped the walls.'

'You do have other talents,' said Harry.

'Do I?' said Anneliese.

'Believe me,' said Harry, his smile sending a message.

His wife returned his smile.

It had been Anneliese's idea to invite Polly and Boots. She and Polly had found a liking for each other during the wedding reception, since when, on Polly's initiative, they had enjoyed several shared excursions to the West End, usually to shop and have lunch, and once to see a matinee performance of a Terence Rattigan play.

The October day was bright but crisp when Polly and Boots arrived at the agreed time of three-thirty. Boots was intrigued by the fact that his hosts' house in Camberwell Road put them among the kind of cockneys he had known so well during the years before, during and after the First World War. Now, however, the people were better dressed and better off, although without being affluent.

Harry and Anneliese greeted their guests warmly. Anneliese thought Boots an arresting and distinguished man, his easy smile infectious. Harry thought him entirely likeable, and he saw Polly as an elegant and cultured woman. Cindy, who had met them at the wedding reception, now found herself very impressed.

'I remember you, Cindy,' smiled Polly.

'Yes, how are you, please?' said Cindy.

'Delighted to see you again,' said Boots.

'Polly, where are the twins?' asked Anneliese.

'Oh, they'll be here any moment,' said Polly, and Cindy thought what a posh voice she had. Not many like that were heard in Camberwell.

'They preferred to cycle here,' said Boots. 'We overtook them on the way. But they'll be here any moment.'

They went in to the sitting room, and the twins arrived with a jangle of bicycle bells. Harry let them in. He saw a boy in a Sunday suit, and a girl in a pretty Sunday frock.

'Hello and welcome,' he said.

'Oh, are you Mr Stevens?' asked Gemma.

'I am,' smiled Harry.

'Oh, jolly good,' said Gemma, 'we've come to the right house, then.'

'We saw Dad's car outside,' said James. He was like his father with his dark brown hair, grey eyes and features already firm. Gemma was like her mother, and had the kind of piquant looks that reminded Boots of Polly during her years as a flapper.

125

Cindy appeared in the hall.

'Hello, I'm Cindy,' she said, 'are you two the twins?'

'By an accident of birth,' said James, verbally profound on occasions.

'Well, if you're an accident, I'm not,' said Gemma, and confided to Cindy that her brother was a bit daft at times. And a bit of a show-off, she said.

Cindy eyed James with girlish interest. He didn't actually look daft, he looked as if he had a knowing and cheeky grin lurking about.

'Come and say hello to my wife,' said Harry. Anneliese, together with Polly and Boots, came out into the hall then, to see what was going on.

'What's keeping you?' asked Polly of the twins.

'Gemma's talking,' said James.

'Me?' said Gemma. 'You talk all the time.'

Harry said, 'Well, James and Gemma, meet my wife, Anneliese.'

'Oh, hello, Mrs Stevens,' said Gemma.

'I think you're Gemma and James,' smiled Anneliese.

'Pleased to meet you, Mrs Stevens,' said James.

'They came on their bikes,' said Cindy.

'Yes, we've both got new bikes, one each,' said James.

'Crikey, I don't even have an old one,' said

Cindy. Her loving dad was against letting his cherished daughter risk her limbs on any bike amid the busy traffic of the area, and Anneliese went along with that.

'When's tea?' asked James directly.

'At five,' said Harry.

'Well, it's only just gone half-past three,' said James, 'so I daresay Gemma will lend her bike for half an hour to Cindy, if she'd like a ride.'

'Yes, would you like that, Cindy?' asked Gemma.

'Well,' said Cindy uncertainly, glancing at her dad.

'Cindy,' smiled Harry, 'if James will take care of you, you can go.'

'Yes, go with her, James,' said Boots, 'but don't take her through the traffic.'

'No, all right, Dad,' said James. 'Come on, Cindy.'

'Oh, great,' said Cindy.

'Just half an hour, mind,' said Polly.

'Hearing you, Mum,' said James, and off he went with Cindy. The bikes were outside, near the Austin, and they wheeled them through the alleyway to the road, where Boots's car was parked. 'Now,' said James, 'd'you know how to get into the saddle?'

'Blessed cheek, of course I do,' said Cindy, 'I've had a few rides on friends' bikes, but don't tell my dad.'

'All right,' said James, 'mount up, then. I

127

like a girl who knows what she's doing.'

'I ignore boys who don't know anything about girls,' said Cindy.

'Good-oh,' said James.

'What d'you mean, good-oh?' asked Cindy.

'Oh, just that we needn't spend time standing about,' said James. 'Let's start riding. Come on. I'll lead.'

'You think,' said Cindy.

They mounted and pedalled away, Cindy exhilarated enough to let this saucebox see she wasn't going to be an obedient follower. She caught him up and cycled side by side with him. James, good-natured, accepted her company and made no attempt to forge ahead.

'How old are you?' asked James.

'Just thirteen,' said Cindy.

Since he and Gemma had their birthdays coming up in December, James said, 'I'm nearly that age myself.'

'You look a good fourteen,' said Cindy, as they turned off the main road and headed for the quiet area around Myatts Fields, a park. 'So you must be growing older quicker than most people.'

'What a prospect,' said James.

'What d'you mean?' asked Cindy.

'Well, I might be having to shave by the New Year,' said James. 'And bald by Easter.'

'What a laugh,' said Cindy, as they

pedalled through side streets. James, as always, relished the exercise, and Cindy was her energetic self. Street kids whooped as she flashed by with her legs showing. One called after her.

'Oi, can I mind yer bike, darling?'

Another bawled, 'Bet yer mum don't know you're showing yer tent pegs.'

'There's more saucy kids in Camberwell than kippers in Billingsgate,' said Cindy. 'Well, that's what my dad always says.'

'There's saucy kids everywhere,' said James. 'Fortunately, I grew out of being one myself, due to my own dad giving me a talking-to. You ever had a talking-to from yours?'

'My dad didn't have to,' said Cindy, 'he didn't need to.'

They reached the park, very quiet on this Sunday afternoon, and raced around outside it. On one of their circuits, an old bloke in a cap stepped into the road, held up his mittened hand and compelled them to stop.

'Now then, now then, what's yer game?' he asked. He had bristling whiskers.

'We're just riding around,' said James.

'Oh, you are, are yer?' said the old bloke.

'Yes, just that,' said James.

'It ain't allowed,' said the old bloke.

'I beg to differ,' said James.

'Oh, you do, do yer?'

'With respect, of course,' said James.

'What ain't allowed is sixty miles an hour,' said the old bloke.

James said, 'I could point out–'

'Oh, you're going to be saucy, are yer?'

'I could point out that no-one could do sixty miles an hour on a bike,' said James.

'And my dad wouldn't let me, even if I could,' said Cindy.

'Hello, she's saucy too, is she?' said the old bloke.

'She's only saying sixty miles an hour can't be done,' said James politely.

'I ain't believing it, not after seeing you two going like your rear ends was on fire,' said the old bloke. Cindy giggled. She was used to the cockney characters of Camberwell and what they could come out with. 'Dangerous to human life, riding like that, yer know.' The old bloke shook his head. 'I ain't personally keen on being knocked down by two bikes all at once. Didn't yer think of what me old dutch would've said if she'd come out and found me laying here with wheel marks all over me chest?'

'To be truthful, no,' said James, intrigued by this, one of his few real encounters with typical cockneys. His dad had once taken him and Gemma to a Walworth street market to meet a stallholder called Ma Earnshaw, whom he'd known long ago. She'd been all of a cockney character, and had sold his dad any amount of hard-to-come-by oranges for old times' sake. He and Gemma had also met Cassie and Freddy Brown, Freddy being the younger brother of Aunt Susie, and Cassie having been known to the Adams family from the time when she was a lively young cockney girl. She was still as lively as a collie, but she wasn't the kind of out-and-out cockney character that this old bloke was.

'No, I'm afraid we didn't think of that at all.' James was still polite.

'Oh, you didn't, didn't yer?' said the old bloke.

'Well, we honestly didn't think of knocking anyone down,' said Cindy. 'My dad's always been strict about things like that. He told me once never to knock anyone down with a bike.'

'Well, I admire yer dad, then,' said the old bloke. 'All right, young 'uns, off yer go now, and mind yer speed.'

'Goodbye,' said Cindy.

'So long,' said James.

They remounted. A boy carrying a stick came out of the park as they rode by. Devilish, he pushed the stick between the spokes of Cindy's front wheels. The bike fell, Cindy with it.

'Oi, yer young perisher! I'll knock yer bleedin' bonce off!' The old bloke, yelling, came charging up, shaking a fist. The boy scarpered. The old bloke and James bent over Cindy, sprawling and winded.

'Cindy?' said James in concern.

'You ain't injured, are yer, girlie?' The old bloke was just as concerned.

'I'm all right, I just want to get my breath back,' said Cindy, and they helped her to her feet. She blinked. 'Oh, is your sister's bike damaged?' she said to James.

James took a look. There was no damage.

'No need to worry about that, Cindy,' he said. 'You sure you're not hurt?'

'Come a purler, she did, poor young gal,' said the old bloke. 'Would yer like to come indoors with me and let the old lady fan yer a bit?'

'Thanks, but no, I'm really all right,' said Cindy, brushing herself down.

'Young perisher,' growled the old bloke, looking in the direction of the boy's disappearing act. 'I'll have the law on him.'

'James, we'd best get back now,' said Cindy.

'Yes, we'd better,' said James, helping her to right the fallen bike. 'So long again, mister.'

'Goodbye,' said Cindy, and she and James rode off.

She was looking a little shaken up, so he said, 'Cindy, you sure you're OK?'

'Yes, honest,' said Cindy, 'and I'm getting my breath back now. Listen, don't tell my dad, he never did like me riding a bike in Camberwell.'

'I won't say a word, Cindy, not unless you've got some bruises that show,' said James.

Cindy laughed.

'If I have, I'm not going to show you,' she said. They were pedalling steadily.

'My sister had a bruise there once,' said James.

'Where was there?'

'On her bottom,' said James.

Cindy giggled. When they arrived back at the house, she said, 'I might let you come and see me sometimes, which I wouldn't with other boys.'

'That's nice of you, Cindy,' said James, 'but—'

'Of course, I don't mean I'm inviting you to be my boyfriend,' said Cindy.

'Well,' said James, 'I don't suppose you're old enough to have one, not yet.'

'Did I say I was?'

'No, but—'

'Still, if you're old enough, so am I,' said Cindy.

'Oh, I don't have a girlfriend,' said James, 'I don't think I'd be able to cope with one until I'm sixteen.'

'Sixteen?' said Cindy. 'You'll be sort of wise and capable by then, will you?'

'Grown-up,' said James solemnly. 'Well, girls are a bit complicated. It's not like making friends with a bicycle.'

'I should think it isn't,' said Cindy. 'If you don't know it, let me tell you girls are girls, not bicycles.'

'Well, yes,' said James, 'I'm not disputing that, I'm only saying they're different from boys.'

'Oh, really?' said Cindy. 'When did you find that out?'

'Kind of gradually,' said James. 'Now, about coming to see you sometimes, I'm not sure if Cathy Davidson would like that.'

'Who's she?' asked Cindy.

'Oh, a girl I walk home from school with,' said James. 'She's definitely a bit complicated. Well, I think she wants to marry me.'

'Marry you?' said Cindy. 'I never heard anything more potty.'

'Nor me,' said James, 'but there you are, a feller never knows what to expect from girls.'

'At my age, I wouldn't have silly ideas about marrying,' said Cindy. 'I wouldn't think about that till I was at least nineteen.'

'Very sensible,' said James.

'Are you going to come and see me sometimes or not?' demanded Cindy, who thought him very advanced for his age. She liked that. It was obvious, of course, that the girl he'd mentioned had a crush on him.

James glanced at her. She had quite an air, lots of self-confidence and talked more sensibly than Cathy. Like his parents, he

134

enjoyed conversation, which his mum said was more important to civilization than television. People, she said, could do without television, but not without talking to each other. If you didn't make conversation, she said, you ended up being a dull old prune. Well, he thought, a feller ought to widen his circle of talking acquaintances, even if one of them was a girl who'd be bound to turn out complicated.

'All right, Cindy,' he said, 'I think I might come and see you sometimes.'

'Excuse me,' said Cindy, 'it's not might, it's either yes or no.'

'Yes, then,' said James. Cindy smiled and they entered the house to join their parents.

Chapter Ten

Anneliese had given a new look to the old house. The rooms she had occupied as a tenant on the first floor had been turned into bedrooms. The ground-floor bedrooms used by Harry and Cindy had become, respectively, a lounge and a dining room. The bills for conversion costs had made Harry scratch his head and consult his bank balance. Anneliese took the bills away from him, told him to concentrate on his writing, and wait for her to remind him to settle up a little at a time. She settled the lot herself, of course, as soon as Harry had forgotten about them. His writing so absorbed him that his forgetfulness was an everyday occurrence. That, to her, was all part of his endearing make-up. She accepted, ruefully at times, that thoroughness, not an easy-going nature, was a very German characteristic. And no German had ever been more thorough than Himmler, who she hoped was now burning in hell.

Over Sunday tea in the dining room, the conversation was anecdotal. Polly and Boots, and their hosts, all owned unforgettable memories of wartime incidents, and if

Anneliese felt that Germany's defeat was touched with shame, she could nevertheless recount stories concerning her nursing experiences that were neither shameful nor unhappy.

Harry and Boots developed a very easy relationship, while Polly and Anneliese were already firm friends. Anneliese wanted to know what the famous Battle of Britain had really been like.

'Hairy,' said Polly.

'High in the sky,' said Boots.

'Ask me about the Battle of the Atlantic,' said Harry, ex-Navy, 'that was hairy too and deep in the sea.'

'Excuse me,' said Gemma, who thought it was well past time to get the conversation up to date, 'but what about all this new music?'

'Ashamed as I am to admit it,' said Boots, 'I know nothing.'

'Yes, you do, Daddy,' said Gemma, 'we all saw the concert on television a little while ago.'

'Did we?' said Boots. 'Then I must have meant I know next to nothing.'

Anneliese smiled. She was finding Polly's husband a man whose sense of humour was ever-present, but never in any irritating way. His eyes reflected a lurking smile. His lazy left eye, of a slightly darker grey than the right, was nearly blind, a souvenir of the

137

1914–18 trench war. Anneliese marvelled at the fact that it still looked as expressive as his sound eye. The man himself was delightful, and so was his vivacious and witty wife.

'Daddy, you're a fraud,' said Gemma. 'How can you know next to nothing about Bill Haley and his Comets when you saw them perform on television?'

'I'm confused,' said Boots, 'I thought that was Alexander's Ragtime Band.'

'What's Alexander's Ragtime Band?' asked Cindy.

'A hundred years old,' said James, 'and they've all got long white beards and rheumatism. I once read in a magazine that they played in Berlin at a command performance for the German Emperor.'

'Did they?' said Anneliese, her hair a wealth of shining gold. 'Well, I suppose that was nearly a hundred years ago.'

'Don't take any notice, Mrs Stevens,' said Gemma, 'my brother's showing off. Well, more than that. He's got a screw loose, poor boy.'

'I thought Mrs Stevens might have known about that command performance,' said James, never one to lose his way, any more than Boots was. Indeed, Polly was thinking just how much her son was like his father.

'James, I'm afraid I don't know,' said Anneliese.

Cindy had her say.

'Well, of course, Mummy, you simply couldn't know unless you had a long white beard and rheumatism yourself, just like that band,' she said. 'I mean, if it's a hundred years old, well.'

Gemma shrieked with laughter, Harry grinned, Boots smiled, Polly looked tickled, James looked solemn and Anneliese looked as if her new life was one of sheer delight. Some Germans might lack a sense of humour, according to outsiders, but Berliners didn't, and Anneliese was a Berliner.

'I assure you, Cindy,' she said, 'it was well before my time.'

'Well, I don't know what's funny about it, then,' said Cindy.

'Excuse me, Mrs Stevens,' said Gemma, 'but could I please have another slice of cake?'

'With pleasure,' said Anneliese.

'It's Mummy's German carrot cake,' said Cindy proudly.

'May I have seconds too?' asked Boots.

'And me,' said James.

Polly, having considered the calorie intake, nevertheless asked for another slice, but of a small size.

'And could I have some more tea, please?' said Gemma.

'It's my belief,' said Harry, 'that all nations would benefit if they went in for Sunday tea instead of spice and garlic. It's spice and garlic that make people fiery. And what does being fiery lead to? I put the question seriously.'

'Well, old sport,' said Polly, 'let's jump from comical white beards to something seriously improving. What's the answer?'

'Short tempers and loaded guns,' said Anneliese. 'Am I right, Harry?'

'Seriously right,' said Harry, and Anneliese cut the required further helpings of cake amid an atmosphere of pure homely enjoyment and nonstop chatter.

It was a prolonged occasion, and if a typically traditional English one, it was far from being formal or stuffy. Everyone had a tongue, and everyone used it. Laughter ran about unchecked. The stimulation came from mutual likings and interests, and from a fund of anecdotes, plus a riot of discussion and argument when Polly eventually reintroduced the subject of rock and roll. The perfect way to arrange a peaceful life, she said, was to keep that kind of so-called music out of one's living room. Gemma and James erupted.

It was seven-thirty before Polly, Boots and the twins finally took their leave. They did so then to avoid overstaying their welcome, by which time Polly had arranged for Anneliese to come and have lunch with her, much to the latter's pleasure.

After saying goodbye to the guests, Anneliese had a moment of reflection. English Sunday tea with visitors? she thought. It was a source of amusement to many people of other countries. To Americans, it was strong black coffee that had helped their pioneers tame the Wild West. We all have much to learn, thought Anneliese, and I am learning happily. I would love it if Harry and I could have Polly and Boots to many Sunday teas.

Polly, Boots and their twins. If, in drastically different circumstances, they had lived under Hitler, would they have come to admire Himmler and his SS? Would Boots, as an SS colonel, have watched dead Jews tumbling into stinking pits without a flicker of compassion?

Who could seriously answer that question? One could only thank circumstances for the fact that people like Polly and Boots, and their twins, had never had to be tested.

One could not thank God, for God had departed the world all through the cruellest war ever known. God had left millions of innocent men, women and children at the mercy of madmen.

The twins made a quick dash for home on their bikes. Polly and Boots began the return in their car.

'I really do find Anneliese and Harry quite delightful,' said Polly.

'There was a time,' said Boots, 'when I thought that Germans as a whole were the complete reversal of delightful.'

'When the Belsen concentration camp was uncovered?' said Polly, as they motored towards Denmark Hill.

'Since when I've had the enormous pleasure of discovering there are enchanting exceptions,' said Boots.

'Enchanting?' said Polly. 'Pardon my fury, but there'll be blood all over our hall carpet if you're telling me you'd like to go to bed with Anneliese.'

'Put your dagger away, Polly old girl,' said Boots, 'you know there's no need for it.'

'That's my faithful old scout,' said Polly, and wound the window down to call to Gemma and James as they overtook them. 'Last ones home put the cat out!'

'We don't have a cat!' yelled Gemma.

'Aren't you lucky?' laughed Polly. 'Boots, I must phone Felicity tomorrow morning.'

'About something special?' said Boots. 'Like Alexander's Ragtime Band or modern rock and rollers?'

'We've just gnawed all that down to the bone,' said Polly. 'No, I'm having Anneliese to lunch on Wednesday, and I'm going to invite Felicity and Patsy too.'

'Good God, that's enough for a hen party,' said Boots. 'Hardly your style, is it?'

'Well, not so much hen parties as knitting

142

circles,' said Polly. 'You see, old fruit, Anneliese would like to meet Felicity again, and Patsy wants to meet Anneliese. I'll persuade Flossie to cook something special. What a treasure she is. We should increase her wages.'

'We did so at Christmas,' said Boots, 'by fifty per cent.'

'Did we?' said Polly. 'Yes, so we did. Rattling good show, old bean.'

'D'you think Felicity will survive a lunch party?' asked Boots. 'I always have a feeling that any kind of party gives her a sense of frustration.'

'Not lunch for four,' said Polly, 'and not when the other three are known to her. In any case, old scout, she likes a challenge, and never ducks one.'

'True,' said Boots.

'I've a feeling,' said Polly, 'that Anneliese's experiences as a nurse have given her an instinctive wish to be able to help Felicity.'

'Only an outstanding ophthalmic surgeon can do that, if at all,' said Boots.

'Well, you remember, of course, the time when Tim, as a wounded prisoner of war, was nursed by Anneliese in the German hospital at Benghazi,' said Polly. 'It gave her a special regard for Tim, and it distressed her when she discovered his wife had been blinded in a German air raid. Most Germans would have pointed to what Allied bombing raids did to their own people.'

'Anneliese has been so disillusioned by Himmler and his SS that she thinks differently from most Germans,' said Boots.

'That's one reason why I feel she'd love to be able to wave a wand and cure Felicity's blindness,' said Polly. 'What would Himmler the hyena have thought of a perfect Aryan woman playing fairy godmother to a former ATS officer, old top? In your great majesty, tell me that.'

'In my great majesty, I'm stuck,' said Boots. 'Well, arrange your lunch. I presume you'll all be quite happy enjoying one of Flossie's special menus while I'm having a sandwich and a beer at the pub?'

'Oh, we'll think pleasant thoughts of you, old boy,' said Polly.

Breakfast over the next morning, Monday, Boots made ready to leave. The twins were on their way to school, Flossie working in the kitchen. Polly followed Boots through the hall to see him off. She rarely failed to do that, however suburban and mundane Bloomsbury intellectuals might have regarded the gesture. In any case, she thought them a pack of frightful snobs.

The phone rang as Boots opened the front door. Polly answered it.

'Hello? Felicity? Yes?'

It was a quick conversation, ended when

Polly said she was going to phone back later. She turned to Boots, waiting at the open door.

'Anything wrong?' he said.

'No, only that Tim's on his way to the office, but has left his briefcase behind,' said Polly. 'Maggie spotted it, and as you haven't left yet, Felicity wants to know if you'd call in on your own way to work and pick it up, which you will, won't you, old love?'

'No problem,' said Boots and kissed her goodbye. Polly liked the fact that he never pecked. He kissed, and always warmly.

It was Felicity herself who answered the door to Boots. She was waiting in the hall, the briefcase on a chair, ready to hand, and she had no difficulty in getting to the door.

'Is it you, Boots?'

'None other,' said Boots.

The open door let in the morning brightness, and Felicity had a sudden sense of light dawning. Incredibly, out of it came a vision of unhindered clarity, that of Boots, her father-in-law. There was no blurring, no mistiness, only the well-defined features of the man she regarded with great affection. Arresting, distinguished, with a fine firm mouth and deep grey eyes, and she could even see that the left, the impaired one, was a little deeper than the right. Never during her recent visions had she experienced a

145

clearer image.

She stared, mesmerized, her heart racing.

'Oh, my God,' she breathed.

'Felicity?' Boots guessed she was having one of her promising moments.

'Boots, I'm seeing you, I'm seeing you!' Felicity let emotion run away with her.

'Stay still,' said Boots, instinctively feeling that was what she should do, that movement would disturb whatever lifted her blindness for a brief while.

But Felicity went over the top. She flung her arms around him.

'Hold me, hold me.'

'Hang on,' said Boots, deeply touched.

'I mean I'm seeing you clearly – oh–' The clarity went, the image blurred and faded. 'Oh, bloody hell, I've lost you.' She detached herself.

Boots closed the door, led her to the chair, took the briefcase off, and made her sit down.

'Felicity, are you saying you had a clear image, a definitely clear one?'

'Yes, wonderfully clear, and for the very first time,' said Felicity, voice husky with emotion.

Since the moment was hardly one of gloom, Boots introduced a lighter note.

'Was it a shock?' he asked.

'A shock?'

'Were you disappointed?'

'Disappointed?' said Felicity. 'What d'you mean? Oh, your image. No, of course not. You are just as people say you are. Boots, in its clarity, that was my most hopeful moment ever. Don't go. Stay a while. No, what am I saying?'

'Nothing I wouldn't expect,' said Boots. 'And yes, it has to be a moment of great hope. I can believe that, so can you and Tim. And Jennifer. Of course I'll stay, if that's what you'd really like – I'll give Tim a ring from here.'

'No, I'm being silly,' said Felicity, but she felt warmed by his presence and his understanding, and by the fact that she now knew exactly what he was like. It could have been Jennifer if the girl had departed late for school. Her daughter's image was her prior wish, but all the same, it had been such a pleasure to see her renowned father-in-law, the man for whom the whole family had such an affection. Felicity knew he was fifty-eight, but he hadn't looked it. What was Polly like? Did she match up to her husband in her looks? 'Oh, my thoughts are running away with me,' she said. 'There's no need to stay, I'm feeling wonderful now.'

'Quite sure?' asked Boots.

'Positive,' said Felicity.

'I'll tell Tim as soon as I reach the offices,' said Boots, 'and I fancy he'll phone you. Oh, and you can expect a call from Polly.

She's invited Anneliese Stevens to lunch on Wednesday, and would like you to join them. And Patsy.'

'What?' said Felicity, coming to her feet.

'Lunch with Polly,' said Boots. 'Wednesday. You can use the occasion to celebrate the best moment you've had so far. You'll go, of course?'

'I can't wait to meet Tim's ex-German army nurse again,' said Felicity.

'Goodbye, then, dear girl,' said Boots, and planted a warm kiss on her cheek.

'I'm so glad I shared that moment with you,' said Felicity.

'My privilege, your happy prospects,' said Boots. He picked up the briefcase and left.

Tim phoned a little later, and Felicity added breathless details to those he had received from Boots. Tim said they should get in touch with Sir Charles Morgan, her specialist, and find out what he had to say about this new development.

'I'll ring him, Puss.'

'No, let me,' said Felicity, 'I've got all day to track him down.'

'Well, do that for sure, won't you?' said Tim. 'By the way, what did you think of my old dad in the few seconds of seeing him?'

'I'm happy to say I now know why I remember you as a good-looking bloke,' said Felicity. 'You take after him. Well, you did then, and I hope you still do.'

'You've got prospects now of finding out,' said Tim, 'but remember I'm thirteen years older since you last saw me.'

'So am I,' said Felicity. 'Does it show?'

'Well, to be frank,' said Tim, 'no.'

'I like that kind of frankness,' said Felicity, 'even if it's a lie.'

Chapter Eleven

Sammy's office phone rang.

'Hello?'

'Sammy?' It was Tommy.

'Something up?' said Sammy.

'You know I phoned Burridge on Friday to tell him our workforce would accept union cards?' said Tommy. 'Well, would you Adam-and-Eve it, he still sent the pickets round. They arrived first thing this morning, well before work started. I talked to them, pointing out we'd agreed things with Burridge. They gave me the raspberry, the saucy sods, and they're making sure nothing's going to come in or go out.'

'Are you giving me a bad start to the week?' asked Sammy.

'I'm giving you facts,' said Tommy. 'I can't reach Burridge on the phone. He's out. Our machinists are spitting needles, I'm spitting iron filings.'

'What's that large lump of leftover porridge up to?' said Sammy. 'Him and his bowler hat. Leave it with me, Tommy. I'll try and get hold of him and I'll call you back.'

'Right,' said Tommy.

Sammy put a call through to Burridge's

office in Bethnal Green, and his switchboard girl connected him.

'Mr Burridge?'

'Who's asking?' said a man's voice.

'Tell him Sammy Adams.'

'Has he heard of you?'

'Don't dislocate my funny bone, whoever you are. Just get him on the line.'

'Sorry, he's out.'

'Well, get him back in, pronto.'

'Is that an order?' The voice was sarcastic. I've got a right one here, thought Sammy.

'Don't give me problems, sonny, just tell me where I can get hold of Bowler Hat,' he said.

'Eh? What?'

'Burridge.'

'I've no idea where he is right now– No, wait, he's just come in.'

'Put him on,' said Sammy, blood up. He heard the murmur of voices, and a moment later Burridge was on the line.

'Who's that?'

'Sammy Adams.'

'Oh, hello, Sammy, nice morning.'

'Never mind the weather,' said Sammy. 'What's the idea, sending the pickets when you know we've agreed to unionize our workforce?'

'Ah,' said Burridge.

'Ah my bleedin' elbow,' said Sammy, 'you were supposed to send your officials round

151

with application forms and union cards, not surround the factory with pickets and placards. Get 'em out.'

'Half a mo, Sammy,' said Burridge, and Sammy heard the murmur of voices again. Then Burridge was back on the line. 'Just a token demonstration, Sammy, according to my assistant, which we sometimes do to let a factory's bosses know what to expect if they're thinking of welshing on an agreement.'

'That's a fact, is it?' said Sammy. 'Right, listen to this. If those pickets don't disappear fast inside the next fifteen minutes, you'll find a newspaper reporter on your doorstep asking awkward questions about illegal token demonstrations. I ain't unfamiliar with the *Daily Express*.' He was totally unfamiliar with its editor and its news editor, but not with the paper's Fleet Street phone number. 'Got that?'

'Now, Sammy, we don't want aggravation–'

'You've got it,' said Sammy, 'I'm personally aggravated all over.'

'Just an oversight this end, Sammy, and of course, I can dismiss the pickets as a gesture of goodwill,' said Burridge.

'Goodwill my Aunt Fanny,' said Sammy, 'get 'em off. You're taking liberties. Illegal liberties.'

'Right you are, Sammy,' said Burridge, 'and I'll send a couple of officials round with forms and union cards.'

'You do that, and quick,' said Sammy, and slammed the phone down.

Rachel Goodman entered his office.

'Sammy?' she said.

'Well?' said Sammy.

'You're all flushed,' said Rachel.

'You want to ask why?' said Sammy.

'I can't help myself,' said Rachel, still a warm-looking woman at fifty-two. A widow, she was much coveted by certain mature gentlemen who, as either widowers or bachelors, were certain that as a wife she would, in bed, be a far more welcome companion than a hot-water bottle or a new-fangled electric blanket. One could think about such comforts and still be a gentleman. Unfortunately for any of their hopes and wishes, Rachel was too content to think of marrying again. As the secretary of the Adams empire, she had the kind of relationship with Sammy that, although platonic, was all she asked for. She had no intention of ever giving Susie cause for suspicion or worry. 'Yes, tell me why, Sammy,' she said.

Sammy told her. Rachel said surrender to trade union demands could mean regular headaches.

'Don't I know it,' gloomed Sammy. 'Look at what the dockers' union is doing to London Docks, getting the men to walk out in the middle of turning a ship round. What kind of a carry-on is that?'

'I suppose it comes from years of the dockers getting a bad deal and no real job security,' said Rachel. 'My life, Sammy, what docker ever had the chance of buying his own house? Low wages, rotten hours, and always regarded as casual labour.'

'See your point, Rachel old friend,' said Sammy, 'which means that if the dockland bosses still won't give the men better prospects, then they're short of business savvy. Still, I ain't in love with what Burridge and his bowler hat think is going to be good for our workers. Next time a picket turns up, I'll get Tommy to arm the machinists with a cartload of rotten veg.'

'You won't do any such thing, Sammy,' said Rachel.

'Well, you can bet I'll give it some thought,' said Sammy. 'Now, what can I do you for, Rachel?'

'I've just had Mr Bunlap on the phone,' said Rachel.

'Who?'

'Mr Bunlap.'

'Is that a name or a Chinese doughnut?' asked Sammy.

'It's the name, Sammy, of a Bethnal Green Council official,' said Rachel.

'Good grief,' said Sammy. A little grin arrived, and Rachel smiled.

'He wanted to speak to Tim or Daniel,' she said, 'but they're both with the architects this morning.'

'So he spoke to you,' said Sammy. 'What about? Our application for the factory extension?'

'Yes,' said Rachel, 'and he was kind enough to inform me the planning committee will be delighted to favourably consider the application, and would like Tim and Daniel to attend a meeting, the date to be arranged. The committee's interested in the fact that the extension will provide more jobs.'

'Well, well,' said Sammy, 'we don't often get phone calls like that from council officials. I think I'm already fond of Mr Bunlap. If he phones again, give him my compliments, and ask how his missus and his little Bunlaps are doing.'

'I should do such a thing?' smiled Rachel.

'Kind enquiries like that could help us get on the right side of a council official,' said Sammy. 'Which I recommend.'

'My life,' said Rachel, 'can I hear myself saying, "Mr Bunlap, dear sir, how is Mrs Bunlap and all your little Bunlaps?"'

'Well, you've got the voice for it, Rachel,' said Sammy.

'Now I must get back to my office and my pile of work, so don't keep me talking, Sammy.'

'Pardon me,' said Sammy, as she walked to

the door, 'but I think you're being cheeky.'

'Enjoy a nice busy day, Sammy,' smiled Rachel, and disappeared.

Sammy's phone rang a few minutes later. Tommy was back on the line.

'What happened between you and Burridge, Sammy?'

'I think I dented his bowler hat,' said Sammy.

'You did all of that,' said Tommy. 'A bloke's just turned up on a bike and called off the pickets.'

'Already?' said Sammy.

'Already,' said Tommy, 'which has helped cure my headaches, including the one I had over Alice and that couple of Bristol gorillas.'

'No worries, Tommy, I'd always bet on Alice being able to fight her corner,' said Sammy.

'As for Burridge calling off the pickets, I must be a living marvel when it comes to denting trade union bowler hats, if you'll excuse me mentioning it.'

'Keep it up,' said Tommy.

'When Burridge's officials arrive with forms and union cards, give 'em a cup of tea,' said Sammy.

'With sugar?' asked Tommy in sarky vein.

'Like plumbers and gas fitters,' said Sammy, 'trade union officials faint at their work if they don't get a cup of tea.'

'Do me a favour,' said Tommy, 'tell me a funny story.'

'Sorry, Tommy old mate, I've got work to do,' said Sammy, and they rang off.

Later, after two trade union officials had arrived at the Bethnal Green factory, Mrs Mavis Percy, the chargehand of the first-floor workshop of machinists and seamstresses, came to see Tommy. Mavis, a forthright woman of thirty-three, was a typical East End cockney, cheerful, good-hearted and resilient, moulded in similar fashion to dear old Gertie Roper, now enjoying retirement.

Mavis had just been elected by the first-floor workers to be their shop steward on account of her popularity, even if she wouldn't tolerate any slacking. At the moment, she looked a bit cross.

'Mister Tommy?'

'What's up, Mavis?' asked Tommy, always a receptive boss.

'The girls have asked me to tell you, Mister Tommy, that they don't like this trade union lark, and nor don't I,' said Mavis.

'Well, no-one was in favour, I grant,' said Tommy, 'but we had no option, y'know. And we're not in yet, not till everyone's officially joined and been given a union card.'

Mavis said that was all very well, but the girls were upset because when they arrived

157

this morning, the pickets got loud and saucy with them, and pushy too.

'Very upsetting, it was,' she said.

'Saucy and pushy,' said Tommy. 'They took liberties, you mean?'

'Not them kind of liberties,' said Mavis. If they had, she went on, there'd have been some teeth knocked out and a lot of blood. No, it was being catcalled and pushed around that upset them. It wasn't what they were used to at the Adams factory.

'Well, I knew there'd been trouble,' said Tommy, 'I didn't get any good mornings meself when I arrived. Why didn't you let me know then?'

Mavis said the girls didn't want to worry him, but now they'd asked her to tell him, and also to let him know that if it happened again, they weren't going to take it lying down, not when they were being poked by the banners of them hooligan pickets.

That made Tommy cough.

'Er – poked, Mavis?' he said.

'Good as,' said Mavis.

'Well, I don't like the sound of that, Mavis, no, I don't,' said Tommy.

'Nor don't I,' said Mavis, and impressed on him the fact that they were only joining the union because he'd said the factory might be in trouble if they didn't. Well, what the girls got this morning was a lot of trouble.

'I'll sort it out, Mavis, I'll see it doesn't

happen again,' said Tommy.

'We're all signing up just now,' said Mavis, 'but I can't say we're joyful, like. Will you make sure we don't get pushed and poked any more, Mister Tommy?'

Tommy coughed again.

'Leave it with me, Mavis,' he said. He thought his reliable first-floor chargehand looked as cross as if her bosom itself had been poked. Not a nice thing to happen to any good woman.

Mavis pointed out that they worked for him and his brothers, not for no union, and they liked it that way. So did all the other workers in the factory.

'You're good bosses, Mister Tommy,' she said.

Tommy appreciated that. He knew, as did Sammy and Boots, that there weren't many East End workers who had kind words to say about any bosses. The East End was a hotbed of trade union banners and the Red Flag. It had been the men and women of the East End who'd given Mosley and his Blackshirts a walloping welter of bloody noses during the years leading up to the war against Hitler and his Nazis. The Adams workers were non-union and non-belligerent simply because Sammy believed in the labourer being worthy of his hire.

'Mavis, none of you–' Tommy coughed yet again. 'None of you will get banners poking at you again, I'll make sure of that.'

'Well, me and the girls will be obliged, Mister Tommy, not half we won't,' said Mavis, and carried the good news forthwith to the machinists and seamstresses on both the ground floor and the first floor.

Chapter Twelve

'Eh?' Mr Barney Burridge, the Bethnal Green trade union official of distinction, looked up from his desk, his bowler hat tipped back, a sign that he was exercising his mental faculties, which were by no means inferior. 'Who wants to see me, did you say?'

'Tommy Adams and escort,' said his assistant.

'Escort? Tommy Adams is here with a couple of coppers, d'you mean? He's taking this morning's token demo as seriously as that? Don't tell me they've got a warrant.'

'No, no coppers, no warrant, Barney, just a young bloke with a clever look. And Tommy Adams, like I said.'

'Right, send 'em in, but first tell the young bloke to leave his clever look on a peg. I don't want it in my office.'

'Noted,' said the assistant, and sent in Tommy, accompanied by his nephew Jimmy, the factory's personnel manager who, at twenty-four, was no more short of savvy than was Sammy, his dad.

'Morning to yer, Tommy,' said Burridge heartily, 'and half a mo, is that young Jimmy?'

'That's him,' said Tommy, a broad-shouldered stalwart in hat and overcoat.

'Morning, Mr Burridge,' said Jimmy, a leaner version of his uncle.

'Well, gents, what can I do for you on this happy Monday morning?' offered Burridge.

'More than a bit,' said Tommy.

'A lot more, seeing how you mucked us about with your illegal pickets first thing,' said Jimmy.

'Now now, sonny, only what you might regard as the result of an oversight,' said Burridge, 'and I called 'em off, didn't I?'

'Not before they upset our arriving machinists,' said Tommy.

'And mortified them,' said Jimmy.

'Mortified?' said Burridge.

'And aggravated them as well,' said Jimmy.

'I'll have you know it's against the law to poke workers with banners,' said Tommy.

'Especially workers of the female gender,' said Jimmy. He and Tommy had decided on a two-pronged attack.

'Now look here,' said Burridge, 'I grant you pickets like to do their job with a bit of brotherly enthusiasm and a few official banners–'

'A bit more than that,' said Tommy.

'A lot more,' said Jimmy.

'Hold on, hold on,' said Burridge, 'would you mind talking to me one at a time, instead of both at once?'

162

'Both at once?' queried Tommy.

'It hasn't happened yet,' said Jimmy.

'It feels like it has,' said Burridge. 'Might I ask, Tommy mate, if this here call represents an official complaint about this morning's picketing? Or are you just dropping a friendly word in me ear?'

'Oh, it's official,' said Tommy.

'That's why there's two of us,' said Jimmy, 'and on top of the complaint we've got something else to say.'

'Pardon me, gents, but you'll have to make an appointment to see me official,' said Burridge.

'This is official now,' said Tommy, and addressed the Bowler Hat crisply to the effect that if any trouble came about that meant regular interference with output, certain steps would have to be taken.

At which Jimmy declared that such steps would mean a conference with other factory owners suffering interference with output.

'Suffering?' said Burridge, bowler hat quivering a little. 'Factory bosses suffering? You're coming it a bit, sonny, and I ain't partial to having to listen.'

Tommy pointed out that Jimmy hadn't finished, and Jimmy said no, he hadn't, and that a conference with other aggravated factory owners would take place with the aim of a collective shutdown.

'A whatter?' said Burridge.

'Some trade union practices can mean taking control of our workers away from us, and get up our noses according,' said Tommy.

'Like illegal picketing and ordering walkouts without notice,' said Jimmy.

'Now see here,' said Burridge, 'all union practices are carried out in strict accordance with laid-down rules and regulations, which I've pointed out before. If certain actions cause a little inconvenience to the bosses, you can lay the offence on your own doorsteps. It's common knowledge that factory owners specialize in provoking union action.'

'Well, I'm going to be provoking right now,' said Tommy.

'Which means a fight,' said Jimmy.

'Threats, is it?' said Burridge.

'You bet,' said Tommy, 'the threat of a collective shutdown that will put thousands of trade union workers out of a job short-term or long-term.'

'We've already spoken to some other owners,' said Jimmy, 'and had a promising response.' Which was a bit of a fib, but put some meat on the bone.

'Sonny, you're talking out of turn,' said Burridge, 'like your Uncle Tommy's other brother I was unfortunate enough to meet last week. A colonel, wasn't he?'

'My Uncle Boots?' said Jimmy. 'Good as a general, so consider yourself privileged. He won the crossing of the Rhine on his own.

Well, almost. His influence with other factory owners and his MP is what you'd call phenomenal.' Which was a compliment to Boots, but a definite fib.

'Now look here, Tommy,' said Burridge, 'what's this lippy lad's real trade? A comedian?'

'He's got medals as a negotiator,' said Tommy. 'Well, that's it. You know the score now. Too much union interference, including hustling our machinists and demands for on-the-spot walkouts, and there'll be a collective shutdown.'

'Thousands out of work,' said Jimmy. 'We're having explanatory leaflets printed to be distributed among the workforces of other factories.'

'I'll fight yer to a frazzle,' said Burridge, 'and let me tell you that next time I lose a fight on behalf of the workers' trade union brotherhood will be the first.'

'Hope it won't hurt too much,' said Tommy, 'or land you in hospital.'

'If it does, what would you like after your operation, grapes or flowers?' asked Jimmy.

At such saucy talk, Burridge's bowler hat fell off. He felt a deep sense of aggravation at this lack of respect. Nor did he relish the vision of thousands of workers being shut out. The lurking trade union Commies might like that, but the workers wouldn't. Who'd get the blame? He could do the

165

obvious and lay it on the bosses. But more likely he'd have to shoulder it himself, which would mean big brother Jack Jones having him on the carpet.

'Now don't let's be hasty, Tommy,' he said, 'you know me, always willing to negotiate. That's what got me where I am, principal area negotiator, noted for being reasonable.'

'Good,' said Tommy, 'but we've done ours.'

'Done your what?' asked Burridge.

'Our negotiations,' said Jimmy. 'Good morning to you, Mr Burridge.'

'Got to get back,' said Tommy.

Burridge sat still for several moments after they'd left, then came to and bawled for his assistant, who appeared in leisurely time.

'What's up?'

'Listen, Trotter, if Tommy Adams and his office boy call again, don't let 'em in. And now you're here, where's me bleedin' bowler?'

'On the floor,' said Trotter.

'Well, how did we do?' asked Jimmy of his Uncle Tommy on their way back to the factory.

'We made a start,' said Tommy, 'but that don't mean we've won. Trade union officials are never pushovers, and you've got to realize that ninety-nine out of every hundred workers favour unions. Can't blame 'em. If it wasn't for the unions, most workers would

166

still have their backs to the wall. Even in my lifetime I can remember workers' kids in Whitechapel going barefoot on account of their dads not being able to afford boots or shoes. Those were the days of the East End sweatshops, Jimmy lad, which your dad said was never going to be the way he'd run a factory.'

'I know about that, of course, but not first-hand,' said Jimmy. They were walking through an area much improved by post-war development of bombed sites. The quality of life for the workers and their families had also improved, their existence no longer charac-terized by exploitation. Here and there the faces of West Indian immigrants could be seen among the busy workers of building contractors. Employment in the building trade was high, despite continuing restric-tions on the import of seasoned timber.

'All we've done with Burridge, Jimmy me lad,' said Tommy, 'has been to give him cause to treat us a bit gentle, maybe, which is what your Uncle Boots had in mind when we were talking about Burridge last week. You and me, we might've shell-shocked his bowler hat a bit, but when he's come to, he won't fall ill about any prospective shutdown. He'll know we wouldn't get more than two or three factory owners to side with us, and we'd need twenty at least. If things do hot up, we'll get your Uncle Boots

167

to point us to another move. He can always think up something. How's Clare?'

'Blooming,' said Jimmy.

'Eh?' said Tommy. 'Does that mean–?'

'No,' said Jimmy. 'We've decided to enjoy our first three years of married life on our own. Clare says she'd like that. She thinks that not until the end of three years will she fancy a change from seeing just my face at breakfast and I'll fancy the patter of tiny feet following me up the garden path.'

'Three years, eh?' Tommy grinned. 'That'll suit your grandma. She's dizzy at the moment trying to keep up with one more great-grandchild after another.'

Jimmy laughed.

'Grandma ought to know by now that her family's procreative talents equal maximum fertility,' he said.

'So help me,' said Tommy, 'some of you young 'uns have got the gift of the gab all right. Don't let your grandma hear you talk like that, or she'll think it's Frenchified bad language of the kind she says she's had to listen to from your Uncle Boots ever since he was being educated. Still, you'll do her a favour if you and Clare don't have any kids just yet. She's still trying to count what she has already.'

'If I know Grandma,' said Jimmy, 'she's got them all in her birthday book. Grandma's an old darling.'

'One of the old brigade, Jimmy lad,' said Tommy, 'and so's Grandpa Finch.'

They entered the factory and were immediately greeted by the satisfying sound of a busy hum.

Felicity succeeded in getting through to Sir Charles Morgan's receptionist at his private consulting rooms in Langham Place. The helpful lady informed Felicity that Sir Charles was conducting two operations that morning at the London Eye Clinic, and would be there for the better part of the day. She gave Felicity the phone number.

Felicity managed to reach Sir Charles at noon. He received the call in one of the hospital consulting rooms, where he was having a coffee following completion of the operations. He listened to Felicity's recounting of the few wonderful seconds when her vision was faultless. He said that such a revelation was not an unexpected development, and to make an appointment to visit him when it happened again.

'Not until then?' said Felicity.

'Quite so, Mrs Adams. That would be best.' Sir Charles sounded somewhat fatigued. 'Don't worry if it doesn't repeat itself as soon as you'd like.'

'Very well,' said Felicity, 'thank you, Sir Charles.'

She felt a little disappointed.

Earlier, however, she had enjoyed a lively phone conversation with Polly concerning the proposed ladies' hen party for Wednesday. Felicity was all for meeting the personal challenge, and happy to know there would be four of them, including Anneliese, who had played her own kind of part in Tim's wartime life. Towards the end of the conversation, Felicity mentioned what had happened when Boots called to pick up Tim's briefcase.

'Felicity? You actually had a clear sight of my old man?' said Polly.

'Yes, I actually did for about thirty seconds,' said Felicity.

'Absolutely great,' said Polly. 'Ye gods, what am I saying? That's my daughter talking. But what does it matter, I'm delighted for you, Felicity, although I think fate should have been generous enough to let you see Jennifer instead of my hoary old warrior.'

'Polly, he's a lovely man,' said Felicity.

'My dear, you're preaching to the converted,' said Polly. 'Wednesday now – I'll come and pick you up at twelve. Anneliese and Patsy will be arriving here at twelve-thirty.'

'I'll appreciate the lift,' said Felicity, 'and I'm looking forward to the lunch party.'

'With the right amount of wine, we could all get squiffy,' said Polly.

'Count me in, Polly,' said Felicity. She always called Tim's stepmother by her

Christian name, knowing she wanted nothing to do with being addressed as mother-in-law. It was one of her little vanities.

When Tim arrived home, Felicity let him know what Sir Charles Morgan had proposed, a consultation when clarity of vision happened again. Tim was as disappointed as she herself was.

'I don't think that's a very positive reaction, Puss.'

'Oh, Mummy's used to disappointments,' said Jennifer, an articulate nine-year-old whose understanding of her mother's disability was that of a child who had always lived with it.

'Sir Charles did sound a little tired,' said Felicity. 'He'd just finished two operations.'

'As many as two?' said Tim. 'I've known army surgeons having to operate all day in a Red Cross marquee fitted up as an emergency field hospital, and still able to come out of it with a positive attitude.'

'But, Daddy,' said Jennifer, 'Mummy has to do what her doctors say.'

'I know she does,' said Tim, 'and I know we have to go along with that.'

'Gosh, wasn't it wonderful, that she saw Uncle Boots?' said Jennifer.

'Uncle Boots is your granddad,' said Tim.

'Oh, but everyone calls him uncle,' said Jennifer.

Tim glanced at Felicity. She seemed a little far away, and he felt she was almost certainly thinking the moment would have been that much more wonderful if it had allowed her to see her daughter.

Chapter Thirteen

Leaving the factory at the end of his day's work, Jimmy headed for his home in Bow. He had broken away from South London. Since his job was in Bethnal Green and since Clare's parents, as well as her grandparents, Gertie and Bert Roper, all lived in Bow, Jimmy had decided to favour her by buying a house close to Victoria Park. That delighted Clare. Their typically solid Victorian terraced house had actually been purchased by the Adams property company, at Sammy's paternal suggestion, and Jimmy was making the required monthly payments at simple interest. The property company had made the same arrangements for other couples in the family, on the basis of long-term profit. Sammy believed in family charity, but not at a loss. He considered any kind of loss to be a businessman's worst enemy.

Clare had helped to hang new wallpaper, apply new paint and to modernize the kitchen and scullery. And a contractor had knocked down the dividing wall between the upstairs loo and a box of a bedroom to create a spacious and good-looking bathroom, with both bath and shower. Accordingly, the young couple's bank balance had been hammered a bit, but Clare managed the household budget as if born to it. East End housewives, beginners or otherwise, had that kind of gift.

Hearing Jimmy arriving home, she went quickly to meet him as he came in out of the damp autumn evening. She still thought him a young woman's best gift, although she was not unaware of her own worth.

'Jimmy.' She kissed him. 'Oh, I like it when you come home.'

'Home smells warm,' said Jimmy, 'and you feel warm. How's your day been?'

'Active,' said Clare, 'I've been in the garden again.'

'In this weather?' said Jimmy.

'Well, it's only been a bit damp, not actually rainy,' said Clare. It was from Jimmy that she'd acquired her interest in gardening. Together they were designing a new look to what had been a bit of an uninspiring garden. Jimmy had called it a rubbish dump, but it had promise and provided enough ground for a sizeable vegetable plot, something on which they were both keen. She had been digging the selected plot over today, a job she and Jimmy had started at the weekend. She had continued clearing it of square feet of tangled grass turves, cut out with her spade, to uncover more of what was obviously rich dark soil.

That's virgin soil, Jimmy had said at the weekend. Clare said virgin soil? D'you mean it's never had flowers or onions make love to it? And Jimmy, of course, being a typical Adams, said flowers would have been acceptable but not all virgin earth wanted to make love with an onion. This virgin plot will, when we grow our own onions, said Clare. A lively cockney, she had gradually made herself verbally equal to Jimmy's sallies.

'I suppose I ought to pay you extra for your gardening,' he said.

'No, of course not,' said Clare, 'it's me labour of love. Jimmy, when the summer comes we'll have our own flowers and things.'

'What things?' asked Jimmy, as they entered their redesigned kitchen.

'Onions,' said Clare, and laughed. 'Won't we?'

'Count on it,' said Jimmy. 'What's cooking?'

'A lamb casserole, with dumplings,' said Clare.

'That's my girl,' said Jimmy. He looked her over. She was a lovely young wife, eyes bright, figure worth a mention, and auburn tints enriching her dark hair.

'Now then,' said Clare.

'Now then what?' said Jimmy.

'I know that look,' said Clare, warm winter sweater fitting her a treat.

'It's my sorry look,' said Jimmy.

'Sorry?' said Clare, who always enjoyed

these moments of daily reunion with her entertaining husband.

'Yes, sorry for all the other blokes,' said Jimmy.

'What other blokes?' said Clare, pretty sure the answer was going to be a lemon.

'All those who've got dumpy wives who keep cats,' said Jimmy.

'D'you know what I like most about you?' said Clare.

'Tell me, don't keep me in suspense,' said Jimmy.

'Your daft jokes,' said Clare.

'Tell you what, you sexpot,' said Jimmy. 'Supper smells ready now, so let's have it, then stoke up the living-room fire, sit around it, get warmed up and play cards.'

'What cards?' asked Clare.

'Strip poker?' suggested Jimmy.

'Oh, me gawd,' said Clare, 'I knew I was right about that look in your eye. Still, I'm going to call your bluff, so all right, yes, let's get warmed up round the fire after supper and play strip poker. But you'll need to get good cards, not half you won't.'

'Specially good cards?' said Jimmy.

'You bet, lovey, because I'm going to wear four vests and six pairs of knickers as well as all me other clothes,' said Clare.

The kitchen resounded to Jimmy's shouts of laughter.

In the Camberwell home of Harry and Anneliese Stevens, the evening meal of grilled salmon cutlets and seafood sauce, with duchesse potato cakes and lightly steamed broccoli, was a triumph of Anneliese's culinary talents. She eschewed the traditional German dishes that were loaded with mounds of potatoes. This particular meal was being enjoyed in celebratory fashion, accompanied by a bottle of white wine. Harry's first novel, a thriller, had been accepted for publication, and he'd received an advance of seven hundred and fifty pounds. Anneliese was delighted for him.

'Crikey, isn't this high living?' said Cindy. 'Daddy, I suppose you realize this is the first wine I've ever had?'

'Is it?' said Harry.

'Blessed if I know how you remember anything sometimes,' said Cindy, but fondly.

'Oh, it's part of why we both love him,' said Anneliese.

'Well, since I've just remembered something I'd forgotten,' said Harry, 'let me act on it.' He put his knife and fork down, took out his wallet from the inside pocket of his jacket, and extracted a white banknote. He'd been to the bank early in the day to deposit his advance cheque and to draw some money. On his way back home he'd bought a huge bouquet of flowers for Anneliese, which touched her to the quick. 'Cindy, this is for you,' he said, and put the banknote beside her plate. It was a white fiver.

Cindy stared at it.

'It's for me?' she breathed. 'A whole five pounds?'

'For everything you've done for me,' said Harry.

'Oh, crikey,' said Cindy, eyes shining. Her pocket money had improved since the marriage, because her stepmother was so generous, but five pounds from her dad, well, that was a fortune. 'Daddy, I don't know how to thank you, except perhaps I could do the ironing for Mummy every week. I'd be blissed, honest.'

'That's sweet of you, Cindy,' smiled Anneliese, her understanding of the English language and its colloquialisms rapidly progressing to the level of her pronunciation. 'But we shan't ask that of you, not after you spent years doing it for your father. You deserve to enjoy time with your friends now.'

'That reminds me,' said Cindy, 'I think I'll phone that boy.'

'What boy?' asked Harry, on guard in respect of his young daughter's social relationships. He knew neighbouring cockney lads were fast workers with girls who had reached their teens.

'Oh, you know,' said Cindy, 'that boy James who had a bike ride with me when his family came to Sunday tea.'

'Ah, that one, yes,' said Anneliese. 'That one,' she added with a smile. 'I see. Well, shall we drink to friendships and your father's success as a novelist, Cindy?'

'Oh, yes, not half,' said Cindy, 'except it's best if we don't mention the title of the book. It's sort of not in keeping with your flowers, Mummy, or my lovely whole fiver.'

The title of the thriller was *Murder on the Night Train*.

Tuesday.

In Bristol, the suspects had been formally identified by the bank cashier who, under the threat of the revolver, had been forced to hand over a huge amount of cash. His positive recognition of the men at an identity parade spared Alice and Fergus from having to do so. What they had done was to make formal statements to the police at the station, at the request of Chief Inspector Bradley.

The newspapers were following proceedings, reporting that the police had still not found the missing revolver.

At home, Chinese Lady was suggesting to her husband that Alice ought not to be living in a foreign place like Bristol. Sir Edwin ventured to say that Bristol, as a long-established English city and port, was hardly foreign.

'Still, you know what I mean,' said Lady Finch, 'it's not like Southend or Margate.'

'True,' said Sir Edwin, 'neither Southend

nor Margate is a port, Maisie.'

'I don't know why Alice can't get a job in London and live in Herne Hill, Edwin. Herne Hill is so respectable. You don't get bank robbers hanging about, waiting to frighten people to death. Nor don't I know why she doesn't get married and settle down proper, like.'

Unmarried men or women of normal physique were a dubious lot to Chinese Lady. She considered them slightly suspect.

'Alice wants to make the most of her university education,' said Sir Edwin. 'I imagine she's an excellent teacher.'

Chinese Lady sniffed. She wasn't in favour of any of her female brood spending their lives teaching. That was for other women.

In the Bethnal Green factory, all the workers now had union cards and the unwanted privilege of paying weekly union dues, which, of course, they considered a liberty. Still, if being unionized kept the factory out of trouble, well, they'd go along with it.

That evening, young James answered the ringing phone.

'Hello, Mr James Adams here.'

'Mr who?' said Cindy. 'Crikey, you don't half fancy yourself.'

'I think I know you,' said James.

'I should think you do or I wouldn't be

phoning you,' said Cindy.

'Wait a tick,' said James, 'are you that girl Cindy Stevens?'

'Well, it's not that soppy girl who thinks she wants to marry you,' said Cindy. 'Why d'you go out with soppy girls?'

'I don't go out with any girls,' said James, 'I'm not old enough yet. A feller doesn't know what to make of any girl when he's only just about thirteen. Didn't I mention that?'

'Yes, and you sounded barmy,' said Cindy.

'Oh, there's a lot like me in my grandma's family,' said James. 'My dad informed me of that, but he told me not to worry, that people a bit barmy were easier to get on with than people who were stone cold sober.'

'Oh, well, never mind,' said Cindy, 'I expect you'll get over it one day. Listen, you can come and see me on Saturday.'

'I'll give it some serious thought,' said James.

'Do you have to talk like you were ninety?' asked Cindy. 'Just say when, can't you?'

'When,' said James. Cindy couldn't help herself. She giggled.

'Listen,' she said, 'my dad won't like it if you mess me about.'

'Well, all right,' said James, 'seeing I don't want your dad to thump me, I'll come over on Saturday morning. It can't be the afternoon, I'm playing football for the school.'

'Football?' said Cindy, disgusted. 'That

kicking game?'

'I like it,' said James.

'Well, I hope it won't always get in the way of our meetings,' said Cindy, whose years of housekeeping for her dad had made her a decisive young lady. Which meant a bit bossy. 'All right, Saturday morning, then. Say half-past ten. If it's raining I'll let you have coffee with me until it stops and then we can go out. Don't be late. Well, goodbye for the present.'

'So long, Cindy,' said James, and put the phone down.

'What was all that about?' asked Polly, entering the hall.

'I think I've just been railroaded,' said James.

'Young man,' said Polly, 'your tongue is running ahead of your age.'

'Is that good?' asked James.

'It means that, like your father and your Uncle Sammy, you'll never be lost for words,' said Polly.

'That's good, then,' said James.

Polly smiled.

'Who's railroaded you?' she asked.

'That girl Cindy Stevens,' said James. 'She wants me to go and see her on Saturday morning, and before I could say no I said yes.'

'I see,' said Polly. 'That's being railroaded, is it, young sport?'

'I'm going to get confused,' said James.

'What with Cathy still talking as if she wants to marry me and Cindy wanting me to keep her company now and again, I won't be able to cope. As I've said before, I'm not old enough.'

'You're right, dear boy, you're not,' said Polly, 'but you aren't doing badly. By the time you're eighteen, some girls won't know what's hitting them.'

'You will have your little joke, Mum,' said James.

'Hey, you James,' called Gemma, 'come and help me do up the parcel for Flossie's birthday.' She was referring to Flossie Cuthbert, their mother's daily maid. 'You've got to put your finger on the string.'

'There, I told you, Mum,' said James. 'Girls. I can't even cope with Gemma.'

'Rotten hard luck, old lad,' said Polly.

With little Sylvia tucked up in her cot for the night, Lulu came down from checking on the poppet to open up a fireside conversation with Paul.

'Is there something you want to tell me?' she asked, curling up in her armchair. Her spectacles were shining earnestly, which told Paul she was probably looking for a discussion on Socialism. His own support for the Labour Party was still of a loyal kind, but his first priority was enjoyably directed at his responsibilities as a husband and father.

'I was wondering if we could afford a television set,' he said, not for the first time.

'We're not going to spend money on a medium designed to control the minds of people and turn them into goggle-eyed robots,' said Lulu. 'Haven't I said so before?'

'Frequently,' said Paul, 'but I'm told there are some interesting evening discussions on television, with smart women like Barbara Castle to the fore.'

'Well, I admire Barbara Castle, she's a top-ranking Labour MP,' said Lulu, 'but not a reason for having a capitalist television set.'

'We could shop around for a Socialist one,' said Paul. 'I wonder if we could get hold of an imported Russian one that'll give us pictures of happy workers gallivanting through whacking great fields of grain?'

'Is that supposed to be funny?' asked Lulu.

'No, just a thought,' said Paul.

'Haven't you anything to tell me about your family's factory now that the workforce is unionized?' asked Lulu.

'Lulu, I don't work at the factory,' said Paul, 'I'm assistant to Tim and Daniel in the property company.'

'But you get all the factory news, don't you?' said Lulu.

'Will it surprise you that I don't?' said Paul.

'Well, you should,' said Lulu.

'I'll speak to Uncle Sammy about it, and

perhaps he'll let me have a daily bulletin to bring home to you,' said Paul.

'I'd simply like to know if the factory's workers are that much happier under the protection of the union,' said Lulu.

'All I know is that they were happy enough before,' said Paul.

'I bet,' said Lulu. 'They had no real rights before.'

'As far as I'm aware,' said Paul, 'they never asked for any. Just their well-earned wages.'

'Out of fear of their bosses, of course,' said Lulu.

'Lulu, their bosses are my dad directly, and Uncle Boots and Uncle Sammy indirectly,' said Paul, 'and none of them would ever put their hobnails in, especially not my dad.'

'Keep your shirt on,' said Lulu, 'I'm only enquiring after the welfare of the workers.'

'What about my welfare?' asked Paul.

'Yours?' said Lulu.

'Yes, you've worked a crafty flanker on me,' said Paul. 'I'm now doing all the supper cooking, as well as my share of bathing our little lady. Not that I mind that. She's an angel, and my only problem is to make sure she doesn't slip through my fingers and bump her bum in her bath bowl.'

'Listen, flannelhead,' said Lulu, 'do I have to remind you I'm looking after her all day every day? And that I've had to put my political career into cold storage? Perhaps for several years?'

'Be frozen solid by then,' murmured Paul, a grin on his face.

'What's that?' demanded Lulu, her spectacles casting the light of dark suspicion, if that was possible. 'What did you say?'

'Oh, just a sympathetic word about your refrigerated career,' said Paul.

'You're grinning,' said Lulu.

'That's as much as I can manage,' said Paul. 'There's too much strife in the world to feel like laughing. Cyprus, French Algeria, Malaya, the Elephant and Castle–'

'The Elephant and Castle?' said Lulu.

'Yup,' said Paul. 'Haven't you heard that people were chucking bricks there today?'

'Fascists?' said Lulu.

'No, the Old Kent Road cockneys,' said Paul. 'They're fed up with hoardings and scaffolding, and with the development that's taking the old Elephant and Castle away from them.'

'Hooray and three cheers,' said Lulu, 'they're rising up against profiteering despoilers of the old and familiar.'

'It was Fatty Goering's bombers that first took the old place away from the people,' said Paul. 'They want it back. The pity is that the young people there like the idea of a completely new look that includes a modern complex of shops, offices and cafés with jukeboxes.'

186

'Nickelodeons,' said Lulu.

'That's it, a popular record at sixpence a time in the slot,' said Paul. 'Point is, will the old people and the young start throwing bricks at each other around the Elephant and Castle? Tricky. And then there's my sister Alice and that bank robbery that could have done her some grievous bodily harm.'

'Everything you're saying points to male aggression,' said Lulu. 'We need a parliament of women. It would spread light and compassion, and turn male belligerence into something much more acceptable. What a liability some men are.'

'Are you including me?' asked Paul.

'You?' said Lulu. 'No, of course not. You're a sweetie. And it doesn't hurt me to say so.'

'For that,' said Paul, 'I'll bath both you and our little lady when I get home tomorrow. That'll include powdering both your bottoms.'

Lulu, her glasses twinkling, said, 'I can hardly wait.'

She was going through quite a happy time as a mother. As for being a wife, well, she'd managed to get Paul usefully domesticated, the objective of many modern wives who had chucked the 'little woman' label into the waste bin.

One day wives would be on top.

On top?

Lulu gave a girlish giggle.

Chapter Fourteen

Wednesday.

The ladies' lunch party was in full swing, Polly hostess to Felicity, Anneliese and Patsy. Flossie had come up trumps by securing two young Norfolk ducks, one from her own family's butcher, and the other from Polly's butcher. She roasted them without the addition of any fat. Result, duck meat moistly tender, but not greasy, served with a delicious sauce that contained the juice of an orange, accompanied by roast potatoes and melting creamed cauliflower. Flossie had suggested green peas, tasty with duck. Polly said no, that Felicity couldn't cope with peas, unless she used a spoon, as she did at home. She avoided that in company.

Two bottles of chilled white wine from Bordeaux complemented the meal, Polly lavish in her filling and refilling of glasses.

No-one fussed Felicity. Fussing suggested she was helpless, and that could irritate her. Certainly, she was coping very well with her meal, and nothing fell off her fork.

Patsy, Sammy's frisky American daughter-in-law, was wholly intrigued to meet Anneliese, and in her frank way wanted to know about post-war Germany, as well as Anneliese's experiences as a German army nurse.

'No, no, I have spoken of those experiences so many times that I shall bore everyone,' said Anneliese.

'But I haven't heard about them,' said Patsy, thinking this striking German woman, golden-haired and blue-eyed, must have been seen as one of Himmler's Aryan goddesses during the heyday of Nazi power. 'Or what you went through immediately after the war.'

'Patsy, I'm afraid that my memories of post-war Germany are best kept to myself,' said Anneliese. 'They would make even one of your Goons weep.' The Goons were a popular comedy team whose weekly show went out on BBC radio.

'Anneliese, you listen to the Goons and understand their humour?' said Felicity.

'Not half,' said Anneliese, and looked surprised as this aroused laughter. 'What have I said?'

'Something I fancy you've heard Cindy say,' said Polly. 'It's a cockney expression, meaning – um–'

'Not half,' said Felicity.

'Or a bit of all right,' said Polly.

'Oh, I'm beginning to understand cockney speech now,' said Anneliese.

'To get back to Patsy's interest in your

experiences,' said Polly, 'at least tell her how you came to meet Tim.'

'You would like to hear that?' said Anneliese to Patsy.

'Not half,' said Patsy. That caused more laughter. 'It's OK, guys, I've picked up some cockney myself. Now, can I hear from you, Anneliese?'

Anneliese smiled. She wondered if her lunch companions were aware of just how much her existence had changed since her arrival in England, how much she loved her life with Harry and Cindy, and how much she welcomed new friendships, especially with the men and women who were related to Tim's remarkable grandmother. He had introduced her to that lady some months ago.

'Very well,' she said, and told of the time when a badly wounded prisoner of war, a British commando, was brought for treatment to the German-run hospital in Benghazi. He was Lieutenant Tim Adams at the time. She spoke of his fight to survive his wounds and how, during his slow recovery, he was not as respectful to her as he should have been. He made jokes. One day, when taking his temperature, she asked him why it was up, and he said because the orderly had brought him a bottle half an hour ago, that it was still between his legs, and the strain of trying to remove it without spilling it was sending him on the road to disaster. 'Yes, something like that,' she said, 'you can believe me, Patsy.'

Patsy shrieked, Polly smiled, and Felicity said, 'I can and do.'

'Yes, he was very amusing,' said Anneliese, 'but he had a sad secret that he told no-one. That his wife had been blinded when caught in a German air raid.'

'Anneliese, don't remind me of the evening it happened,' said Felicity, 'it still makes me curse.'

'It was a terrible war, yes, terrible,' said Anneliese soberly.

'Well, we aren't here to make ourselves miz,' said Polly, 'but to welcome you as one of us.'

Anneliese said, 'One of you means–?'

'Oh, together we stand, divided we fall,' said Polly, 'which in turn means that together we can keep one step ahead of our men.' She laughed. 'Fat chance any woman has of keeping one step ahead of mine. What an old darling, he was born a front runner.'

'So was Daniel,' said Patsy. 'My stars, why did I marry a guy who's a natural smarty-pants?'

'Luck of the draw, Patsy,' said Polly. 'It was either Daniel or a Boston cowboy, I suppose. Let's drink to our struggle to hold our own with our men.' She refilled glasses.

Felicity had momentarily lost touch with

hers. She groped for it. Anneliese, next to her, lightly pushed the glass until it touched Felicity's fingers. Felicity lifted it.

'I'm drinking to a vision of my daughter,' she said.

'Ah, so?' said Anneliese. 'A lovely thought. We should all drink to that, I think.'

Which they did. Flossie, having cleared away plates and cutlery of the main course, brought in the dessert, a simple concoction of autumn raspberries and ice cream, much appreciated after the deliciously rich roast duck.

'Patsy,' said Polly, 'did you know that on Monday morning, Felicity had a clear vision of Boots?'

'Clear?' said Patsy. 'Really clear?'

'For a brief while,' said Felicity. 'My best moment ever.'

'Oh, marvellous,' said Patsy, 'and it reminds me that when I mentioned in a letter to my pa that you were getting images now and again, he wrote to say there are now several great eye surgeons practising in the States. He said that experiments during the war on blinded GIs pushed research to the limit, and that some very successful operations are now being performed on people blinded by accident or by war wounds. Felicity, you could be one such case.'

'By going to America?' said Felicity. She spooned raspberries and ice cream into her mouth, giving herself time to think. Then, overbright, she laughed. 'What a hope.'

'It's one you should consider,' said Polly.

'I'd have to talk to my own surgeon first,' said Felicity.

'Where's my handbag?' said Patsy. It was on a chair by the sideboard. 'Excuse me, guys, but I must show you something.'

She came to her feet, crossed to the chair and brought her handbag with her. She opened it and extracted a newspaper clipping. 'Felicity, my pa enclosed this from *The New York Times*. It's all about Dr Paul Rokovsky, a Ukrainian physician and eye surgeon, who was forced to work for German medical units during the war and emigrated to America in 1946. Now he carries out successful operations on blinded GI veterans.'

'Patsy, let me see,' said Polly. Patsy gave her the clipping and she read it. 'Well, Felicity dear girl, if this is true, you've something seriously promising to think about.'

'Sir Charles Morgan advised me to wait until I get another clear vision,' said Felicity.

'Wait for what?' asked Patsy.

'For a new consultation,' said Felicity.

'Well, I guess he knows what he's talking about,' said Patsy.

'I still think you should consider consulting this American genius, if Sir Charles has no objection,' said Polly. 'There's a photograph, and he looks the perfect medicine man, if a bit hairy.'

'May I see?' asked Anneliese, and Polly passed her the clipping. Anneliese read the eulogistic write-up and studied the photograph of a heavily bearded middle-aged man in spectacles.

'Where are we now?' asked Felicity.

'Figuratively, we're in New York,' said Polly.

'We sure are, Felicity, and thinking of you,' said Patsy.

Anneliese, still absorbed in the write-up and the photograph, said, 'If I were blind and there was the chance of a cure, I'd go anywhere for a consultation that could lead to a successful operation. Felicity, you must show this newspaper cutting to Tim.'

'And tell him to blow the expense?' said Felicity.

'Yes, of course,' said Anneliese, 'for what does the cost matter?'

'Make it the least of your worries, Felicity,' said Polly, who knew Boots would happily finance any possible operation, wherever it took place. So would she herself, since she had recently benefited richly from her late father's will. She was delighted that her lunch party had opened up a new avenue of hope for her stepdaughter-in-law.

Patsy, although aware that American medical fees could cost as much as an arm and a leg, said, 'Go for it, Felicity.'

'I'll speak to Tim,' said Felicity.

Anneliese, who knew many Ukrainians had freely thrown in their lot with the Germans in the hope that their nation would become independent, took one more look at the photograph, then said, 'Here's the newspaper cutting.' She folded it and placed it in Felicity's hand.

'Let's finish the wine,' said Polly.

They did so, and Polly uncorked a third bottle when Anneliese announced that her husband had had his first novel accepted for publication. Questions were asked about it and answers given in a spirit of animation and enjoyment, but it was only Patsy who became a little squiffy.

Anneliese was in a thoughtful mood when she arrived home in the family car, so much so that she narrowly missed scraping one side of the alley that led to the house.

It was nearly four o'clock when she let herself in.

'Harry?' No answer. She listened. She climbed the stairs to the landing, from where she heard the faint sounds of a typewriter. Harry was at work on another novel. She smiled, and put her thoughts aside. 'Harry?'

He came out of the top-floor room that she and Cindy now called his den or his study. He looked down at her. As usual, his thick hair was a little untidy, a pencil stuck behind his ear. His brown cardigan was worn loosely, and he was hardly a figure to make a London tailor's eyes light up. But she would not have changed him for any matinee idol.

'You're back,' he said, and came down the stairs to kiss her. She put her arms around him and gave him an affectionate hug.

'What's the time?'

'Don't you know?' she asked, still smiling.

'Two-thirty? Three?'

'Nearly four,' she said. When he was writing, time escaped him.

'Four?' said Harry. 'Bit of a long lunch, wasn't it?'

'Oh, it simply went on and on,' she said. 'Polly was charming, and I've a new friend in Patsy, and a closer friend in Felicity. I must tell you about Felicity.'

'Tell me over a pot of tea,' said Harry. 'I'll make it, while you take your hat and coat off and drop them somewhere.'

'I'll freshen up,' said Anneliese.

Cindy arrived home from school then. She had a friend with her, Judith Keller, a Jewish girl, who had shown flickers of concern at being told Cindy's stepmother was German. Cindy assured her that her dad's new wife was a lovely lady, nothing like the awful Germans one read about. Come and meet her, she said. Judith said all right, but as soon as she entered the house with Cindy, she let her reservations be heard.

'No, I don't want to,' she burst out, and turned and ran.

Cindy sighed. Other friends and other people found it hard to believe that her stepmother was German.

However, by the time the tea was made, Cindy had settled down with her dad to listen to what Anneliese had to say about a New York doctor and what he might be able to do for Felicity Adams.

Harry said surely a blind woman who kept having moments when she could see, however vaguely, had to be a case of real interest to any eminent eye specialist, particularly since she had just experienced a few moments of clear sight.

'Golly, if it was me I'd be giddy with hope,' said Cindy. 'But to have to go all the way to America? How far is that?'

'Well, New York's a couple of thousand miles,' said Harry.

Anneliese, her reservations about the Ukrainian doctor put aside, said the tribute to his skill was so glowing that she hoped Tim would make sure a consultation was arranged for Felicity in New York. Harry said that if a diagnosis suggested a cure was possible, Felicity would obviously have to stay there for some time.

Anneliese responded impulsively.

'Harry, I would gladly pay all fees,' she said.

'But not advisable or necessary,' said Harry. 'The whole family's big in business, and they'd never consider accepting financial help from anyone outside. I'll wager they could finance Felicity and Tim's stay in New York over and over again. I imagine Tim would go too.'

'Yes, I'm sure he would,' said Anneliese.

'You've a special interest in Felicity, haven't you?' said Harry.

'It was her husband who first made me think hard and seriously about what Hitler was doing to Germany and its people,' said Anneliese.

'You still think yourself as guilty as the worst of his followers,' said Harry, 'and you aren't. You're a sweet woman and all you were guilty of was allowing yourself to be hypnotized. Cindy and I count ourselves lucky from the first day you came to lodge with us.'

'Mummy, we love you,' said Cindy.

'Then I'm the lucky one, darling, wonderfully so,' said Anneliese. 'I simply feel I'd do anything to help Felicity regain her sight.'

'Wish her well, then, but don't set your hopes too high,' said Harry.

When Daniel arrived home that evening, he

found his children, Arabella and Andrew, building a Meccano castle in the lounge. Patsy was curled up on the settee, asleep.

'Arabella, what's up with your mother?' he asked.

'She's tired,' said Arabella.

'What's she been doing, then?' said Daniel. 'Trying to run a four-minute mile? Can't be done. Well, it hasn't been done so far. Patsy?'

He touched her shoulder. She opened sleepy eyes.

'Who's that?' she murmured.

'Me,' said Daniel.

'Don't know you,' murmured Patsy, 'get lost.'

'Not in front of the children,' said Daniel. Remembering she'd had a special lunch date at Polly's, he grinned. He knew that when Polly entertained, she did so lavishly. 'Kids,' he said, 'I think your mother's tipsy.'

'Tipsy?' said Andrew, four years old.

'Yes, sad but true,' said Daniel. 'Patsy?'

'Go away,' sighed Patsy.

'What about supper?' asked Daniel.

'Ugh,' said Patsy.

'All right, stay there,' said Daniel. 'Come on, kids, let's see what we can rustle up for supper.'

'Yes, let's,' said Arabella, now six, 'I'm starving.'

'So am I,' said Andrew, 'but I don't want

any greens.'

'Tell you what, young 'un,' said Daniel, 'how about you and me popping out and bringing back fish and chips?'

'Oh, I'll come,' said Andrew.

'While we're out,' said Daniel, 'Arabella will make sure your mother doesn't fall off the settee, won't you, poppet?'

'Of course, Daddy,' said Arabella. 'Well, I mean, if she does fall off, I don't think I'll be able to pick her up.'

'We won't be long,' said Daniel. 'Patsy?'

'Mmmm?' murmured Patsy.

'I don't suppose you fancy some fish and chips, do you?'

Patsy opened wine-bedewed eyes once more.

'Ugh,' she said again. 'What are you, a ghoul?'

Daniel, grinning broadly, left the house in company with Andrew. I need to have a word with Aunt Polly, he thought, and find out how much plonk she poured into Patsy, and tell her to give her Coca-Cola next time.

That evening, of course, Felicity had a long talk with Tim. Tim, much impressed by the newspaper write-up of Dr Paul Rokovsky, whose practice was in New York, insisted that they must get Sir Charles Morgan to concede to their wish for a second opinion.

'I'll try to reach him tomorrow, Puss,' he said, his mind made up, 'and I'll let him know I'll definitely go with you.'

'Tim, the time we spend in New York and an operation itself, could cost a fortune,' said Felicity.

'Well,' said young Jennifer in stout-hearted fashion, 'I don't think we ought to worry about money. And I won't be an expense myself, I could stay with Grandma and Grandpa.'

'We'll manage,' said Tim, 'we can't pass up a chance like this, can we, Little Puss?'

'No, course we can't, Daddy,' said Jennifer.

Tim phoned Boots later. His dad had heard about the newspaper report from Polly, and was fully aware of what it might mean for Felicity. He said he supposed the reason why Sir Charles Morgan himself couldn't do what was necessary was because he specialized mainly in cataract operations. Wasn't that so? Tim said yes, but he was still a renowned ophthalmologist.

'Well, Tim old lad,' said Boots, 'in regard to a possible consultation with this New York specialist, I've already agreed with Polly that you and Felicity must go. Don't worry about the cost. This is a family matter all the way.'

'We may be talking about thousands of dollars,' said Tim.

'We'll cover that with pounds sterling,' said Boots. 'The Government will allow an outflow of sterling under these circumstances.' There was a Treasury limit on the amount of currency private individuals could ordinarily take out of the country.

'I'm going to give in to family generosity,' said Tim, sensibly opting to be practical.

'Grandma Finch will beat you with her brolly if you don't,' said Boots.

'What a great old lady, hope she lives for ever,' said Tim. 'And thanks, Pa old sport, you'll save me from pawning our new set of kitchen saucepans.'

'You're welcome,' said Boots. 'Love to Felicity.'

Chapter Fifteen

Anneliese woke up in the middle of the night, not by reason of a nightmarish dream, but because of a subconscious projection of an image into her mind, the image of a man she and her army medical team had encountered during the German army's disorganized retreat from Stalin's limitless hordes.

The encounter came about after the Auschwitz extermination camp had been evacuated, when most of its surviving inmates had been summarily murdered. That frightful place had left one more searing mark on Anneliese's conscience, and had filled the members of the medical team with horror and disgust. Several SS officers from the camp, plainly petrified at the possibility of being caught by the Russians, attached themselves to the medical convoy, insisting on sharing their lumbering transport, consisting of worn and battered ambulances and horse-drawn peasant carts.

Russian guns roared at a distance, shelling the remnants of a German armoured division that was far ahead and making for Berlin, as was the straggling column of exhausted refugees and ragged military personnel. None dared stop, except for brief hours at night, for by day the Russians were always too close. Those who did stop, who simply collapsed, had to be left to the mercies of the Red Army.

There were two doctors among the SS officers from Auschwitz, neither of whom endeared himself to the strictly principled medical team that had always acted as an honourable unit of mercy, no matter what the circumstances. Major Karl Hubert, in charge of the unit, and weary to the bone, objected to the presence of the SS doctors and their arrogance. He knew them, he told Anneliese and other nurses, to be responsible for indescribably cruel experiments on concentration camp inmates. One was Dr Hans Beck, a neurologist, the other Dr Gerhard Fischer, an ophthalmologist and physician. Anneliese took note of them both as two more hateful cyphers of what to her had become the loathsome ideology of Nazism. Dr Fischer, an impressive-looking man with a moustache, was particularly arrogant, boasting that in the medical research centre at Auschwitz, he had advanced the cause of ophthalmic surgery in a remarkable way.

'Yes, some of us know,' Major Hubert told him, 'and we know how. We of this medical unit will stop running when we reach

Berlin. You will have to run for the rest of your life, for the Allies will be hunting you and Dr Beck as war criminals.'

Wide awake, and remembering all this, Anneliese stared at the dark ceiling, with Harry breathing evenly beside her. That photograph of Dr Paul Rokovsky in the newspaper clipping. She was certain that she now knew who he really was, and she also knew why her inspection of the reproduced photograph had stirred her instincts and given her food for thought. In her mind, it had now become a likeness of Dr Gerhard Fischer. He looked much older, was heavily bearded, and the spectacles added their own change to his appearance, but she had no doubts about his real identity. Not now. He was among the many Nazi war criminals who had slipped the Allied net, changed their identities and begun new lives abroad.

It might be the middle of the night, but her mind was clear and positive. The New York eye specialist Felicity had been urged to consult was one of the sadistic doctors who had experimented in hideous fashion on Jewish inmates of Auschwitz, the most notorious of Himmler's extermination camps.

My God, she thought, what must I do?

Knowing she was not going to be able to get to sleep again, she slipped quietly from the bed without disturbing Harry. She donned her winter dressing gown, put her feet into her slippers and went silently down through the darkness to the kitchen. Closing the door, she switched on the light and began to make some strong coffee.

Thoughts chased around and put her into mental turmoil. If the man who now called himself Dr Paul Rokovsky could operate successfully on Felicity, must I keep quiet for her sake, or must I go to the American Embassy and denounce him?

That question would not let go of her mind.

She was on her second cup of coffee when the door opened and Harry, in his dressing gown, showed himself.

'Anneliese? What's all this? Aren't you well?' His concern touched her.

'Close the door, Harry,' she whispered, 'I have something I must tell you, and I'm glad you're the kind of man I can tell.'

And so she told him.

At the end, he said, 'You need do nothing about this, either now or in the immediate future. You can think about it – we can both think about it and take our time, since it's pretty obvious Felicity and Tim won't be going to New York tomorrow or even next week. Arrangements for a consultation in New York will take their own time.'

'Harry, you think I should say nothing to

them, nothing at all?' said Anneliese.

'Well, some might argue that they've a right to know and a right to make up their own minds,' said Harry. 'Let's give ourselves a week to decide whether to tell them or not. By the way, you're absolutely sure this doctor in New York is – what was his name?'

'Gerhard Fischer, an SS doctor of the Auschwitz extermination camp,' said Anneliese. 'Yes, I'm quite sure.'

'Dear God, I feel for you,' said Harry, thinking of the horrendous nature of Himmler's crimes. 'Perhaps the full depths of these atrocities will never be plumbed. Cindy's history lessons are taking in Oliver Cromwell and the Civil War. Cromwell was a cymbal-clashing republican, a witch-hunter and a grim Puritan, but a saint compared to some of the characters she'll learn about when she reaches the history of the Second World War.'

'She won't like it,' said Anneliese.

'There's one person who might help you make a decision,' said Harry.

'Who?' asked Anneliese.

'Tim's father,' said Harry. 'Boots. He's a man of great experience, with a knowledge of a wartime hell himself. He was there when Belsen was uncovered. Polly told us, if you remember.'

'Oh, yes, so she did,' said Anneliese.

'Other than with Boots,' said Harry, 'not a

word about all this outside these four walls.'

'No, darling, not a word,' said Anneliese, and they went back to bed.

By Friday, Tim had been able to speak to Sir Charles Morgan, and the consultant had promised to unearth more facts concerning the reputation and prowess of Dr Paul Rokovsky. Certainly, he said, if this man's skills and qualifications did prove excellent, there'd be no objection to Felicity consulting him.

'How soon, would you say?' asked Tim, phoning from the office he shared with his co-director, cousin Daniel.

'Patience, Mr Adams, patience,' said Sir Charles, 'but I shan't dawdle, I assure you. I have contacts among the New York medical profession.'

'Thanks, we'll wait to hear from you,' said Tim, and rang off. Sir Charles was a busy man.

'What prospects?' asked Daniel.

'He's going to make a check on Dr Rokovsky's skills,' said Tim.

'More waiting, then,' said Daniel.

'Can't be helped, I suppose,' said Tim, 'but Felicity's naturally on tenterhooks, and so am I.'

'Tenterhooks can be like a rash,' said Daniel, 'so best of luck to both of you.'

'Felicity can do with all the luck going,'

said Tim. 'Where are we today, Daniel?'

'Still waiting to see the Bethnal Green planning committee,' said Daniel.

'Oh, yes, Mr Bunlap's committee,' said Tim.

'Dad's convinced Bunlap is a Chinese doughnut,' said Daniel.

Tim smiled, his thoughts on New York.

Saturday morning, ten-thirty.

It was raining when James arrived at Cindy's home in Camberwell Road. Cindy answered the door to him.

'Oh, you've come,' she said.

'In hope that the rain might stop sometime soon,' said James, slipping off his mac and removing his cap. Well, thought Cindy, I must say he's a bit of an improvement on most boys, but fancy that girl talking about marrying him. How soppy can you get?

'The rain better had stop,' she said. 'Oh, you can come in, Mr James Adams.'

'Very kind of you, Miss Cindy Stevens,' said James, stepping in and bowing.

'Don't start showing off already,' said Cindy. 'Come and say hello to me mum and dad, then we'll have some coffee. That's if it's still raining.'

Anneliese was in the kitchen, baking cakes as an antidote to the rainy morning, and looking decoratively goddess-like in a brightly patterned apron.

'Hello, James,' she said.

'Good morning, Mrs Stevens, how are you today?' greeted James cordially.

'I'm very well, thank you,' smiled Anneliese, 'and how are you?'

'Showing off,' said Cindy, 'and he keeps talking like he's ninety years old.'

'Do you, James?' asked Anneliese, liking the good-looking boy.

'It's what Cindy thinks,' said James, 'but as I mentioned to my mother, I don't understand girls. Mrs Stevens, your oven's sending out a lovely aroma.'

'I'm baking a fruit cake,' said Anneliese.

'Mum, could James and me have some coffee until the rain stops?' asked Cindy.

'I'm brewing some for all of us,' said Anneliese. The percolator was gently bubbling. 'Would you call your father? The rain's sent him up to his typewriter.'

Cindy went to the foot of the stairs, followed by James. She called up.

'Daddy! Coffee's ready! Come on down!'

From above, Harry's deep masculine voice was heard.

'Coming, Cindy.'

'Yes, and now, not next week,' called Cindy. 'He's a bit airy-fairy, my dad,' she said to James.

'So's mine,' said James. 'Still, that's better than being a fusspot.'

'Let's go in the living room and we can

talk till the rain stops,' said Cindy.

Harry brought them coffee in a little while. He found Cindy giving James what sounded like the story of her school life. He said hello to the boy and left the young pair to their get-together.

'I think those two like each other,' he said to Anneliese.

The rain kept on, making the day uninviting. It seemed all too obvious that November was just around the corner, waiting to make a nuisance of itself. Old men were wearing their long johns, and old ladies were guarding their chilblains. November was no respecter of the elderly. In fact, when it was in its sourest mood, it had no qualms about hastening their funerals.

Cindy was hogging the conversation, not only to stop James doing so himself, but also to let him know what her school life was like. She had reached the stage of declaring it great. Great? said James. Yes, said Cindy, all her teachers thought she was clever enough to be famous by the time she was in her twenties. James said that was amazing. Yes, said Cindy, but don't interrupt, it's not good manners.

'Bother the rain,' she said, 'especially as I was going to take you shopping with me.'

'Shopping?' said James in horror. 'Shopping?'

'Yes, I've got some lovely extra pocket money from my dad for being a help to him,' said Cindy. 'And for being brilliant in my term exams,' she added, just to let James know she was entitled to his respect. 'So I'm going to buy a new dress, new stockings and new shoes.'

'Could you count me out?' said James, slightly hoarse.

'Not if the rain stops and we get some sunshine,' said Cindy. 'Sunshine's just right for that kind of shopping. Rain's sort of depressing. So if it rains all morning, you'll have to come next Saturday instead.'

'And go shopping with you?' said James, frankly alarmed.

'Yes, it'll be fun,' said Cindy.

'Would you mind if–'

'When I'm trying dresses on, you can give me your opinion,' said Cindy.

'I'll be a mile away,' said James, 'and still running.'

'Don't you like shopping?' asked Cindy.

'Only in hardware stores,' said James.

'Oh, you'll soon get to like dress shops,' said Cindy. 'And shoe shops.'

'I've got serious doubts,' said James, and while the rain kept falling he and Cindy debated what there was to like about a girl taking a feller shopping. Cindy came up with positive points. James remained negative.

Not until he returned home at twelve-thirty

did the rain clouds finally break.

'Had a happy morning?' said Boots.

'What a question,' said James.

'I agree,' said Polly. 'There's never anything happy about a morning as wet as this.'

'Still,' said Gemma, 'I expect James had a nice time with Cindy. That boy of ours, Daddy, having a girlfriend at his age.'

'Allow me to tell you what Cindy had in mind for me,' said James.

'What?' asked Gemma, who liked to know everything.

'Shopping,' said James.

'Shopping?' said Polly.

'Shopping?' said Gemma.

'Not your style, James?' said Boots.

James explained why it was that the planned excursion would have taken him in and out of dress shops and shoe shops. He was saved only by the rain, and was there something in the house what would cure him of a fainting feeling?

'Is it as bad as that?' smiled Polly.

'Worse,' said James. 'The outing's only postponed. Till next Saturday. I'll have to fall ill. I tell you, Dad, I'm never going to be able to cope with girls.'

'Console yourself with the fact that you're not the only one,' said Boots. 'You'd be hard-pressed to find any of us who could even cope with a seven-year-old Goldilocks.'

'Rhubarb,' said Polly.

'Lie low, James old chap,' said Boots. 'In a crisis, be neither seen nor heard.'

'Some hopes,' said Gemma, 'that boy can't stop being seen and heard all the time.'

'I think I'll go and lie down,' said James.

Anneliese phoned Boots later that day and asked if he could possibly find time to see her about a confidential matter.

'You sound as if you've something serious on your mind,' said Boots.

'Yes, I have,' said Anneliese.

'If I can help, I will,' said Boots, 'but why me?'

'Because you're Tim's father,' said Anneliese, her lightly accented voice vibrant in her earnestness, 'and this concerns Tim. Yes, and Felicity. I would like a private meeting with you. Could you possibly agree to that?'

'Well, look here,' said Boots, 'how about Monday lunchtime? You know where our business offices are, and there's a pub immediately opposite. In the saloon bar we can tuck ourselves away and not be overheard. It's not far from where you live. Would you fancy a ham sandwich made with crusty new bread, and any kind of drink you favour?'

That intrigued Anneliese. An English pub lunch? With Tim's father, a man of engaging goodwill? How would it compare with a large stein of foaming lager and hot sausages in a Munich beer hall, her companion one of its jolly, jovial but paunchy patrons? The prospective comparison was irresistible.

'Boots, I would be happy to meet you there,' she said.

'Shall we make it early to ensure we can secure a corner table?' said Boots. 'Say twelve-fifteen?'

'Yes,' said Anneliese.

'I'll wait outside for you,' said Boots.

'Thank you so much,' said Anneliese.

'Monday lunchtime, then,' said Boots.

Polly, when told of the assignment, said, 'Not on your life, old bun.'

'I've promised,' said Boots.

'To have a private chinwag with her in a secluded corner?' said Polly. 'Nothing doing.'

'State the reason for your objections,' said Boots.

'She's too young–'

'She's over thirty.'

'She's still too young, and far too exotic,' said Polly, 'and although I like her, I don't trust any woman who wants to be alone with you.'

'You can trust me,' said Boots, 'especially in a saloon bar.'

'That won't stop her playing footsie with you,' said Polly.

'Anneliese is a happily married woman,' said Boots.

'So am I,' said Polly. 'Saints alive, I never thought in my wild twenties that I'd be the kind to qualify for this happy-ever-after stuff. Fair enough, old soldier, give Anneliese your ear, then, but what exactly is her problem?'

'I've no idea, except that it concerns Felicity and Tim,' said Boots.

'So you mentioned,' murmured Polly, eyeing him wryly. He was still an arresting man, and she could never help thinking that every attractive woman had sexy ideas about him. 'Well, Felicity and Tim are the topic of the moment, so all right, old playmate, go and meet Anneliese on Monday and find out what she has to say about them.'

Chapter Sixteen

In Bristol, Alice received a phone call from Fergus.

'Oh, so there you are,' she said as an opener.

'Aye, here I am, Alice,' said Fergus.

'You've taken your time,' said Alice who, much to her annoyance, had found herself becoming fretful at not hearing from him.

'I've been infernally busy at the factory,' said Fergus.

'You could at least have found time to ring and ask me about my bruises,' said Alice.

'Well, shame on me,' said Fergus, 'how are they?'

'Invisible now,' said Alice.

'Have you heard from the police at all?' asked Fergus.

'Yes, to tell me the date of the trial at Bristol Crown Court,' said Alice.

'Same with me, January ten,' said Fergus.

'They hope by then to have found the gun. The hell-hounds obviously threw it away or buried it. I'll pick you up on the day of the trial, Alice, and drive you to the court.'

'Well, thanks very much,' said Alice. 'Is that all?'

'All?' said Fergus.

'Aren't you going to see me until then?'

'Alice, I did tell you I had no wish to intrude on your life again,' said Fergus.

'Don't be silly,' said Alice. 'We've known each other for ages, and we're friends. Friends aren't intrusions. Come and take me out tonight. To the Old Vic. *Macbeth* is still playing, and although it's Saturday, we can still get gallery seats.'

'Alice, I wouldna want to cut out any special friend of yours,' said Fergus.

'What's happened to you?' asked Alice. 'You were never as retiring as this. Anyway, all friends are special.'

'In that case,' said Fergus, 'I'll come and pick you up this evening.'

'Seven-thirty,' said Alice.

'I'll be there,' said Fergus, still cautious about resuming a close relationship with her. He was all too sure he still wanted her as his wife, and just as sure that she'd back off.

Alice rang the theatre, gave her name and address, informed the booking clerk she was a member of the Old Vic patrons' society, and was told they'd reserve two gallery seats for her. The rest of the house was full, as usual for a Saturday evening.

The evening proved a pleasure for her. Fergus was kind, entertaining and not in the least his once presumptuous self. They enjoyed Shakespeare's dark towering epic of the ambitious Macbeth and his even more ambitious wife. Afterwards, Fergus drove her back to her flat, where Alice provided tea and smoked salmon sandwiches. They talked about their encounter with the violent bank robbers, and about her family. Fergus had discovered a liking for her parents, Tommy and Vi Adams, and wanted to know how they were.

It was nearly midnight before he left.

Alice, seeing him out of the house, said with a smile, 'It didn't hurt, did it?'

'The evening?' said Fergus.

'Taking me out.'

'Alice, have you still no attachments?'

'Attachments?'

'Aye. Your own kind of man, y'ken.'

'I have friends, that's all.'

'And your books?'

'Fergus, stop being trivial,' said Alice, 'come and take me out again next Saturday, and phone me in between.'

'So I will, lassie, so I will,' said Fergus, and left with the feeling that his cautious approach could get to the stage of falling apart.

Alice went to bed with a smile and a hot-water bottle.

Annabelle, the elder daughter of Lizzy and

Ned, had her son Philip home for the weekend. Philip, eighteen, was training to become an RAF fighter pilot, but it has to be said that his attachment to his Service career was rivalled by his feelings for Phoebe, the seventeen-year-old adopted daughter of Sammy and Susie, and as pretty as a dark-eyed sunflower.

By Sunday afternoon, Annabelle and her husband, Nick Harrison, had seen very little of Philip. He had spent most of his time with Phoebe at her home, including taking Sunday dinner with her family.

'When that young man's on his weekend leaves,' Annabelle said to Nick, 'we only see him at bedtime and breakfast.' Annabelle, nearly thirty-eight, was the image of her mother Lizzy at that age, full-bosomed, chestnut-haired and brown-eyed. But, unlike Lizzy, she'd become a little bossy.

Nick, forty-two and still vigorous, said, 'Well, you know, Annabelle, a young bloke with stars in his eyes isn't quite the same as an old married codger like me.'

'Still, he ought to spend a bit more time in his own home,' said Annabelle.

'He's got dancing feet,' said Nick, who had been a fighter pilot himself. His wartime exploits, especially in the air over beleaguered Malta, had earned him medals, 'So has Phoebe.'

'Philip shouldn't get too serious about

Phoebe,' said Annabelle, 'they're cousins.'

'Not really,' said Nick, 'Phoebe's adopted.'

At this moment, in Sammy and Susie's home, Phoebe and Philip were sharing a settee in the warm comfort of the lounge – parlour to Susie because of her Walworth upbringing. Philip had just kissed Phoebe.

'Now don't I keep telling you you mustn't do that?' said Phoebe, bright, perky and intelligent.

'Why not?' asked Philip.

'Don't I keep reminding you we're cousins?' said Phoebe.

'And don't I keep reminding you we're not blood cousins?' said Philip.

'Oh, yes, so you do,' said Phoebe. These exchanges were of a kind she often initiated. 'All right, then.'

'All right what?' said Philip, lean, lanky and homely, and basically a decent type of bloke.

'You can do it again, then,' said Phoebe. So Philip kissed her again, which made her lips go dewy. 'I didn't mean like that,' she said.

'It tasted fine to me,' said Philip. 'Listen, I've been thinking.'

'What about?' asked Phoebe.

'I've been thinking that when I get my wings and my rank as a pilot officer, I'll be considered A1 and capable.'

'Get you,' said Phoebe. 'Capable of what?'

'Making my own decisions,' said Philip.

'Unlikely,' said Phoebe. 'It's a well-known fact that most boys don't mature until they're about forty.'

'It's not well known to me,' said Philip. 'And what about girls, might I enquire?'

'Oh, most girls are like me,' said Phoebe, 'and I'm already mature.'

Philip laughed.

'Tell me another,' he said.

'Well, come on,' said Phoebe, 'what decisions did you have in mind?'

'About you, to start with,' said Philip. 'I was thinking that in a couple of years I might have an urgent feeling about asking you to marry me.'

'In a couple of years?' said Phoebe. 'All right, let's wait till then.' At the moment, she had no serious thoughts concerning marriage. She liked her life as it was now, spent with the people she loved the most, her adoptive parents, and working in her dad's firm as an aspiring bookkeeper. She was good at figures. It was a life without strain, troubles or complications. 'Meanwhile,' she said blithely, 'you can still take me dancing whenever you're on leave.'

'Ta,' said Philip.

'Don't mention it,' said Phoebe. 'Mind, that doesn't mean you can keep on kissing me like you just did. It's been happening far too often, and for months now.'

'I'll make it just once in a while,' said Philip.

'Oh, all right, do it again now, then,' said Phoebe. She liked him kissing her. There was no strain about that, either.

'Here we are, lovey,' said Lizzy, handing her husband a hot bedtime drink of Horlicks. It would help him to sleep. Ned, comfy in a fireside armchair, took the steaming mug.

'Eliza, you're a treasure,' he said.

Lizzy, sitting down opposite him, with her own drink, had made up her mind ages ago to give him all the care she could. She knew he was never going to be very active again. His heart played up as soon as he attempted to do more than he should. He was nearly sixty, only two years senior to Boots, but looked much older, poor dear, his face lined, hair grey and thinning. Chinese Lady, during one of her frequent visits, had actually tried a light-hearted aside, telling her not to let Ned go bald, as there hadn't ever been baldness in the family. You're joking, Mum, Lizzy had said. Well, I don't want to be a wet blanket about Ned losing his hair, said Chinese Lady, it's always best to have a little joke now and again. Little jokes from her were a rarity, and hilarious jokes had never happened. Living and surviving had always been a serious business to Chinese Lady. Lizzy thought that her three brothers must have got their sense of humour from their dad. Corporal Daniel Adams, her mother's first husband, must have been a bit of a comic.

'Ned,' she said, 'I think your hair's stopped falling out.'

Ned laughed. His fireside hours with Lizzy in the evenings were always of a Darby and Joan kind, of being comfortable with each other. Companions. That was what it had come down to now, when all their children were married and living their own lives.

'Is there much left to fall out, Eliza?' he asked.

'Of course there is,' said Lizzy, 'you've still got lots.'

'Well, I'll do my best to hang onto it,' said Ned, sipping his Horlicks, which he secretly thought did expectant mothers more good than himself. But it did seem to help him get to sleep. 'Particularly as your mother's against me going bald.'

'Oh, you heard her the other day, did you?' said Lizzy.

'I've never liked to miss any of your mum's pearls of wisdom,' said Ned.

'Pearls of wisdom?' said Lizzy, taking her turn to laugh. 'Go on with you, Ned Somers. Oh, what d'you think about this business of Felicity hoping to see an eye specialist in New York?'

'If she does see him by the time she gets

there,' said Ned, 'she won't need any consultation. She can turn round and come straight back, except what woman would want to miss out on doing the rounds of the New York shops and getting chummy with their Irish cops?'

'Now you're having your little joke,' said Lizzy.

'Felicity's hopes are no joke,' said Ned, 'and I'm wishing her the best of luck.'

'We all are,' said Lizzy. 'There, that's good,' she added as he finished his nightcap. She took the empty mug from him. 'We'll go up now.'

Ned used the poker to clear the ashes from the fire. They both liked an old-fashioned fire, and were able to buy and burn smokeless fuel now.

A few minutes later, with the downstairs lights switched off, and an empty milk bottle put out for the milkman, they went up to bed for about the fourteen-thousandth time in their thirty-eight-year-old marriage, and it didn't seem a night too much.

Chapter Seventeen

Monday, twelve-thirty.

Anneliese and Boots had met at the pub, Anneliese opting to dress without ostentation. Her coat was dark grey, with a black velvet collar, and on her blonde hair she wore a black beret, the kind made popular by Marlene Dietrich. She and Boots were tucked away in a corner of the saloon, on red-padded wall seats. Her coat was open now, and off her shoulders, revealing a wine-coloured dress. Joe, the barman, had served them their ham sandwiches, with a small dressed salad each. The salads were an innovation in an establishment that rarely changed any of its Edwardian customs.

Anneliese had a glass of wine, another innovation, and Boots had a glass of old ale.

'Now,' he said, 'tell me what's on your mind, Anneliese.'

Anneliese felt as relaxed with this man as she did with Harry. And as the saloon was only half-full, with no-one crowding them, it wasn't difficult to unburden herself.

'It concerns the doctor mentioned in *The New York Times*,' she said. 'The report described him as a Ukrainian immigrant applying for American citizenship.' And she went on to tell Boots of the German retreat from the Russian hordes, and her medical team's encounter with several SS officers from Auschwitz, two of whom were doctors, specialists in their fields. One was a Dr Gerhard Fischer, an eye specialist, whom the leader of her medical team knew to be responsible for hideous research experiments on Jewish inmates. That disgusting man now called himself Dr Paul Rokovsky, and was the eye surgeon Felicity hoped to consult, she said. Boots noted voice vibrations of emotion. Her half-eaten sandwich and salad now lay untouched.

'And you're worried about Felicity placing herself in the hands of a man who's almost certainly been classed as a war criminal?' he said.

'You are quick in understanding that,' she said.

'My dear lady,' said Boots, 'your problem is obvious, and also damned tricky. Have you heard of being on the horns of a dilemma?'

'I've come across it in English literature,' said Anneliese.

'It means not knowing which way to turn,' said Boots, and took a mouthful of old ale. 'Yes, damned tricky. But there's one way of looking at it.'

'Tell me,' said Anneliese.

'We have a doctor, an ophthalmologist, who might be able to restore Felicity's sight,' said Boots. 'And perhaps he's able to do that because of the experiments he conducted on suffering Jews, poor devils. Should we let Felicity take advantage of that? She was blinded by a bomb blast during a German air raid, so is she entitled to be cured by a German doctor, even if he is a war criminal? She and Tim need not know that, or that he's German.'

'Boots, how immoral would that be when you and I, and Harry too, would know the cure would be at the expense of perhaps a thousand innocent victims?' said Anneliese.

'There's the tricky factor,' said Boots, 'there's the horns of a dilemma on which you and I, and Harry, are all perched now. The other option, of course, would be to tell Tim and Felicity, and make it their dilemma.'

'Could we do that to them?' asked Anneliese.

'I don't think so,' said Boots. 'At this stage, with Felicity's London consultant about to enquire into the New York doctor's credentials, it would be a little too much for her. I suggest, Anneliese, that we leave things as they are for the time being. Let's see what comes of the enquiries. Tim will be keeping me informed of developments, and I'll keep in touch with you.'

'I suppose that if only Tim were told, he would hate to have to make a decision himself,' said Anneliese.

'It would be the most difficult decision of his life,' said Boots.

'Boots, what a terrible inheritance Himmler and his SS exterminators left to the world,' said Anneliese, voice low and intense. 'Will the world ever forgive my country?'

'It will forgive women like you, Anneliese, and men like Count von Stauffenberg, who did his best to rid Germany of Hitler,' said Boots.

'That is what Harry tells me,' said Anneliese. 'You do me a great kindness in telling me so too. Thank you, Boots, for meeting me and allowing me to confide in you.'

'Dear lady, what are friends for?' smiled Boots. 'Come and have tea with Polly and me next Sunday. Bring Harry, of course, and Cindy.'

'Boots, we would love to,' said Anneliese, blue eyes coming to life.

'By the way,' said Boots, 'I'll have to let Polly know of our discussion.'

'Yes, of course,' said Anneliese.

On her arrival back home, Anneliese gave Harry an account of her meeting with Boots, and told him why they had decided to do nothing for the time being.

'Very wise,' said Harry, 'and better than

dropping a bomb on Felicity and Tim.'

'That might still happen,' said Anneliese.

'I wouldn't want to be the one to set the fuse,' said Harry.

'No, who would?' said Anneliese. 'Oh, we're invited to tea with Polly and Boots next Sunday.'

'Well, as you know, I'm all in favour of the civilizing influence of Sunday teas,' said Harry.

'So am I,' said Anneliese, 'they remind me of my English grandmother and her addiction to her English teapot. How sad that, like the rest of the family, she became devoted to Hitler.'

'It's all over for her now,' said Harry, 'and so it is for you.'

'Yes, how glad I am that I'm still alive,' said Anneliese, and kissed him.

James had Cathy Davidson with him when he arrived home from school.

'What's the idea, my lad?' asked Polly, collaring him in the hall after he had shown Cathy into the living room. 'Why have you brought Mrs Davidson's little Goldilocks home?'

'To tell you the honest truth, Mum,' said James, 'she brought me.'

'Oh?' said Polly. 'And how did she manage that?'

'It just happened,' said James. 'Well, at the

risk of being boring, I do keep pointing out to you and Dad that I can't cope with girls. Anyway, Cathy would like a cup of tea and a slice of cake. Oh, and to talk about me and her making a secret pact.'

'A secret pact?' said Polly. 'I'm shuddering.'

'I'm confused,' said James. 'I mean, a secret pact about keeping a promise to marry her when we're old enough?'

'You made that promise, you young wretch?' said Polly, looking him in the eye.

'No, she wants me to make it now, while we're having tea and cake,' said James.

'Only over my dead body,' said Polly. 'Fiery green sea serpents, haven't your father and I told you more than once that you are never going to have Mrs Davidson as your mother-in-law?'

'Well, you've told me, Mum, but I don't think Dad has,' said James. 'He's sort of airy-fairy about it. Can I ask Flossie to do the tea and cake now? Then I'll see if I can get Cathy talking about football or cricket or something.'

Polly laughed, softly. Both her twins were endearing, James so like his father in looks and whimsies.

'Go on, then,' she said.

Secret pacts.

Delicious, as long as this one didn't last.

Later, when Boots was home, Polly received

details of his lunchtime discussion with Anneliese.

'Listen, old fruit bun,' she said, 'it was bad enough James bringing Cathy Davidson home to talk about a secret marriage–'

'A what?' said Boots.

'Never mind, you know the ideas that girl gets,' said Polly. 'I simply didn't expect you to bring home a bombshell yourself. My God, Anneliese has turned a prospect into a crisis, hasn't she?'

'She's unhappy about it,' said Boots, 'but felt she had to speak out.'

'Anneliese's permanent problem is her conscience,' said Polly. 'She's one of the few Germans who changed their minds about Hitler. I'm delighted she's married to Harry Stevens, he's her shield and comfort. So, you suggested nothing should be done for the time being?'

'I thought the best thing was to see how events develop,' said Boots.

'There's a wise old owl,' said Polly. 'We can all sit back in the hope that no-one will have to make a decision.'

'Dr Paul Rokovsky could, of course, drop dead from overwork,' said Boots.

'Is he overworked, do we know?' asked Polly.

'I've no idea,' said Boots, 'it was just a thought. However, that would hardly cause Felicity to jump for joy.'

Polly asked if he had thought about the fact that since Dr Paul Rokovsky was applying for American citizenship, his background would be thoroughly investigated by the American authorities. Boots said that was a point. Polly said skeletons might be falling out of the cupboard right now. Boots said that was a further reason to let events unfold and to simply wait.

'I can't disagree,' said Polly.

'By the way,' said Boots, 'I've invited Anneliese to tea next Sunday, along with Harry and Cindy.'

'How delightful,' said Polly, 'except that I'll have to try my hand at baking a cake. Oh, well, I'll give it a jolly old go on Saturday, with Flossie's help. Incidentally, it's snowing in New York.'

'That'll make things slippery for the doctor,' said Boots.

On Wednesday afternoon, Tim and Daniel, co-directors of Adams Property Company, having been informed of the date and time of their meeting with Bethnal Green Council's planning committee, arrived punctually at two-thirty. The subject was the proposed extension to the Adams factory. The planning committee was mainly interested in the prospects of an extra workforce, which Tim and Daniel guaranteed. The interview, accordingly, was unusually brief, but it was also entirely satisfactory, for they were advised that their application for the extension was granted, and official notification by post would follow.

On their return to the Camberwell offices, they gave the news to Sammy, and Sammy sat back in his chair the better to observe his son and his nephew.

'Well, well, me lads,' he said.

'You're not going to make a speech, are you, Dad?' said Daniel.

'I ain't one for making speeches,' said Sammy, 'they take a long time, and I don't ever have a long time except for my Sunday dinners at home as a compliment to Susie's cooking. I'd just like to say you two cockalorums are a credit to your dads, of which I'm one, as your respected mum will tell you, Daniel. Believe me, getting the better of any council bowler hats is nearly up with getting the better of trade union bowler hats, and accordingly—'

'Uncle Sammy,' said Tim, 'I think you're making a speech.'

'Never been known, not in office hours,' said Sammy. 'Just saying you two have done a first-class job and accordingly I'll recommend to Boots that the firm strikes a medal, one each for both of you.'

'Gold?' said Tim.

'Eh?' said Sammy.

'Gold medals, Dad?' said Daniel.

'Don't make that kind of joke,' said Sammy, 'I might have a careless moment and take it seriously. Let's just clap hands that we've had a good week so far, especially seeing Barney Burridge has now stopped trying to teach me how to suck a lemon, and you two have won an application for required planning permission. Now you can ask one of the girls to make you a cup of tea, with two biscuits each. There you are, that's all, me lads, short and sweet.'

'Short and sweet?' Daniel grinned. 'You could have fooled me, Dad.'

'No sauce,' said Sammy. 'Tim,' he said, turning sober, 'give Felicity my fond regards and tell her I'm keeping my fingers crossed for her.'

'She's still getting blurred images,' said Tim, 'and still hoping this doctor in New York can work wonders for her. We're waiting, of course, for Sir Charles Morgan to recommend him for a consultation. If that comes about, we'll fly off to New York. You'll be able to manage here without me for a while?'

'Under those circs, we'll manage, Tim,' said Sammy. 'Young Paul's capable now of doing some of your work, and Daniel can double up on his.'

'For double salary, Dad?' said Daniel.

'There you go again, with your jokes,' said Sammy. 'You could catch me out one day, and I'd wake up the next morning feeling someone had taken advantage of me. Go on, toddle off, you two, and have some tea and biscuits.'

'Pity you were never able to join the army, Uncle Sammy,' said Tim, 'you'd have made a caring sergeant major.'

'Fortunately, your dad wouldn't let me,' said Sammy. 'He knew it could have meant the business falling down dead.' Rachel Goodman would have said that was true, that the business and Sammy were indivisible, that neither could exist without the other. Sammy, in delivering the remark, only showed a good-natured grin. 'Go on, hoppit,' he said.

Cindy, coming home from school, saw a large sheet of paper stuck on a wall of the alley. There were words in large bold capitals.

GO HOME NAZI BITCH.

Cindy tore it from the wall, ripped it to pieces, screwed them into a ball and dropped it in the dustbin. That, however, didn't prevent her from being upset.

She said nothing to her dad and step-mother.

Chapter Eighteen

'Edwin,' said Chinese Lady at breakfast the next morning, 'I don't like thinking about Felicity and Tim having to go all the way to America to see some foreign doctor.'

'Worry not, Maisie,' said Sir Edwin, rarely other than calm when dealing with her agitations, 'Daniel and Patsy, and their children, made the journey last year, and all returned safe and sound. None of them went missing.'

'I should hope not, the very idea,' said Chinese Lady. 'But it's different for Felicity, being blind. She could step off a kerb and get knocked down by one of them dangerous New York taxis I've heard about.'

'Tim will see that she doesn't,' said Sir Edwin.

'I'd feel better about it if that foreign doctor came over here to see Felicity,' said Chinese Lady.

'I'm sure that would suit her,' said Sir Edwin, 'but not sure it would suit him. Let's comfort ourselves with the knowledge that Felicity's still in the care of her London specialist.'

'Well, all right, if you say so, Edwin,' said

Chinese Lady.

Breakfast over, Sir Edwin answered a knock on the front door. Boots showed himself.

'Morning, Edwin,' he said, 'not a good one.'

It was cloudy and drizzling. November had made its unwelcome entrance.

'The forecast is promising an improvement,' said Sir Edwin. 'Come in, Boots.'

'Can you spare me ten minutes before I push off to the office?' said Boots, stepping in. He took off his homburg and shook it free of rainy beads.

'Say hello to your mother first,' smiled Sir Edwin, 'she's in her kitchen. Then we'll chat in my study.'

Boots said hello to Chinese Lady, who wanted to know, of course, the reason for his call. Boots said he simply wanted a chat with Edwin before going on to his office.

'Well, I'm sure Edwin will enjoy that while I'm washing up the breakfast things,' said Chinese Lady.

'How's he been lately?' asked Boots. He and his brothers and sister were all keenly aware that their respected stepfather was eighty-one.

'Oh, he's been fine,' said Chinese Lady, 'and we still do our daily walks. Mind, he misses Sir Henry, they used to see each other a lot.'

'We all miss Sir Henry,' said Boots, 'Polly especially.'

'I always said Polly was more caring than some people thought,' said Chinese Lady.

'So she is,' said Boots, and went to join his stepfather.

In the study, Sir Edwin said, 'Do I presume you've something on your mind, Boots?'

'I want to ask a favour of you,' said Boots.

'Fire away,' said Sir Edwin.

'Can you find out for me if your old department knows anything about a German SS medical officer, Dr Gerhard Fischer, who conducted experiments on Jewish inmates at Auschwitz?'

'That's a tall order, Boots old fellow,' said Sir Edwin.

'If it's too tall, I'll excuse you,' said Boots.

'We're talking about M15 files, of course,' said Sir Edwin. 'Some of those are very high up. Are you going to give me a reason for this request?'

'Not yet, if that's all right with you,' said Boots.

'Well, I shan't push you,' said Sir Edwin, 'I've known you for too long to feel your reason isn't a good one. I can contact an old colleague who's well placed to help, if he's disposed to. First, let me ask you a question. Do you know if this doctor is officially classed as a war criminal, or a suspected one?'

'No, I don't know,' said Boots, 'that's what I'm asking you to find out. I fancy he is. I'd like to be certain. What I do know is that he's alive and well, and practising his profession.'

'I see.' Sir Edwin smiled. His relationship with Boots went back forty-two years, to the time when Chinese Lady's eldest son was a bright, enquiring schoolboy, fascinated by life and all its wonders. 'Well, leave it with me, Boots, and I'll see what I can do. What was the man's name again?'

'Gerhard Fischer.' Boots spelled it out, and Sir Edwin noted it down. 'I'm obliged, Edwin, but don't worry if no information is forthcoming. But if it is, I'll let you know sometime why I wanted it.'

'I'll be happy with that, Boots.'

They parted, Boots to go on to the company offices, Sir Edwin to make a phone call to his old colleague George Coleman, head of a department in M15.

Later, over coffee with Chinese Lady, he told her he was going up to town after lunch to meet an old government colleague. Chinese Lady, used to his occasional reunions with such people, asked if he was sure he'd be all right, and Sir Edwin said yes, he would, since the clouds were breaking and November was actually dispensing some sunshine. Chinese Lady said it would be nice for him to spend a little

240

time with his old friend, but to make sure to get back home before any fog came down.

'I don't trust this sunshine,' she said, 'you know what November's like.'

'An enemy of the people,' smiled Sir Edwin.

'Edwin, what did you and Boots talk about?'

'He had Christmas in mind,' said Sir Edwin, on the assumption that most people were beginning to think about that Christian festival.

And Chinese Lady assumed the conversation had been about what Polly and Boots would be buying her for a Christmas present. Edwin, of course, would know what to tell Boots, because he knew what she would like.

What would she like?

Oh, anything nice.

If certain people had a problem concerning Felicity and Tim, Rosie and Matthew had a problem concerning their West Indian workers, Joe and Hortense Robinson. Joe and Hortense had asked if their two nephews, recently arrived from the West Indies, could come and spend a weekend with them in the farmhouse annexe. Rosie and Matt had consented. It was now twelve days since the young men, Herby and Grant, had arrived, and they were still resident,

241

spending their time following their aunt and uncle about, or wandering around the sheep and exploring the village. Matt, deciding he had to speak to Joe, pointed out that a weekend hadn't meant a fortnight. When would Herby and Grant be on their way?

'Ah, Mista Chapman, sir, I'll ask my old lady,' said Joe.

Hortense spoke to Rosie and Matthew later.

'It's like this, Miz Chapman, Mista Chapman, them poor boys, they don't have nowhere to live,' she said.

'Well, I'm sorry about that,' said Rosie, 'but really, they can't live here.'

'But, Miz Chapman, me and Joe, we got room for them in the annexe, and we feed them ourselves.' Hortense was apologetic and also unhappy.

'Hortense,' said Matt, 'forget making that a permanent arrangement. Those young men need jobs and their own place.'

'They can't get no jobs,' said Hortense, 'but they is willing to work for you, then they can stay, ain't that so, Miz Chapman?'

'No, Hortense, it isn't,' said Rosie firmly. 'We don't need any more help. Don't they know London hospitals have all kinds of jobs available for unskilled workers?'

'They like it here,' said Hortense.

'No, they can't stay, Hortense,' said Matt. 'We'll give them until Saturday, then they must go. Where are they now?'

'They done gone down by the shop,' said Hortense.

'Hortense, they're lazing about,' said Rosie.

'Miz Chapman, Joe and me, we could give them a talking-to,' said Hortense, 'but I ain't sure they'll listen.'

'They'll still have to go,' said Rosie.

'Miz Chapman, maybe Mista Chapman can talk turkey to them,' said Hortense, looking as if that prospect would solve the problem and ease her discomfiture.

'Do they have any money?' asked Matt.

'Only that ole dole money they go and pick up once a week,' said Hortense.

'Hortense, they haven't left here since they arrived, except to visit the village store,' said Matt. 'But if they're entitled to collect the dole, then they've had jobs.'

'Not good jobs,' said Hortense, 'not like Joe and me have got here.'

'Hortense, see that they leave on Saturday, or I will talk to them,' said Matt, which sent Hortense off sighing.

'Matt, I'm disappointed in them,' said Rosie. 'They're trying to land us with their nephews.'

'It's probably because of family ties,' said Matt, 'but of course, we can't take them on. And they strike me as being a couple of work-shy young men.'

'Perhaps they're finding it difficult to settle,' said Rosie. 'It can't be easy for any of the West Indians who come here from sunny Jamaica.'

'I'd miss the coconuts myself,' said Matt.

Mr George Coleman, sixtyish but still a valuable asset to M15, received Sir Edwin in his office, and shook his hand vigorously.

'Happy to see you, Edwin old chap – you're carrying your years like a two-year-old. Take a seat. I don't have much time, but I can always find enough for you. Let's see, what was it about?'

'The man I mentioned on the phone,' said Sir Edwin. 'Gerhard Fischer, who practised at Auschwitz.'

'Oh, yes,' said George. 'Right, yes. I went to work on this as soon as I came off the phone.' He opened up a file that lay on his desk. 'Dr Gerhard Fischer. Born in Dresden 1897, Dresden Medical Academy from 1923 to 1929, set up practice as a general physician in 1931, began a course in ophthalmic surgery in 1933, joined the Nazi Party the same year, and was posted in 1937 as an SS medical officer to Dachau concentration camp, where he first began experiments on inmates. In 1941 he was sent to Auschwitz as assistant to Dr Mengele, a sadistic bugger of infinite savagery. There he performed every kind of experiment as an ophthalmic surgeon on twins and on men and women, all under Mengele. In September '45 he was documented as a major war criminal, along with Mengele, but they both avoided capture. It's assumed they're somewhere in America, probably the Argentine. So there you are, Edwin. Incidentally, I've given you this information out of the goodness of my heart, but it stops there. Now I want to know what it means to you. I hope you're going to tell me you know where the hell-hound is.'

'If I could tell you that, George, I would,' said Sir Edwin.

'You're handing me a lemon?' said George.

'I'm asking you to trust me,' said Sir Edwin. 'I've a feeling I'll be able to tell you sometime in the near future why the information is wanted.'

That's all?' said George. 'Edwin, you've diddled me. That information is classified.'

'It's safe with me,' said Sir Edwin, putting his own trust in Boots.

'Well, I tell you, none of this is going down on paper for you,' said George. 'What you've heard is what you've got. Damned if you aren't still a deep one, Edwin you old sod. I'll wait with interest to hear from you. Now, stay a few minutes longer and have a cup of tea with me.'

'Delighted,' said Sir Edwin, 'and if there are biscuits, George, remember Osbornes are my favourite.'

George laughed.

'Bloody good to see you, my old friend,' he said, 'even if you've made a monkey out of me.'

'Not my idea at all,' said Sir Edwin, 'rely on that.'

On his way home on the bus, he did some thinking. So, the man Boots wanted to know about, Dr Gerhard Fischer, was definitely and officially classed as a war criminal, on a par with the notorious Dr Josef Mengele, said to be still at large in South America.

What was Boots's interest in him? It had to be of a very intriguing kind, or he would not have kept the reason to himself. Was it something to do with his time at the uncovered Belsen concentration camp? Could Dr Gerhard Fischer have been there, and had Boots actually seen him recently? In Dulwich? Very unlikely, since Boots would surely have said so.

I'd like to know, said Sir Edwin to himself. So would M15, of course.

He phoned Boots that evening.

'Hello?'

'Boots, my dear fellow,' said Sir Edwin, 'would you care to drop in again on your way to the offices in the morning?'

'You've clicked?' said Boots.

'I'll let you know tomorrow morning,' said

246

Sir Edwin.

'I'll be there,' said Boots. 'Say about nine?'

'I'll have finished breakfast by then.'

'First-class,' said Boots, instinctively sure his worldly stepfather had news for him.

'So there you are,' said Sir Edwin the following morning, 'and I want you to know that what I've just told you is classified information.'

'It would be if it came from MI5, of course,' said Boots, 'although I'd point out that similar information about the master sadist, Dr Mengele, has circulated worldwide.' But, obviously, the change of name and nationality did point to a murky past. The information his stepfather had obtained was no more than could have been expected. I'm back where I started, he thought.

'What are you going to do with it?' asked Sir Edwin.

'Not very much,' said Boots, 'and I'll tell you why.' He acquainted his stepfather with all the facts. Sir Edwin expelled a low whistle.

'Boots, if Anneliese Stevens has correctly identified this man in New York as Dr Gerhard Fischer, then you and your friends have a problem indeed,' he said. 'To tell Felicity and Tim, or not to tell them?'

'Yes, that's the question,' said Boots. 'We're all playing Hamlet. So are you, now

247

that you know. It's the very devil.'

'I suggest waiting on Felicity's London consultant, since he's making his own enquiries,' said Sir Edwin. 'If he discovers the New York ophthalmologist has a suspect history, I'm sure he won't hesitate to tell Felicity.'

'Which will mean she and Tim will have to make a difficult decision,' said Boots.

'Don't you think Sir Charles will make it for them, Boots? By not giving his approval for any second opinion from a practitioner suspected of being a war criminal?'

'That's it, we'll have to continue playing a waiting game,' said Boots. 'God knows for how long.'

'I feel for everyone concerned,' said Sir Edwin, 'and I shan't tell your mother.'

'Spare her,' said Boots. He came to his feet. 'Edwin, my thanks for your invaluable help and advice.'

'I think our opinions coincide, Boots,' said Sir Edwin, and saw him out. 'By the way,' he said, 'would you and Polly buy your mother a white summer handbag as a Christmas present?'

Boots smiled.

'I think I understand,' he said.

'And one more thing,' said Sir Edwin. 'It's just occurred to me, can your friend Mrs Stevens really be sure she's able to correctly identify a man from a newspaper photograph, a man she hasn't seen since the German retreat of 1945?'

'That's one more point worth thinking about,' said Boots.

After his stepson had gone, Sir Edwin wrote a confidential letter to his old colleague George Coleman, telling him that the information he had given was already known to a certain third party, that it was safe with him, and no more need be said. On his morning walk with Chinese Lady, he posted it to George's private address. During the walk he told her that his second little chat with Boots definitely concerned Christmas.

Chapter Nineteen

Major Gorringe, retired army officer, and a bluff old codger, was a friend and neighbour of Rosie and Matthew's. He often dropped in on their farm, usually for a chat. It provided a welcome change from coping with the idiosyncrasies of his wife Mildred.

Today, his call was of a different kind. Rosie was grading eggs, Matt far up the field, replacing a broken hinge on the gate, through which Hortense and Joe had just driven the sheep to graze in the adjacent field. Their nephews were nowhere to be seen.

Major Gorringe had a protesting look on his ruddy face.

'I say, Rosie old girl,' he said, 'sorry to interrupt and all that, but it's bit much, y'know.'

'What's a bit much?' asked Rosie, looking as classy as ever, even in her smock.

'All these darkies of yours,' said the major, 'a regular tribe according to Mildred. She says she's feeling surrounded.'

'Well, we do have two extra to Hortense and Joe,' said Rosie. 'Their nephews.'

'I say, not permanent,' protested the major.

250

'They're visiting,' said Rosie, a little fed up with the situation, 'but they'll be gone by the weekend.'

'Good, that's the stuff,' said the major. 'I'll tell Mildred it'll be safe for her to come out at night from next week. Sensitive woman, y'know. Well, that's it, Rosie, regards to Matt.'

'Goodbye, Major,' said Rosie, and the old soldier departed at a brisk semi-trot.

The extension phone in the shed tinkled. Rosie picked it up.

'Woldingham Poultry Farm,' she said.

'Mrs Chapman?'

'Yes?'

'Mr Harris here.' Mr Harris was proprietor of the village store. 'Look, Mrs Chapman, those two young West Indians. They were in here a few minutes ago, looking around. They bought a tin of baked beans, paid for it, but pocketed two bars of chocolate on their way out. I gave 'em a shout, but away they went. Now, I could have them for shoplifting, but thought I'd talk to you first.'

'Mr Harris, I'm dreadfully sorry,' said Rosie, 'and you can be sure the chocolate will be paid for, and those young men dressed down.'

'I'll leave it with you, Mrs Chapman, and much obliged.'

Blow this, thought Rosie, as she put the phone down. Hearing footsteps, she emerged

251

from the shed and saw Herby and Grant beginning a stroll up the field to the gate. From there, she knew, they would enter the other field and waste the time of Joe and Hortense by talking to them.

She called.

'Herby! Grant! Come back here!'

'You want something, Miz Chapman?' called Grant.

'I want you, both of you, right now,' said Rosie.

They strolled back, two young men in their early twenties, overcoats wrapped around them, caps firmly pulled down over their heads.

From the gate, Matt watched. He saw Rosie standing stiff and erect, and knew something was up. He put his tools down and quickly caught up with the leisurely young men as they reached his wife. He could move fast, despite a gammy ankle he'd had since a boy.

'Rosie, what's going on?' he asked.

'You'll be surprised,' said Rosie, and addressed the young men. 'Where are the chocolate bars?'

'Miz Chapman, I ain't familiar with no chocolate bars,' said Herby.

'Nor ain't I,' said Grant.

'Don't give me fairy stories,' said Rosie, 'there's a witness who saw you slip them into your pockets. Turn out your pockets.'

'Rosie?' said Matt.

'These bright boys have been shoplifting at the store,' said Rosie. 'Turn out your pockets,' she repeated.

'No good doing that,' said Grant.

'We done ate them,' said Herby.

'Right,' said Matt, 'both of you pack your things and go. I'll give you ten minutes.'

'But we ain't got nowhere to go,' said Grant.

'That's your problem,' said Matt.

The chickens, hundreds of them, stopped pecking away in the field to indulge in a cacophony of squawking. One of the ferrets, used for nailing rabbits, was crouching and eyeing the hens.

'Mista Chapman,' said Herby, 'you ain't kicking us out, are you?'

'I am,' said Matt, 'and if you aren't out of here inside ten minutes, I'll burn the breeches off your backsides.'

'That's mighty hard, Mista Chapman,' said Grant.

'You'll have to grin and bear it,' said Matt.

It took the young men twenty minutes to pack and leave, and Matt watched them go until they disappeared into the morning mist. Then he took a quick walk to the store, apologized to the proprietor for what had happened, told him the young men had left the district, and paid for the chocolate.

When Hortense and Joe were advised at

253

lunchtime of the departure of their nephews and why, their reaction was surprising. Hortense beamed and Joe looked happy for the first time since the arrival of Herby and Grant.

'Miz Chapman, you saying them scallywags have done gone?' said Hortense.

'Mr Chapman saw them off himself,' said Rosie.

'I sure am glad to hear it,' said Joe.

'You're surprising me,' said Rosie.

'Joe,' said Hortense, 'you speak up.'

And Joe said Herby and Grant were a packet of trouble, that when they asked to visit for a weekend and then stayed on it was because the police in Lambeth were after them for shoplifting. They'd begged to lie low here at the farm, and acted cussed when Hortense said no. But seeing as they were related and in trouble, Hortense didn't have the heart to keep saying no, especially as the boys promised to behave once the trouble blew over.

'Miz Chapman,' said Joe, 'it was mighty upsetting for Hortense, who didn't want Herby and Grant falling into the hands of the police, and nor liking it that you and Mista Chapman were getting riled about them staying on. Now she's good and happy that Mista Chapman got rid of them.'

'Mind, I ain't happy that them boys look like they're born for trouble,' said Hortense.

'Nor that they done wrong in the store.'

'That's been settled,' said Rosie. 'You can relax now, Hortense, and you too, Joe. Go and have your lunch, while I call Mr Chapman up.'

'Miz Chapman,' said Joe, 'Hortense and me is mighty grateful you don't hold them boys against us.'

'I'm mighty grateful that they've gone,' said Rosie, and smiled to show there were no hard feelings. That made Hortense beam again.

'I think I need to speak to Anneliese,' said Boots to Polly that evening.

'If you're thinking of taking her to see that film starring Marlene Dietrich,' said Polly, 'I'll load my shotgun.'

'You don't have a shotgun,' said Boots, 'and I'm not thinking of taking her anywhere. Um, have I heard of Marlene Dietrich?'

'She's only a top film star and the epitome of the Eighth Army's wartime icon, "Lili Marlene,"' said Polly.

'The lady they pinched from the Afrika Korps?' said Boots.

'So I believe,' said Polly.

'Interesting,' said Boots. 'No, I think I need to ask Anneliese if she's absolutely sure that from a newspaper photograph she can recognize a man she last saw nine years ago.'

'What made you think of that?' asked Polly.

255

'Edwin made the point when I was talking to him about a suitable Christmas present for Chinese Lady,' said Boots. 'He recommended a white handbag for summer outings.'

'That's useful to know,' said Polly, 'but I still object to your habit of always referring to your respected mother as Chinese Lady.'

'She admires the Chinese,' said Boots.

'Not Miaow she doesn't,' said Polly.

'Somebody's Chinese cat?' said Boots.

'Funny man, don't you know it's what she calls Mao Tse-tung?' said Polly. 'She thinks he's China's Hitler.'

'Good grief, if she's scanning her newspaper to find out what's going on in China, she's into politics at last,' said Boots.

'No, she's into a new phase of not liking what's coming out of her wireless,' said Polly. 'Well, phone Anneliese, then, and ask her about the newspaper photograph.'

Boots did so, and Anneliese said she would never forget the face of Dr Gerhard Fischer, and that the newspaper photograph had stirred her memory to the point where she was finally able to discount his large beard and his spectacles. Yes, she was quite sure the man was Fischer.

'Sorry to have troubled you, Anneliese,' said Boots, 'but I thought I'd ask.'

'Oh, it's no trouble, I'm always happy to talk to you,' said Anneliese, 'and Harry and

I, with Cindy, are looking forward to seeing you and Polly for tea next Sunday.'

'Fine,' said Boots, and acquainted Polly with the news that Anneliese was positive about her identification.

'I see,' said Polly. 'I wonder, how long will it be before Sir Charles Morgan comes up with some information?'

'Your guess is as good as mine, Polly old girl.'

'Noted, Boots old scout,' said Polly.

James was spared the ordeal of having to go shopping with Cindy. She phoned to say she'd bought all she wanted, and that, anyway, she was going out on Saturday with some schoolfriends.

'You can go and see that soppy girl you go out with, the one who wants to marry you, if you like,' she said.

'Well, that's kind of you,' said James, 'but I don't go out with her or any girl. I must emphasize once more I'm not old enough.'

'Crikey, you're still talking like you were ninety,' said Cindy, 'and that's old enough all right.'

'Oh, I don't think I'll be going out with girls when I'm that age,' said James, 'I expect to be a bit tottery by then.'

'Oh, my, fancy that, what a shame,' said Cindy. 'Well, I'll have to say goodbye now. Goodbye.'

'So long,' said James.

Polly, of course, wanted to know what the call was all about, and James was able to tell her his life had been spared.

'Say that again,' said Polly.

'Yes, I don't have to go shopping with Cindy on Saturday,' said James.

'And that's saving your life, is it?' smiled Polly.

'Good as,' said James.

'That boy,' said Gemma, shaking her head like a soulful old lady, 'he'll fall over himself one day.'

'I think he'll be able to pick himself up,' said Boots.

'Well, of course, you have to think like that, Daddy,' said Gemma, 'you're his father.'

Boots exchanged a smile with Polly. Their thoughts coincided. What had they got in their twins? A couple of precocious wags.

On cue, James switched on the television set so that the family could catch a comedy show featuring a professional wag, one Jimmy Edwards.

Brigitte Bardot was getting rave notices on account of her kittenish air of subtle French sexuality. Jimmy Adams thought he and his young wife Clare ought to acquaint themselves with this latest cinematic sensation.

'Let's go and see that Brigitte Bardot film

up in town tomorrow evening,' he said.

'But it's in French, and I don't speak that,' said Clare.

'Well, I think I could get by with my schoolboy French,' said Jimmy. 'You could bring your knitting.'

'Oh, I'd like that, wouldn't I, especially as I don't do knitting,' said Clare. 'I do pencil sketches.'

'So you do,' said Jimmy. She had a gift for that. 'Clare, I want you to keep every sketch. I've got a feeling you'll be rich and famous one day. Then we can retire to our yacht and motor round the Mediterranean coast in our Rolls-Royce.'

'It'll sink,' said Clare.

'I mean the coastal roads,' said Jimmy. 'Still, it's no good bringing your sketchbook to the cinema, you won't be able to see.'

'Crikey, you're brilliant,' said Clare.

'Now and again, perhaps,' said Jimmy. 'Anyway, saucy chops, about tomorrow evening. Let's go to the local flicks instead and see the latest Humphrey Bogart film. You like old Humph. How's that?'

'Oh, I'm thrilled you still care,' said Clare.

'Who wouldn't?' said Jimmy. 'I honestly don't feel I need Brigitte Bardot all that much. Done any good baking today, gorgeous?'

'Yes, a Victoria sponge sandwich with raspberry jam,' said Clare. 'They're simple.'

'You're not, you're up with Mrs Beeton,' said Jimmy. 'Let's have a cup of tea, then, and a large slice of sponge sandwich. If I'd known marrying you was going to be this good, I'd have done it on Boxing Day instead of waiting till Easter.'

Clare laughed.

'I'll put the kettle on in a tick,' she said. 'Jimmy, is there any news about Felicity going to America?'

'New news, you mean?' said Jimmy. Everyone in the family seemed to be thinking of cousin Tim's wife. 'No, not as far as I know. She's still having to wait.'

'Life's not been much fun for her,' said Clare.

'She and Tim work things out between them, and make the most of what they've got,' said Jimmy. 'You could say they're both tough old soldiers.'

'You and me, we're lucky, Jimmy,' said Clare. 'I'll make the pot of tea now and bring it in time for the news.' The nine o'clock news was due on the telly in five minutes. Out to the kitchen she went. Unlike Lulu, she never asked for kitchen equality. She might consider herself modern, but she wasn't hooked, as certain intellectual women were, on what was beginning to make the men of America nervous, the faint clash of cymbals heralding the outbreak of a battle of the sexes. In any case, it was only causing minor ripples in the UK.

Jimmy thought about people who were lucky. That was something to reflect on. He was lucky himself, with his family. His mum and dad had never had a shouting match in all the years he could remember. Well, his mum knew just how to handle his dad if he looked like losing his rag. Then there were his sisters Bess and Paula, both happily married, and Phoebe growing up to be anything but a problem to a bloke. More of a tease. As for his brother Daniel, he had the kind of relationship with his American wife Patsy that was a laugh all the way. Yes, the lucky side of a feller's life began with a happy family background, and continued if he married a girl like Clare, a born cockney, sparkling with enthusiasm.

He switched the television on just as she re-entered the living room with the evening tea tray.

'I was thinking about Felicity having to go to America, to a doctor,' she said, 'and that made me think oh, crikey, wouldn't I like to go to America to see the sights.'

'When you're rich and famous, we'll go together,' said Jimmy, 'in our own cruise liner.'

'Oh, it's a cruise liner now, on top of a yacht and a Rolls-Royce, is it?' said Clare.

'Would you fancy a castle as well?' asked Jimmy.

'I'll tell you something, Jimmy love,' she said, 'I don't want anything except what I've got already.'

'There's one thing about you my dad would consider special,' said Jimmy.

'And what's that?' asked Clare, pouring the tea.

'You're not expensive to keep,' said Jimmy.

'Oh, that's now,' smiled Clare, 'so don't place your bets yet.'

The news came on. It was all about Chairman Mao and his Chinese People's Republic posing a threat to world peace.

'Jimmy, switch it off,' said Clare, 'I'm fed up with him and his Communism.'

Which was very much in keeping with what Chinese Lady was saying to Sir Edwin about the nine o'clock radio news.

'I don't want to listen to talk about that Miaow, Edwin, it's like having that man Hitler coming out of our wireless again.'

She had always respected the Chinese, ever since she had taken her Monday wash to Mr Wong Fu's Chinese Laundry in Walworth. That had been as long ago as before the German Kaiser's war, and Mr Wong Fu had been a gentleman. It was a disappointment to realize Chairman Mao wasn't.

Chapter Twenty

Saturday morning.

As Cindy left the house to meet her schoolfriends, she noticed a sheet of paper stuck on the front door. The wording on it was bold.

GO HOME JEW-KILLER.

Cindy flushed to her roots, snatched the paper free of the door, and did to it what she'd done to a similar loutish notice a few days ago. She tore it up, screwed it up, and put it in the dustbin.

But it spoiled her outing.

Upstairs, Anneliese, tidying the main bedroom, glanced out of the window. There was nothing much to see, no garden, no shining waters, and not even much of a back yard. Just a high brick wall.

No, I mustn't wish for something more. The house itself is enough. It's a very good-looking house. But many English families have gardens. Little gardens, medium gardens and even large gardens, all beautifully kept and ablaze with flowers in the summer.

Perhaps, yes, perhaps one day I might ask Harry if he would like to have a garden with a little summer house in which he could do his writing when the weather tempts him to. No, that would sound premeditated. So I'll just make a casual suggestion that he might like to have a garden. Yes, would you like to have a garden, Harry? A simple suggestion, and I must make it sound as if I had only just thought of it.

But would he want to move away from the home he had shared with his first wife, the wife who left it to him? I know he has his memories, he's that kind of man. There is nothing practical or calculating about him. Or covetous. Ah, I know, of course, what his English people would call him. A softie. But he's still a man for all that, better by far than many other men I've known. Only the German army doctors I knew have my respect and affection, and perhaps some of my wounded patients.

Would you like a little garden, Harry?

'Anneliese?' He was calling to her from down below.

She went out to the landing.

'Yes, Harry?'

'Are you going shopping this morning?'

'Yes, after we've had coffee.'

'Good. I'll come with you. It's not a bad day, considering the time of the year, and I feel like an outing.'

Anneliese smiled down at him.

'With me and my shopping bag?' she asked.

'We'll have lunch out somewhere,' said

264

Harry, 'you, me and your shopping bag.'

'Harry, you're the dearest man.'

'Good God,' said Harry, 'my ship's captain thought the reverse of me.'

'Where is he now?' asked Anneliese.

'He's a vice admiral in command of a desk at the Admiralty,' said Harry.

'Serve him right,' said Anneliese, 'he's an idiot.'

Harry laughed.

His entertaining German wife was a delight. Who'd have thought it after so many photographs had been shown of burly, coarse-looking women guards of concentration camps? But then, of course, there were the pictures of German maidens at physical exercise in pre-war years, every one an Aryan goddess.

Bloody marvels, he thought, I'm married to one of them, I've got my own Aryan goddess. How did that happen right here in old cockney Camberwell?

Search me.

Chinese Lady and Sir Edwin were having morning coffee with Felicity, Tim and Jennifer, whose home in Poplar Walk wasn't far from theirs in Red Post Hill. Chinese Lady had knitted a black-and-white woollen hat with a bobble for Jennifer, a popular winter head-covering for girls. Tim had said bring it on Saturday morning and have coffee with us. Sir Edwin had managed the walk very well, particularly as the morning weather offered some weak but acceptable sunshine. November was having a forgetful moment, but Sir Edwin suspected it would come to later on and foul the evening with fog. Smokeless fuel was the answer, or central heating, but neither of these solutions was advancing with speed. Far from it.

Jennifer was delighted with the woollen hat and wore it while they were all enjoying coffee.

After some minutes of chat, Chinese Lady asked a question.

'Felicity,' she said a little tentatively, 'has anything been happening lately?'

Everyone knew what she meant, Felicity most of all.

'Not a blind thing, Grandma,' she said, which took Chinese Lady aback, but tickled Tim and Jennifer, who were both used to Felicity's ability to be droll about herself.

'Oh, I didn't mean to upset you, Felicity dear,' said Chinese Lady.

'You haven't upset me, Grandma,' said Felicity, 'I fielded the question honestly.'

Fielded the question? Chinese Lady wondered what 'fielded' meant exactly. Wasn't it something to do with cricket?

'Oh, you're saying you haven't had any of your hopeful seeings lately?' she enquired.

'Nothing since I had that clear sight of

Boots,' said Felicity, which was depressingly true. No blurred visions and certainly no repeat of momentary clarity had occurred.

'Mummy's waiting for good news from her specialist,' said Jennifer, very much up with everyone's wish for that.

'Patience is sometimes hard to contain,' said Sir Edwin, one of the few outside of Tim and Felicity who knew just how complicated were the present circumstances. His own hope at the moment was for the doctor in New York to be a genuine Ukrainian immigrant, and that Anneliese Stevens had made a mistake.

'Oh, I'm sold on patience, Grandpa,' said Felicity.

'Well, I don't know anyone I could be more admiring of,' said Chinese Lady fervently. 'You ought to be given–' She stopped herself from saying 'a medal'. What good would any medal be to a blind woman? Just a lump of copper or something. 'Yes, you ought to be given some good news, Felicity.'

'And so say all of us, Grandma,' said Jennifer.

Tim was a little silent. It worried him that Felicity had had no moments of vision, limited or otherwise, for quite some time now. Had everything during the many preceding months been in the nature of a false dawn? After all, in the beginning, every examination she'd had at the hospital near

Farnham had resulted in opinions from experts that she'd be permanently blind. Curse false dawns, he thought, they've given her the kind of hope she naturally doesn't want to let go of. Come on, Sir Charles Morgan, let's hear from you.

On the way home with Sir Edwin later, Chinese Lady said, 'It's all very hard on Felicity.'

'I'm sure we can always rely on her to face up to disappointments and setbacks, Maisie,' said Sir Edwin, as reassuring as ever. He thought that if any person blinded by accident had moments of vision, however blurred or vague, then there had to be hope. He knew Sir Charles Morgan had spoken some time ago of a natural healing process. If that was so, perhaps nature would get a move on and eliminate any need to go to New York and consult a doctor who might be a war criminal. 'Felicity has her fair share of courage.'

'Well, yes, she's always been brave about her blindness,' said Chinese Lady, 'but I can't help worrying about her having to go all the way to America for an operation, and then there's Alice having to go to the trial of those thieving hooligans in January. I'm sure that's worrying to Tommy and Vi– Oh, look at those two and their November guy, Edwin.'

On the other side of Red Post Hill, a girl

and boy in jeans and jerseys were pulling a little wooden home-made cart in which sat their version of Guy Fawkes. Their version looked more like a scarecrow than an effigy of the conspirator who had plotted to blow up the Houses of Parliament almost three hundred and fifty years ago. Spotting the elderly couple, the girl called.

'Thruppence for the guy, mister?'

'Thruppence?' said Chinese Lady. She and Sir Edwin stopped. 'It used to be a penny.'

The boy and girl crossed the road, pulling their cart with them. Guy Fawkes swayed a bit.

'Well, yer see, missus,' said the boy, 'it's inflation.'

'Inflation?' said Chinese Lady.

'There's been a war, yer know,' said the boy, 'and that's what done it. Me dad said so. He was in the war, missus, and he's got photos to prove it. And Sally's aunt was a cook in the ATS, wasn't she, Sally?'

'Yes, she did rice puddings and stewed prunes for the soldiers,' said the girl. She looked up at Sir Edwin. 'We don't mind just tuppence, if yer like, mister, it's fireworks night tonight.'

'And we've come all the way from Camberwell,' said the boy. 'Well, people round 'ere are richer than in Camberwell, so me dad said.'

'In that case,' said Sir Edwin, 'will this do?' He extracted a shilling from his pocket.

'Crikey, a bob?' said the boy.

'And yer don't want no change?' said the girl.

'Enjoy your fireworks,' said Sir Edwin, parting with the shilling.

'You're a sport, mister,' said the boy, and off he and the girl went in perky fashion with their cart, in which even the scarecrow Guy Fawkes joggled happily, obviously unaware it was to be consigned to the flames in the evening.

'Well, that was nice of you, Edwin,' said Chinese Lady, 'but I don't know why there's still children about that are poor. It wasn't what the Government promised after the war.'

'They did implement some of the recommendations of the Beveridge Report, like our National Health Service,' said Sir Edwin, 'but most promises from politicians, Maisie, are made to win votes. Keeping them is another matter.'

'It didn't ought to be allowed,' said Chinese Lady. 'I wouldn't want any of my family making promises they couldn't keep.'

'Fortunately, Maisie, no-one in the family is a politician,' said Sir Edwin.

'Except Tommy told me his daughter-in-law Lulu, that's married to Paul, wants to be one,' said Chinese Lady, 'and her with a

270

baby to look after and all.'

'I believe that some women these days are looking for something more than domestic duties,' said Sir Edwin.

'I don't know what good it will do them,' grumbled Chinese Lady. 'Lizzy never wanted to be more than a wife and mother, nor did Vi and Susie. I don't know what ideas must have got into Lulu when she was growing up.'

'Perhaps, as the daughter of her father, she decided she'd like to follow in his footsteps,' said Sir Edwin. 'He's been a Labour MP for many years.'

'Oh, now look who's coming our way,' said Chinese Lady.

Two middle-aged neighbours, Mr and Mrs Dennis, were turning out of their gate. Chinese Lady knew what was going to be said.

'Good morning, Lady Finch,' said Mr Dennis, raising his hat as he and his wife approached.

'Good morning, Sir Edwin,' said Mrs Dennis coyly.

'Good morning,' said Sir Edwin, and made sure by deft movement that he and Chinese Lady were able to bypass these neighbours before a conversation could develop, a conversation in which Mrs Dennis would drop several verbal curtseys.

Chinese Lady was faintly blushing. She

271

had been far more comfortable with the boy and girl from Camberwell than with neighbours who were always addressing her and Edwin by their titles, which she found embarrassing.

'I'll never get used to being a Lady,' she said, not for the first time.

'My dear, you were born a lady,' said Sir Edwin, which was his usual response. He knew the kind of remark that would come next, and it did.

'Edwin, I was born of my parents that were poor but honest.'

Chapter Twenty-One

In Bristol, Chief Inspector Bradley, accompanied by a sergeant, made a call on Alice, who let them into her flat with her curiosity uppermost.

'Why this call, Chief Inspector?' she asked. She looked tidily well dressed in a grey costume. She didn't go in for what she thought of as girlish flounces.

'We've a problem, Miss Adams,' said Bradley.

'What problem?' asked Alice.

'Mr Edwards, the bank cashier, has advised us he can't, after all, be sure that the men he pointed out at the identity parade really were the two who committed the robbery. He says, after thinking it over, that he might be mistaken.'

'But didn't he see them when they took their masks off just before they ran out of the bank?' questioned Alice.

'He said he did, yes, but is having second thoughts about being sure of himself at the trial. He feels he won't be able to identify them for certain. The defence will make the most of that.'

'The poor man's nervous,' said Alice.

'Well, whatever is making him unsure,' said Bradley, 'it means we'd be obliged if you and Mr MacAllister would attend a new identity parade on Monday afternoon. D'you see, Miss Adams, we now need a positive identification from one of you two, preferably from both. In fact, if one of you is uncertain, that'll make uncertainty the best part of the defence.'

'I don't think you'll find either Mr MacAllister or myself uncertain,' said Alice. 'Attending the process means I'll have to take the afternoon off from my school duties. However, I can't say no, and I'm sure Mr MacAllister will co-operate. I'm seeing him this evening. Would you like me to tell him all this, Chief Inspector?'

'Thank you, Miss Adams, that would save me a trip to Filton,' said Bradley, 'but I must ask you to let me know if he can't make it.'

'I'll let you know,' said Alice.

'I'm obliged,' said Bradley. 'Thanks again. The identity parade will begin at the station at three. Are you absolutely confident you'll recognize the men?'

'Absolutely,' said Alice.

'Well, if Mr MacAllister is just as confident,' said Bradley, 'we'll look forward to a positive recognition at the trial.'

'By the way,' said Alice, 'have you found the revolver yet?'

'Not yet, damn it.' The chief inspector

274

grimaced. 'But we will.'

Fergus, who had arranged to take Alice out for dinner in the evening, called for her at seven. While he was more hopeful about her feelings towards him, he was friendly rather than outgoing. Caution was still the name of the game, since he wanted to do nothing that would cause another rift.

On the way to the restaurant in his car, Alice told him of her conversation with Chief Inspector Bradley. Fergus said he couldn't understand how the bank cashier, having formally identified the men, had decided he was now doubtful.

'Decided?' said Alice. 'Does one decide to have doubts?'

'Well, he's decided he's no' going to be sure at the trial,' said Fergus. 'It could, I suppose, be due to the fact that he only saw their faces for a few seconds.'

Alice said that was why they were required to attend an identity parade at three on Monday afternoon. Could Fergus make it? Fergus said it was something to get out of the way, and that he'd call for her at two-thirty and drive her to the station.

'You're being very nice to me lately, Fergus,' smiled Alice, as he drove his Austin slowly through the damp, lamp-lit streets of the city, a bus lumbering in front of him and two cars crawling on his tail. 'How many times now have you called for me and driven me here and there?'

'I havena counted,' said Fergus, 'but each time has been very sociable, Alice.'

'Except the time when we ran into Bill Sikes and Charlie Peace,' said Alice. 'That's what my father calls them.'

'Whisht, we'll nail those hellhounds at the identity parade,' said Fergus.

'Let's forget them for the moment,' said Alice. 'Tell me, how are things going at your new factory?'

'In stop-go fashion, damn it,' said Fergus. With the bus pulling up at a stop, he skirted it and left it behind. He said in some disgust that the skilled men fitting machinery were downing tools and walking out on the job for every kind of trade union reason. These last few years, he said, had seen trade union workers holding back the productive progress of this country by their bloody-mindedness. Germany had already overtaken the UK, and that from a country pulverized by the war.

'In his last letter to me,' said Alice, 'my dad mentioned the family's garments factory has been unionized and he's now waiting for trouble.'

'I dinna doubt he'll get it,' said Fergus. 'Our unions are packed with Communists, the kind who'd like to see us as a Socialist republic. To achieve that, y'ken, they first need to close down every factory and put millions of men and women out of work. They'll blame our capitalist system and call for a workers' revolution.'

'It'll never happen,' said Alice, 'the people of this country simply aren't revolutionaries.'

'Aye, we're a cautious lot,' said Fergus.

They arrived at the restaurant then, and Fergus parked the car. He and Alice, alighting, were happy to make their way through the murk and to enter the warm, well-lit restaurant. Its welcoming atmosphere embraced them.

From another car, parked a few moments later, two men followed them in.

Alice and Fergus made a very pleasant occasion of their time in the restaurant, enjoying their choices from a menu that, despite the restrictions of continuing post-war austerity, was diverse enough to satisfy all diners generally, although Alice did hear one man voice a plaintive protest at the absence of fillet steak.

She and Fergus had a table for two, and Fergus noted with pleasure that Alice's dress of rich maroon, without fussy trimmings, gave her an attractive look of simplicity and charm. They shared a bottle of rosé wine with their main course of roast Welsh lamb. Alice favoured pink wine, although, in her conservative way, she was a modest imbiber.

They talked about the era in which they were living, the Fifties, and its social advances that were making young people more adventurous and women more ambitious.

'I think my family are being left behind,' said Alice.

'Why?' asked Fergus, whose Scots relatives in the main were still sticking dourly to old values.

'They live by the standards of my paternal grandmother,' said Alice with a smile.

'And what standards are those?' asked Fergus, who had met Grandma Finch more than once.

'Victorian,' said Alice.

'Victorian, oh, aye,' said Fergus, dark features easing into amusement.

'Everyone must know his or her place, and not step out of it,' said Alice.

'And the young ones must be seen but no heard?' said Fergus.

'No, not quite as rigid as that,' said Alice. 'Grandma doesn't believe in silence at any family gathering, except from her wireless, which she thinks is an invention civilization could well have done without. She's a wonderful old lady, and everyone in the family regards her with admiration and respect. Well, I think you know that, Fergus.'

'Aye, I know her well, and her large family,' said Fergus.

Alice said that those who became members of the family through marriage, such as Patsy from America and Helene from France, were simply absorbed into it and took on its values. Even upper-class Aunt Polly, married to Uncle Boots, was now as much an Adams as any of them.

'It's diverting in its way, Fergus.'

'I fancy,' said Fergus, 'that you're the exception, that you've stepped out of your place.'

'I do have a feeling I'm a disappointment to my parents,' said Alice. 'First, because I've chosen a career, and second, because I've also chosen to live in Bristol and not in South London.'

'I think there's a third reason,' said Fergus.

'And what do you think that is?' asked Alice.

'You're no' a wife and mother,' said Fergus, 'and I fancy your grandmother considers every woman should be a wife and mother.'

'Yes, that comes from her Victorian attitude,' said Alice.

'Well, these days I suppose young people are beginning to form their own values,' said Fergus, 'and live their own kind of lives, no' their grandmothers'.'

'Are your grandparents Victorian?' asked Alice.

'Lassie, my grandparents still believe in fire and brimstone, as preached by John

Knox, the pulpit thunderer who denounced Mary, Queen of Scots as a wanton wench four hundred years ago,' said Fergus.

'Oh, yes, poor Mary,' said Alice amid the clatter and chatter of diners mixing non-stop conversation with busy application of their knives and forks. 'But what do you believe in?'

'Live and let live,' said Fergus.

'That's accepting the way other people live?' said Alice.

'I'll no' say that about those who rob banks, steal my car and lay dirty hands on you, Alice,' said Fergus.

'Fergus, you've become very civilized,' said Alice.

'I'm an improvement on what I was?' said Fergus.

'Well, there were times when I did think you a little overbearing,' said Alice.

'Those were the days when you were giving me black marks?' said Fergus, who might have said they were also the days when she came over as a bit of a madam.

'More than a few,' said Alice. She smiled. 'But not now.'

They left a little later to have coffee at Alice's flat, at her suggestion. As they went out of the restaurant they were followed by two men who had been dining not far from them. When they reached the car, the men were close behind them.

'Just a moment, guv,' said one man.

'You've got a problem?' said Fergus, turning.

'No problem, guv, just like to talk to you, yer know,' said the second man.

Londoners, thought Fergus, with something on their minds.

'Send me a postcard,' he said.

'Got no time for that, cully. Just want to have a word with you and this 'ere female lady about Monday afternoon at the main Bristol police station. If yer get me.'

It wasn't difficult then for Alice and Fergus to realize that the men behind bars had friends, and that these characters were two of them. Fergus wondered how the hell they'd come to know he and Alice were involved, and how, for that matter, they'd traced them. Both men were tall, husky and darkly overcoated. Their trilby hats were pulled well down, their features in shadow. They were all too remindful of the thugs who had staged the bank hold-up.

'We're leaving,' said Fergus, taking hold of the handle of the car's passenger door. 'Get in, Alice.'

A large hand planted itself on the door.

'Now we don't want no fuss, mate,' said the owner of the mitt.

'Not when there's a tidy lump of the ready on offer to you and the lady,' said the other man.

'Oh, aye?' said Fergus, tensing on the balls of his feet. 'How do we earn it?'

'It won't cause yer no sweat. Just don't do a recognizing job on certain friends of ours come Monday af'ernoon.'

'You know about that?' said Alice, nerves on edge.

'Don't ask questions, lady, we ain't staying 'ere all night.'

'Is your offer one we can turn down?' asked Fergus.

'It won't pay yer to.'

'I think this is called intimidation of witnesses,' said Alice, and it then occurred to her that perhaps the bank clerk had become unsure of himself by reason of such intimidation.

'How much is on offer?' asked Fergus.

'Half a monkey apiece.'

Five hundred pounds in all?

Fergus whistled.

'Tempting,' he said, with Alice suspecting, and hoping he was merely playing for time. 'Very tempting.'

'It ain't a jar of jam.'

'When would we get paid?' asked Fergus.

'As soon as we know you've done us the favour.'

'Right,' said Fergus, 'be outside the police station when the identity parade is over and listen to the police informing the press of the outcome.'

'Got yer, mate.'

'Then when do we get the money?' asked Fergus.

'You'll get it. Well, if you don't, you won't play come the trial, will yer?'

'Understood,' said Fergus. 'D'you mind if I take this lady home now?'

'Our pleasure, guy. Nice to have met yer. Take care, eh? No tricks, or else.'

'Rely on us,' said Fergus.

The two men watched as he and Alice entered the car, and they stayed watching as Fergus drove out of the parking area into the damp misty night.

When they were clear and away, Alice said, 'Fergus, I hope you were only joking in all your exchanges with those beetle-browed hustlers.'

'What they were after, Alice, was no' my idea of a joke,' said Fergus.

'Why did you tell them you were taking me home?'

'To find out if it tempted them to follow us,' said Fergus, 'so let me know if they are, will you, Alice?'

Alice turned her head and kept her eyes on what was visible through the back window. All she could see was the blurred glimmer of a wet road. There was nothing behind them at the moment except the murk of the night.

'What are you going to do?' she asked.

'Drop in at the police station,' said Fergus. 'Aye, we'll do that, Alice, if we aren't followed.'

'There's nothing in sight yet,' said Alice. The hour was late, the traffic desultory on the other side of the road.

'Keep looking,' said Fergus.

'I don't suppose Chief Inspector Bradley will be at the station,' said Alice. 'He's the one to talk to, isn't he? I'm assuming you intend to report those men.'

'I'm thinking those men had a hand in plotting the bank robbery,' said Fergus, 'and that they've had the kind of wee chat with the cashier they've just had with us.'

'That occurred to me too – Fergus, there's something coming now.' Alice, spotting headlights, tensed.

'Well, if it sits on our tail, I'll turn off for your place,' said Fergus.

The car came up fast. Fergus, driving steadily, made no attempt to increase his speed. At his back, the headlights flashed, and the car, a sports model with its hood up, overtook him rapidly. He glanced, so did Alice. They glimpsed a young man and a girl, scarves wrapped around their necks.

'Students,' said Fergus.

'Out on the tiles,' said Alice, relieved, and they watched the car vanish into the misty night. With no vehicle behind them, Fergus drove on to the police station.

Chapter Twenty-Two

The night duty sergeant, on happy terms with a cup of hot tea, put it aside with obvious sorrow and came to his feet. He approached the window.

'Don't tell me you're another car accident,' he said, 'I've already had two. It's that kind of dirty night.'

'Are there any CID officers around?' asked Fergus.

'The usual night team, sir.'

'Would Chief Inspector Bradley be one of them?'

'He might have been called in if instead of a couple of car collisions, there'd been a murder or a spot of nasty GBH,' said the sergeant. 'Which don't happen every night, Bristol not being New York or Chicago. Can I help, sir?'

'It's like this, y'ken,' said Fergus, and briefly explained the reason for wanting to see the chief inspector. The duty sergeant raised his eyebrows and set his mouth in a grim line.

'We've got the makings of a criminal offence,' he said. 'The kind,' he added, with the authority of an officer who knew his stuff, 'that seriously subverts the law.'

'I couldn't have put that better myself,' said Alice, 'I'm a teacher.'

Fergus pointed out that Chief Inspector Bradley had advised Miss Adams that the bank cashier had backed away from his positive identification of the arrested robbers.

'So he has, sir, which sent a lot of language flying about in the station. And what've we got now, eh?'

'The possibility that the men who spoke to us outside the restaurant have already spoken to the cashier, and showed him their knuckledusters,' said Fergus.

'They showed them to you and Miss Adams, sir?'

'No, just their teeth, you might say,' said Fergus. 'Can you get hold of the chief inspector? We need to talk to him before Monday.'

'Take a seat, Mr MacAllister, and I'll try to get him on the phone.'

The sergeant made the phone call. It woke up Chief Inspector Bradley. He listened to the sergeant while growling under his breath. Before the call was finished, the sergeant beckoned Alice and Fergus back to the window.

'Well?' said Alice.

'Miss Adams, if you and Mr MacAllister could come to this station at ten tomorrow morning,' said the sergeant, 'Chief Inspector Bradley will see you then.'

Fergus looked at Alice.

'If that's suitable,' he said, 'I'll pick you up at about twenty to ten.'

'I'll be ready,' said Alice. She smiled. 'It's my duty, after all, to do what I can to frustrate a criminal subversion of the law, even on my Sunday rest day.'

'Highly creditable, Miss Adams,' said the sergeant, and picked up the phone again. 'They'll be here, sir. Yes, ten o'clock. Right, sir, I'll tell 'em.' He replaced the phone. 'Miss Adams, Mr MacAllister, the chief inspector says watch your backs.'

'Understood,' said Fergus.

He and Alice left. A drizzle was falling, and the Austin was wetly glimmering in the light cast by the station windows. Fergus looked around to check there were no hovering shadows.

'In a way,' said Alice, 'I wish the chief inspector hadn't mentioned our backs. It's making shivers run down my spine.'

'Let me get you home,' said Fergus, and they put themselves in the car. Another tense moment arrived, for two burly figures emerged out of the November darkness.

'Oh, no,' breathed Alice, but then she saw the glistening capes of two uniformed policemen, who passed by to enter the station. 'False alarm,' she said.

'Aye,' said Fergus. He started the car, switched on his headlights and headed for Alice's flat.

'Can we hope those men have taken you at your word, that you'll do what they want, and that they won't appear until the identity parade is over?' she said.

'I'm counting on it,' said Fergus, 'but a pound to a wee bawbee, Alice, that they'll be somewhere close by before, during and after our time in the police station on Monday afternoon.'

'Fergus, you're a cool customer,' said Alice.

'That I'm no',' said Fergus, 'my nerves are raw.'

The drive, however, was uneventful, and when they arrived, he accompanied her up the steps to the front door of the apartment house.

'You'll come up for coffee?' said Alice.

'Thanking you, Alice, but I'll no' do that,' said Fergus, 'it's late and well past the time for drinking coffee, and you'll be tired, I'm thinking.'

'I am now,' said Alice, 'and I expect you are too.'

'I wonder how those men knew we'd be together this evening?' said Fergus. 'Ah, well, now's no' the time to discuss it. Tomorrow morning, I'll pick you up at twenty to ten, as arranged.'

'Yes,' said Alice. 'Goodnight, Fergus, I'm glad I didn't have to stand up to those men alone.' And she lifted her face for a kiss. His lips landed on hers for a brief second. 'Heavens, that's a kiss on a night like we've had?' she said.

He kissed her again, more definitely, then said, 'Get you to your bed, Alice.'

He left then, before his feelings took over. He was still sure it was right to avoid rushing her in any way at all.

At eleven o'clock in her Camberwell home, Cindy was still awake. Moreover, she was awake in an armchair in the living room, a woollen dressing gown around her. It was not too cold, for the fire was still lingering. She had kept herself awake in her bed, and sneaked down silently fifteen minutes ago, when the house was quiet. She chose the living room because it was closest to the front door. She was in darkness, for she hadn't switched the light on.

It was Saturday night. People were out late on Saturday nights. She was listening and waiting, waiting for someone to approach the front door. She thought it might happen, and she wasn't frightened by the possibility. She was too angry. She wanted to catch whoever was responsible for those rotten posters. Anyone who knew her step-mother would also know she just wasn't the kind of German who'd do awful things to Jewish people. She'd been a nurse in the war, she'd cared for wounded soldiers, including an enemy one, and she was ashamed of what Hitler's beastly SS had done to innocent people.

Cindy, born in 1941, couldn't remember anything about the war, any more than she could remember her dead mother, although sometimes there were vague images in her mind. She could remember her dad taking care of her when she was a little girl and walking her to school when she was old enough to start attending classes. And he was there to take her home when classes ended. She grew up devoted to him, and by the time she was ten she was already learning to cook for both of them.

He was easy to care for, and always said he had little cause for grumbling, except he did remark once that he didn't think much of God's kingdom on the day her mother died. Still, he'd got over that to become a kind of contented man. And now that he had a new wife, a lovely lady, he was a happy man, especially as his first novel was going to be published.

Cindy didn't want him, or her kind stepmother, to find out about those posters. There'd been three now, and she was sure they'd keep appearing, that one would stare her stepmother in the face any day soon, unless she herself could find out who was responsible.

So she waited and listened, a torch in her hand and pinching herself occasionally to keep awake, although she was quite prepared for nothing to happen.

However, when she knew it must be close to half-past eleven, she did hear a sound, the sound of someone creeping up the steps to the front door. Heels clicked on the steps. She still wasn't frightened, she was a young lady determined to protect her dad and stepmother from distress.

She came to her feet, and with her eyes used to the darkness, she padded silently from the room in her slippers. She reached the front door. Yes, there were definite sounds, there was someone out there. She concentrated on listening, and heard what she thought was the quite clear little rustle of paper. She pulled the front door open and switched on the torch. It caught a dark figure and illuminated him, a lanky youth in an overcoat and cap. He was in the act of squeezing glue from a tube onto a large sheet of white paper. He froze in the light of the torch.

'Got you!' hissed Cindy. 'Give it here.' She snatched the poster from his nerveless hand. 'Oh, you rotten beast, it's you, Joey Marsh.'

Joey Marsh, son of a local plumber, was

seventeen and precocious. At the moment, however, he was far from his cocky self. He was stuck to the doorstep in shock, the beam of the torch lighting up his gaping mouth. He struggled and found his voice. It wasn't at its usual pitch, it was kind of wet, and all he was capable of were a few gurgling words.

'I gotter go.'

'Oh, no, you don't,' hissed Cindy. She put the poster under her right arm and used her left hand to grab his jacket. 'You're a creep, Joey Marsh, and nasty as well, writing wicked things about my nice kind mum.'

'It wasn't me,' complained Joey, 'so would yer let go of me jacket?'

'No, I wouldn't,' breathed Cindy, 'and keep your voice down or you'll wake up my dad. Then he'll come down and smash your face in. And what d'you mean, it wasn't you? I've just caught you, haven't I?'

'I mean it wasn't me that wrote the stuff,' said Joey. He may have been seventeen and lanky, but was no match right now for thirteen-year-old Cindy, who was on the warpath.

'Who did, then?' she asked, keeping a tight hold of his jacket and the light on his face.

'Ain't telling,' said Joey.

'You'd better,' said Cindy, 'or there'll be a bobby knocking on your door tomorrow because even if it is Sunday, I'll be down at the police station showing them this poster and telling them who I caught trying to stick it on our door. I bet your fingerprints will be on it, especially if you've been eating fish and chips. You smell as if you have.'

She let go of his jacket, took the poster from under her arm, and by the light of the torch she read what was on it.

WHO DONE THE JEWS IN?

''Ere, look 'ere, Cindy, I tell yer honest, I didn't write it,' said Joey.

'Who did, then?' demanded Cindy, fighting a fiery battle on behalf of her dad and stepmother.

'Well if yer must know, it was me dad,' said Joey. 'He hates Germans.'

'Why, did they torture him, then?' asked Cindy. 'Was he in the war, like my dad was?'

'Well, no, he was doing plumbing jobs on injured pipes,' said Joey. 'There was injured pipes all over London on account of them German bombs. Yerse, and injured people too, as well as dead ones. Course, you wouldn't know about that–'

'Of course I would,' said Cindy, 'everyone knows about the bombs. And now I know about your rotten dad and his rotten posters. I'm getting cold, so come in here.' Taking hold of Joey's jacket again, she pulled him into the hall and switched off the torch. 'Now, just keep your voice down,' she whispered, 'unless you want my dad to come down and sock you one.'

'Look, I gotter get home, Cindy–'

'Never mind that,' whispered Cindy, 'just listen. You tell your dad I'm keeping this poster, and if any more get stuck on our wall or door, I'm taking them all to the police station. And tell him too that my mum's a kind woman. She was a German army nurse in the war, and when she found out about the concentration camps, it made her sick and she's never stopped grieving for all those poor Jewish people.'

'Crikey, Cindy, you can't 'alf talk to a bloke,' whispered Joey. 'Still, all right, I'll tell me dad. You ain't going to the cops tomorrer, are yer?'

'I just told you, I'll only go if any more of your dad's rotten posters get stuck anywhere,' breathed Cindy.

'Got yer, Cindy,' said Joey, and Cindy let him go then.

Quietly, she returned to her bedroom, taking the poster with her. She folded it up, and tucked it away out of sight in the bottom drawer of a tallboy. Then she simply fell into bed. She thought for a little while about the possibility that there might be other people, besides Joey's dad, with unkind ideas about her stepmother. It worried her, but sleep claimed her and the worries went away.

Chapter Twenty-Three

Sunday morning. The weather was filthy, but Chief Inspector Bradley was at the station when Alice and Fergus arrived. He greeted them briskly, then said, 'If what Sergeant Woodley told me last night is correct, there's something that needs serious investigation.'

'Dirty work at the crossroads?' suggested Alice.

'That's one way of putting it,' said Bradley. 'Let me hear what you and Mr MacAllister have to tell me yourselves, then we'll review probables and possibles. We'll use an interview room.'

In the interview room, Alice let Fergus recount all that took place outside the restaurant last night. The chief inspector's expression conveyed a mixture of personal disbelief and official disgust.

'Have I got a pack of London gangsters in my city?' he said. 'I agree with you, those two men last night could have been the partners of the arrested pair, they could have been one half of a four-man plot to rob the bank. Bank robberies at the point of a gun turn me sour.'

Alice said she couldn't understand how the men came to know she and Fergus were the principal witnesses, along with the bank cashier. It was obviously easy enough to make contact with the cashier, but how did the men trace her and Fergus?

'Aye, a good question,' said Fergus.

The chief inspector, looking ready to spit iron filings, said, 'Dirty money talks to any person open to bribery, even to–' He checked, looking as if his teeth were grinding the iron filings. 'I'll find out,' he muttered. Then he asked Fergus what he had meant by advising the men that if they listened to what was said to the press about the result of the identity parade, they'd know if the bribe had worked.

'You and Miss Adams are going to correctly identify the arrested men, aren't you, for God's sake?' he growled.

'That's what we need to talk to you about,' said Fergus.

The following discussion was lengthy, and punctuated at intervals by some strong language from the chief inspector that wasn't in keeping with the Sabbath.

However, in the end, agreement was reached.

Fergus then drove Alice home, and there she cooked lunch for both of them. Fergus helped. My bonny Alice, he thought, is mellowing. She's softer in her moods and far less challenging. I think I'll start riding a horse called Good Hope. I could win the Derby on it.

Matthew was in the yard at the rear of the farmhouse, cleaning mud off his gumboots. It was twelve-thirty, time for lunch, and the weather had improved. He heard the kitchen waste pipe of the annexe delivering water into the drain. Hortense was at work preparing lunch for herself and Joe, probably. He smiled. They liked spicy pickle and mustard cauliflower with their food.

His boots clean, he entered the farmhouse kitchen. Rosie was there, and the children, Emily and Giles.

'Mummy's doing lunch,' said Emily, eleven and a bit of a tomboy.

'It's onion soup and rolls,' said Giles, twelve and already muscular from the help he gave to his parents in their open-air work.

Lunch on winter days was always simple and quick, so that more work could be done while the light lasted. Rosie served a substantial evening meal accordingly. She was invariably in command of her daily routine and her family. Rarely did she have flustered moments, and Matt sometimes thought she could have made a name for herself in the great world of commerce. She wasn't, however, that kind of woman. He knew this was her world, the farm, the family and her unvarying attachment to her relatives, especially Boots, her adoptive father. Not many evenings went by without a phone call to one or the other of them. Rosie was a woman of abiding affection and loyalty, and the kids adored her.

'Sit,' she said, 'sit, everyone, and put on your bibs and tuckers.'

'We don't have bibs and tuckers,' said Emily, named after Rosie's late adoptive mother.

'Napkins, then,' said Rosie, and ladled thick creamy onion soup into the bowls. 'Anyone who finishes up with soup on dress or shirt will get seven days in the chicken house.'

'The chickens won't like that,' said Giles, 'it'll crowd them out.'

'Right first time,' said Matt. 'Chickens are fussy about interlopers who use their elbows.'

'I'll talk to them,' said Rosie. 'Begin, everyone, I want the meal to be over in fifteen minutes, but beware of gobbling. It's bad manners.'

Soup and rolls were consumed hungrily. Rosie served second helpings of the soup, and that too went down a treat, although it stretched fifteen minutes to twenty. Then out went Matt and Giles to see that the hens and their chicks returned squawking to their wired-off enclosure before the loitering foxes took advantage of the twilight to get at them. The hens and chicks would stay out until then if allowed to, for there were good pickings to peck at in the grass of the field all year round. By late afternoon, there were always foxes on the prowl, no matter what preventive measures Matt set up. They weren't only greedy for chickens, they were as crafty at outwitting defences as old Mother Riley was at shoplifting.

Up came Joe and Hortense, Joe with two ferrets in a sack, and Hortense with two rabbits in another sack. Among their other duties, the West Indian couple, and the ferrets, were the prime enemy of rabbits that proliferated, despite the presence of foxes.

'Haven't you had lunch yet?' asked Matt.

'Jest going up for it, Mista Chapman,' said Hortense.

'We've had onion soup,' said Giles.

'Ain't that mighty good for a belly on a cold day?' grinned Joe, and he and Hortense continued on their way to the annexe.

After a moment, Matt said, 'Start the roundup, Giles, but don't give the chicks heart failure. I'll be back in a few ticks.'

'OK, Dad,' said Giles.

Matt went up in the wake of Hortense and Joe, having remembered something – the annexe waste pipe delivering water into the drain. He arrived in the yard at a moment when he heard Hortense shout in the kitchen. He opened the back door, and stepped in. There, seated at the kitchen table, were the nephews, Herby and Grant, munching cold pie.

Hortense, rageful, turned to Matt.

'Mista Chapman, ain't this doing me and Joe no favour?' she burst out. 'Look at them two rascals, they done come back again.'

'And we didn't give 'em no invitation,' said Joe, 'they sneaked in behind our backs.'

'So I see,' said Matt.

'Mister, we don't have nowhere to go,' said Herby, and took another bite at his wedge of pie.

'We ain't got no bed,' said Grant through a mouthful.

'I'm minded to skin the pair of you alive,' said Matt, looking as if he'd first boil them. But his mood changed and took on a more humane approach. 'Now look, you can stay here for the rest of the day and for the night, but out you go in the morning, you hear that?'

'You're talking clear,' said Grant, 'but we still ain't got nowhere to go.'

'What's your trade?' asked Matt.

'Bricklaying,' said Herby. 'Grant and me both.'

'Joe, are they good at it?' asked Matt.

'When they ain't laying around,' said Joe.

'Can't get no job in London,' said Grant.

'At bricklaying?' said Matt. 'Yes, you can.

I'll drive both of you to the Croydon Labour Exchange tomorrow morning, and you'll apply. There's a demand for brickies, providing you are good at it.'

'They're good all right, Mista Chapman,' said Hortense, 'except they been bone idle since coming to London and reckoning on picking up a passel of gold off the streets.'

'That's got to stop,' said Matt, 'or I'll let the police know where they can pick up a couple of shoplifters.'

'Hey, mister, that ain't nice,' said Herby.

'In Croydon tomorrow, you'll apply for jobs, you hear?' said Matt. 'And you'll find lodgings.'

'That ain't easy, neither,' said Grant.

'I'll really burn your breeches if you don't keep trying,' said Matt.

Hortense gave a little chuckle.

'Mista Chapman, you sure do talk loud and clear to these here rascals,' she said.

'Well, you and Joe keep an eye on them and don't let them get near the village store,' said Matt, and departed to let Rosie know Herby and Grant had turned up again, and what he proposed to do about it.

Rosie said that made sense, and that she was tickled to know her children's father wasn't just a pretty face. Matt said his face had never been pretty, even as a child with curly hair.

'Well, never mind, old thing,' said Rosie,

'you're still favourite with me and the kids.'

'Who could ask for more?' said Matt.

'I know what I could ask for myself,' said Rosie.

'And what's that?'

'I could ask you to make sure you do get Herby and Grant off the backs of Hortense and Joe,' said Rosie. 'Without being a complete rotter, of course.'

'Dump them at the Croydon Labour Exchange with a few kind words?' said Matt.

'No, see that they get jobs and lodgings as well,' said Rosie, 'otherwise they'll come back here again.'

'That could take me all day,' said Matt.

'I'll excuse you for time off work,' said Rosie, 'for the sake of Joe and Hortense.'

'Burn my shirt-tails, Rosie, if you don't still knock holes in my head,' said Matt.

'And blow my blushes, Matt, if you don't still come after me,' said Rosie.

They laughed, then Matt went to rejoin Giles, while Rosie found Emily and took her to the shed to see how many eggs Joe and Hortense had collected during the morning. At this time of the year laying always fell off a bit. Even so, a single crate of eggs was a good return for November. All needed to be inspected and graded for customers, especially those who asked for a good proportion of double yolks.

302

Hortense and Joe gave their nephews lunch, then took them into the field adjacent the main one, put shears into their hands and made them trim tall evergreen hedges. Joe was pleasantly surprised to find that they worked efficiently and vigorously. That Mister Chapman, he knew how to talk turkey to them boys, he sure did.

Polly and Boots, at Sunday dinner with the twins, looked up as James said he had some news for them.

'Good or bad?' said Boots.

'Bad news on Sundays is out, out,' said Polly.

James chewed thoughtfully on a piece of roast chicken. Rosie regularly delivered chickens, plump and dressed, to family members who phoned their orders.

'Well, it's like this,' he said, 'I saw Cathy this morning–'

'That's not news, that's boring,' said Gemma.

'And I've just remembered what she told me,' said James.

'And what did she tell you?' asked Boots.

'If it was anything to do with marrying you next week, dear boy,' said Polly, 'the answer's never during any week.'

'Mum,' said Gemma, 'that stuff's even more boring.'

'She told me,' said James, 'that she and her

mum are moving to Paris in the New Year.'

'Paris? Paris?' said Gemma.

'Paris sounds divine,' said Polly, 'it's far far away, but why there?'

'Her mum's met a millionaire French count,' said James, 'and he's found a house for her. One of his own houses, by the Serpentine.'

'I thought the Serpentine was in Hyde Park,' said Boots.

'Did I say the Serpentine?' said James. 'I meant the Seine. I'm confused. Well, I always am after being talked to by Cathy. It makes me feel I'll have a mixed-up future. Oh, and Mrs Davidson has already sold her house in Dulwich.'

'This is wonderful news,' said Polly. 'Boots, open a bottle of wine.'

'Let's stay with what's on the table,' said Boots. A bottle of chilled white wine was present, and only half empty.

'Paris,' murmured Polly, 'far far away. Absolute bliss. Children, we can now do away with the drawbridge and the moat, and no longer will we need to lock your father up in the walk-in larder. The spider has caught a rich French count, poor blighter. James, what will happen to Cathy?'

'Oh, she'll go to a school for English children in Paris,' said James.

'Better and better,' said Polly.

'Mind you,' said James, 'she's going to

make me swear a solemn oath to marry her in Paris when I'm old enough.'

'Not while I live and breathe,' said Polly. 'Don't you dare, James, don't you dare.'

'Mummy, do be your age,' said Gemma, 'you know how daft James can be. He could swear six solemn oaths, and not one would mean anything. Honest, Dad, I don't know how I came to have a brother as potty as James.'

'Luck of the draw,' said Boots.

'I'd feel happier if Cathy ended up in darkest Africa instead of Paris,' said Polly.

'And lost in the jungle?' smiled Boots.

'The point is,' mused James, 'I feel I'm going to get confused again before the day is out.'

'Why?' asked Gemma.

'That girl Cindy is coming here to tea this afternoon, with her parents,' said James.

Polly laughed. Cindy might very well be a confusion to James, but her charming German stepmother was no spider.

Chapter Twenty-Four

The afternoon became so mellow and kind that people might have thought November was preening itself if they hadn't known it was more likely to be stirring its fiendish pot of pea-soup fog. Pea-soup fogs were still its speciality.

Late in the afternoon, when the light was fading, Harry, at the wheel of the family car, was driving Anneliese, Cindy and himself to Sunday tea with Polly and Boots. The sun, mild though it was and sinking, still softened the vista as he entered Denmark Hill from Camberwell Road. Anneliese was immediately conscious of a change from the built-up area of central Camberwell to the open aspect of the broad thoroughfare lined with trees and handsome houses. Evergreen hedges guarded front gardens, and the fading sunshine touched windows with a soft gleam.

'This is always such a pleasant area, Harry,' she said.

'It's for families generally better off than most of those in Camberwell,' said Harry. 'In Queen Victoria's time it was open fields.'

'Well, nothing stays the same, Daddy,' said

Cindy from the back. 'Our history teacher said that if it did, there wouldn't be a single house anywhere, just caves.'

'And fig leaves?' said Harry.

'No, no, Cindy, it's impossible for nothing to change,' said Anneliese, 'evolution is proof of that.'

'Oh, our class isn't into evolution yet,' said Cindy.

'If it hadn't worked,' said Harry, 'we'd still be monkeying about in trees instead of being on our way to Sunday tea with friends.'

The car reached Sunray Avenue on the left of the hill. Standing by the gate of the house on the corner was a FOR SALE board. Anneliese did not miss it. She reacted at once, on impulse.

'Harry, look, such a nice house for sale.'

'Yes, I did notice,' said Harry, driving on.

It came then, the wishful thought that had been hovering in her mind.

'Harry, wouldn't you like a house with a garden?'

'Eh?' said Harry.

'Crikey, yes,' said Cindy, fastening eagerly onto the prospect of a move from Camberwell Road. 'Daddy, a garden and deckchairs and flowers, you've got to like that.'

'Sell up for the sake of a garden?' said Harry.

Anneliese, knowing the house in Camberwell had special memories for him, did not intend to press or push him.

'It's only a thought,' she said.

'It might be, but it's a happy one,' said Harry.

'Harry?'

'Oh, good old Dad,' said Cindy, very taken indeed with what a move could mean. No more funny looks from some people, and definitely no more spiteful posters. 'I'd love a garden myself and I'd help you with it.'

'All right, pet, we'll give the idea serious thought,' said Harry.

'Harry, you mean that?' said Anneliese.

'It's time we had a garden to sit in on summer afternoons,' said Harry. Truthfully, he might never have thought about it himself. He was always content with what was in hand. But now that the idea had been planted by Anneliese, he found he liked it. He liked all the ideas she had had and acted on in respect of making the Camberwell Road house brighter and better. 'Yes, a happy thought of yours, Anneliese.'

'Darling, a garden really would be nice,' she said.

'Not half, you bet,' said the delighted Cindy.

'Well, wife and child,' said Harry, turning into Red Post Hill, 'we'll put our present old shack on the market and see what the owners are asking for the house on the corner of Sunray Avenue.'

308

'Sunray Avenue?' said Anneliese.

'Yes, that's the name of the road,' said Harry.

'I didn't notice,' said Anneliese, her English more natural week by week, 'but such a lovely name and so in keeping with summer gardens.'

'What d'you say to that, Cindy?' asked Harry.

'That you must make sure we get the house,' said Cindy. 'I shan't mind riding to school on a bus.'

Anneliese turned her head and glanced at Cindy. Her lovable stepdaughter gave her a delighted smile. Anneliese returned it. There was mutual if silent acknowledgement that together they could persuade Harry to pursue the matter.

On went the car to the house in East Dulwich Grove, where Polly, Boots and the twins received their visitors with the friendliest greetings. Anneliese warmed again to Tim's distinguished father, and to Polly, now a fascinating companion on their periodical trips to town.

Cindy came face to face with James.

'Oh, hello,' she said.

'A pleasure, Miss Stevens,' said James, and bowed.

Gemma rolled her eyes at the show-off.

'Where can we talk?' asked Cindy.

'Now?' said James.

'Well, now or after tea,' said Cindy. 'Somewhere quiet.'

Boots coughed, Polly blinked, Harry grinned and Anneliese said, 'Cindy, this isn't our house.'

'Well, yes, I know,' said Cindy, 'so I'm not sure where somewhere quiet is.'

'You can talk now,' said Boots, 'in the living room or the garden shed. Try the lounge, James, it's damp in the shed, and we won't be serving tea just yet.'

'Oh, right,' said James. 'This way, Cindy.'

The amused grown-ups watched them making for the living room. Gemma was still rolling her eyes.

In the well-appointed room, designed by Polly to offer colour and comfort, in addition to the entertainment value of radio and television, Cindy said, 'Crikey, you don't half have a posh house.'

'It's just another house,' said James, 'and I like yours just as much.'

'But we don't have a garden,' said Cindy, 'or even a decent back yard, just enough space for hanging the Monday washing. Mind, my mum, sends most to the laundry. D'you send much of yours to a laundry?'

'Well, I don't, not personally,' said James, 'we all leave it to Flossie to sort out.'

'Who's Flossie?' asked Cindy, looking pretty in a patterned Sunday frock.

'Oh, she's Mum's daily help,' said James.

310

'D'you have a butler as well?' asked Cindy, glancing around.

'Well, no, we've got Dad,' said James. 'I think Mum prefers him to a butler.'

'I must say he's very nice,' said Cindy. 'Anyway, before we all have tea, I want to tell you there's a film on at the Camberwell cinema that I want to see. It's starting tomorrow. It's called *Genevieve*, and it's supposed to be ever so funny. You can take me next Saturday afternoon. Dad says it'll be all right for me to go with you. You can call for me at half-past one. You won't be doing anything with that soppy girl who wants to marry you, will you?'

James, surfacing after being swamped by this tidal wave, said, 'I give you my word, I don't do anything with any girls. My mum would have a fit if I did at my age or any age, and my dad would do a lot of head-shaking.'

'Well, that's all right, then,' said Cindy, 'I'll be able to trust you. Did I say call for me at half-past one? Yes, I did. So don't be late.'

'I'll have to ask you to excuse me,' said James. 'I don't think I'll be well enough to leave my bed next Saturday.'

'How can you know now what you'll be feeling like next Saturday?' asked Cindy.

'It's a sort of instinct,' said James.

'Crikey, you can't have that kind of instinct at your age,' said Cindy, 'you have to wait till you've had proper experience of

311

life. What're you looking like that for?'

'Already, I don't feel well,' said James. He had an idea that Cindy was going to be another Cathy.

'Well, I just don't know I ever met a pottier boy,' said Cindy.

The talk went on in this way, James holding his own only with a struggle.

In the lounge the conversation was on a different level. Anneliese and Harry were telling Polly and Boots about the house up for sale on the corner of Sunray Avenue. Anneliese advanced the cause by asking if Polly and Boots happened to know the owners and what their asking price was.

'So sorry, but I've no idea,' said Polly. 'Do you know, Boots?'

'No, I'm afraid not,' said Boots, 'but my brother Tommy might. He lives almost opposite Sunray Avenue. Would you like me to phone him before Polly serves tea?'

'Oh, we're not desperate,' said Harry.

'But it would be nice if we had that information,' said Anneliese, and Boots suspected she was keen for Harry to make the purchase.

'Well, sit back,' he said, 'and I'll make the call.'

He did so. Tommy answered.

'Hello, who's that?'

'Your mother's eldest son,' said Boots.

'You're not having a Sunday afternoon

nap?' said Tommy.

'So far,' said Boots, 'I've avoided that old man's habit. Polly says she'll prang me with her garden fork if she catches me at it.'

'What's she worried about?' asked Tommy. 'You're not old yet. None of us are. Well, Chinese Lady's getting on a bit, but she was born a lot earlier than we were. Anyway, what can I do for you?'

'Tell me,' said Boots, 'do you know who owns the house that's up for sale on the corner of Sunray Avenue?'

'The Herbisons?' said Tommy. 'Yes, Vi and me know 'em. Nice couple in their sixties and retired. They're selling up and moving to the Isle of Wight.'

'Do you know their asking price?'

'Three and a half thousand,' said Tommy, 'and they're looking for a quick sale. So they'll probably come down a hundred or so. Mind, it could've been bought for a thousand before the war. Here, half a mo, you enquiring on behalf of yourself and Polly?'

'No, on behalf of Harry and Anneliese Stevens,' said Boots.

'Well, they're a nice couple too,' said Tommy. He and Vi, along with other members of the family, had met them at Tim and Felicity's home. 'Don't they live in Camberwell Road?'

'Yes, with only half a back yard,' said

Boots. 'They'd like a garden.'

'Blimey, that takes me back a few years to our back yard in Walworth,' said Tommy, 'and our Lizzy pining for a house with a garden and a bathroom. Y'know, Ned did her proud when he married her.'

'A tale of happy ever after,' said Boots. 'By the way, do you also know who the agents are?'

'Yes, Parrish and Partners, near Herne Hill station,' said Tommy. 'What d'you want to know next? Who pinched Nell Gwynn's oranges?'

'I know that one,' said Boots. 'Charlie. Thanks for all the info, Tommy. Love to Vi.'

'That'll make her blush,' said Tommy.

It didn't. Placid Vi just smiled. She was getting tea ready. Her mum would come down for that, as she always did on Sundays. Known to the family as Aunt Victoria, she was a mellow old lady these days, but still careful not to drop her aitches.

'What did Boots want, Tommy?' Vi asked. Tommy told her, and Vi had a moment's thought before saying, 'Isn't Anneliese Stevens German?'

'Yes, but you'd never think it,' said Tommy.

'Tommy, Mr and Mrs Herbison are Jewish,' said Vi.

'Oh, blimey, so they are,' said Tommy.

'If you see them, don't tell them Anneliese is German,' said Vi. 'I don't think they'd like

314

selling their house to anyone from Germany.'

'Vi, I'll mind my own business,' said Tommy.

Polly put the kettle on, and Boots passed Tommy's information to Harry and Anneliese. Anneliese asked if three and a half thousand pounds was a fair price, since she knew nothing about English house values. Harry said it was fair and reasonable, which gave Anneliese another moment of happy anticipation.

'I'll phone the agents tomorrow morning,' said Harry, 'and find out when we can look the house over. How's that?'

'Promising, isn't it?' smiled Anneliese. 'Boots,' she said in quieter vein, 'I must ask, is there any further news on Felicity?'

'Felicity's still in the middle of a waiting game,' said Boots.

'It must be a damned rough game,' said Harry.

Polly appeared at the open door.

'Tea's ready. Where's Gemma?'

'I've an idea she's listening at the keyhole of the living-room door,' said Boots.

'Heavens,' said Polly, 'is Cindy still talking to James?'

'If he's not yet deaf,' said Harry, smiling.

Polly turned.

'Gemma,' she called, 'wherever you are and whatever you're doing, stop doing it and tell Cindy and James that tea's ready.'

'Oh, jolly good, Mama,' called Gemma. She entered the dining room a minute later, with Cindy and James. James looked as if he'd recovered. Cindy looked as if something had gone wrong.

'Cindy, what have you been saying to James?' asked Anneliese, as they all seated themselves.

'Oh, nothing much, just about going to see that film next Saturday," said Cindy.

'James, what film is this?' asked Polly.

'*Genevieve*,' said James, 'but I can't go, I remembered five minutes ago that I'm playing football, and I can't be excused by the sports master unless there's something like a family wedding or funeral taking place.'

'I see,' said Polly.

'Fancy having to play that kicking game instead of going to the pictures,' said Cindy.

'There's always another time,' said Boots.

'Oh, are we having tea now?' said James. 'Well, I'll have some, Mother, then I think I'll go to bed.'

'Would you let us all know why?' asked Boots.

'Yes, I don't feel well,' said James, who'd been under the cosh from Cindy, especially when he remembered about the school football match. 'I think I'll be like it all day.'

Gemma rolled her eyes yet again, Cindy

316

giggled, and the grown-ups laughed.

James was having another spell of confusion.

Or so his manner implied.

Boots and Polly, of course, didn't believe it. If anyone knew how to manage his life at the near age of thirteen, it was their forward-thinking son.

And Gemma, of course, knew her brother was a daft show-off.

Chapter Twenty-Five

Monday morning. The lady clerical officer at the Croydon Labour Exchange, turning up a file, had no difficulty in finding building firms that had vacancies for bricklayers. Matthew stood by as Grant and Herby were handed cards that invited them to apply at one particular firm in West Croydon, the working-class area of the town.

Matt drove the young men there. He told them that if they were accepted, to ask the boss if he knew of suitable lodgings. In they went, and after twenty minutes out they came.

'Well?' said Matt, standing by his car.

'Mister, we got the jobs,' said Grant.

'We is starting tomorrow,' said Herby.

They both looked pleased with themselves.

'How about lodgings?' asked Matt.

'The man, he didn't know any,' said Herby.

'Right,' said Matt, 'get in the car and I'll drive you around. We'll do some looking and knocking on doors.'

He spent the rest of the morning with them, watching as they knocked on doors without any luck. Prospective landladies took on a negative look as soon as they saw the colour of their skins. Matt sighed. There was a lot of colour bar about. Eventually, he called it a day, drove them to a café, told them to get something to eat, and to wait for him outside the café after the meal.

'We ain't in good with money,' said Grant.

'You're both broke?' said Matt.

'We sure is,' said Herby.

'I thought you were collecting the dole.'

'It got stopped,' said Grant.

Matt wondered if it had ever started for them, and if they'd existed on shoplifting. However, he gave them ten shillings. He watched them enter the cafe, speculating on whether or not the proprietor served black immigrants. Not all café owners gave a welcome to these people from the West Indies, who were landing in the UK every week.

Herby and Grant did not emerge from the café, and Matt, satisfied they were getting a meal, drove to the nearest public phone box. From there he rang Rosie to let her know what progress he'd made with the young men.

'They've got jobs but no accommodation?' said Rosie.

'That's how things are at the moment,' said Matt.

'Well, Matt old horse,' said Rosie, 'don't come home until they're fixed up with lodgings.'

'You're joking,' said Matt. 'There's an old Dorset saying. "When the day be up the spout, 'tis time to be up and out."'

'Not yet, keep trying,' said Rosie.

'Damn my bootlaces, Rosie, I haven't had any lunch yet,' said Matt.

'I feel for you,' said Rosie, 'but there's an old cockney saying. "When yer back's to the wall, mate, keep on fighting yer fate."'

'Rosie, you just made that up.'

'Same to you, lovey,' said Rosie, 'so keep trying, or Herby and Grant will follow you home.'

'I'll kill 'em,' said Matt, and rang off.

He returned to the café. There was no sign of Herby and Grant. He put his head in. They weren't there, but a pleasant smell of fried eggs and bacon existed.

Standing on the pavement, he looked around. He saw various people, the homely kind that dwelt in this semi-industrial area between West Croydon and Selhurst, with its small factories and old-looking houses. He spotted a couple of immigrants, but not Herby and Grant.

After a while, he entered the café, a quite acceptable establishment. Several patrons were enjoying a lunchtime snack. Behind the counter, with its hot cooking plate, stood the proprietor, portly, bald and chubby-cheeked.

'Excuse me,' said Matt.

'What for?'

'I'm looking for a couple of West Indians,' said Matt. 'They came in here for a meal.'

'Yup, there were two. Fried bacon and eggs, with baked beans.' The proprietor was genial and forthcoming.

'When did they leave?' asked Matt.

'They ain't left yet.'

'Can you tell me where they are, then?'

'Up next to the roof,' said the proprietor, bald head shining, chubby cheeks slightly flushed from the heat of his hotplate.

'Come again?' said Matt.

'They're renting the attic.'

'They're what?' said Matt.

'You speaking of two darkies names of Herby and Grant Robinson?'

'They're the johnnies,' said Matt.

'That's them, then, up in the attic, having paid me a week's rent of ten bob in advance. They seem decent lads. Would you be the gent that's going to pay for their meal? They said you would.'

What a pair of roll-me-overs, thought Matt, but a smile appeared.

'How much?' he asked.

'Four and fourpence. They had a packet of crisps as well.'

Cheap at the price, thought Matt, if they've landed lodgings. He paid up.

'Much obliged,' said the proprietor. 'You can go up, if you want. Through that door and turn right. Three flights of stairs.'

From the outside, Matt had noticed there were two floors above the shop, topped by a sloping attic with a little window.

'Thanks,' he said, and climbed the stairs to the top landing, where the door of the attic was directly in front of him. He pushed it open and walked in. There were two truckle-beds, a couple of chairs and a chest of drawers. Herby and Grant were sitting on one bed, chewing potato crisps.

'Hey, Mister Chapman, us is fixed up, see?' said Grant.

'I do see,' said Matt, 'but if I remember right, I asked you to wait outside for me.'

'Sure you did,' said Herby, 'but the man, he done told us not to go till the meals got paid for.'

'Fair enough,' said Matt. 'Seeing you're fixed up here, I'm happy, and so are you two, I hope. I'll come after you if you don't pay your rent regularly every week, but I'll say nothing about your dodgy performance in getting me to pay for your meals and those potato crisps, on top of using my ten bob for a week's advance rent.'

'That's mighty obliging, Mister Chapman,' said Grant.

'You can visit your aunt and uncle now and again,' said Matt. 'On Sundays. But if you give them trouble, watch out for fire in your breeches. So long, then, and keep those jobs you've got.'

'You done us a pretty good turn, Mister Chapman,' said Herby.

'It's something you could have done for yourselves,' said Matt, and went down to the café, where he ordered a snack of hot sausages, baked beans and tomatoes. It was that kind of menu, typical of a London café. Hungry, and satisfied with the day's outcome, he enjoyed the meal, and made friends with the proprietor, who promised to keep a fatherly eye on his West Indian lodgers. Matt said he'd be grateful for that, since many of these immigrants were having a hard time. The proprietor said he understood, and wanted Matt to know he didn't have anything against them himself.

Matt arrived back at the farm by late afternoon, where he was able to let Rosie, Hortense and Joe know that Herby and Grant were fixed up with jobs and lodgings. Hortense and Joe expressed gratitude and relief, and when they went back to their work, Hortense was beaming.

'Matt, what a lovely chap you are,' said Rosie. 'How would you like something dear to the heart of Grandmother Finch?'

'Her best aspidistra?' said Matt.

'No, a pot of hot steaming tea,' said Rosie.

'What a lifeline,' said Matt. 'There's another old Dorset saying. "At the end of the day–"'

'I've heard it, ten times,' said Rosie, 'but you're still a good old bloke.'

At three o'clock, the arranged identity parade took place at the main Bristol police station. Alice made her inspection of the lined-up men. She then notified Chief Inspector Bradley of her selection. Numbers three and eight. Fergus followed, and he too informed the chief inspector that numbers three and eight were the men he and Alice had come up against on the day of the robbery.

At half-past three, the chief inspector spoke to the journalists waiting outside the station.

'What's the verdict, Chief Inspector?'

'Negative.'

'Eh?'

'The suspects will still be charged. The bag containing the loot has been found, and the revolver.' They'd been found lodged high up a tree.

'You're going to charge them without–'

'They'll be committed for trial next month. That's all, gentlemen.'

A small young man, hovering, slipped away. A plain-clothes policeman, standing at a bus stop across the street, made a move. Chief Inspector Bradley went back into the station, and there enjoyed a cup of tea with Alice and Fergus, who had wisely opted not to show themselves to the journalists.

'You think you're on the ball, Chief Inspector?' said Fergus.

'I know my sergeant is now on the tail of a little chap with quick feet.'

'The men themselves weren't around?' said Fergus.

'Not according to my eyesight,' said Bradley, 'but I'll lay odds on the shifty little bugger being their go-between for a quid or two. Now, let's hope the message he carries to them will mean neither of you will suffer grievous bodily harm. And let's also hope he'll lead my sergeant to where they're living at the moment. Then we can keep tabs on them.'

'You're not going to arrest them?' said Alice.

'Miss Adams, I want that arrest to take place when they're handing over the bribe either to you or Mr MacAllister. Catch 'em red-handed, and we've got a case that'll back up your evidence.'

'Aye,' said Fergus, 'but what happens when the press finds out you fooled them with your announcement that the outcome of the identity parade was negative?'

'Well, it was negative in its way,' said Bradley. 'For the suspects. No, the press will be informed after the trial why I made that kind of announcement. Look, be ready at any time for the hustlers to call on one of you.'

'Chief Inspector, we still don't know how they traced us,' said Alice.

'I know,' said Bradley, looking ferocious. 'One of the uniformed constables here has been suspended from duty.'

Fergus knew what that meant, and why the chief inspector had been grinding iron filings. He'd had the unusual experience of finding there was a bent copper in the station.

'I'm sorry you've had that kind of blow, Chief Inspector,' said Alice.

'So am I,' ground Bradley. 'You'll know now how you and Mr MacAllister were traced. Those men tracked you until they caught you together. Well, it's our turn to do the tracking. They'll be watched night and day until we nail them in the act of handing the bribe money to one of you. And that won't be long.'

'I'm wishing you luck,' said Fergus, and he and Alice left then.

'Fergus, when d'you think it will happen?' asked Alice.

'It'll no' be next week,' said Fergus. 'Once this go-between has informed them that the result of the identity parade was negative, they'll want to contact you or me without wasting time. Alice, I think I'd better keep you company all day.'

'You're welcome to,' said Alice. 'Let's go back to my flat now and prepare something to eat.'

'I'll no' turn down that offer,' said Fergus.

Alice smiled.

The moment of confrontation happened thirty minutes after darkness fell that evening.

Alice's bell rang.

'Fergus?' she said. Her protective Scot was still with her.

'I'll come down with you,' said Fergus.

Down they went. Alice opened the door. There they were, two dark and bulky figures, overcoated and the brims of their hats well down.

'I think we've met before,' said Alice, quite composed, while Fergus looked beyond the men for signs of a further presence, but the darkness was impenetrable. However, he and Alice, and the men, were illuminated by the hall light.

'Here,' said one man brusquely, and thrust a fat envelope at Alice.

'What's this?' asked Alice.

'As agreed,' said the second man. 'Take it.'

Alice put out a hand. The envelope was delivered. From out of the darkness, rubber-soled boots silently pounded, and up the stone steps to the house rushed four plain-clothes men.

There was a roar from one suspect, and a raging fight on the doorstep. Blows were taken and given, and it ended with professional armlocks and the application of handcuffs. The men were then told they were under arrest for an attempt to bribe witnesses, and cautioned.

A dark police van drew up outside the house.

'You all right, Miss Adams?' enquired the CID officer in charge of the squad.

'Relieved,' said Alice.

'We'll take that,' said the officer, and Alice handed him the fat envelope. He opened it and by the light of the hall disclosed the contents, a wad of banknotes. 'See that?' he said to the arrested men.

'So what?' said one.

'Prime evidence,' said the officer. 'Take 'em away, Sergeant.'

'I dinna know I ever saw a smarter piece of work,' said Fergus, as the arrested men were taken down to the van, their blasphemous outpourings shocking to the ears of old ladies who cherished the more righteous Victorian values. Happily, no such ladies were about.

'Just one more job, sir.'

'All the same, give Chief Inspector Bradley our compliments,' said Fergus.

'That reminds me, sir. The chief inspector suggests that when this gang of four finish their prison sentences, it might be advisable for you and Miss Adams to have changed your addresses.'

'That'll be in more than a few years' time, won't it?' said Alice.

'These kind of crooks have long memories, Miss Adams, and they won't forget you and Mr MacAllister identified two of them as the hold-up pair at the trial, as we're sure you will.'

'You can be sure,' said Fergus.

'Goodnight, sir. Goodnight, miss.' The CID officer descended the steps to the van, in which the arrested men were now securely locked with their police escorts.

'Well, Fergus?' said Alice, closing the door.

'Whisht, Alice lassie, I feel I need a wee dram or two,' said Fergus.

'I don't keep strong drink,' said Alice, 'so let's go to a pub and celebrate.'

'Am I hearing you?' said Fergus.

'You should be,' said Alice, 'I'm speaking loud and clear in my fashion, and I think I fancy a gin and tonic.'

'Alice, you don't drink.'

'Well, I'm in the mood to make a start,' said Alice.

'I'm thinking gin and tonic willna be the right kind of start,' said Fergus.

'Why?'

'It'll go to your head,' said Fergus.

'Oh, let my head make a start too,' said Alice.

They enjoyed an hour in a warm and cosy

pub, and Alice actually had two gin and tonics. Neither went to her head, but both increased her festive mood, which Fergus thought confirmed her changed attitude to life outside her books. When he took her back to her flat and said goodnight to her, she kissed him with warmth.

'You're a fine young lady, Alice,' he said.

'Come again tomorrow evening,' said Alice.

'Will I bring a bottle of gin and some tonic water?' asked Fergus.

'Thank you, but no,' said Alice, 'just yourself.'

'I like it fine, Alice, that you're no' a woman who'll take to drink,' said Fergus, and departed smiling.

Chapter Twenty-Six

A little after nine on Wednesday evening, Tim took a phone call.

'Mr Adams?' The voice was pleasant and cultured.

'Speaking,' said Tim. His own voice was like his father's, easy, vibrant and well articulated, although Emily, his late mother, had been an irrepressible cockney with the quick, sometimes rushed, delivery of her kind.

'Sir Charles Morgan here. Sorry to call you at this time in the evening, but I've had a busy day.'

'It's not late,' said Tim, 'and if you've some news to impart, the time's irrelevant.'

'I do have some news,' said Sir Charles, 'obtained by a New York ophthalmologist I came to know when we were both students at St Mary's Hospital in London.'

'He's written you about Dr Paul Rokovsky?' said Tim, quickening.

'He has, Mr Adams, and I'm delighted to tell you that his knowledge and assessment of this specialist is very much as you and I, and Mrs Adams, hoped for. He's certainly a Ukrainian, there's no argument about that.'

And Sir Charles went on to say the man's credentials were of the highest, and that his experiences and successes when compelled to work with German medical units during Hitler's Russian campaign were fully substantiated by documents. The American immigration authorities had nothing against him, and his application for American nationality was currently under sympathetic consideration. The United States had welcomed an influx of medical and scientific specialists from devastated Europe after the war had ended.

Tim, who knew America had made a point of collaring many of Germany's leading scientists and research chemists immediately following the ceasefire, said, 'And Dr Paul Rokovsky has made a name for himself in New York?'

'Indeed,' said Sir Charles, 'and I think it worthwhile to help Mrs Adams secure an appointment with him. At the same time, I must tell you my old friend advises me that most of Dr Rokovsky's successful operations have been performed on American soldiers whose blindness hasn't been total. However, there have been one or two cases where the condition appeared to be permanent. So I'm perfectly happy for Mrs Adams to consult him.'

'That's great news,' said Tim. 'After all, in view of the fact that my wife has experienced these periodical moments of vision, we could perhaps say her own blindness is no longer total.'

'Has she had one of these moments since I last spoke to her?' enquired Sir Charles.

'If you'd asked me that question yesterday, or even this afternoon,' said Tim, 'I'd have had to say no. But this evening, at supper-time, she suddenly had one of her blurred visions. That was the first for some weeks. She intended to phone you tomorrow, although you did say you were only interested in another clear vision.'

'I assure you, all blurred visions still have their possibilities,' said Sir Charles. 'If you'll leave matters with me, I'll try to arrange the New York appointment myself and then let you know the date. Mrs Adams, I presume, is ready to make the necessary flight to New York sometime in the near future?'

'It's what we've been waiting for,' said Tim. 'I'm damned grateful to you for all you're doing.'

'I'm doing nothing that I shouldn't do,' said Sir Charles, 'or that I wouldn't want to. I have a great admiration for your wife, and I should like to think that my hopes for a restoration of her sight are no less than hers or yours.'

'I appreciate that, very much,' said Tim.

'Then goodnight, Mr Adams, and I'll be in touch with you again as soon as I can.'

'Thanks,' said Tim.

He rejoined Felicity in the living room. She was listening to a concert on the radio. Maggie Forbes, their invaluable live-in help, was up in her room, and Jennifer was in bed.

'Who was that on the phone?' asked Felicity.

'Sir Charles Morgan,' said Tim.

Felicity sat up.

'Tell me what he said.'

Tim told her. Felicity uttered what could only be described as an exclamation mark.

'The prospect excites you, Puss?' said Tim.

'Tim,' she breathed, 'he's recommending an appointment with Dr Rokovsky, he's actually going to arrange one?'

'With his blessing,' said Tim. 'What do we say about that? New York, here we come?'

'I'm already flying high,' said Felicity, glowing. 'Isn't it the cat's whiskers? And we won't have to worry about Jennifer, Maggie will be here to look after her.'

'I'm thinking of adopting Maggie,' said Tim.

'As your concubine?' said Felicity. 'You'll be lucky. Try bringing her a special present from New York, you sheik of Araby. Tim, I feel high. I could jump over the moon.'

'I'll be with you,' said Tim, 'so let's hope for an easy landing.'

They talked with enthusiasm and at length

about the prospect of a successful operation, and Felicity, of course, could hardly sleep that night.

Next morning at the office, Tim let Boots and Sammy know about developments.

'I'm delighted,' said Boots, while thinking that Anneliese must have been definitely mistaken in identifying Rokovsky as a former SS doctor and a war criminal. If not, could the American investigating authorities have been fooled?

'On behalf of my own feelings, I second Boots's compliments,' said Sammy.

'That's your seal of approval for the trip, is it, Uncle Sammy?' said Tim.

'Plus my best wishes for Felicity, you bet,' said Sammy. 'Mind, you'd better warn her in advance that if she gets to see again, she might have a shock when she finds out what we all look like.'

'There's nothing wrong with Aunt Susie's looks,' said Tim, 'or Aunt Lizzy's or Aunt Vi's. Or my stepmother's or–'

'Don't make a list, Tim,' said Sammy, 'or those you leave out might get to hear. Stone me, I never knew any family that got to hear things quicker than ours. Must be something to do with everyone being pathetic.'

'I think you mean telepathic, Sammy,' said Boots.

'Well, you'd know, of course, old mate,'

said Sammy. 'That education of yours is always breaking out. Anyway, Tim, you just tell Felicity good luck from one and all. I can confidently speak for everyone.'

Rachel entered the office at that point, and when she too was informed of developments, she demonstrated her happy reaction by kissing Tim.

'Lovely news,' she said, and Tim, riding high, kissed her in return, on her cheek.

'Might I ask what's going on?' enquired Sammy.

'Nothing one wouldn't expect,' smiled Boots.

'Now, Boots, you know kissing and suchlike ain't allowed in office hours,' said Sammy.

'There's always an exception,' said Boots.

'Half a mo, Tim, where you off to?' asked Sammy. His nephew, coat over his arm, hat in his hand, was making for the door.

'I'm off to Bethnal Green with Daniel and our architects,' said Tim. He and Daniel were losing no time in finalizing everything that would allow work on the factory extension to begin before Christmas.

'Oh, right,' said Sammy, 'off you go, then, me lad.'

Tim turned at the door.

'Dad,' he said amiably, 'would you let Uncle Sammy know I'm getting on a bit?'

He was thirty-three and every inch a

336

mature veteran of the war.

'Point taken, Tim,' said Boots, and his son disappeared.

'Speaking personal,' said Sammy, 'it's my belief that kids grow up when our backs are turned. Little kids one minute, then when you next turn round, there they are wearing bowler hats or nylon stockings and fancy frocks. Depending, of course, on their – um–'

'Gender?' said Boots helpfully.

'Like I already mentioned, we're all thankful for your education, Boots,' said Sammy. 'But what I mean is – well, take Rachel for a start. When I first met her down the market in Kaiser Bill's war, there she was, a young girlie in a gymslip.'

'My best Sunday frock, I think, Sammy,' said Rachel.

'I ain't arguing,' said Sammy, 'I'm saying that next time I turned round, Boots, I don't know where the time had gone, but she looked like the Queen of Sheba.'

'Thank you, Sammy,' said Rachel.

'Be of good cheer, Sammy,' said Boots, 'she still looks like the Queen of Sheba.'

'Boots, you dear man,' said Rachel.

'Then there was Susie – no, wait a tick.' Sammy took a look at his watch. 'Here, can anyone tell me why we're all standing about?' he complained. 'I've got work to do concerning posters for our shops' New Year sales.'

337

'And I need to speak to you or Boots about some outstanding debtors,' said Rachel.

'We've got outstanding debtors serious?' said Sammy. 'I ain't ever been fond of that, it can lead to a bankrupt condition. Rachel, before the roof falls in on my head and yours as well, kindly acquaint me with details.'

'Sammy, that's what I'm here for,' said Rachel.

'I've a phone call to make,' said Boots, and went back to his office where, with the assistance of the switchboard girl, he was connected with Felicity.

'Good morning, daughter-in-law.'

'Boots?'

'I've had the good news from Tim, and I'm delighted.'

'Thank you,' said Felicity. 'Myself, I feel one over.'

'Well, it's time you had that kind of feeling,' said Boots. 'As for New York and what it means, I'd like to talk to you and Tim about how to meet the costs of everything. This evening, say?'

'Boots, come and talk to me now,' said Felicity. 'No, I mean later. That is, instead of going to your pub, come and have lunch with me.'

'Done,' said Boots, 'I'll spend my lunch hour with you, then. I'll arrive about twelve-thirty. How will that do?'

'Lovely,' said Felicity, and they rang off.

'Maggie? Maggie?'

'Yes, mum?' Maggie's plump and indispensable self appeared in the hall.

Felicity turned in the direction of the voice.

'Maggie, my father-in-law is coming to lunch,' she said. 'Can we do something nice?'

'Well, I always say something nice ought to be put before a nice gent like your father-in-law,' said Maggie. 'Fish, mum?'

'No bones, Maggie, I can't manage fish-bones,' said Felicity. 'They get up my nose, blow it.'

'There's some nice plaice fillets in the fridge, mum,' said Maggie. 'I could do them poached.'

'I think poached plaice for a man like my father-in-law would be too bland, don't you?' said Felicity.

'Well, poached salmon would be all right for anyone, mum, but I see what you mean about poached plaice fillets,' said Maggie. 'Grilled, say, with a bit of butter? We could spare a bit, and I could do creamed and peppered potatoes, a few runner beans and a fish sauce to go with it.'

'Maggie, you're a treasure,' said Felicity.

'Mum, I ain't ever been happier,' said Maggie, 'specially now you're going to New York to see a doctor that might be able to operate.'

'Fingers crossed,' said Felicity.

'Parrish and Partners,' said the receptionist, answering a phone call.

'Oh, good show,' said Harry airily. 'I'd like to speak to one of the partners about a house on your books.'

'Certainly, sir. Hold the line for a moment.'

Harry was put through to Mr Percy Parrish, who welcomed his call as if it was coming from a dear old schoolfriend. Harry described the location of the house in question.

'Mr Stevens, I'm happy to inform you that that property is high on our list, a most desirable residence in a charming neighbourhood, equipped with modern gas-fired central heating, excellent amenities, a delightful south-facing kitchen, four bedrooms, a garage, a—'

'Fine,' said Harry, interrupting the sales flow. 'When can you arrange for my wife and me to see it?'

'Tomorrow morning, Mr Stevens, when I'll be happy to meet you there and to introduce you to the owners, Mr and Mrs Herbison. May I ask if you'll be requiring a mortgage?'

'No, we shall pay in full on completion day,' said Harry. Anneliese had persuaded him to see the advantage of using her bank account to ensure firm agreement with the owners. Harry could settle with her when their own house was sold. Harry, not sure that their Camberwell Road property would attract a quick sale, saw the sense of that. But he also saw they were unlikely to receive an offer of more than half the cost of the Sunray Avenue house. Camberwell Road was the central point of a working-class area. So Anneliese said what was wrong with joint ownership? That would be fair, Harry, she said, if you paid me back half the cost. And Cindy said if half the people in the world were fair with the other half, there wouldn't be all the trouble there was, like wars and quarrels and hollering. Harry couldn't argue against that pearl of wisdom, and didn't. 'Yes, Mr Parrish, we'll settle on completion.'

'Excellent, Mr Stevens, excellent. That will be to your advantage if you decide to purchase, and I'm sure, yes, quite sure you'll like the property. Shall we say ten-thirty tomorrow morning, then?'

'Fine,' said Harry.

Boots arrived on the dot. Felicity herself let him in, thinking, as she opened the door, that if yesterday's glad tidings were going to be topped by a second clear vision of her father-in-law, what could be more encouraging or more of a wonder than that?

It didn't happen, however. Her eyes

remained obdurately sightless. But she sensed his presence on the doorstep, and his greeting confirmed it.

'Hello, dear girl.'

Her response to that was quick and light-hearted.

'Oh, to be a girl again, now that spring is here.'

'It isn't,' said Boots, 'but Christmas is on the way.'

'Come in, come in,' said Felicity.

Boots entered and delivered a kiss on her cheek. She responded to that too, by giving him an impulsive hug.

'I see you're still in high spirits,' he said.

'I'd be a dull old lady if I weren't,' she said. 'Come and have lunch. It's ready, and I've opened a bottle of white wine.' Extracting a cork was something she could manage. 'Then we can talk.'

Maggie served the meal, and blushed a little when Boots said how good it looked.

'Oh, the proof's in the eating, Mr Adams,' she said.

'I don't think I'll have any bother getting this down, Maggie,' said Boots.

The lunch began and so did the talk. At first, it was all about the promising prospects in New York, and whether a satisfactory consultation could lead quickly to an operation or a long stay before it took place. Boots said either was possible. In the meantime, all costs relating to travel, hotel, consultation and an operation itself, had to be considered.

'They won't be small,' said Felicity.

'No,' said Boots, 'and the fact is that with Tim still making monthly payments to the property company for your house, he'll be hard-pushed to meet the costs himself. I did say I would look after all expenses, and I now want you to know I'll finance you and Tim from the moment you board the plane until the day you return. You are not to have any worries about this, none at all.'

'Tim told me a little while ago that you intended to take care of the expenses if the New York trip came about,' said Felicity. She reached across the table, searched for and found his hand, and pressed it. 'You're the dearest man.'

'When I look back on my life and my family,' said Boots, 'I realize I'm a very fortunate one. I think of my first wife, Emily, and how damned unlucky she was to have died in her prime. I think of millions of Jewish people who died for no other reason than being Jewish. Thousands of their children, Felicity, and even babes in arms, all murdered. But here I am myself, alive and enjoying this lunch.'

'And here I am, enjoying it with you,' said Felicity.

A little emotion prevailed for a moment,

then Boots said he wanted her and Tim to be prepared for a disappointment if Dr Rokovsky's diagnosis turned out to be negative. Felicity said she was living on optimism. They talked some more, this time about the fact that she'd had many moments of temporary vision, which they both agreed were grounds for optimism.

They finished lunch and the wine, then Boots left to return to his office. Felicity said goodbye to him at the door, thanking him for coming. She sighed after he had gone, for he always boosted her morale. He was such a fine man to have as a father-in-law.

Chapter Twenty-Seven

Boots, arriving home that evening, told Polly of Sir Charles Morgan's report on the man in New York.

'Which means, Polly, that there's now nothing to stand in the way of Felicity consulting him.'

'He isn't a German, then, with a suspect past?' said Polly.

'Not according to Sir Charles's contact in New York, a medical man himself,' said Boots.

'So Anneliese was mistaken in identifying him as a doctor of infernal practices at Auschwitz?' said Polly.

'It seems so,' said Boots.

'Well, rousing cheers, old scout,' said Polly, 'and even if her mistake means embarrassment for Anneliese, she'll have the consolation of knowing Felicity's now able to travel to New York on a hope and a prayer.'

'I wonder,' mused Boots, 'was it her worst memories of SS excesses that caused Anneliese to see a war criminal in a newspaper photograph of a European immigrant in America? An immigrant who happens to be a doctor and a specialist in the field of ophthalmic surgery?'

'And is actually a Ukrainian doctor practising legitimately in New York?' said Polly.

'It's possible she made that mistake out of imagination,' said Boots.

'Well, let's forgive our charming German friend for that, and be glad for Felicity,' said Polly. 'She needs to hang onto this possibility of a cure. God, what must it be like for her never to have seen her own daughter?'

'Hellish at times,' said Boots.

'Boots old ducky, the twins have been asking after their Aunt Felicity,' said Polly, 'so it'll make them happy to be told this news.'

'Tell them as soon as they've finished their homework,' said Boots. 'I'll phone Anneliese.'

'Oh, ask her if she'd like to come up to town in a week or so and do some Christmas shopping with me,' said Polly.

'I'll ask her,' said Boots, and made the call.

It was Cindy who answered.

'Hello, it's Miss Cindy Stevens here.'

Boots smiled. Here was a young miss with a future.

'Good evening, Miss Stevens,' he said, 'it's Mr Robert Adams here, Tim's father.'

'Oh, great. You can call me Cindy.'

'Well, is your mother there, Cindy?'

'I'll call her,' said Cindy, and Boots heard her yell, 'Mummy, you're wanted! It's Mr Adams, Tim's dad.'

Anneliese arrived on the phone.

'Boots?'

'How are you?' asked Boots.

'I'm preparing supper with support from Harry and Cindy,' said Anneliese.

'Then I won't keep you,' said Boots. 'I simply want to tell you that Felicity's London specialist has a report from an old colleague in New York. It clears Dr Rokovsky and an appointment for Felicity to consult him can now be arranged.'

'Oh,' said Anneliese, obviously taken aback.

'It seems there are no grounds for suspicion,' said Boots.

'Then I must have made a mistake,' said Anneliese. 'I'm so sorry, since I know it's caused you worry.'

'Mistakes like that are easily made,' said Boots. 'Sir Charles Morgan, the London specialist, is arranging the appointment himself. I thought you'd like to know.'

'That's so kind of you,' said Anneliese, her light accent more pronounced because of her sensitive reaction to the report. 'I'm very happy for Felicity, yes, but embarrassed for my mistake.'

Remembering Polly had suggested this was how the German woman would feel, Boots said, 'Anneliese, you can't be blamed for thinking a certain man's photograph was that of someone you met when the German

347

armies were in turmoil and retreat from the Russians. They were hideous days for you, and I know they were burned into your memory.'

'I'm thankful you did not tell Tim and Felicity,' said Anneliese, 'it would have killed their hopes at the time. Thank you for keeping quiet.'

'Apart from this news,' said Boots, 'I'm to tell you Polly would like you to go to town with her to do some Christmas shopping in a week or so. If you fancy the idea, she'll let you know exactly when.'

'Boots, I would really love that,' said Anneliese, instantly happier.

'Polly will see you do,' said Boots. 'Now I'll let you get back to your kitchen.'

'Oh, I can spare a few more moments to let you know Harry has arranged with the agents for us to look over that house tomorrow,' said Anneliese. 'We shall meet the owners there.'

'I hope you find the place, and the garden, to your liking,' said Boots. 'Goodbye, Anneliese, and regards to Harry.'

'You and Polly, you are such good friends,' said Anneliese.

The next morning, Chinese Lady was having her usual breakfast-time talk with her husband. She liked to start the day on a chatty note. That, plus breakfast and two cups of tea, put her in form for the rest of the day. Many other couples didn't go in for breakfast talk at all. Tongues were still drugged from sleep, and talk seemed an interference with the process of gradually coming to life. Chinese Lady, however, came to life as soon as she opened her eyes. And Sir Edwin, as a very polite and civilized man, was always willing to participate.

'Edwin,' she said, as she poured their first cups of tea, 'what a blessing that there's this doctor in New York that might cure Felicity's blindness.'

'A great blessing, Maisie, full of promise,' said Sir Edwin.

'But I don't like thinking about her and Tim having to go all that way,' said Chinese Lady. 'When I asked Boots, he told me it was over two thousand miles. That must be nearly as far as Australia.'

'Not quite, Maisie,' said Sir Edwin. 'In fact, a short distance by comparison.'

'I don't know how you can call it short, Edwin.'

'I did say by comparison,' said Sir Edwin.

'All the same, I wish they only had to go to King's College Hospital by Ruskin Park,' said Chinese Lady.

'Much more convenient, of course, but not as exciting as going to New York,' said Sir Edwin. 'New York is hailed as a city of vigorous life, towering skyscrapers and splendid entertainment. And, I believe, T-bone steaks.'

'T-bone steaks?' said Chinese Lady.

'I know, scarcely seen in this country for many years,' said Sir Edwin.

'Nor a decent rib of beef, neither,' said Chinese Lady. 'You'd think, like I mentioned to Lizzy the other day, that they'd stopped growing beef in this country. Next thing you know, we'll have to make do with whale steaks again, like we did during the war, which I never took to. Nor did you. Edwin, where was I?'

'In New York, my dear.'

'Oh, yes, so I was. About them skyscrapers, Felicity wouldn't be able to see any, even if they were as high as the moon.' That logical comment induced in Sir Edwin a smile of appreciation.

'Very true, Maisie, as things are,' he said, 'but what if an operation proved successful?'

'Well, when we go to church on Sunday,' said Chinese Lady, 'we'd best say a prayer for her. I suppose being able to see a skyscraper would be exciting for someone that hadn't seen anything for years and years.'

'But not, I fancy, as exciting as being able to see her husband and daughter,' said Sir Edwin.

'I'm glad you said that, Edwin.' Chinese Lady then frowned. 'I ought to have said it myself. I must be getting a big vague, though

I don't know why. I'm not old yet.'

Sir Edwin smiled again. One had to admire any woman of seventy-eight who insisted she wasn't yet old.

Anneliese and Harry arrived at the house on the corner of Sunray Avenue. The morning was hardly encouraging. It was damp and dull. But the house, with its pre-war frontage of a central door and bay windows on either side, looked welcoming. Lace curtains, of the kind that so upset the aesthetic tastes of the artists, writers and poets of Bloomsbury, hung delicately inside the windows.

Mr Parrish was waiting for them on the doorstep. Fortyish, his moustache was neatly trimmed, his well-fitting overcoat and stylish trilby giving him a spruce appearance. He smiled as Anneliese and Harry walked up the path from the front gate, and he stepped forward to greet them.

'Mr Stevens? Mrs Stevens?'

'Mr Parrish?' said Harry. 'Good morning to you.'

'Happy to make your acquaintance,' said Mr Parrish, and shook hands with them. 'Mr and Mrs Herbison are waiting to meet you and to show you around. This way.' The front door was ajar, and he pushed it open. He stood aside, and Harry and Anneliese entered. They were at once conscious of a house warmed by central heating, and of a

351

square hall with parquet flooring, also a sign of pre-war suburban property development.

The owners appeared, an elderly couple, the woman homely in a jumper and skirt, her husband grey-haired and still a handsome man. He welcomed Anneliese and Harry in pleasant fashion as Mr Parrish made the introductions, while his wife regarded them with interest.

'Not a very nice morning,' said Mr Herbison.

'Typical of November,' said Harry, 'it's never been known to show a liking for people.'

'Our number one enemy, would you say?' smiled Mr Herbison.

'Certainly, I don't call it friendly,' said Harry, 'and I hope it doesn't follow you to the Isle of Wight, where I believe you intend to retire.'

'Oh, we're looking forward to that,' said Mrs Herbison.

'It has a very attractive sound, the Isle of Wight,' said Anneliese.

'Have you never been there?' asked Mr Herbison.

'No, not yet,' said Anneliese, her light accent discernible.

'It's lovely and quiet,' said Mrs Herbison.

'Delightful,' said Mr Parrish. 'Shall we – er–?'

'Yes, of course,' said Mr Herbison, and

addressed the prospective purchasers. 'Allow my wife and myself the pleasure of showing you round.'

The tour began. The house, fully detached, was roomy and well kept. Everything, in fact, was spotless, and the furnishings were tasteful. There was one part of the ground floor which Anneliese thought she would like to change: she would have the wall dividing the modest dining room from the kitchen knocked down. Then one would create a large open-plan kitchen with a dining area, a feature she had noticed in magazine photographs of modern American houses.

Upstairs, there were four bedrooms, two of which were very spacious, a bathroom, an airing cupboard and a useful landing cupboard. All bedrooms were nicely furnished and carpeted. While there was nothing imposing about the house, there was also nothing with which to find serious fault.

Mr Parrish did not attempt to make the tour one of pressurizing sales talk. He did point out the merits of the property, but only in a reasonable way. Perhaps he guessed that Harry and Anneliese were the kind of people who could make up their own minds about the place. And Mr and Mrs Herbison were content to only answer questions, Mrs Herbison glancing at Anneliese with growing interest.

From a back bedroom window, Harry and

Anneliese observed the garden. The rectangular lawn was trim, shrubberies and flower beds tidily kept, although forlorn with winter. They noted a garden shed and a small timber-built greenhouse. At this point the owners and Mr Parrish disappeared to give them a chance to discuss the pros and cons in private.

'Well, Anneliese?' said Harry.

'What do you think?' asked Anneliese.

'I know what we're after, a house with a garden,' said Harry.

'There's the garden,' said Anneliese, 'and we must think about what it would be like in the spring and summer.'

'Very much like a garden,' said Harry.

'Oh, very perceptive, Harry.'

'The house itself, it's nice enough without any outstanding features,' said Harry.

'I could design features,' said Anneliese, 'such as turning the kitchen into a much larger and more attractive one by arranging to do away with the wall dividing it from the dining room. And having a bathroom and shower built into the main bedroom.'

'You've ambitious ideas for the place?' said Harry.

'You have ideas you turn into plots for your stories,' said Anneliese. 'I have ideas for interior design.'

That was true. She had given their Camberwell house character, although unable to suggest any way of improving their tiny back yard, which remained an eyesore.

'And you'd like to follow up these ideas?' said Harry.

'It's such a pleasant area here,' she said, still disinclined to push him. She wanted him to be sure of himself, and to have no regrets about leaving the house he had inherited from his first wife. If Cindy thought her stepmother was oblivious of certain anti-German feelings among people in their immediate neighbourhood, she was mistaken. Anneliese was looking for a new neighbourhood, where she would not feel so crowded or so sensitive. Here, she would still be close to London's West End and its shops and theatres, all so attractive to her, especially now that she and Polly went there together with enjoyable regularity. She had long recognized that Polly's background was upper class, and since she herself came from an aristocratic German family, she saw Polly as a kindred spirit and a delightful friend.

'Well, don't let's hum and ha,' said Harry, 'let's make an offer. After all, Cindy can still get to school from here.'

Mr Parrish appeared.

'How are you finding things?' he asked.

'Favourable,' said Harry.

'I'm delighted to hear you say so,' said the agent.

'It's on the market at three and a half

thousand?' said Harry.

'In view of the fact that you have funds available to pay in full on completion,' said Mr Parrish, 'I could negotiate favourably with you on behalf of the owners.'

'Such nice people,' murmured Anneliese. Knowing Harry wouldn't haggle, she was willing to do so herself. 'We could make an offer of three thousand, two hundred and fifty, don't you think so, Harry?'

'Would that interest the Herbisons, Mr Parrish?' asked Harry.

'I'm sure it would, since they're hoping for a quick sale,' said Mr Parrish. He smiled. 'If they do accept, we must avoid completion on a Saturday. It's their Sabbath, and although they aren't obsessively strict, they do nothing tantamount to business on that day.'

'You mean they're Jewish?' said Harry.

'That's right,' said Mr Parrish. Anneliese bit her lip. 'Shall we go down and talk to them?'

'A good idea if we can get agreement today,' said Harry, glancing at Anneliese. He hadn't missed her moment of discomfiture. He wondered if such reactions would ever leave her.

They went down, and in the pleasant lounge, Mr Parrish mediated on behalf of both vendors and purchasers. When he mentioned the offer of three thousand, two hundred and fifty pounds, the Herbisons looked at each other, but made no comment. Harry said they need not decide now, that they could take their time.

'Mr Herbison, perhaps you and your wife would like to have a few minutes to yourselves,' said Mr Parrish, pleasant and tactful rather than voluble and pushy, even though he hoped for a quick sale satisfactory to all.

'We'll wait in the hall,' said Harry, and he and Anneliese left the lounge.

'Well,' said Mr Herbison.

'Mrs Stevens isn't English, is she?' said Mrs Herbison to Mr Parrish.

'I did notice she had an accent,' said Mr Parrish.

'I don't think it was a French accent,' said Mr Herbison.

'One of the East European countries that suffered under Hitler's atrocious armies, perhaps?' said Mr Parrish.

'I'll never never forgive Hitler and the German people,' said Mrs Herbison.

'I've a feeling Mrs Stevens is Polish,' said Mr Herbison.

'If so, such a charming woman did well to escape both Hitler and Stalin,' said Mr Parrish. 'As to the offer, I think it worth considering, especially as Mr Stevens is financially able to ensure a quick completion, which, I believe, is what you'd like. However,

357

I'll leave you to think it over. Mr Stevens did say you can take your time.'

'No, you needn't leave,' said Mr Herbison. 'We can't overlook the advantage of a quick sale.'

'We'll accept, shall we, instead of delaying, or waiting for another offer?' said Mrs Herbison.

'I think so, yes,' said Mr Herbison.

'Splendid,' said Mr Parrish.

Which meant that when Harry and Anneliese left fifteen minutes later, agreement had been reached and they were in line for a move from Camberwell Road. Neither Mr Herbison nor his wife had asked Anneliese her country of origin. They were simply too polite. They might not have been if they'd suspected Anneliese was German.

Cindy, on arrival home from school, received the news with delight. She hugged her stepmother, kissed her dad and gave him her blessing.

'Oh, we're going to be really happy now,' she said.

'We're not there yet,' said Harry, 'but I don't think there'll be any real snags.'

'You'll soon get over them,' said Cindy, then paused for thought. 'Mind, I don't know if it'll suit me, living closer to that boy James. You know, the one who talks like he's an old man.'

'Do I know someone who talks like an old

lady?' murmured Harry.

'Yes, course you do, Daddy,' said Cindy, 'Mrs Goodwin that comes round collecting for Dr Barnardo's. She's old.'

'Well, all of forty-five,' said Harry.

'Poor old thing,' said Cindy. 'Daddy, I still can't believe that boy James has to kick a ball about on Saturday afternoons unless there's a family funeral.'

'Life's full of the unbelievable, Cindy pet,' said Harry.

Anneliese laughed. Harry and Cindy were so droll.

Chapter Twenty-Eight

In Bristol, Fergus was working his head off to get the new factory fully equipped for production. With the help of his manager, he had recruited a skilled labour force that was scheduled to begin work on the first Monday in December, three weeks later than originally proposed. From Aberdeen, his father was delivering growling complaints into the telephone. Fergus, however, was at the mercy of the equipment workers who seemed to think go-slow periods were natural in this day and age. The contractors offered apologies, which were no consolation to Fergus, and he responded to the effect that by the terms of the contract, they had already forfeited ten per cent of their fee. Sammy and Tommy would have sympathized with his frustrations.

Alice did her very best for him on the evenings when he brought his headaches to her flat. She had discovered a quite effective cure. She had purchased a bottle of Johnnie Walker whisky, and encouraged Fergus to help himself to a wee dram or two on these social occasions.

Fergus had become the pleasantest man,

no longer pushy and intrusive, and Alice was progressively warming to him. On the evenings when pressure of work kept him away, she felt disappointment.

Fergus, of course, was making himself part of her life, and doing so with canny Scottish flair. His objective was marriage. Alice, despite all her bluestocking characteristics, was the only woman he had ever really wanted. So he proceeded slowly and carefully in his subtle courtship of her. True, he kissed her warmly every time he said goodnight, and was noting her increasing responsiveness, but neither mentioned what such kisses would have meant to other couples.

Alice was asking questions of herself.

Did she want marriage, and to Fergus? She hadn't wanted it at the time their previous relationship broke up.

She knew who'd be delighted if she did marry.

Her old-fashioned mum and dad.

Tommy and Vi, in fact, had long accepted that their daughter wasn't of the marrying kind. And having received a long and chatty letter from her, they were talking about her life in Bristol.

'She's not home-loving, that's for sure,' said Tommy. 'It beats me, I tell you. I mean, she couldn't have a better home than this.'

He and Vi were proud of their fine house on Denmark Hill.

'Well, we've been saying for ages that she's entitled to live her own kind of life,' said Vi. 'Mind, it's sad that it's taken her away from us.'

'Yes, and look what's happened because we haven't been able to keep an eye on her,' said Tommy.

'Tommy love, I don't know any parents could expect to keep an eye on a daughter who's twenty-nine,' said Vi.

'Ought to have got married years ago,' muttered Tommy, 'then she'd have had a husband to keep an eye on her. And to see she didn't get in the way of a couple of thieving bank robbers. All that learning didn't help. Now she says she and Fergus have got to wait till January for the trial. But she doesn't say what she feels about having to hang about all that time.'

'Oh, well, she was never impatient,' said Vi, 'she'll just get on with things.'

'With her teaching job?' said Tommy. He muttered again, then growled, 'Be a sight better for her if Fergus bundled her up and took her off to Gretna Green.'

'What's that, Tommy, what did you say?' asked Vi. 'Did I hear you mention Gretna Green?'

'I can't tell a porkie,' replied Tommy. 'What I said was she'd be better off if Fergus took her up to Gretna Green and married her. Before she could argue the toss with him.'

'Tommy love, don't be silly,' said Vi. 'Even if Fergus managed to get her there, Alice wouldn't let him marry her if she didn't want that.'

'Pity,' said Tommy. He and Vi had the attitude to marriage of their kind, that it was the natural state for men and women. And, of course, their own marriage and the marriages of so many of their relations were of a stable nature, never mind the ups and downs. It was true that in the old days when their world was confined to Walworth and Camberwell, they had known wives and husbands to holler at each other, with some wives going as far as to bash husbands with frying pans. But they all stuck it out, they all grew old together. It never occurred to Tommy or Vi that Alice, out in the wider world, might have become acquainted with people who had a much more modern and independent outlook on life, an outlook that did not see marriage as the be-all and end-all of their existence.

But then, neither did it occur to them that Fergus, a man they had known as a plain-speaking Scot, was now conducting a subtle campaign in his renewed relationship with Alice. Mind, she had said nice things about him in her letter, although nothing that

363

pointed to a wedding ring.

'I just hope that when the trial takes place, those robbers are put away for years,' said Vi.

'With hard labour,' said Tommy.

Anneliese kept thinking about the doctor in New York, and the fact that Sir Charles Morgan was now arranging for Felicity to consult him. She could not help feeling very uncomfortable about what was now obvious, that she had made a bad mistake in identifying him as an SS doctor who had used children and adults for his medical experiments at Auschwitz. She suspected now that Boots was right, that her obsession with the fiendish excesses of the SS had caused her imagination to work against her.

She could only hope the Ukrainian doctor would be able to perform a successful operation on Felicity. That would make up for everything of an unhappy nature.

Towards the end of the week, a parcel arrived for Harry at breakfast time. Opening it, he disclosed a copy of his first novel, with a letter from his publishers. It said this was an advance copy, and that his full quota of author's copies would be sent next week, a few days before the official publication date, when it was hoped he and his wife would attend a celebratory reception at the offices.

There it was, the novel, its colourful jacket pristine, its title bold:

MURDER ON THE NIGHT TRAIN

'Harry!' Anneliese exclaimed her delight and excitement. 'How wonderful.'

Harry himself felt a surge of pleasure, and not a little excitement of his own. It was, after all, quite a step up from magazine short stories.

'Crikey, Daddy, you'll be famous,' said Cindy, taking hold of the book for a close look.

'Only if the critics like it and a million people buy it,' said Harry.

'Cindy, let me see it,' said Anneliese, and Cindy passed it to her. Anneliese studied the jacket, then turned pages, her eyes shining for Harry. 'How much is it?' she asked.

'Four pounds and fifteen shillings,' said Harry.

'Wow, if a million people buy it, that'll mean over four million pounds,' breathed Cindy. 'Daddy, we could buy a castle and stables, and have six horses and a butler.'

'Hardly,' said Harry. 'I'm entitled only to seven and a half per cent, and I'll be lucky if I get sales of more than a few thousand. And that'll be mainly for the paperback edition, which will probably go on sale for about two bob.'

'Crikey, what a swindle,' said Cindy. 'Still, never mind, Daddy, you'll still be famous.

Could I take the book to school today and show it to the teachers and my class?'

Anneliese smiled.

'Oh, you'd like to be famous too, Cindy?'

'Not half,' said Cindy. 'Well, we'll all be famous.'

'I don't think you should show it around your school, pet,' said Harry. 'It'll look like swank, or at least as if you're showing off.'

'No, I'll just be proud,' said Cindy.

'Then there's the possibility that it might come back with bits of school dinner sticking to it,' said Harry.

'As if I'd let that happen,' said Cindy. 'Still, perhaps some of the girls might think I'm swanking.'

'Harry, let her take one when you receive the others,' said Anneliese. 'I think Cindy has a right to be proud and to show the book to her friends.'

'Fair enough,' said Harry.

'Oh, groovy,' said Cindy.

'Let me tell you what we'll do to celebrate as a family,' said Harry. 'We'll all go up West on Saturday afternoon to see the matinee performance of *South Pacific*.'

'Harry, will you be able to get tickets at such short notice?' asked Anneliese. 'I think you'll find the show is playing to full houses.'

'I've already got the tickets,' said Harry. 'I knew an advance copy of the novel was coming sometime this week. After the show, we'll all go to Simpson's in the Strand and enjoy one of their hot roasts. I've booked a table. What d'you think of that, my angels?'

'Oh, wow, smashing,' said Cindy.

'Harry, you are quite the nicest man I have ever known,' said Anneliese.

'Crikey, the time, if I don't get a move on, I'll be late for school,' said Cindy, and jumped up. 'Daddy, I really am proud of you,' she said, and kissed the top of his head. 'Bye-bye.' She kissed her stepmother. 'Well, now look, Daddy, Mum's already got her nose in the book.'

'There'll be fireworks if it ends up with marmalade all over it,' said Harry.

On Saturday they had a wonderful time at the theatre, where they enjoyed a sparkling performance by Mary Martin, playing the lead in *South Pacific*. And that was topped by an early supper at Simpson's, which Anneliese thought delightful and Cindy thought magical. Harry ended up as much the most popular man in the lives of his wife and daughter, not a bad achievement for an airy-fairy bloke who sometimes forgot what time of the day it was.

First thing on Monday morning, the area trade union leader, Mr Barney Burridge, paid the Adams factory in Bethnal Green the compliment of calling in person, complete with bowler hat. He asked to see Tommy, and was shown in.

'Morning, Tommy me old mate, how's yer workload?'

'As much as we can cope with,' said Tommy, 'and might I ask the reason for you enquiring?'

'Well, it's like this,' said Burridge, taking a seat without being invited. 'The workforce of the Peterson factory happens to be coming out in legitimate protest about conditions, the kind that mean they're working elbow to elbow and can't swing a kitten, let alone a cat. It's making them sweat, and as yer know, Tommy, those old sweatshop conditions ain't allowed these days.'

'What's all this got to do with us?' asked Tommy, growling a bit.

'Well, I've got me officials talking to other workforces about coming out in support, which is a legal step. I'm calling on you meself – any tea going, by the way?'

'We give our workers coffee in the mornings,' said Tommy, 'and listen here, if you've come to ask them to do a walkout on me, I ain't in favour.'

'Now, Tommy, I've come to put me request to you personally,' said Burridge. 'All right, I'll have a cup of coffee.'

'You're too early,' said Tommy. 'Ten o'clock's the time, and I've got to tell you I don't want to be requested.'

'Tommy, is it helpful to talk like that?' said Burridge, pained beneath his bowler. The bowler remained expressionless. Some bowlers could reflect their owners' moods, such as City bowlers. City bowlers could look perky or worried, according to the state of the stock market. 'We've got to have solidarity, y'know.'

'I've got it,' said Tommy, 'I've got a workforce as solid as they come on behalf of production.'

'I'm speaking of union solidarity,' said Burridge.

'Thought you'd come to that,' said Tommy.

'My pleasure,' said Burridge, who knew the Adams set-up with its large factory was important to Bethnal Green, and would be more so when the extension was built and buzzing. 'Now, your workers being unionized at last, they've got a duty to support their brothers and sisters. Or, well, I ain't keen on upsetting them, Tommy, but I've got to mention that if they don't support the strikers, they'll have to put up with some unkind language from pickets.'

'Funny thing,' said Tommy, 'I thought you'd come to pickets as well. Might I ask about the language?'

'Well, they can expect to be called blacklegs and scabs,' said Burridge.

'Thought so,' said Tommy.

'Not nice, I agree,' said Burridge, 'but it's the degree of honest umbrage that brings it on, y'know.'

'When's the Peterson workforce coming out?' asked Tommy.

'As soon as they don't start work on Thursday morning,' said Burridge.

'As soon as they don't what?' asked Tommy.

'Let's say just before they start work,' said Burridge. 'We've given the management due notice, as is required.'

'All right, leave it with me,' said Tommy.

'Knew you'd co-operate, Tommy,' said Burridge, and since he felt he wasn't going to be invited to stay for coffee, he departed, his bowler hat heading for a nearby café.

Tommy sat musing, talking to himself. I've got trouble, union trouble, which Boots and Sammy and me knew we'd get. I don't like trouble, I like a quiet life. I'm not an awkward bloke, or Vi wouldn't have stuck with me all these years, and there's been a lot of them. Sometimes, when I think of the days when I ran Sammy's market stall for him, it seems like a hundred years. And sometimes it seems like only yesterday. That don't alter the fact that Vi and me have come a long way and never had a rough and tumble. One of the best is Vi, a real comfort to a bloke, but what I need now is a brain. I've got my own, but I'm not proud, and I know it ain't up with Sammy's or Boots's.

He phoned the head office at Camberwell.

'Adams Enterprises, good morning,' said the switchboard girl.

'Tommy Adams here.'

'Oh, good morning, Mister Tommy.'

'Same to you, Lily,' said Tommy. 'Put me through to brother Sammy.'

'I'm afraid Mister Sammy's doing a round of the shops, but Mr Adams is in.'

Tommy grinned to himself, knowing how it got up Sammy's nose that it was only Boots whom the staff referred to as Mr Adams.

'He'll do, Lily.' In fact, thought Tommy, Boots's brain nearly always has the edge.

'Hello, Tommy?' said Boots.

'Glad you're awake,' said Tommy.

'So am I,' said Boots, 'it means I'm still alive.' That remark, or something like it, was often made by Boots, and Tommy knew it meant he was never less than bloody grateful for surviving two wars that had cost the lives of unlucky millions, including six million Jews. The Herbisons, whose house Harry and Anneliese Stevens wanted to buy, were Jewish. Did they know yet that Anneliese was German? Well, I ain't going to tell them, thought Tommy. 'Where are you, still there, Tommy, or gone away?' asked Boots.

Tommy, coming to, said, 'Still here, Boots, just thinking.'

'What's on your mind, then?'

'Union trouble,' said Tommy, and explained. Boots said it was no more than they'd all expected from time to time, once the workforce had been unionized. Tommy said he knew that twice over, but what was the answer?

'It's with Peterson's,' said Boots.

'What help is that?' asked Tommy.

'What kind of factory have they got?' asked Boots.

'A going one,' said Tommy.

'I mean, d'you know if Burridge is on firm ground, Tommy? Are the workers squeezed for space? Do they sweat?'

'Well, I know they don't have as much room as our girls,' said Tommy, 'but I haven't heard any serious complaint.'

'Right,' said Boots, 'give me the phone number of the local branch of the Factory Inspectorate. They're bound to have offices in that industrial area. And you're bound to have their address and phone number on one of your files, aren't you? With the name of the bloke in charge.'

'Got you,' said Tommy. His office door was open. Burridge had departed without closing it. He saw his nephew Jimmy passing by. 'Jimmy!'

'At your service,' said Jimmy, putting his head in.

'Your filing system – look up the name and phone number of the local Inspector of Factories. Your Uncle Boots wants it pronto.'

'Pronto's coming it a bit, but for Uncle Boots I'll perform a miracle,' said Jimmy, and vanished.

Only a minute later, Boots had the required information embracing phone number and name of the chief officer, D. Wheeler. Thirty minutes after that, he rang Tommy back.

'Got the answer, Boots?' said Tommy.

'I can tell you I've had a very interesting and rewarding conversation with Deirdre,' said Boots.

'Eh?' said Tommy.

'Deirdre,' repeated Boots, and explained that D. Wheeler turned out to be a Miss Deirdre Wheeler, senior officer of the branch in question. Tommy said trust you to land on a female. Boots said landing on females was something any respectable married man should avoid, otherwise he'd be in trouble not only with the law, but his wife as well. Tommy said now tell me a bedtime story.

The issue, said Boots, was whether conditions for the workers at Peterson's really were of a sweatshop kind. If so, no factory inspector would have issued a certificate. It so happened, according to Deirdre–

'Is this going to be serious?' asked Tommy.

'Satisfying,' said Boots, and continued. It so happened, he said, that the lady, not being the usual kind of reserved Civil Servant, was forthcoming with the information that no inspection had taken place at Peterson's factory since 1947.

'Do you have a problem about that, Mr Adams?' she had asked.

'Indirectly, yes,' said Boots. 'The workforce at our own factory in Bethnal Green is being asked to support a strike at Peterson's over what the union claims are sweatshop conditions. I thought, naturally, that that suggested the factory wasn't up to scratch. Is it possible for you to make a further inspection before Thursday?'

'Well, I really don't know—'

'Believe me, I'd be extremely grateful,' said Boots, 'and your office would be able to satisfy itself in the matter of either renewing Peterson's certificate or cancelling it until necessary improvements were made.'

'Oh, yes, I see,' said Miss Deirdre Wheeler, and Boots supposed she saw all too well that the reputation of the Inspectorate was at stake. 'Yes, I understand, Mr Adams.'

'It's a pleasure to have spoken to you,' said Boots. 'One isn't always so lucky. Would it be impertinent to ask you to let me know the outcome?'

'Strictly, the outcome should only be known to Peterson's management,' said Miss Wheeler.

'Of course,' said Boots, 'one must observe the rules. I wouldn't dream of quarrelling with strictly.'

'Perhaps in this case—'

'How kind,' said Boots.

'I'll arrange an official visit to Peterson's factory for tomorrow or Wednesday,' said Miss Wheeler. 'Advance notification, of course, isn't necessary.'

'So I believe,' said Boots. Such officials invariably arrived without warning. Regulations allowed them to catch factory owners with their pants down, in a manner of speaking. 'Well, I'll leave the matter with you, Miss Wheeler. My thanks for such helpful co-operation. Again, a pleasure to have talked to you.'

'Not at all,' said Miss Wheeler. 'What is your phone number?'

Boots, seeing this as an implication that she would get back to him, gave it. The lady said goodbye and rang off.

Tommy, having received the gist of this, said, 'Well, if I knew how you manage to make women talk sweet, I'd go in for some of it meself. Listen, all this knocks Burridge off his perch. He can't call a strike if Peterson's factory is passed OK for the workers, nor if improvements are ordered and started. Peterson's can lay the workers off legit, y'know, while the job's being done.'

'I do know,' said Boots, 'and certainly, there'd be no point in going on strike pending job completion. What we'd like, of course, is to be able to give Burridge the news before Thursday morning.'

'Which news Deirdre might come up with in good time?' said Tommy.

'I've a feeling she will,' said Boots. 'I'll contact you when she does.'

'Good on yer,' said Tommy, 'and I won't mention to Polly that you talked sweet to her. How is Polly, by the way?'

'Alive and well, and keeping her fingers crossed for Felicity,' said Boots.

'Well, we all are,' said Tommy. 'Anyway, ta for doing a good job, Boots.'

'You're welcome,' said Boots.

Chapter Twenty-Nine

On Tuesday afternoon, Sir Charles Morgan made a further phone call to Felicity. He was, he said, pleased to inform her that he'd arranged for the consultation in New York to take place on the sixth of January. It was the earliest date available, since Dr Rokovsky was not only very busy, he was also scheduled for a lecture tour in California during the better part of December.

Felicity, taking a leap into excitement, said, 'Oh, that's great news, Sir Charles. I shan't mind waiting until January.'

'It's a positive first step,' said Sir Charles, and suggested she and Tim ought to be in New York by not later than the second or third of January to give her time to orientate herself. Also, she could expect to find New York very cold. Felicity said she would prepare for that, and get Tim to book an overnight flight some days in advance of the consultation. Sir Charles said he would mail her all relevant details, and include a letter from himself for Dr Rokovsky. He also said the extent of her stay would depend on what Dr Rokovsky decided after making his diagnosis. Felicity thanked him excessively for everything. He wished her the very best of luck and said goodbye.

Felicity could not resist the immediate temptation of ringing Tim at the office. Tim, of course, went over the moon with her, an accomplishment not every couple could achieve from the intangible springboard of a telephone line. He said he'd book an overnight flight from London Airport four days in advance of the consultation. That, he said, would give them time not only to acclimatize but to see the sights of the skyscraper city.

'Lead the way, lover,' said Felicity, 'but you'll have to do the seeing for me.'

The following day, Miss Deirdre Wheeler contacted Boots to let him know the inspection of Peterson's factory had taken place, and that the only alteration necessary was the removal of eight workbenches to an area at the back of the main workshop. The management had now effected the change. Would that eliminate the indirect problem Mr Adams had spoken about?

'I'm sure it will,' said Boots. 'Miss Wheeler, I'm delighted with your co-operation and efficiency.'

'Thank you, Mr Adams. Goodbye.'

Boots passed the good news to Tommy. Tommy phoned Barney Burridge, who did not think the news good at all. He suggested sabotage had taken place and said he would like to know who'd done it.

'I don't get you,' said Tommy, 'what sabotage you talking about?'

'Sabotage of a proposed protest strike on the part of certain workers that happen to be sweating at their jobs,' said Burridge.

'You've got me there,' said Tommy. 'I only know what Peterson's management came up with about fifteen minutes ago, that their workers have now got more room.'

Burridge said what he'd like to know was why Tommy got in touch with Peterson's. Tommy stretched the truth a bit. He said he'd had the proposed strike on his mind, and simply decided to find out why Peterson's had let working conditions get so bad. He was informed about the visit of two inspectors, and what had been done. He didn't say Boots had informed him.

'Now, now, Tommy,' said Burridge, 'like I've told you before, I wasn't born yesterday, y'know.'

'That's a coincidence,' said Tommy, 'nor was I. But I still ain't guilty of any sabotage. Bobby Adams, a nephew of mine, was, but only during the war, when he sort of lurked about with the French Resistance.'

'All right, so you've got a war hero in yer family,' said Burridge, 'but I still wasn't born yesterday. To me sorrow, I've got to conclude you've had some little talks with the local factory inspectors.'

'On me honour, and on the Bible, if you like,' said Tommy, 'I haven't seen or spoken to any of 'em since this factory of ours was built and ready for production, when they certified us.' He coughed and hastily retracted. 'I mean the factory.'

'Well, someone got to be a clever Dick,' said Burridge, good fellowship on the wane.

'Leave off,' said Tommy. 'Blimey, you ought to be happy that your union members at Peterson's don't work in sweatshop conditions, and don't need to lose wages by going on strike.'

'Well, I'm happy about that, naturally, of course I am,' said Burridge, 'but I—' He growled under his breath.

Yes, I know, not half I do, thought Tommy, you'd be happier if they had a reason to strike.

'Cheer up, Barney,' he said, 'Christmas is coming.'

'I'm relieved it's not tomorrow,' said Burridge, 'I don't feel like crackers right now. Or Christmas pudden. All right, so long, Tommy.' He rang off.

One up to me, thought Tommy. And Boots.

Sammy, of course, when he heard all about this from Boots, showed a grin a mile wide.

'Got to hand it to you, Boots old cock,

you've never been just a pretty face,' he said. 'You're a thinking bloke as well.'

'So you've said before, Sammy.'

'Well, it's all in the family, Boots, so hang onto it,' said Sammy. 'By the way, I like the news Tim gave me about Felicity and New York, don't you?'

'It's the kind of news they've been hoping for, Sammy.'

'Could be a happy New Year for those two, Boots.'

'And for little Jennifer,' said Boots.

'Hello?'

It was evening, and Anneliese had answered the ringing phone.

'Polly here, Anneliese.'

'Oh, how nice,' said Anneliese.

'I thought you'd like to know that Sir Charles Morgan has arranged for Felicity to see Dr Rokovsky in New York on the sixth of January,' said Polly.

'Ah, yes?' said Anneliese. 'I'm very happy to know that, I really am. It must mean so much to her.'

'You can be sure of that,' said Polly. 'Now, about our excursion to town for Christmas shopping, and a swanky lunch for two discriminating ladies whose husbands are easy-going enough to let us wander into the wilds of the West End with open cheque-books. I have a date to suggest.'

'A moment while I take all that in,' said Anneliese. She laughed. 'Yes, I've taken it in, so which day do you wish to suggest?'

'Today week?' said Polly.

'Yes, that will be fine,' said Anneliese.

'I'll pick you up in my car at ten,' said Polly.

'Ten, yes,' said Anneliese, 'I am looking forward to it already.'

'Be happy, ducky,' said Polly.

'Polly, I am a woman blessed,' said Anneliese, 'and very happy for Harry now that his first novel has been published.'

'Oh, yes, congratulations to you both,' said Polly. 'Wildly exciting. Boots and I mean to buy a copy as soon as it appears in our bookshop.'

'No, you are not to,' said Anneliese. 'Harry has several author's copies and is going to give you one.'

'Signed, please,' said Polly.

'Everything that is happening makes me think I have so much where before I only had years of nightmares,' said Anneliese.

Polly thought of her own years, the years when all she wanted was a man who belonged to someone else. They had not given her nightmares, but they had been tortuous. Perhaps no woman should want a man as much as she had wanted Boots. It reduced her and wrecked her self-esteem. Only eventual possession made her normal again. Normal, but with a lovely touch of giddy delight.

'Oh, you and I, Anneliese, we're both blessed,' she said lightly. 'By the way, did you and Harry find that house in Sunray Avenue to your liking?'

'Polly, we made an offer there and then,' said Anneliese, 'and the owners accepted. But I felt very uncomfortable when Harry and I were talking to the agent about our offer. He said the owners were Jewish.'

'That opened up a raw nerve, did it?' said Polly. 'Such moments shouldn't. You've nothing on your conscience.'

'Hitler's Germany is on my conscience,' said Anneliese.

'Did you tell the agent you were German?' asked Polly.

'No, I–'

'Well, don't,' said Polly. 'Let the owners go happily off to their retirement in the Isle of Wight. Ignorance is bliss, ducky, and should be for a retired couple.'

'But would they sell the house to us if they weren't ignorant, if they did know I was German?' asked Anneliese.

'You're not,' said Polly, 'you're here, you're happily married and you're the grand-daughter of an English lady from Bath. You couldn't be more English than that, unless she'd been your mother. Buy the house and enjoy the garden. I'll come round and show you how to grow your own vegetables. Boots says my runner beans would win prizes every year.'

'I find it fascinating that a woman like you grows vegetables,' said Anneliese.

'What kind of a woman do you think I am, then?' asked Polly, tickled.

'Well, you are so – so–'

'Upper crust?' Polly laughed. Her voice always gave away her aristocratic roots, although she was entirely cosmopolitan in her outlook. 'In the summer of 1914, ducky, I was a debutante in ostrich feathers, and very upper crust, don't you know. Only a month later, the First World War reared its ugly head. I joined an ambulance unit, and the day I arrived in France was the day I left ostrich feathers behind me for ever.'

'Perhaps my earlier years were like yours,' said Anneliese, 'but while your ostrich feathers probably came to no harm, mine were trampled in the mud and crushed by Himmler's jackboots. Do you understand what I mean?'

'Yes, but forget Himmler, forget his jackboots,' said Polly. 'I repeat, you're here, and your life belongs with Harry and Cindy, not with the swastika. That's dead and buried, thank God and all His angels. Next week you and I go Christmas shopping to buy something special for our families, and perhaps something extra special for our-

384

selves. We deserve it.'

'Polly, such a good friend you are,' said Anneliese, and then heard a girl's voice interrupt.

'Mummy, are you going to be on the phone all night? Only we're all waiting to start this game of Monopoly.'

'I'll be right with you, Gemma,' said Polly. 'Anneliese, I must ring off now.'

'Thank you for calling me,' said Anneliese. She replaced the phone and went up to Harry's study to tell him that an appointment with Dr Rokovsky in New York had been fixed for Felicity. Harry, expressing heartfelt approval, refrained from making any mention of Anneliese's identification mistake. He knew how upset she was about that. 'And next week,' she said, 'Polly and I are going to do Christmas shopping in the West End.'

'Rather you than me,' said Harry, 'Christmas shopping isn't my cup of tea.'

'Such a funny expression, your cup of tea,' said Anneliese.

'Well, m'lady, you know how barmy the English are,' said Harry.

'I am not always believing that,' said Anneliese, 'but I know I like barmy much better than proper.'

'Meaning Germans are more proper than barmy?' smiled Harry.

'Do you think I am?' asked Anneliese.

'No, I don't,' said Harry, 'I think you're the cat's whiskers.'

'I know what that means,' said Anneliese. 'Harry?'

'Well?' said Harry, divorced from his typewriter for the moment.

'All men should be like you. Tell me, please, what are you writing?'

'The same new thriller I started months ago,' said Harry. 'And yesterday's high jinks inspired me to get a move on.' Yesterday, he and Anneliese had attended the publishers' reception to celebrate the issue of his first novel. They'd both been fêted, and Anneliese had been asked what she thought of her talented husband. Anneliese replied that she thought him the kind of man any woman would like as a husband, which was why she married him before someone else did. Later, a friendly bloke with a Mexican moustache told Harry how divinely lucky he was. Harry said for getting my novel published? No, anyone can write a novel, said the friendly bloke, but you alone, my dear fellow, are married to exquisite poetry in its divinest form. Which made Harry think him one of those avant-garde characters of Chelsea who talked like a bunch of lilies. Still, it was decent of him to say something like that about a woman he knew to be German. Anneliese's origins had inevitably come to light at the reception, but no-one had shown any distaste or shock. Harry knew from what his agent had told him, that publishers' head offices were full of liberals.

'I wonder how your first novel will sell?' mused Anneliese.

'Let's wait and see,' said Harry.

Chapter Thirty

The following Monday, Harry signed the contract for the purchase of the house in Sunray Avenue, when his solicitor advised him he would do his best to advance the completion date. Meanwhile, Harry had put his own house on the market, with Parrish and Partners as the agents.

The next day, Anneliese, who had been a little edgy, combined a local shopping excursion with a visit to her doctor, a second visit. The shopping was a sociable and pleasant chore, for the shopkeepers had come to like her, despite knowing she was German. The visit to the doctor was quite different, however, and when she emerged from the surgery, she made her way home like a woman in a daze.

'Harry!' She called up to him as soon as she entered the hall. 'Harry!'

'What's up, is the house on fire?' called Harry, coming out of his study. 'I hope not, we've got prospective purchasers arriving this evening.'

'Harry, come down!'

Harry descended the stairs. Anneliese was waiting for him on the ground floor, her face flushed.

'Anneliese, have you got a fever, is it flu?'

'No, nothing like that.' Anneliese took a deep breath. 'Harry, what do you think? I'm going to have a baby.'

'You're what?' said Harry, mouth falling open.

'Darling, I'm pregnant. Dr Stockwell says so.

'You've been to see him?' said Harry. 'You didn't mention it.'

'No, I thought – oh, I thought all the wrong things, that the test was bound to be negative,' said Anneliese, sounding breathless.

'You had a test?' said Harry, trying to take in this hair-raising news from his wife, now in her thirty-seventh year. 'You didn't mention that, either.'

'No. Well, you see, I couldn't believe what it might mean,' said Anneliese, blue eyes dark with emotion. 'Harry, it isn't negative. I really am going to have a baby.'

'God save all sinking ships,' said Harry, 'what a fantastic woman you are.' He swept her into his arms.

'Harry, you're pleased?'

'I'll say I am, I'm tickled up to my ears.'

'And do you think Cindy will mind?'

'If I know Cindy, she'll be tickled up to her pigtails,' said Harry.

'Harry, I felt I must be dreaming,' said Anneliese. 'But imagine, it's true. I'm to

389

have your child, an English child.'

'A second great-grandchild of the one-time lady of Bath, the English grandmother of you and your sister,' smiled Harry. Her sister Brigid had a little girl.

'Oh, yes, how happy Grandmama would be,' said Anneliese. 'And I must phone Brigid this afternoon. Harry, I am now thinking there is something we really must have.'

'A pram?' said Harry.

'That in time, yes,' said Anneliese, 'but I meant the garden of the house in Sunray Avenue. It would be much much better for the child and for Cindy than a back yard.'

'Roses round the door, and garden deckchairs, here we come,' said Harry, and kissed her like a man of great good fortune.

Cindy received the happy news when she arrived home from school, and, as Harry had predicted, she was tickled all over. Which delighted Anneliese. A woman could never be sure of a stepdaughter's reactions.

Days went by.

Anneliese and Polly enjoyed their Christmas shopping expedition in the West End. They spent the morning in Bond Street dress shops that offered the very latest in French fashions. Such shops were delightfully familiar to Polly and remindful to Anneliese of the elegant pre-war establishments on

Berlin's Unter den Linden. Anneliese did not fail to notice how gushingly Polly was received and fussed over. Polly took all that in her stride, introducing Anneliese as a friend with a highly discriminating taste for fashion wear. So show us nothing that too many other women are wearing, she said. By too many, she meant not more than one.

They bought dresses, separates, and hats. After lunch, they would buy Christmas presents for Boots and Harry, and for Cindy and the twins. Polly drove her car around, parking in outrageous fashion on yellow lines outside some shops. However, traffic in the West End, apart from hordes of buses and proliferating taxis, was not what it obviously threatened to be in the future. Even so, that did not prevent Polly from having a confrontation with one of the West End's new symbols of the law, traffic wardens. However, she refrained from argument, and accepted a ticket with such a sweet smile that the warden looked as if he had been the one to commit an offence.

Later, when Polly arrived with Anneliese at a chic Mayfair restaurant for lunch, she parked outside as if she owned the place. A smart, gold-braided doorman stepped forward and opened the driver's door.

'Would madam mind moving forward a few yards to leave room for taxis to drop off customers?' he asked politely.

'Happily, old sport,' said Polly. He closed the door and Polly did as requested. He opened her door again, and she and Anneliese alighted. 'Would you keep an eye on my old banger?' asked Polly. It was laden with parcels.

'Certainly, madam, with pleasure,' said the doorman, correctly sensing a decent tip.

'There's a good old scout,' said Polly.

How easily she relates to people of all kinds, thought Anneliese, and who would think she was approaching sixty?

It was over lunch that she told Polly she was expecting Harry's child. Polly, absolutely enchanted, at once suggested ordering a bottle of champagne.

'Polly, no, no,' said Anneliese, 'we have this bottle of wine to finish, and more shopping to do. To share a whole bottle of champagne as well as the wine would make us – well–'

'Squiffy?' said Polly.

'That is the same as being drunk?' said Anneliese.

'Not a bit, just happy,' said Polly, 'and the occasion calls for the bubbly and for us to let our hair down. Let's leave the wine, ducky, let's go for the bubbly.'

So they had champagne and an extended lunch, extended to the point where Polly suggested doing the rest of the shopping next week. She wished, she said, to be home before the twins arrived back from school at about four-thirty. It was a thing with her, to always be there for Gemma and James, unless circumstances were exceptional.

When they left the restaurant at three-twenty, the brief November daylight was beginning to fade. The doorman received his tip, a large one, and noted the two elegant ladies had far more sparkle than the weather. Neither, however, was tipsy. Vitality, that was what it was. The younger one, a blonde, gave him imaginative thoughts of what he'd like for Christmas, not half.

When they reached the Elephant and Castle and its reshaped exits in the afternoon gloom, Polly took the one into the Walworth Road. Driving towards Camberwell, thoughts of Emily, Boots's first wife, entered her mind. Walworth was where she had been born and bred, and where, as the girl next door, she had grown up with Boots to become his wife, the mother of Tim, the adoptive mother of darling Rosie and the stepmother of melodramatic Eloise. Emily. A lively and irrepressible cockney woman who always had her suspicions about my feelings for Boots, she mused. Emily. Killed during a German daylight raid, and now at rest in Southwark Cemetery. How tragic, and why do I always feel guilty about her death? Because I know that if it hadn't happened, I would never have had Boots, or Gemma and

James. I would now be a crotchety and bitter old has-been, without–

'Polly!'

Anneliese's warning came just in time. Polly jammed her foot on the brake, and the car came to a shuddering halt only inches from a crawling lorry. Unfortunately, the driver of the car that was on her tail, seeing warning brake lights too late, could not avoid a minor collision.

'Oh, dear,' said Anneliese.

'Are you all right?' asked Polly, concerned for Anneliese's delicate condition.

'I am fine, yes, really, and feeling sympathy for your embarrassment,' said Anneliese.

'Oh, well, now for the reckoning,' said Polly. 'Sit tight, Anneliese.' She alighted. The angry driver of the other car, a gleaming black Daimler, was already out. Pedestrians stopped to watch as the drivers confronted each other. Both were women.

'You are an idiot,' said the offended one, 'you–' She gaped. 'Oh, is this true?'

'Dear Mrs Davidson, can it be?' said Polly, gazing at a flushed face beneath a mink fur hat. Yes, it was true, here was Mrs Davidson, the mother of Cathy. She was a handsome woman with Russian blood, a fancy for Boots, and a house and a millionaire sugar daddy in Paris. 'I'm terribly sorry,' said Polly, 'and must apologize for pulling up so suddenly. Is there much damage?'

She noted no more than a slightly dented bumper, while ignoring onlookers hoping to see something like a female boxing match. Traffic was skirting the stationary cars, male drivers grinning.

Mrs Davidson, wrapped in furs, was quivering a bit. Confusion had arrived to interfere with vexation.

'Mrs Adams, you must realize I had no chance of avoiding hitting you,' she said.

You would have had every chance, if you hadn't been riding on my tail, thought Polly. And in such collisions, responsibility was always that of the following driver. There was a dent in the rear of her own car, but she smiled sweetly.

'Dear Mrs Davidson, I really am so sorry,' she said. 'Please send me the bill for the repairs. Yes, you must. It's extraordinary to meet you like this. I thought you were in Paris.'

'I've had to come back for a week, by the car ferry, to settle certain things with my solicitors,' said Mrs Davidson. 'It's really most irritating.'

She means me, thought Polly, not her legal affairs.

'Well, let's go on our way and not encumber the traffic any more, shall we, dear lady? I do wish this reunion had been a happier one. Don't forget to send me the repair bill – oh, and do remember us to Cathy.'

'Yes, very well,' said Mrs Davidson, and without asking after Boots or the twins, she got back into her car.

'Goodbye,' called Polly, and Mrs Davidson made a gesture with her gloved right hand. Polly slipped back into her own car, started the engine and drove away. Mrs Davidson followed, but at a distance.

'Polly, what happened?' asked Anneliese, who had been tempted to get out and witness the exchanges.

'One of those coincidences that make some of us believe the world is too small,' said Polly, and explained.

'The woman is Russian?' said Anneliese.

'A quarter Russian,' said Polly.

'Ah, so?' said Anneliese. 'That is enough to make me spit. Why did you offer to pay for the damage?'

'Because, ducky, I dislike the lady, but would rather do the civilized thing than punch her on the nose.'

Anneliese smiled.

'Polly, you are very civilized,' she said. 'Tell me, was it the champagne that made you almost hit the truck?'

'Good heavens, no,' said Polly, entering Camberwell Road, 'it was thoughts of a woman I once knew, a woman who used to live around here.'

'And where is she now?' asked Anneliese.

'In her grave,' said Polly, and sighed a little.

In a while, she signalled a right turn, moved to the crown of the road, and with oncoming traffic at a distance, drove carefully through the alleyway to park the car in the spacious front yard of Harry's house. 'There, Anneliese,' she said, 'you're home, with your parcels.'

'Except for the accident, it's been a wonderful day,' said Anneliese.

'One could say you've wet your baby's head with champagne,' said Polly. 'We'll do the rest of our shopping next week, by which time, with Mrs Davidson back in Paris, we'll avoid having her climb up our backs.'

They looked at each other and laughed.

Boots and the twins were intrigued by Polly's account of her clash with Mrs Davidson in the Walworth Road.

'How did she take it?' asked Boots.

'With flashing eyes until she saw I was the guilty party,' said Polly. 'Then our confrontation became civilized.' She smiled. 'Up to a point,' she added. 'There's a dent in the back of my old banger.'

'And she has a bent bumper?' said Boots.

'Better than a punch on her nose,' said Polly.

'Mummy!' exclaimed Gemma in protest. 'You simply couldn't do that in front of people.'

'Oh, I think the people looking on hoped I

would,' said Polly.

'Instead of which you offered to pay her costs?' said Boots.

'It settled the confrontation,' said Polly.

'Very civilized,' said Boots.

'Yes, Anneliese thought so,' said Polly. 'By the way, she's happily expectant.'

'Well, bless the lady,' said Boots.

'I suppose you know what it means,' said Gemma to her brother.

'She's expecting a postal order?' said James.

'You're hopeless,' said Gemma. 'It means she's going to have a baby.'

'Well, it's nothing to do with me,' said James.

'Daddy, that son of yours is getting pottier,' said Gemma.

'Most dads have some kind of problem,' said Boots, 'but other things make up for it.'

'I had a postcard of the Eiffel Tower from Cathy the other day,' mused James.

'Yes, we know,' said Gemma, 'she told you she was having a wonderful time and signed it as your sweetheart.'

'That confused me a bit,' said James.

'It scared me,' said Polly. 'James, for the umpteenth time let me remind you that this family is never ever going to be related to Mrs Davidson.'

'Right, Mum, I've got your meaning,' said James. 'Well, I've had it for some time now.'

'We all have,' said Boots.

'Supper's nearly on the table!' Flossie made herself heard from the kitchen.

'I like our Flossie,' said James.

'Then you'd best marry her instead of Cathy Davidson when you're older,' said Gemma.

'Anything for a quiet life, James,' said Boots, as they made their way to the dining room.

Chapter Thirty-One

December arrived and with it, a letter for Phoebe from Philip. She read it at breakfast.

'Dear Phoebe,

'I'm officially hospitalized, having fallen when getting out of the plane on my first training flight. I don't know how it happened, I was all right one sec, then doubled up on the ground the next. My instructor wasn't a bit pleased, and when my sergeant came up he talked about certain cadets being on a par with clumsy camels. Actually, I couldn't repeat his exact words, not to a girl as young and innocent as you, but I could confide them to your dad when I next see him.

'It all means I won't be able to have any weekend leaves until my leg's working again. That's gloomy, that is, and it's making me think about you keeping safe and sound yourself, so don't go out in the fog in case you walk into a lamp-post and get yourself wounded. When I've been measured for crutches, I'll hop to a phone box and ring you. If my present condition upsets you, be brave and don't faint. If you want to write a letter of sympathy, I'll be pleased to hear from you. You needn't send any grapes. Love, Philip.

'PS. You needn't tell my parents, I've written to them as well.'

'I can't believe this,' said Phoebe to her mum and dad.

'What's the letter all about, then?' asked Sammy.

'And who's it from?' asked Susie, looking every inch an attractive woman of forty-five, which was nice going considering she was fifty.

'It's from Philip,' said Phoebe, 'and he's been acting like a clumsy camel.'

'He says so, does he?' asked Sammy, enjoying his breakfast of bacon and egg. Susie was never short of eggs. Rosie and Matthew kept her supplied, as they did with other members of the family, all at an agreed price. 'Might I ask what this particular clumsy camel has been up to?'

'It's his sergeant who called him that,' said Phoebe, 'and I'll tell you what he's been up to. He broke his leg falling off a training plane.'

'He did what?' said Susie. 'D'you mean when the plane was up in the air?'

'No, when it was on the ground,' said Phoebe, 'and now he's in hospital feeling sorry for himself and hoping I'll write him a letter of sympathy.'

'Well, you should,' said Susie. 'After all, he is your boyfriend.'

'Oh, would you say that's official?' asked Phoebe.

'Boyfriends aren't official,' said Susie, 'they're simply nice to have around.'

'I mean, do you and Daddy approve?' asked Phoebe.

'Of course,' said Susie.

'Oh, I'll write him a letter of sympathy, then,' said Phoebe.

'You were going to, anyway, weren't you?' said Sammy.

'Yes, but sort of formal,' said Phoebe.

'What's sort of formal?' asked Sammy, a grin lurking. His adopted daughter was a bit of a character. Talk about the family being full up with characters of the female kind, right up to Chinese Lady herself. 'Come on, what's sort of formal?'

'Well, it means you sign yourself "yours faithfully",' said Phoebe.

'And now?' said Susie.

'I can sign it "your comfort in adversity",' said Phoebe. Susie shrieked with laughter, and Sammy's grin broke out. 'I didn't say anything funny,' said Phoebe.

'Yes, you did, and you know it, you tease,' said Susie.

'Phoebe, me pet, finish your breakfast,' said Sammy, 'we'll be leaving for the office in five minutes.'

'Yes, Dad,' said Phoebe. 'Oh, by the way, Philip's broken leg has made him think about my welfare, and he says I'm not to go out in the fog in case I walk into a lamppost and wound myself.'

Collapse of her mum and dad.

It made her dad a bit late driving her to their work.

Much to Felicity's excitement, she experienced that which Sir Charles Morgan had considered a definite step towards a natural healing process. She had a second clear vision while groping for a hankie in a top drawer of her dressing table. With the hankie in her hand, it suddenly leapt to her eyes, the white cambric lace-hemmed and almost dazzling. There it was. Her breath rushed from her as she glanced towards the mirror, and the mirror reflected her own self in an ivy-green dress. She stared at her face, and wondered dizzily why it was that after years of stumbling around in the dark she showed no lines, no haggard hollows. For a long minute, the vision remained clear before darkness slowly descended again. The excitement affected her knees, weakening them, and she sat down at the dressing table. She drew in needed breath.

Surely, this meant that the New York doctor would diagnose the present condition of her eyes as favourable for an operation.

The excitement took her downstairs to the telephone, and she made a call to the private consulting rooms of Sir Charles Morgan. Informed by the receptionist that he was unavailable at the moment, she left a message. He rang back late in the afternoon, listened intently to her and asked questions. Felicity left him in no doubt of the clarity of her vision and of the exciting fact that it had lasted a full minute. Sir Charles said she must emphasize that when the consultation with Dr Rokovsky took place. His own hopes on her behalf were now higher, stronger, he said. He then added that his interest in her case and the advances Dr Rokovsky had made in ophthalmic surgery were such that he himself would be in New York on the fourth of January. He had, in fact, been invited to be present at the consultation on the sixth and would spend several days studying Dr Rokovsky's techniques, not yet known in the UK.

'Sir Charles, you'll really be there?' said Felicity.

'Studying something as important as this to the ophthalmic practitioners of Britain can't be resisted,' said Sir Charles. 'My diary for January has been adjusted.'

'I'm delighted you'll be there,' said Felicity.

She had much to talk about with Tim when

he arrived home. Tim's excitement matched her own. Jennifer made her own contribution to the happy hour, that of a girl who would have gladly given up all future Christmas and birthday presents in return for the restoration of her mother's sight.

On attaining the age of thirteen, Gemma and James were given a birthday party. No, not a tea party. As teenagers now, it was a buffet supper party, to which they invited the best of their respective schoolfriends, as well as Giles and Emily, the children of Rosie and Matthew. And after some hesitation, James also invited Cindy.

On receiving the invitation over the phone, Cindy said, 'Well, thanks ever so much, I'll be pleased to come, especially as it's your thirteenth and not your ninetieth. Will you make a speech?'

'I probably will, on my ninetieth,' said James, 'but I won't be up to it on my thirteenth.'

'Oh, good,' said Cindy. 'By the way, I'll be living nearer you the day before your birthday.'

'Will you?' said James, wondering if that was good or bad news.

'Yes, that's when Mum and Dad and me will be moving into our new house in Sunray Avenue,' said Cindy. Completion had been effected with payment in full, and Anneliese and Harry were now busy ordering new furniture and fittings, the furniture to augment what they would take from their present house, for which an offer had been received, an offer in cash. The prospective buyers were Mr and Mrs George Hooper. George Hooper was a spiv, and a Camberwell Road residence would suit him very nicely, thank you. Camberwell and Peckham were where he did the bulk of his spivving. Harry, however, liked the bloke and his missus enough to consider favourably letting them have the house that had once belonged to his first wife.

'Sunray Avenue's a lot nearer,' said James.

'Yes, but that doesn't mean you can keep coming and knocking on our door every day.'

'Well, I'll make a promise,' said James, 'I'll hardly ever come knocking at all.'

'Oh, I'll let you know when you can,' said Cindy blithely.

The party was a roaring success, mainly because Polly and Boots allowed one of the guests to bring a record player with loudspeakers, plus a collection of currently popular records. The large lounge exploded with rock and roll numbers, and vibrated to dancing feet.

So roaring was the success that Polly retired temporarily to the kitchen, where she informed Flossie that if anyone desperately needed to see her, she'd be in the walk-in pantry with the door closed, and keeping company with headache pills. Flossie, who had volunteered to stay on and prepare the buffet supper herself, said, 'Oh, you'll be nice and comfy in there, Mrs Adams, I'll get you a chair.'

'Don't bother, Flossie, I'm not serious,' said Polly.

'My, but there's a real thumping going on in the parlour,' said Flossie.

'Don't be surprised if it's the heads of teenagers hitting the ceiling,' said Polly. 'Flossie, has all the food been taken in?'

'Taken in?' said Flossie. 'It's been taken in, mum, and it's all gone, hot sausages, salmon salad, chicken drumsticks, ham rolls and everything else.'

'Oh, Lord,' said Polly, 'd'you think we gave them enough?'

'Enough?' said Flossie. 'I should think every one of them youngsters has got through a hundredweight of food – well, more than a few pounds, at least.'

Polly smiled and returned to the fray. Rosie and Matthew, who had arrived with Giles and Emily, were helping Boots to keep twenty young revellers from actually bringing the ceiling down. James, she noted, was going great with Cindy, and Gemma with Giles.

Above the din came a violent thumping sound.

'What's that?' gasped Rosie. If it startled her, it didn't intimidate the kids. They kept going. The violent sound repeated itself.

'That,' said Matt, 'is a thunderous knocking, Boots. On your front door.'

'So it is,' said Boots, and went to investigate. On the doorstep stood two uniformed police constables, one a woman. 'Ah,' said Boots.

'Are you the owner of this house, sir?' asked the policeman.

'I am,' said Boots, guessing what was coming.

'We've been trying to raise you for five minutes, sir,' said the policewoman.

'So sorry,' said Boots, 'there's a teenage birthday party going on.'

'So we can hear,' said the policeman, 'and I'm afraid it's been disturbing some of your neighbours. We've received complaints at the station.'

'Can you tone it down, sir?' asked the policewoman.

'I can and will,' said Boots. 'What's the time?'

'Nearly ten, sir,' said the policeman.

'Right, time to end the party,' said Boots. 'Sorry for the din, and I'll apologize to the neighbours tomorrow.'

'Thank you,' said the policewoman, who

looked as if she wouldn't mind joining the party herself, as long as she could kick up her heels with the house-owner.

'Goodnight,' said Boots.

'Goodnight, sir.'

Boots closed the door and rejoined Rosie, Matt and Polly. He told them the police had called about the noise, and that the party had to end. It was scheduled to end, in any event, at ten, when some parents would be calling to collect their offspring.

Organizing a peaceful departure of the pumped-up guests was easier said than done. Rosie and Matt played an heroic part, but well before the last of the youngsters had gone or been picked up by parents, Polly and Boots had skilfully withdrawn from the noisy hall to the kitchen.

'Ye gods, I feel trampled,' said Polly.

'I feel old,' said Boots.

'Teenagers, for God's sake,' said Polly.

'The shape of things to come?' said Boots.

'I hope not,' said Polly, 'or they'll blow up this island and we'll sink. Is the house still standing, old fruit?'

'The roof's still trembling,' said Boots, 'but the walls are staying put.' He smiled. 'Happy kids' birthday, Polly old dear.'

Polly put one hand on the back of his neck, drew his head down and kissed him.

'Love you and the kids, even if I am feeling my age,' she said. 'What's going to happen

409

next year, when they'll be fourteen?'

'We'll hire the Tower of London,' said Boots. 'They won't be heard there, except by the ghost of Anne Boleyn, and I don't suppose she'll care.'

On a Friday evening, a week or so before Christmas, Lulu and Paul were entertaining her father, John Saunders, Labour MP, and her stepmother, Sylvia, a lively woman in her late thirties, who was touched that her stepdaughter had named little Sylvia after her. Lulu, in fact, had named the child first after Mrs Pankhurst's elder daughter Sylvia, a fiery suffragette with Communist leanings, and only secondly after her stepmother. However, she did not tell her stepmother that.

Paul and his father-in-law were drinking beer, Sylvia was enjoying her favourite tipple, gin and tonic, and Lulu, being a nursing mother, was making do with lemonade. In any case, she had reservations about gin and tonic, for although she liked its refreshing sparkle, she knew the working classes regarded it as fit only for middle-class poofs.

She was talking politics, of course, and had reached the point where she was declaring disaster for the country under Churchill's Conservative government.

'You've got to admit it, Churchill's past it,' she said.

'There's still a bit of life left in the old dog,' said Paul.

'And to be frank, I've got a soft spot for him,' said John. He was known as Honest John, since he always spoke his mind. That kept him on the backbenches. MPs who spoke their minds during a debate, or outside the House, were slightly suspect to Party leaders. 'I can't deny the inspiration of his wartime leadership.'

'Whatever our political views, we can't deny his place in history,' said Sylvia, who, before her marriage, had worked at the House of Commons as a member of the Labour Party's secretariat.

'In any case,' said Honest John, 'the old boy's due to retire and to give way to Anthony Eden.'

'Eden?' said Lulu. 'Brilliant for the country, I don't think.'

'Could we have the news?' suggested Honest John. The time was close to nine o'clock. 'I believe there might be a definite announcement about Churchill's retirement.'

'Let's listen,' said Paul, and switched on the radio. They caught the news. It mostly related to the cold war, about which Churchill had warned the world during his 'Iron Curtain' speech in 1946.

There was no reference to his proposed retirement, but there was a footnote to the main news. It concerned two more gunshot murders in New York during the afternoon, and the fact that that swarming American city was becoming the murder capital of the world. There had been thirty-three during the last few weeks. The news of these latest homicides had just come in, said the announcer, but there were no details yet.

Lulu switched the radio off.

'That was an indication of what rampant capitalism can do to a people,' she said. 'Foster corruption and monopolies, increase the divide between rich and poor, encourage gangsters and bring about the use of guns.'

'Fortunately,' said Sylvia, 'we don't have that kind of capitalism or that kind of people in this country. Now, if I may, I'm going up to peep in on little Sylvia. She's a symbol of the country's peaceful future, and I haven't seen her for ages.'

'If you wake her up,' said Paul, 'you'll find this won't be a peaceful evening. She's a yell when woken up.'

Near to midnight in the house on Red Post Hill, Sir Edwin Finch, dressing gown over his pyjamas, was out of bed and down in the kitchen. Not for the first time in recent months, he was finding it difficult to get to sleep. Philosophically, he accepted the generalization that some ageing men and women didn't need as much sleep as younger people.

412

It seemed he was now one of them.

He had just had a sleeping pill, knowing that would send him off until about eight in the morning. He was giving the pill time to take effect before going back to bed. He switched on the radio to catch the midnight news, the last before the station closed down.

That news too was mainly about incidents connected with the cold war. Sir Edwin sighed at the propensity of international politicians to disagree with each other. He alerted when the footnote to the news came through. The announcer was now able to give details of the two murders in New York, one a gangland slaying, the other concerning a doctor who had been shot and killed when leaving a hospital in Westchester, a superior residential suburb of New York.

Sir Edwin listened transfixed to the details. The doctor, one Paul Rokovsky, a Ukrainian immigrant, was a top ophthalmic surgeon, responsible for a number of successful operations on blinded war veterans. His murderer was a young Jewish man, who stepped into his path, and cried dramatically in the hearing of passers-by, 'Vengeance for my brother and sister, Dr Gerhard Fischer, murderer of little children!' The announcer said the young man then shot the doctor dead at point-blank range. He was now under arrest, and enquiries of a very complex kind were going on.

Sir Edwin sat in shock, oblivious to the radio closing down by the playing of the national anthem.

Dear God, he thought, was Anneliese Stevens right, after all, in identifying Dr Paul Rokovsky as Dr Gerhard Fischer, responsible for hideous medical experiments at Auschwitz? Whether she was or not, Dr Paul Rokovsky was now dead, and Felicity's hopes had died with him.

Who was going to be first in the family to hear the news in the morning, and who was going to be the first to tell Tim and Felicity, if they hadn't heard it themselves?

One thing was sure. The family would rally to Felicity, and give her all the support she needed, although she was not a woman who would cry out for comforting. Her strength of character had served her for years, and would do so now. Must do so.

Sir Edwin went slowly up the stairs and back to bed.

The publishers hope that this book has given you enjoyable reading. Large Print Books are especially designed to be as easy to see and hold as possible. If you wish a complete list of our books please ask at your local library or write directly to:

Magna Large Print Books
Magna House, Long Preston,
Skipton, North Yorkshire.
BD23 4ND